PRESSURE BREACH

PRESSURE BREACH

THE BLACK BOX SERIES

KIM SERRANO

S+S

SWITCH + STERN

Pressure Breach

© 2025 Kim Serrano

First edition, published July 2025

Published by Switch + Stern

switchandstern.com

Cover design by Kim Serrano

ISBN: 979-8-9997264-2-1

Printed in the United States of America

CONTENT WARNING

This novel contains mature themes and emotionally intense content. Includes:

- Explicit sex, including hate sex and power play.
- Racialized and gendered power dynamics.
- Corporate violence.
- References to gang activity and past domestic violence (off-page).
- Animal illness.
- Colonial trauma.

Read with care.

1

Vee stood at the arrivals gate, doing her best impression of a person who wasn't spiraling. She glanced down at herself and felt, not for the first time, like a character from a different movie had wandered into the wrong set. Her outfit was a mess of eras—chains, rings on nearly every finger, a battered Bikini Kill tee, leather jacket stiff at the shoulders, combat boots scuffed. The Chanel box bag slung crosswise at her hip wasn't even hers—her best friend Morgan had shoved it at her months ago, with that executive casualness that made it impossible to say no.

Morgan was the nerve center of their messy little triangle. Vee's best friend since high school. Sloane's since Penn. Former Heritage fleet director, current consultant. She was the kind of busy that still made time for group chats and crisis calls. Vee loved her. Sometimes wanted to strangle her. Always listened to her.

The flowers were from the corner market, a fistful of ranunculus and something vaguely green she hadn't identified. She'd kept the receipt. God forbid she lose the tax write-off on her own humiliation.

Her nails glittered faintly—subtle, tasteful, like she wasn't trying too hard. Like she hadn't spent over a year in this maddening cycle of hot-cold-pull-push with Sloane.

She shifted her weight, boots creaking, and let herself spiral a little, because what the hell else was she going to do? She replayed the texts in her head.

Two months. Two whole months since they'd last seen each other at Morgan's wedding, though they'd been texting the whole time—sporadically, but with that bite. Late-night dirty jokes. Flirty memes that hit just wrong enough to keep Vee up at night. Sloane texting her:

Hey, I'll be in Chicago next week. We should grab a drink. Let's talk.

Let's talk.

Vee had spent the last six days doing mental gymnastics over that. Did it mean what she thought it meant? Were they finally going to have the conversation? The capital-T Talk? *The I like you, you like me, maybe we should stop pretending we're just occasional bodies* Talk?

Because they had been occasional bodies. It started through that whole fucked-up whistleblower scandal that had nearly tanked the airline—Sloane was one of Morgan's people, flown in like a precision missile, all ice and Yale Law pedigree and legal authority. And there was Vee, elbow-deep in a stripped-down engine at midnight, grease-streaked and bone-tired, when Sloane—Sloane in heels, in a perfect black pencil dress—walked onto the floor, demanding files nobody else could find.

Later that night, whiskey on Vee's breath, Sloane's tongue in her mouth, hands everywhere, Sloane's body pressed flush to hers in a too-small bathroom stall. That stupid, hot, reckless night had spiraled into a pattern—months of texting, of sneaking off together, of Sloane's hand fisted in Vee's hair, of Sloane's voice gone low and soft, saying, *fuck, don't stop,* before disappearing again for months.

And now, here she was.

Morgan had texted last night:

Emergency came up. Kieran's stuck at Ren's moot court thing. Can you pick Sloane up at the airport?

Sure. Sure, she could pick Sloane up. It wasn't like she had anything better to do. It wasn't like she'd planned her whole outfit with *I'm about to confess my feelings at the airport* energy, wasn't like she'd debated if a bouquet was too much before telling herself to get over it and just buy the fucking flowers.

And then—

Sloane appeared.

Tall, radiant, impossible.

Deep brown skin that seemed to catch and hold the sunlight, hair pulled up into a high, lush bun, curls soft and neat like they'd been styled by a professional two hours ago. Her mouth—Oh, her mouth. Lips painted in some warm, glossy shade that made Vee's brain short-circuit. She was wearing a soft cream sweater, light slacks, flats, of all things, that still left her towering—five-ten barefoot, probably. She looked exactly the same and completely untouchable.

Vee's heart did a pathetic, ugly little lurch.

"Hey," she said, and it came out too quiet, too tentative. She tried again, stronger this time. "Morgan got called into an emergency thing last minute, and Kieran's in Indiana—some law school thing for his kid, I don't know. So I'm here." She held out the flowers. "Welcome back to Chicago."

Sloane's eyes dropped to the flowers. Then back up to

Vee's face. There was a flicker—sharp, unreadable, like a pane of glass catching the sun.

"You shouldn't have," she said, voice low. Cool.

A pause. Just a beat too tight.

"I actually just started seeing someone. It's...new. But serious. I don't want to blindside you."

Vee's brain went sideways. Her ears rang. Not in a poetic, heart-fluttering way, but in the way you get when you stand too close to an air compressor. The words hit, all right. Square in the chest. Except no—this wasn't a hit. This was a goddamn ambush. A low, quiet *fuck you* wrapped in a bow.

"Oh," she heard herself say, like she was in a sitcom where the laugh track had been yanked out at the last second. Her voice sounded small, half-cooked. There was a nod—small, polite, fucking stupid—because what else was she supposed to do? Her throat went dry, and she felt the blood leave her face in one slow, public exhale.

Of course. Of course. Because why wouldn't Sloane— this woman with her perfect skin, her flawless teeth, her neatly packed lawyer energy—have someone else? Some finance guy named Chris, probably. Or better yet, a wellness influencer named Dahlia who did hot yoga and posted cryptic thirst traps with the caption "soft where it counts, unbothered everywhere else."

Vee could feel it happening in real time—the humiliation crystallizing inside her chest.

"I just thought," she tried, her voice catching on the gravel in her chest, "you texted me to talk."

Sloane's mouth—those lips, shiny and perfect, the kind of mouth that had once been wrapped around Vee's fingers —pressed into a line.

"Forget I said that."

Forget.

Oh. Okay. Sure. Let's all just forget.

Vee nodded again, because she was on autopilot now, running on some humiliating emergency generator that powered through sheer force of stubbornness. Her chest felt tight, and she was suddenly, vividly aware of how even at five-seven, and being the tallest girl in her family, she still had to tip her chin up just to meet Sloane's eyes.

"Right," she muttered.

She turned and pressed the flowers—those stupid, too-bright ranunculus, now burning a hole in her hand—into the hands of some guy standing nearby, a random suit who looked vaguely startled, like he hadn't expected to get swept into the drama of the arrivals gate.

"Here," Vee said, voice flat and sharp as a boxcutter. "You look like you could use these."

She didn't look back. She refused to look back. Lot's wife had turned to salt for less, and Vee wasn't about to risk getting calcified in the middle of O'Hare. Because it was always like this. This was the cost of wanting women like this. The waiting rooms, the admissions paperwork, the soft voices of intake nurses asking, "Do you feel like hurting yourself?"—and you're sitting there trying to explain that, no, it wasn't some external threat, it was just *her*. It wasn't a sharp object, it wasn't a high ledge, it wasn't a bottle of pills. It was the way she said your name. It was the text that never came. It was the *"I'm seeing someone."*

This wasn't heartbreak. This was infrastructure failure.

Vee knew the drill. She'd seen friends check in, check out, stabilize, destabilize, patch themselves up, then do it again. *Oh, so you just had a break-up?* Okay, now you're locked in the back room with a cold blanket and a plastic cup of water, whispering your own shame to a stranger who's never been wrecked by a single fucking text.

And yet, if Sloane had turned around—right there at the gate, hair catching the light, mouth soft and perfect, looking at Vee like she meant it—and said, "Let's go somewhere quiet," she'd have followed. No hesitation.

THEY WALKED in silence to the parking garage.

Vee's hands were tight on the wheel as she drove, the sky outside going that deep, endless blue of an early Chicago evening. Sloane sat in the passenger seat, a vision of casual disinterest, scrolling through her phone. Like Vee hadn't just publicly offered her heart in the form of a supermarket bouquet and been slapped across the face with it.

They didn't speak the whole drive to Morgan's place, that old Victorian perched like some gothic cathedral on the West Side, looking down on the skyline like it knew all the secrets and was too tired to give a shit. Vee parked, put the truck in neutral, and sat for a second too long.

Sloane unbuckled her seatbelt.

"Thanks for the ride," she said, not looking at her.

Vee just nodded. Once. Twice. A sharp, automatic tic. She watched Sloane disappear up the steps, her long, impossible legs eating up the distance, her high bun catching the light.

Vee exhaled slow, chest tight, and whispered, to no one in particular, "Motherfucker."

SHE DIDN'T DRIVE STRAIGHT HOME.

Took a few wrong turns on purpose, let the city fall away behind her. Past Pulaski. Past the last gas station with lights still on. Out to Woytek's lot—half-lit, half-forgotten, always open just enough if you knew which gate to push.

She parked the truck, climbed out, and crossed the yard without a word. The side door stuck like it always did. She shouldered it open. Lights off inside—just the security strip near the back, humming low and blue.

She keyed open her bay.

There it was. Low, quiet, parked where she left it. The other car.

Not pretty. Not flashy. But built mean.

She opened the driver's side door. Slid in.

It smelled like rubber and cold vinyl and the kind of adrenaline she never talked about in therapy. She didn't start it yet. Just sat. Hands on the wheel like they still knew what to do.

Her phone buzzed once.

Signal.

A message with nothing but a time and a cross street.

She didn't react. Just turned the key.

The engine purred, low and clean. She eased out of the garage. No music. Didn't head toward the meet. Not yet.

But the car was awake now.

And so was she.

2

The club was a godforsaken shoebox buried in the industrial corridor—some forgotten warehouse off Damen, half-swallowed by viaducts and tagged-up delivery trucks. It still reeked of piss, beer, and black mold, no matter how many Edison bulbs the new owners strung up or how shiny the new sign was. The floor was sticky. The walls sweated. The air was heat, spit, and reverb.

Vee hit the stage like she'd been shot out of a goddamn cannon.

She wasn't thinking about the airport. Not the flowers. Not the way Sloane had said "I'm seeing someone." She was thinking about the mic in her hand, the bass pounding through her ribs, the way the crowd cracked open when she screamed the first line. One of her rings flew off into the dark. Her boots hit the edge of the monitor. She threw her head back and roared.

The pit moved like a living thing.

Sweaty limbs. Boots. Leather. Elbows.

She crowd-surfed over a sea of graying punks with work

boots and bad knees and mouths that still knew every word. They caught her like they always had. Like she never left. She could've cried from the fucking relief of it.

Every breath onstage was a purge.

Screaming until her throat burned? Cheaper than therapy.

Spitting water on the crowd? Communion.

Cussing out some twenty-year-old who tried to grab her ankle mid-solo? Public service.

Her bandmates—Jules on bass, Moni on drums, Bones on guitar—all in their fifties now, all twice divorced or bankrupt or both. But still here. Still her people. Still the loudest, rowdiest, most loyal bastards she knew.

After the fifth song, they called a smoke break.

Vee slipped out back into the alley, hands on her knees, grinning like a maniac, lungs on fire.

Jules lit a cigarette with trembling fingers. "So," she said, puffing. "Where's that hot lawyer girlfriend you were braggin' about last time?"

Vee barked out a laugh that didn't reach her eyes. "She doesn't exist."

Moni squinted. "Wasn't she flyin' in from D.C.?"

"Yeah," Vee muttered. "She landed and told me she was dating someone else."

Bones exhaled. "Damn."

Vee flicked her lighter open. "Whatever."

She went back inside before anyone could get sentimental. Grabbed the mic again, cracked her neck once, and tore into the next set like she was trying to exorcise the ghost of Sloane's lip gloss.

The crowd? Decent. Shoulder to shoulder. Kids with pink mohawks and old punks with belly-length beards. All screaming, all sweating, all still giving a shit after twenty years. Vee hadn't thought they'd remember. But they were here.

They were still showing up for *Kill Fee*.

Back in the early aughts, the band had been a joke that got too loud. They'd played basements and storage units, DIY fests in Gary and Dayton, gigs that paid in drink tickets and black eyes. The Midwest scene had been rough and loving—more duct tape than structure, more mutual aid than career moves. They never blew up, but they didn't burn out either. Just kind of...disappeared, one member at a time. People had kids. Got laid off. Went sober. Got sick.

Now the joke was that they were back together. But the real joke was that they never should've stopped.

Everything had changed.

The scene was different now—less teeth, more content. There were still bands, sure. Still good ones. But the clubs were vanishing. The all-ages spots got bought out. The old flyers were artifacts now, framed on bar walls where they sold twenty-dollar cocktails and called it nostalgia. Places like this one were the exception, not the rule. Every time she played, she wondered if it'd be the last time the floor still held.

She looked around and noticed it—how much older the fans were. How older she was. Laugh lines, crow's feet, knees that creaked louder than her mic check. She didn't feel forty, not really. Just...more haunted. Like every version of herself from nineteen to now was still pressed inside her skin, crowding her ribs. She still wanted the same things—loud music, a cold beer, someone to come home to.

They called it a reunion tour, but that was generous. It was five shows strung together by Facebook comments, wishful thinking, and a shared inability to let go. It barely covered gas, let alone rent. Bones was crashing at his sister's again. Jules picked up bartending shifts and still owed the IRS four grand. Moni was splitting time between public defense and driving Lyft—burning out on both.

Vee was the only one with something close to steady income—and even that came with grease burns, back strain, and bargaining with corporate cowards.

But onstage, none of that mattered. Not for ninety minutes.

The music hit. Her voice ripped through the static. And she remembered what it felt like to matter—to scream something ugly and real and have the room scream it back like they meant it.

She wasn't ready to grow up. Never had been.

And maybe that was the most punk thing left.

THEY ENDED up at Egan's, a washed-out corner bar with no working jukebox. The kind of place where nothing changed but the price of well whiskey.

Vee got carded at the door.

It wasn't even ironic. The kid checking IDs squinted at her like he'd just spotted a minor trying to sneak into a dive with her older sister's passport. From behind, she passed for some skate-rat kid—all sharp elbows and cheap rings, swagger too big for her frame. Up close, maybe twenty-five, tops. If she wasn't talking.

She handed over her license without flinching.

He stared at the birth year. Did the math.

"Damn."

"Yeah," she said. "Sunscreen works."

He waved her through.

Inside, it was the same as always—dim, loud, the air sticky with decades of spilled beer and desperation. A place for has-beens and could've-beens, held together by grit, duct tape, and a loyal, aging bartender who always poured strong.

The band didn't love it, but it was close to the venue.

She was half a drink in when someone clocked her from across the room.

"Holy shit, is that Phan?"

The voice was rough, familiar—cigarette-scraped and Chicago-worn. He had the posture of someone who still hauled parts for a living, hoodie stained at the cuffs, ball cap faded from sun and machine grease. Behind him, a couple others ambled in, already grinning, already half-drunk and carrying that quiet reverence reserved for people who'd bled in the same shop.

"No shit," one of them said, slapping her shoulder like they hadn't all aged a decade. "You still shacked up with the suits over at Heritage? Or did you finally chew through the leash?"

Vee shrugged, took a long sip. Her guilt said enough.

The older guy—gravel voice, thick wrists, laugh lines carved deep—turned to the others. "This is the one I told you about. My old boss. Mean as hell. Smoked me for every shortcut I ever tried to pull."

He grinned, crooked and proud.

"Still went to bat for us when it counted. Got us hazard pay, locked in raises. Took a wrench to the execs and made it look like paperwork."

Vee just raised her glass again, quieter this time. Let them talk. She'd never been good at taking praise while sober.

They bought her drinks without asking. Three shots lined up like they were offering communion. She didn't say no.

"You did good, you know," one of them said, slapping the bar beside her. "Ten years ago? That fight over shop rates? We're still riding that wave. Brought in three new guys this year 'cause of those raises. Kept 'em outta Amazon's claws."

Another one nodded. "And that deal with MRO? Never would've happened without you. Whole damn hangar would get your name tattooed if they knew how to spell it right."

She should've said something. Should've smiled, maybe. But her throat was tight.

Then came the gut punch.

"You hear about Jerry?"

Her fingers went cold around the glass.

"Jerry who?"

"Cortez. Old head. He passed. Last night. Pneumonia, they think. You know how it is—lungs never really recovered after those spray booths."

Vee blinked. Twice. Felt the air thin.

Jerry had been the only one who vouched for her when she first got hired two decades ago. Everyone else thought she was a PR stunt—diversity hire, union bait, whatever. Jerry took her aside the second week, handed her a wrench and said, "Don't let these assholes get to you. You belong here."

She'd carried that sentence like armor. Now he was gone.

She downed another shot. Then another. She lit a cigarette she didn't need.

The guys kept talking, telling stories, their voices getting blurrier with each drink. But she wasn't listening anymore. She was already pulling out her phone, thumb hovering, brain fuzzy but fixed on one thing.

On her.

Sloane.

She slipped outside, sat on the curb with her phone glowing in her palm, and did the dumbest thing imaginable.

She called her.

The line rang once. Twice. Then: "Vee?"

She didn't say anything for a second. Just breathed.

Sloane's voice again, softer: "Are you okay?"

"Why'd you lie to me," Vee said. Her voice didn't shake. "You're not really seeing someone. That's bullshit. You think I'm an idiot but I know your tells."

A pause.

"I'll come get you," Sloane said.

"I'm sitting on the sidewalk," Vee said with a giggle, followed by a hiccup.

"Share your location."

She didn't mean to. But she did.

Thirty minutes later, a black car rolled up.

Sloane stepped out. She was in slate-gray knit pants and a cream long-sleeve so soft it had to be cashmere. The cuffs hugged her wrists, the neckline slouched just enough to expose the hard line of her collarbone. Her bra wasn't visible, but Vee could tell it was there, doing ungodly structural work under that hoodie. Quiet money. Hidden scaffolding.

Vee squinted up at her from the back seat, chin tilted like she was trying to find the hidden catch in a riddle. "You look like you work at Goop," she slurred.

Sloane met it with nothing. "Where do you live?"

Vee waved vaguely. "Off Broadway. Argyle. Above the bakery."

The driver punched the address and pulled off. Vee leaned her head against the window and pretended not to exist. She could feel Sloane watching her, silent and impossible.

They got to the building. Sloane helped her out of the car, one arm slung under Vee's, steadying her like she weighed nothing. The stairwell was dim and too warm. Vee was sweating again. Someone had left a pizza box on the landing, half open. Classy.

"My nephew's supposed to be home," she muttered, keys clinking in her hand. "He's got a midnight curfew."

Sloane glanced at the clock on her phone. "It's two."

"Exactly," Vee growled.

The apartment was dark and still. A pair of Nikes by the door, but no sound. No TikTok bassline, no kitchen light. Vee muttered something about ungrateful little shits and almost tripped over her own boot. Sloane caught her again —efficient, detached. Too careful.

In the bedroom, Vee sank onto the mattress with a groan. Sloane knelt in front of her and tugged her boots off, then her socks. Then—hesitating only briefly—unzipped her jeans and slid them down. The motion was clinical, not cruel. Vee's tank top clung to her damp skin, her bra visible through the fabric. She reached for Sloane, arms looping around her neck, breath hot with whiskey and sweat and something desperate.

Sloane didn't flinch. She just placed a palm gently over Vee's mouth and pressed her backward onto the bed.

"I don't think so," she murmured. "You might not even remember this."

Vee blinked up at her. Frowned. "Fuck you for being decent."

Sloane didn't respond. Just pulled a duvet over her, then set a bottle of Pedialyte and a glass of water on the nightstand like it was nothing.

"You are a forty-year-old woman," Sloane said, low, not quite judging—more like tired of being right.

"Yeah. I'm a forty-year-old woman with three slipped discs, a punk show's worth of adrenaline still in my blood, and a girl who blew up my heart in Terminal 5. What, you thought I'd go home and journal?"

Vee moved too slow, lips slack, eyes glazed but still hitting their mark. She tilted her head back against the pillow and let the words hang. Let them rot the air between them.

"And then I got the news. Someone who mattered—gone. Just like that. Lungs, liver, fuck if I know. So yeah, I lit a cigarette I didn't even want and called you, because I hate myself."

Her laugh was low, ugly, soft around the edges. She gave a loose shrug—sharp with irony and resignation.

"You can call it pathetic. I call it maintenance."

For a second, Sloane didn't move. Just stared at her like she'd been hit. A full-body stillness, the kind Vee had seen in animals right before they bolt or bite. And then—no argument, no lecture—just movement. Sloane grabbed the water from the nightstand and damn near pressed the glass to her lips.

"Drink," she said.

Vee coughed, lips brushing the rim, and drank. Not because she was ready to be obedient, but because Sloane looked like she would make her otherwise. It wasn't sweet. It wasn't caring. It was matter-of-fact. Necessary. Annoyingly righteous.

And still—she was beautiful.

Especially in the half-light of Vee's bedroom, Sloane looked like something carved out of divine punishment. Her curls were loose around her face, soft and full. They framed her high cheekbones, full cheeks, those goddamn lips, always looking glossy even when bare. Her eyes were honey-brown and devastating, the kind of warm that made you think you were safe right before she sentenced you.

Even wasted, even wrecked, even ruined—Vee still wanted her. Wanted to fight her and fuck her and press her down into this mattress and ask why. *Why did you come? Why did you pick up? Why are you still here?*

But all she said was, "Why do you look so guilty?"

Sloane looked at her for a long, unreadable second, then smoothed her expression into something neutral.

"Go to sleep, Vee."

Vee didn't argue. She turned her face toward the wall. Sloane didn't leave. Didn't crawl into bed. Didn't even sit down. She just paced once, checked the door lock, closed the curtains tighter, and pulled the chair from the corner of the room like she was standing night watch.

It wasn't romantic. She stayed, Vee realized later, in case she puked in her sleep. It was just typical Sloane-level due diligence. Had to be.

Vee passed out halfway through resenting her.

The next morning, Sloane was gone.

For a second, Vee thought she'd hallucinated the whole thing—just another mean little brain-movie cooked up from grief and cheap whiskey. Her limbs ached. Her head was a drumline. Her mouth tasted like death.

She groaned and reached blindly for the nightstand.

Pedialyte. Painkillers. Water. All lined up like a care package from someone who didn't know how to say "I'm sorry."

So maybe she hadn't imagined it. Maybe Sloane really had been there, quiet and cold and maddeningly decent.

Vee stared at the bottles for a long second, then muttered, voice shredded and dry:

"What the fuck."

3

Five days later, the sky over Graceland Cemetery was a soft, impersonal gray—the kind that didn't grieve, didn't judge. Just hovered. The trees were summer-thick, old as debts. Angel statues leaned over graves like they were listening. The place was too quiet for someone raised on car alarms, late-night sirens, pit bulls barking at passing bikes.

Vee stood near the back of the crowd. Black boots on damp grass. Hands in the pockets of a thrifted leather jacket that still smelled faintly like last week's gig—cigarettes, beer, the ghost of a bassline. Underneath, she wore a black slip dress with a raw hem and laddered fishnets, one garter peeking through when she moved. The boots were real—steel-toed, scuffed, laced like she meant it. Her hair was down, pin-straight and freshly washed, streaks of old blonde catching in the overcast light.

She wore eyeliner sharp enough to cut glass, mascara still perfect despite the wind. A thin silver chain looped twice around her neck. Two rings on each hand. Her nails were black. She looked like she could throw a punch at a eulogy or give one, if asked.

Funeral appropriate in the loosest possible terms. But dignified—because she chose to be.

People cried. Even the tough ones who'd wrangled engines and contracts and bosses—stood stiff, shaking, holding back until they couldn't. Even the ones who didn't cry let it sit heavy in their throats, faces twisted like grief had grabbed them by the collar and wouldn't let go.

The casket was plain, almost humble. His family had done it right.

The line of cars had curled slow through the cemetery gates—hazards on, headlights burning, cops blocking Montrose so the whole motorcade could pass in peace. Old men in union jackets rode up front with the family. Friends trailed behind in borrowed sedans and washed trucks, radios off, grief quiet and obedient. No one honked. Not in this city. Not for this.

She met the widow at the end of the procession. The woman pulled her in like they hadn't missed a year—same warm hands, same steady grip, same gold cross around her neck from back when the boys were still in high school.

"Vee," she said, smiling like it hurt. "I was hoping you'd come."

Vee didn't trust herself to speak, just nodded.

"You still wearing those boots?" the woman asked, eyeing them. "Jerry used to say you were the only one who could stomp around in non-regs and still outwork every man in the shop."

Vee exhaled a dry laugh. "They're close enough."

"Sure, baby," the woman said with a chuckle. Then: "You know, he talked about you all the time."

Vee looked away. The wind smelled like roses and damp soil. Somewhere, a kid was crying.

"He used to say—when you'd come by, back in the day—he used to say you were like a daughter to him. You know, with all those boys and no girls, he adored you."

Vee didn't move.

A pause. A shift in tone. Not sharp, not accusing. Just... offhand, soft.

"Funny. I hadn't seen you in a while. Guess life gets like that."

That was the knife. Right there. Just a passing observation that gutted her.

"I meant to," Vee said. Quiet, automatic.

"I know," the woman said, and squeezed her hand. "We all do."

Then she let go, and Vee stood there, feeling all the years she didn't show up.

The kids came next. Grown, with their own worry lines and tired backs. They looked like people who knew what hard work did to a body. The grandkids were quiet, too young to understand the weight of this moment. One clutched a folded flag. Another had drawn something on printer paper and left it near the casket—a picture of an airplane with wings like bricks.

At the wake, the house smelled like Lysol. People packed every room. Laughter tangled with grief, heavy as sweat. There was a photo of Jerry above the fireplace—one of him grinning crooked in front of a half-built fuselage, goggles on his forehead like a mechanic superhero.

Vee hung back. She accepted hugs, accepted food, let people talk around her. She drank half a soda she didn't want and watched the way everyone moved around the space like they were orbiting something holy.

Later, a few of the union guys pulled her out onto the porch.

It was dusk. The air smelled like honeysuckle and fresh-cut grief. One of them lit a cigarette and offered her the pack. She shook her head.

The front yard was blooming. Not just blooming—curated. Loved. Roses everywhere, in colors that didn't come from a grocery store bouquet. Deep crimson, coral, butter yellow. Some climbing trellises Jerry probably built himself. Some tucked into planters that looked like weekend projects —wood still sanded smooth, corners braced, nothing fancy but nothing lazy either.

It looked like a life made in tandem. Jerry building. His wife planting. Years of partnership rooted in soil and splinters.

Now half of that was gone.

And the roses still bloomed anyway.

"This ain't right," one of them muttered. "Jerry getting tossed out of this world like that, after everything? After what they did to the booths?"

"He knew the risks," she said. Her voice came out flatter than she meant. "We all did."

"That don't make it right," another one snapped. "And you know it."

The older guy—Donny, maybe, or Miguel—tilted his head. "Look. We been talkin'. And we think it's time."

"For what?"

"For you to come back. Fight again."

Vee rubbed her temple like the request gave her a headache. "Fight...*again*? I just threw hands with a multi-billion-dollar company ten months ago. I'm still coughing up pieces of that."

"And?"

"What do you think this is, a fucking subscription?"

"You walked into a goddamn lion's den and came out breathing," he said. "Now you're gonna tell me you're done?"

"I'm telling you it took something out of me."

He leaned forward, voice lower. "So what? That's the deal. You fight, you lose pieces. But if we don't show up, who the hell will?"

She didn't answer right away. Just stared out at the dark street, the porch light humming above them like a warning.

They weren't asking because it was fair. They were asking because it worked. Because she looked good on camera. Because when she raised hell, people tuned in—and stayed.

"I can't," she said, but it was clear she was going to cave soon. "I can't keep doing this till I'm dead."

They went quiet. Not disappointed. Just respectful. The silence of people who'd lost more than they'd ever gotten back.

Finally, the tallest guy uncapped a flask and handed it around. They each took a sip without saying a word, like communion.

When it came to her, she held it a second too long.

"For what it's worth," one of them said, soft and crooked-grinned, "I can see you still raising hell in a nursing home fifty years from now. Filing OSHA complaints about the jello."

Vee didn't smile, but the breath she let out was less bitter than before.

She took the sip and let it burn.

4

The week dragged like a loaded cart.

Vee didn't sleep so much as reboot. She woke to an overflowing inbox, a crusted coffee ring on the nightstand, and Dolores Huerta—the smaller of her two cats—licking the foil of a forgotten burrito. Eugene V. Debs, the larger one, was sprawled on top of her head. The apartment smelled faintly like takeout. She hissed Dolores off the nightstand, scooped kibble into two bowls, rinsed a mug, poured coffee, jammed a pen behind one ear, and hit the street.

She had a case to build.

Not just a case—stories. Names, dates, photos. Shop floor layouts. Shipment records. Air filters logged and "lost." One guy left the union-paid diner breakfast halfway through—started coughing blood into a napkin. Said he "didn't want to be a downer." Obits with the same damn word in them: *mesothelioma*. The kind of diagnosis that doesn't come from bad luck. The kind that comes from negligence.

It was all there. In the maintenance logs, the parts inventory, the asbestos abatement plan that got quietly downgraded to "recommendations." In the memos that said "cost-prohibitive" and "low likelihood of exposure." In the email chain where someone flagged a deteriorating duct panel—and got ignored. In the hush money NDA one widow sent her lawyer to rip apart.

None of it was new. The risk had been documented years ago. Mitigation protocols filed. Safety trainings scheduled, then canceled. Whistleblowers silenced or shuffled to night shift. One guy got reassigned to desk duty after he filed a complaint—retired early, died within eighteen months.

It could've been caught. Could've been fixed.

It wasn't.

Because someone somewhere decided the retrofit was too expensive. The cleanup too slow. The optics too ugly. So they wrote it off. Took the gamble. Played roulette with other people's lungs.

And now? Now they were dying. Quietly. Expensively. Predictably.

And Vee?

Vee had worked the same hangars. Breathed the same air. Ran the same drills in the belly of the plane—tight, rusted compartments with no real ventilation and no time to wear a mask right. By every rule of exposure, she should've been coughing up pieces of herself by now—waiting on a biopsy, rehearsing her eulogy.

But somehow, she wasn't.

Maybe it was the shift rotation. Maybe it was the months she got pulled for line work at Midway. Maybe it was sheer fucking luck. Her station got upgraded early—new HVAC, new sealants, a contractor who actually gave a shit. She'd complained about it at the time. Called the remodel a waste of funds. Said the new panels made the crawlspaces hotter.

Turns out they probably saved her life.

She didn't like the math of it. Didn't like the way the odds played favorites. She kept waiting for the other shoe to drop—CT scan, shadow, headline. But it never came.

She was fine.

And the ones who weren't?

They'd stood right beside her.

She was mid-video conference call when the front door slammed open like it had any right to. Kha stumbled in, sweat-slick and wide-eyed, hoodie half-off his shoulder, phone dead, eyes bloodshot.

His presence stretched upward—broad-shouldered, built solid—the kind that filled a room whether he intended to or not. Tattoos ran down his arms and climbed the side of his neck. Some looked fresh. Others had the faded, rough-edged look of ink earned in places where choices ran out.

"You must be fucking joking," Vee muttered, muting her call. She didn't turn around. Just stared ahead at her screen while her voice dropped into that low, ancestral octave—the one passed down by women who'd survived colonization, immigration, and raising the dumbass sons of their siblings.

"You come in this house smelling like weed and basement pussy, after not calling for forty-eight hours—you better start running now."

Kha rolled his eyes. Mistake number one.

"I'm not a kid anymore, Auntie Vee."

She stood. Not fast. Not loud. Just precise.

"You're right," she said. "You're not a kid. You're a six-foot-one embarrassment with two working legs and no working brain. Where the fuck were you? You think because you have pubes and a vape you get to disappear? You think if you made your mom bail you out again I wouldn't be right there with her dragging your ass home by the roots?"

"It's not that deep—"

"It's not that deep? Bitch, I will make it shallow."

Then—without breaking eye contact—she reached down, slipped off one of her house slippers, and launched it at his chest. Full force. Perfect aim. Echoed off his sternum like judgment. Kha flinched like he'd been shot.

"Keep talking. I'll throw the other one. And then the air fryer."

He backed up, hands up. "Damn, okay! I was just staying at a girl's place, my phone died—"

"Your brain's been dead. The phone's just catching up. Next time you vanish, I'm not calling you. I'm calling Bà. And I'll put her on speaker. Let's see if your ears survive that before your ego does."

Bà survived the fall of Saigon, three refugee camps, and forty years of back-breaking salon work in Long Beach—when she yelled, it was divine punishment.

That cowed him. He disappeared down the hall, six feet of sulking failure and no upper hand.

Vee sat back down, unmuted. Face smooth. Voice calm.

"So," she said to the baby-faced union organizer still frozen like he'd seen a haunting, "you wanna organize here, you better learn two things: one, you're not smarter than the people who clean your planes. And two, when the brass say no? That's just your cue to dig deeper."

She gave him a once-over—clean button-down, nice watch, earnest panic behind the eyes.

The union had hired themselves a Harvard boy. The kind they could wring dry for two years before he wised up, cut his hair short, and jumped to corporate law with a moral exit interview and a new LinkedIn header.

She'd seen five of him already.

And every single one of them took her word like law.

She didn't even have a college diploma.

But she'd been fighting this place for two decades—long before it rebranded, long before it got shiny logos and DEI pamphlets. Same company. Same rot. Different flavor each year.

She'd led strikes in ninety-degree heat with tear gas still hanging in the air. Held the line through contract freezes, pay gaps, furlough threats. She'd forced management to rewrite the bathroom policy after a trans mechanic got cornered on her break. Put an end to the supervisor who thought back pats belonged south of the shoulder blades.

She knew how to turn a walkout into a headline. Knew how to kill a rumor in under three texts. Which local reporters to feed a quote to when corporate tried to play PR.

She wasn't just here to negotiate. She was here to count the dead.

Half her time was spent tracking down survivors. The other half was convincing them it wasn't their fault.

Her phone stayed hot. Burned through chargers, overheated in her back pocket. She ran meetings in laundromats and wrote statements on bar napkins. Told one grieving daughter to meet her at a dog park and conducted the whole interview with a pit bull in her lap. The dog farted halfway through. They both cried anyway.

The union office stayed open late. She'd crash in the break room sometimes, jacket balled under her head. The admin would leave a note: *Clock out next time, you martyr.* She didn't.

No one mentioned Sloane. Not even Morgan.

Sunday night came and went. The usual. Morgan in leggings, Kieran barefoot in the kitchen, a bottle of wine already open. MILF Fight Club season sixteen on screen. Vee showed up in sweatpants and an ankle brace.

"Round three, I got big titty Debbie," Kieran said, pulling the rack of lamb out of the oven.

The kitchen smelled unfair—rosemary, garlic, Dijon, rendered fat hitting hot metal. He plated like it was a Food Network season finale, arranging the chops with a flourish that made Morgan roll her eyes without looking up from her laptop.

"Incorrect," Vee replied, mouth full. "Debbie can't block for shit. She's gassed by minute five. Lucía takes the win."

"You always bet on the hot one," Morgan said. "Be for real."

"You married the hot one," Vee muttered, and that got a laugh.

Sloane didn't come up. Not once. Not in Morgan's clack-clack multitasking, not in Kieran's wine glass monologue about how every airline CEO should be required to fly middle seat economy once a month or be set on fire. Vee didn't ask. She wasn't going to. She could endure a lot of things—structural failure, toxic exposure, back-to-back shifts—but she wasn't about to ask after someone who walked out without saying goodbye.

Monday blurred. Union work by day, mechanic duties at night. A birdstrike inspection that nearly broke her back.

Late-night parts order from a vendor she hated. Elbow-deep in jet guts by midnight, high on acetone and rage.

And then—Tuesday.

The meeting was set for 9 a.m. sharp. Conference room on the 22nd floor in the Loop. New Heritage brass. New CEO, new COO, all polished and desperate to be liked. They wore Patagonia vests. They thought coffee carts and equity statements could mop up the blood.

Vee walked in with three manila folders and a migraine. Black denim, fitted blazer, and her nails this time were clear of polish and simply cut short and clean. The blazer was stupidly expensive—structured shoulders, high cut, sleek as sin. Morgan had given it to her in a garment bag with no explanation years ago. The tag said something French and judgmental. She'd paired it with a thrifted black silk blouse she'd found for four dollars, still faintly scented like someone else's auntie's perfume, and suede black ankle boots that were clean but heavy. Just enough heel to remind the room she could still kick something over if provoked.

No combat boots this time. No leather jacket armor. But she still looked like someone who'd crash your board meeting and dare you to ask her to leave.

Her hair was clipped back—tight, deliberate—but a few straight strands had fallen loose and framed her face like punctuation. Her eyeliner was sharp. Red lip, matte. Multiple earrings, mismatched on purpose. A silver cuff on one wrist. Rings on almost every finger—thick, scratched, intentional.

It was boardroom friendly.

Barely.

The union guys flanked her—some in suits, some in faded tees, all of them tired. She could feel their expectation like weight in her ribcage. They wanted her to speak. She always spoke. Even when she didn't want to. Even when she was tired of being useful.

A legal assistant opened the door.

"General counsel's here," she chirped.

And then there she was.

Sloane fucking Campbell. She walked in wearing a navy sheath dress—boardroom armor, fitted like it was custom. High neckline, structured shoulders, just enough hem to stay HR-compliant. The kind of dress that didn't ask for power. It assumed it. Her thick curls tied back like it had somewhere to be. Calm as a held breath. No hesitation in the step. Not even a flicker of surprise.

And her body—goddamn her.

Tall, cut, perfectly still. Legs for days and posture like violence. Elegant shoulders, tight waist, that long, clean line down her back Vee used to trace with her mouth. She could still feel the press of her thighs, the grip of those hips. The way Sloane moved: efficient, deliberate, every step a sentence. And that ass—high, perfect, carved like it belonged in a museum.

Sloane sat down at the head of the table like she'd been born there.

Vee didn't react. She short-circuited. For half a second—just one—her entire body went twitchy. Pupils dilated. Pulse in her ears. She felt it, embarrassing and immediate: the urge to bend the woman across from her over the conference table and bite a perfect semicircle into her shoulder.

Next to her, the new union organizer—Noah Feldman-Bloom, fresh out of Harvard and still mixing up Article 34 with the seniority protections—glanced at her and immediately looked away, like he'd just witnessed an HR violation. His clipboard trembled slightly.

And then her brain caught up.

Her hot, aloof, occasionally ruinous situationship had just walked in as opposing fucking counsel.

She felt the tremor somewhere in her spine, the ripple of you've got to be fucking kidding me threatening to break loose. But she swallowed it. Filed it under Later.

Because now? Now she had a room to burn.

5

The folders landed with a sound Sloane recognized instantly: deposition-grade.

Thick paper, heavy spine, the faint acidic smell of toner and threat.

She smoothed her hair behind one ear, adjusted the slim gold watch on her wrist, and centered her pen. Her tone didn't change. It never did.

"We appreciate the union's continued engagement—especially in light of recent emotional escalations."

She didn't say Vee's name. She didn't have to. The tension in the room shifted like pressure dropping before a storm.

Across the table, Vee smiled. Not sweetly. She tilted her head, just slightly, like she was tuning into a private frequency.

Sloane hated how endearing it was.

"You'll have to forgive the escalation, counsel. We're used to watching people die slow."

The word "counsel" landed sharp enough to draw blood. Someone shifted in their chair. No one followed up.

Sloane remained still.

"Then let's move to the proposed timeline for implementing enhanced facility standards. I assume you brought documentation."

Three folders slid across the table. They landed against her legal pad with a satisfying slap.

Noah Feldman-Bloom—the new union hire, visibly sweating—tried to fill the silence with numbers.

Sloane corrected him without looking down.

"That's under OSHA 1910.1001, not .1020. Thirty-day reporting window post-diagnosis."

Vee didn't miss a beat.

"Unless it's a Class III operation. Then it's ten. Which you'd know—if you'd been in the hangar instead of reading about it."

Another silence. This one didn't breathe.

"Fine. We will make a note of it."

Vee, quiet: "You always did like having the last word."

Sloane looked up once. Not long.

"And you always mistake silence for surrender."

Noah tried to pivot.

"So—uh—about the implementation timeline—"

Vee didn't break eye contact.

"Let's get something clear. We're not here to make requests. We're here to confirm your compliance."

Someone knocked over a bottle of water. No one picked it up.

Sloane turned a page, tone perfectly unbothered.

"We're prepared to discuss performance-based retrofits over the next fiscal cycle. With third-party environmental audits."

She didn't say take it or leave it. But she didn't have to.

Her tone had been developed in appellate courtrooms and C-suite briefings. It didn't invite interpretation.

Vee's laugh cracked it open. Not cruel. Just tired.

"You want optics. We want overhaul."

She opened the first folder and laid it flat.

"Two hundred and twenty-five million. That's the projected cost of retrofitting your five major maintenance hubs to match EPA and OSHA standards that haven't hit yet —because your bosses made damn sure of that."

She didn't refer to the entirely new executive suite. She didn't need to.

"New HVAC. Industrial air filtration. Sealant replacements. Full toxic material removal. Training. Site-wide safety protocol rewrites. Internal monitors with third-party oversight."

She opened the second folder.

"On top of that: a long-term healthcare fund. Terminal cases. Diagnosed workers. Ongoing care. Retroactive coverage. Hazard compensation."

The third folder sat unopened. For now.

"And then there's the survivor settlements. For the families. For the widows. For the kids who got handed condolences and NDAs while your board approved dividend increases. That's separate, too."

Finally, she looked at Sloane.

"Itemize it however you want. But you're going to pay."

Sloane's pen stilled. Only for a second.

Her face didn't move, but inside something shifted. An old reflex, maybe. The sense of battle lines hardening.

She'd seen the internal estimates. She knew the site that got the early retrofit. She'd reviewed the email chains flagged for deletion and watched the C-suite twist themselves into knots trying to call a decade of negligence a clerical oversight.

She also knew the politics of saying no.

She'd done the math—cost per family, per facility, per legal hour billed. This was three-pronged: the capital cost of prevention, the long tail of healthcare liability, and the emotional damage settlements meant to make disappear.

Sloane had thought that part of her life was compartmentalized—contained. And yet here she was, walking and talking and delivering a $225 million ultimatum in a fitted blazer.

She turned another page.

Her hand didn't shake. But her mind flickered, uninvited, to Jamaica. The mountain air. The fan spinning above her late uncle's patio. The wide, slow pour of hibiscus tea into sweating glasses. Her aunt's hand on hers, the legal document resting between them like a dare.

"You're the only one who can get us out of this. Help us."

Sloane had nodded. Of course she would.

And now here she was. A general counsel in a rebranded airline that hadn't changed its bones. Playing clean-up with inherited guilt and borrowed polish.

What kind of soap opera was this? What were the odds?

She didn't bother asking. She knew better.

Aviation was a small world. Smaller still if you didn't fit the mold.

And when you crossed three lines in the sand—race, gender, queerness—you stopped being anonymous a long time ago.

It wasn't fate. It wasn't irony. It was the inevitable result of a closed circuit—same faces, same names, same doors held half-open if you were lucky, slammed shut if you weren't.

None of this was coincidence.

Just another ripple in the pattern—one she'd tried to outrun, but that kept catching up anyway.

Sloane let the silence hang.

She didn't look down. Didn't reach for the pen she'd capped minutes ago. She just folded her hands—precisely, palms flat on the table—and smiled.

"These are detailed," she said finally. "Thorough. Unfortunately, many of them are also inadmissible."

Her tone was mild. Almost helpful. The kind of voice she reserved for interns and political appointees with fragile egos.

She tapped the edge of the first folder—twice, lightly.

"This report was filed by an unlicensed contractor. Terminated for cause six weeks before this timestamp. Which, I'll add, has been digitally altered."

She turned to the second.

"The diagnostic statements in here? Not accompanied by medical records. No chain of custody. No witness affirmation. Several of them have already been disqualified by the company's insurer."

Then she glanced at the third. Didn't even touch it.

"And the NDA you cited predates the referenced incident by six months. Which makes it emotionally compelling but legally irrelevant."

The room didn't breathe. Noah looked like he might faint.

Sloane shifted slightly in her chair, legs crossed, eyes sharp and clear as disinfectant.

"If I were litigating this, I'd be asking who assembled this for you. And why they let you walk into a negotiation with it."

A pause. Not smug. Just surgical.

"I'm saying this now because you still have time to revise your approach."

Across the table, Vee didn't move.

Not at first.

Then—slowly, like the motion cost her—she pushed back from the table. Not far. Just enough to sit back, arms crossed, one ringed hand flexing against her sleeve.

Her face was red. Not just from fury—from heat. From knowing she'd been outmaneuvered in front of her people.

"You've already been digging, huh," she said. Low. Controlled. Barely a question.

Sloane held her expression. She didn't answer.

She only tilted her head, just slightly—an almost imperceptible shift. Not denial. Not confirmation. Just the kind of poise that said: *You already know. I don't need to say it.*

Vee looked like she'd been slapped.

And then—cool, almost amused, Sloane said: "There's also the matter of the two individuals you spoke to during your preliminary review. One has since recanted. The other retained private counsel. I'd advise checking who's leaking to whom."

Vee's jaw locked. Her shoulders went rigid.

If Sloane reached out right now—just brushed the side of her face—she was certain Vee would bite her.

But that wasn't what this was.

This was about power. And precision. And letting Vee know—in front of her team—that she'd walked into a fight half-dressed and overconfident.

Sloane picked up her pen again. Slowly.

"We'll take the union's proposal under advisement," she said, with that same inflectionless grace. "But we won't be making any commitments today."

Across the table, Vee was still vibrating. Her chest rising

fast. Color blooming high across her cheekbones, her throat. She looked like a woman about to throw something or fuck someone.

Sloane didn't look away.

She never did.

6

Outside, the air smelled like ambition and exhaust. Sloane adjusted her sunglasses and stepped off the curb, heels slicing clean through the sidewalk grit. The conference room still clung to her like smoke—acrid, oppressive.

Lucretia's touch lingered too: a manicured hand between her shoulder blades, her voice low—"Beautiful work. We'll stall until the board makes me permanent. Keep doing what you're doing."

Which meant: *Keep the union bleeding. Keep the settlements theoretical. Keep Heritage afloat long enough for a rebrand and a bonus cycle.*

So now she was hunting down a $25 salad in heels that hurt. Not because she wanted it. Because she needed the ritual. Something clean, overpriced, and green—proof of discipline in a world built to tempt you into rot.

She felt it then—that sour twist in her stomach, the knowledge that Vee was right. About the cost. About the bodies. About all of it.

But guilt was a luxury.

She'd grown up understanding that women like her didn't get clean wins. Only survival in tailored increments. And every polished decision she made—every calculated cruelty—was another inch of ground clawed from a world built to erase her.

So yes, she felt like shit.

But she wasn't sorry.

Regret didn't keep the lights on. Strategy did.

She turned the corner—and stopped.

Vee's truck was parked crooked at the edge of the street, windows down, engine off. She sat inside like someone who'd forgotten how to leave. Arms slack. Face blank. Her blazer had slipped off one shoulder.

And her eyes—Sloane clocked it instantly—were red. Not high, not hungover. Crying. Not dramatically. Just enough that it lingered in the creases. Evidence of softness, or something like it, fighting to exist in a world that did not reward it.

It should've made her look small.

It didn't.

She looked like a fucking weapon. Like a beautiful, maddening, overpriced piece of protest art. That same impossible face—soft where it shouldn't be, angular where it hurt, with that smug little mouth that never stayed shut long enough to be safe. She still dressed like a juvenile delinquent who'd snuck into a union hall. Still wore her hair like she cut it herself in the bathroom mirror and didn't care how it fell.

And it still worked.

Sloane hated that it still worked.

From across the street, she could feel the heat of her. The same heat from the room, from the fight. From her skin, that one time Sloane had let herself touch it with her mouth, her hands.

It was almost funny. Almost. How Vee could look like she'd been through hell, like she was barely hanging on, and still Sloane felt like the one disarmed.

Because there she was. Sitting still, looking ruined. And Sloane—Sloane was somehow the one who wanted to beg.

She adjusted the strap of her clutch. Swallowed something unprofessional. And kept walking.

Sloane ordered her salad with the same focus she brought to cross-examination: calmly, ruthlessly, and with no room for substitutions.

"Spring mix. Farro. Roasted sweet potato. Extra pickled onion. No almonds. Light vinaigrette."

The cashier didn't even try small talk. Smart.

She stepped aside, tapped her AirPods in. One ring.

"Talk."

Her private investigator's voice came clipped. "The HVAC report the union submitted? The contractor's clean. But the timestamp's off—uploaded six days after the inspection window closed. Makes it technically inadmissible unless they get it re-certified."

"And the survivor affidavits?"

"Five legit. Two flagged. One under active litigation for an unrelated matter. I'm still digging."

Sloane swiped open her encrypted app, read the message from the twins. The diagnostics Vee submitted weren't invalid —they were just...incomplete. Missing sign-off from attending physicians. No sealed affidavits. One file had been submitted post-expiration on the claim window. Another referenced a facility address that had been rezoned six months ago.

It was good work. Just not good enough.

And in Sloane's world, that was fatal.

She closed the chat. Tapped out a thank-you. Put her phone away.

This was the part no one liked admitting: that law was mostly architecture. Not truth. Not justice. Just who could build the cleanest structure before the whole thing caved in. And right now? Vee's case was drywall and crossed fingers.

Sloane's name got called. She collected the compostable box, stepped toward the far corner where the signal was weak and the bathroom door didn't squeak when it closed. She needed five minutes. Just five.

Work-life balance. Or the illusion of it.

The mirror was a little too clean. She washed her hands. Pressed her fingers to her temples like she could exhale a career's worth of ethical compromise.

A stall door clicked open behind her.

Sloane didn't turn. She kept checking herself in the mirror, assuming someone else had entered. Heard running water. The scent of citrus soap—bright, hospital-issue—cut through the air.

And then—

The shove came fast. Not enough to bruise. Just enough to jolt.

Vee stood before her. Eyes blazing. Still red. Still ruinously beautiful. The bathroom door locked automatically behind them.

"What the fuck is wrong with you?"

Sloane didn't move. "You'll need to be more specific."

Vee stepped forward, voice rough. "How can you work for them? How can you sit in that room and act like you don't know what this costs?"

"I do know."

"Then what the fuck are you doing?"

Sloane met her gaze. Steady. Unmoved. "I work for the highest bidder. That's not news."

"Bullshit," Vee snapped. "You're not that kind of person."

"You don't know what kind of person I am."

"I used to."

"No," Sloane said, calm as poison. "You used to sleep with me. That's not the same thing."

Vee's hand twitched at her side. Not violent. Just overwhelmed.

"This is sick," she said. "You sued them barely a year ago. You filed the goddamn injunction."

"And now I'm inside the firewall," Sloane replied. "That's how it works. Enemies closer."

Vee's breath hitched. "How are you so calm?"

Sloane stepped forward, barely closing the distance. "Because it's all a lie. The whole game. You think any of this ends in justice? It ends in settlements. In hush money. In back-channel hires and job changes."

"You think that makes it okay?"

"No," Sloane said. "But it makes it survivable."

Vee stared at her like she didn't recognize the person standing there. Like she'd been handed a body double.

"God," she whispered. "You actually believe that."

"I have to."

And then—it happened.

The second push wasn't calculated. It wasn't posturing.

It was fury. And grief. And every ruined part of Vee that still wanted something from her.

Sloane hit the tile hard enough to feel it in her teeth. She quickly straightened, dusted her blazer with one sharp flick—more signal than cleanup.

"Really."

Dry, flat, said like an exhale. But they both knew the

game. They didn't do softness. They liked control contested, power traded in bruises, and wanting sharpened to a blade.

"Yes," Vee said through gritted teeth. "Really."

They were too close. Breathing the same air. The tension so tight it could snap ribs.

Sloane didn't move. Just looked at her, careful now, voice low.

"Tell me what this is."

A pause. Not refusal—something else.

Vee's hand hovered at her waist. Not holding. Not letting go.

"You already know."

"I want to hear you say it."

Not a command. A check-in, buried under steel.

"I want it," Vee said—her tongue trailing the curve of Sloane's neck before it sharpened into a bite.

Sloane drew in a sharp breath through her nose and closed her eyes.

"Then do it right."

And that was the only permission either of them ever needed.

Vee grabbed her hips in a searing grip and pinned her against the tile—hard. Not mean, not messy. Just decisive. A challenge. Sloane didn't dignify it with a response. She took her time reversing the hold, effortlessly, like shifting the power dynamic in a deposition. Now Vee was the one pressed against tiles, her head only reaching Sloane's chin. Not that height meant anything when the woman could probably deadlift a Vespa with one hand and twist a lug nut with the other. That mechanic strength.

They tussled. Half-fight, half-foreplay, all tension. Vee's blazer hit the ground with a disrespectful slap—no ceremony, just gravity and lust. Sloane couldn't stop herself—

her hands traveled under that black silk top, found Vee's chest, squeezed. Porn star tits, absurd, too perfect for someone who spent her days bent under hoods and half inside engines. Sloane bent low, bit down and sucked, shameless. But while she was indulging, Vee was working.

That goddamn hidden zipper.

Vee got it down, but the architecture of it was too complex for one quick tug, so she gave up and shoved the hem up and snapped her thong clean off like a party trick. Sloane barely had time to hiss, "What the fuck. Are you gonna pay for that?"

"No," Vee said, grinning like a villain in an indie slasher.

Vee reached up, fingers extended. Sloane knew what to do. She wrapped her lips around Vee's index and middle finger, sucked them in slow. Citrus. Soap. Clean in a way that made her filthier by contrast.

Then Vee's hands were on her.

Her fingers slipped between Sloane's thighs like they'd never forgotten the way. When they came back slick, she didn't pause—just pushed in with purpose.

Sloane tensed, muscles clamping instinctively, breath stalling. It should've hurt more. But instead, the pain carved something out of her. She gave. And before she knew it, Vee had twisted her around so her back was to the wall again.

She went loose. Melted.

She reached for Vee's breasts again, greedy, but Vee blocked her—hedged her in, strong and strategic. One leg around Vee's waist, fingers driving in again, not easing or teasing now, but knowing. Fucking her like she had something to prove.

Vee knew exactly where her G-spot was. Didn't waste time. She curled her fingers into it with efficiency—but never quite enough. Always just shy.

Before she realized what was coming out of her mouth, Sloane was panting, begging, unraveling with every near-miss. Vee smirked—ruthless, delighted, chaotic as hell.

Then: both fingers in again. Curling. Persistent. Her palm grinding Sloane's clit. She slammed her hips forward and Sloane shattered—no lead-up, no buildup, just gone. A full-body clench and a long, torn sound she couldn't have held back if she tried.

But Vee wasn't done.

She never was done.

Sloane was already hypersensitive, wrecked, but Vee kept going, expertly riding her through the aftershocks. Kept her right there, teetering, and dragged another orgasm out of her like it was extraction. A rough kiss followed, messy, teeth and tongues, someone bleeding—she didn't know who, didn't care. There was copper on her tongue and heat crawling down her spine and she came again, this one mean and involuntary.

By the time Vee pulled out, Sloane was a wreck of herself. Empty in that immediate, lonely way. She slid down to the floor like a broken statue, limbs shaking, still mostly dressed, hem slanted indecently.

Before she could catch her breath, she looked up and saw Vee at the sink. She washed her hands with the precision of a surgeon—meticulous, mechanical. Not once did she speak. Not even a glance. She finished, dried her hands, and walked out like it meant nothing. Like she hadn't just wrecked Sloane.

7

By the time Sloane stepped off the elevator on the fiftieth floor, her legs had stopped shaking. Mostly.

She moved like nothing had happened. Like she hadn't just been fucked against a mirror in the bathroom of a salad chain that sold quinoa like it was a luxury good. Like she hadn't walked out past a line of women glaring daggers and a teenage employee yelling, "Don't come back." The salad in her hand cost twenty-seven dollars. The indignity had no ceiling.

"Where were you?" her assistant asked the moment she crossed the threshold.

Zora was seated behind her desk, immaculate stiletto nails drumming against a keyboard. Her expression was unreadable in the way only truly beautiful people could pull off.

"You know it's literally my job to fetch that crap for you."

"I needed the walk," Sloane replied, already halfway through her door.

Zora narrowed her eyes, but said nothing. Sloane

respected that. Suspicion without insubordination. It was why she'd hired her.

The office smelled faintly like glass cleaner. Her inbox lit up like a coronial inquest: three escalating emails from Heritage board members and one long, seething manifesto from someone in the union that included the words *press*, *liability*, and *criminal negligence*.

She didn't flinch. She read, responded, and neutralized.

To the board: "Panic is a poor strategy. Sit still."

To the union: "Any external disclosure during pending legal review will result in a countersuit with full injunctive power. Your move."

She did not over-explain. That was a weakness.

Her privately-appointed conference room was already occupied when she entered. The windows framed downtown like a hostage, the view too wide, too quiet.

The hacker twins—El and Andi—sat cross-legged on opposite ends of a window sill, syncing files in eerie unison. Both wore black. Both had that shimmery, half-ethereal presence of people who lived online more than off. They were already tracking metadata from three Heritage employee group chats and an aviation subreddit.

In the window seat lounged her PI—Kenji Miwa, silver-haired, half-buttoned shirt, leather notebook balanced on one knee. He didn't bother pretending to look busy. Just watched her, like he already knew what the next few months will hold.

"You're flushed," El said without looking up.

Andi elbowed them. "Shh!"

They exchanged a glance. Sloane stared back just long enough to make it stop.

Then Zora cleared her throat. "Most important thing of the day—guess who just got dropped off by pet concierge?

Flown private from D.C., mind you, while the rest of us were in economy praying for legroom and dignity."

She wheeled in the travel enclosure—sleek, matte-black, with reinforced corners and chrome accents that caught the office light. Inside, under a battery-run amber heat lamp, a five-foot leucistic ball python lay coiled with the detached elegance of royalty. Her scales were flawless white, nearly iridescent in places, and her eyes were pale gray like polished pearls—no pigment, no pattern, just the soft menace of something that had never needed camouflage to survive.

Sloane didn't pause. Mid-sentence, she unlatched the case with one hand while scrolling through a brief with the other. Her fingers moved with clinical precision, letting the snake rise from the enclosure and wind itself around her wrist, then her arm, then the crook of her neck. Tiberia settled there—slow, deliberate—until she draped across Sloane's collarbones like a scarf made of muscle and myth.

She hadn't wanted Tiberia to spend her first hours in a strange city alone. Sloane wouldn't tolerate it for herself— why would she expect her snake to?

No one in the room raised an eyebrow.

Across from her, one of the twins cleared their throat and muttered, "What do you think, Tiberia? Satisfied with the Q2 forecast?"

The other twin didn't miss a beat. "We can restructure the intel drop if the Queen is displeased."

Kenji didn't even look up from his notepad. "Please advise, ma'am," he said, dry as ash. "We live to serve."

Sloane didn't smile. She turned the page of the report like nothing was out of the ordinary and said, "She approves."

And somehow, they all accepted that.

The meeting continued.

Updates were fast, clinical. Three leaks identified. Two reporters already sniffing around the cancer disclosures.

Then—

"Vee Phan met with a specialist—independent reporter. Covers OSHA, industrial accidents, environmental damage. The kind who digs till someone bleeds."

Sloane frowned, trying not to think about how her hand had been up that same woman's shirt less than thirty minutes earlier.

Kenji glanced up from his notes. "You want me to follow her?"

She kept her expression blank by force. "Obviously."

He raised an eyebrow. "Are you sure?"

She turned her head. "If that was an attempt at subtlety, I'd suggest a different field."

Kenji didn't flinch. "Noted. I'll stick to surveillance."

"And report back," she said, voice even. "Daily."

He nodded, but she didn't like the look he gave her.

After the room cleared, Zora lingered.

"They're getting antsy," she said finally. "Chicago's not their scene. They think you're wasting your firepower on an airline."

Sloane didn't answer right away. Just picked up her salad and set it down without opening it.

"They don't need to understand why we're here," she said. "They just need to do their jobs."

Zora gave a shrug that looked like surrender. "They will. You know they will."

Sloane didn't reply.

She hadn't told any of them the truth.

This wasn't about fixing Heritage and corporate reform.

It wasn't even about the company.

It was about a ledger written before she was born.

A debt disguised as generosity.

A deal her grandfather should've walked away from—and a signature that bound more than just a balance sheet.

She said yes because someone had to pay it off. And she was the last one left who could.

SHE HATED THURSDAYS.

That was the day of the executive roundtable: division heads, regional VPs, overpaid strategists clawed up the ladder or airlifted there by nepotism. The boardroom on the seventieth floor was chilled to preserve egos and orchids. Heritage called it a Weekly Alignment. Sloane called it an air-conditioned act of violence.

At the head sat Lucretia Morrow—interim CEO and Ava Thompkins' favored heir. British-Egyptian, immaculately composed, with the bone structure of a statue looted from its homeland and forced into a pantsuit. She had the stillness of something ancient and heavily surveilled. Her smile never reached her eyes.

Lucretia didn't speak often, but when she did, the room shifted. A tilt of her chin, and someone's quarter got reforecasted. A breath too long, and a VP was quietly exiled to "strategic consultancy."

By 2:15 p.m., they'd slashed union overtime by forty percent, greenlit a vague snack rebrand to "reinforce domestic loyalty," and hired a Yale legacy whose last name caused visible arousal among the board.

No one reacted. Sloane didn't either. She just marked the approvals in the margin—handwriting sharp and neat, like it knew it might one day be used against her.

The meeting ended not with a bang, but with an executive assistant handing out embossed folders and the scent of espresso creeping in from the hallway. Someone made a joke about last quarter's crash being "a controlled landing." There was polite laughter. The kind that smelled like money and mouthwash.

At 6:40 p.m., she left.

Sloane slipped the sleek, heated reptile carrier into the oversized Goyard tote she used for "non-essentials," then slid into the back of the waiting car. Not a look from the driver. Either he was paid too well to react or too tired to care that his passenger was carrying a five-foot snake like a handbag.

Heritage paid for the apartment—a gleaming tower in the Gold Coast, all angles and hush. The view faced Lake Michigan like it was a reward. Floor-to-ceiling windows, polished stone, furniture chosen by someone who'd never met her but had read a portfolio labeled Executive Female, Mid-Thirties, Tasteful Power.

It was too much space. Too much lake. The water stretched out like an accusation.

Near the windows sat a custom-built glass terrarium—temperature-regulated, humidity-controlled, basking lamp pre-installed—discreetly built into the living room architecture like it had always been there. It hadn't. Sloane had negotiated it as part of her relocation package. Tiberia's comfort had been listed under non-negotiable living expenses. Legal hadn't reacted. Heritage wanted her badly enough to build a reptile temple in a penthouse.

She opened the carrier, let Tiberia unwind slowly from her wrist, and placed her inside. The python moved with deliberate grace, adjusting to the new heat gradient like she'd expected nothing less.

Sloane tapped the glass once—soft, almost absent.

"Welcome to your new home," she murmured. "Eleven months. Try to enjoy it more than I will."

She stepped out of her heels in the foyer, the leather sighing softly as if relieved. Walked barefoot across imported Italian stone flooring that—despite the expense—felt no different than the cracked tile in her family's ancestral estate in the Blue Mountains.

A crumbling colonial mansion, reclaimed a century ago with salt and strategy. Her grandfather called it a victory. Her late mother called it a mausoleum with plumbing. Sloane had called it home.

Her phone buzzed. Two unread messages. One from legal. The other from a board member trying to "circle back."

Nothing from Vee. Not that she expected anything.

Instead, she stood by the glass, drink in hand, watching the lake not move.

It was a long way down.

She changed into silence.

Black shorts. Cotton bralette. Hair pinned back. No mirrors. No playlist. Just her pole—matte chrome, floor-to-ceiling, bolted into the bones of the living space like it came with the lease.

She didn't do cardio. Didn't run. Didn't lift. What she did was this.

The speakers clicked on. Philip Glass.

Not for the irony—for the discipline. The relentlessness. The unresolving tension. Each note like a metronome counting down her restraint.

Sometimes she switched to Nicholas Britell when she felt sentimental. Max Richter when she didn't. Today, she chose Glass. Repetition was honesty. Structure was freedom.

She approached the pole like a shrine. One hand. Then the other. She let gravity flirt. Then she denied it.

Climb. Hook. Invert. Fold.

It was choreography, but also war.

And she was good. Not casually good. Not "toned and capable" good. Good like she'd once made an instructor at her old studio pause mid-critique and say, flatly, "If you ever quit law, you could make what you make now."

That had been back in year one—fresh off the bar, still believing she had options.

She'd laughed then.

But here, in the echo of minimalist piano and the clean bite of muscle on metal, it didn't feel like a joke.

And for a split second—one breath, one tremble—she thought of Vee.

The way Vee had looked at her that morning. Open. Furious. Like she was watching Sloane do something dangerous and couldn't decide if she wanted to stop her or hand her more fire.

That morning, Vee's hands had gripped her thighs the same way she gripped the pole now—like control wasn't a request, it was a dare.

Sloane exhaled. Adjusted her grip. Pushed higher.

She didn't need Vee in this space.

But her body remembered her anyway.

And in that moment—balanced mid-air, bruised and breathless—Sloane Campbell felt closer to the truth than she had in weeks.

She showered with the lights off.

She cooked.

Always something simple. Always from scratch. A pot of rice, callaloo with garlic and thyme, a soft-boiled egg sliced clean. Not traditional, maybe. But familiar enough.

She moved with the kind of ease you only get when someone has shown you—not once, but a hundred times—and expected you to remember.

The apartment smelled like something real for the first time all day.

She ate barefoot by the window, Lake Michigan stretching wide and unknowable. Just the dark pressing against the glass and the echo of her own quiet.

Tiberia slept in the terrarium, barely moving, as if to say: *this, at least, is safe.*

When the dishes were done and the air had cooled, she turned out the lights and slipped into bed.

8

Vee hadn't expected to feel good tonight. The workplace exposure mess had dragged into its third week of silence—no progress, no account-ability—and it had been sitting in her chest like wet concrete.

She'd dressed up. A crushed velvet slip dress clung to her hips like it had an agenda. Dark red, almost black. Her lace-up PVC boots were scuffed to hell and still added two inches. Every finger carried a ring—silver, brass, black enamel—like her hands had stories to tell and weren't asking permission.

Her arms were bare. The tattoo on her left bicep glinted under gallery lights: engine parts etched in fine detail, gears and pistons arranged like a blueprint for something holy and half-destroyed.

Neck laced in chains. Red lips catching the neck of the beer bottle.

She knew exactly what she looked like—dangerous, deliberate, untouchable.

But swagger didn't cancel out grief. Or rage. Or how tired she was of waiting for justice to call back.

Still, here she was—beer in hand, standing in a converted auto body shop packed with the Chicago art scene—and somehow, she felt okay.

The space buzzed. Concrete floors, corrugated walls, the smell of hot metal still clinging to the air. There was ambient music looping through a busted PA, and a churro truck parked outside. Half the room looked like they'd wandered off the set of a punk zine from 2007; the other half were clearly in grad school debt denial chic.

And the artist? Rosa fucking Márquez.

Her favorite pain-in-the-ass with a welding torch and a god complex. Her ex. Her old hangar mate. Six years side by side under leaking fuselages and broken union promises—before Rosa walked away from torque wrenches and certification cycles to melt scrap into beauty. Last year, one of her pieces got picked up by LACMA. Vee still hadn't shut up about it.

They hugged the second they locked eyes. No hesitation. No stiff-shouldered half-embrace. A real hug. Arms tight around each other. Face in neck.

Rosa still smelled like iron and incense.

Vee whispered, "I'm so fucking proud of you." Every syllable true.

Rosa grinned into her shoulder. "Told you I'd get out."

"You're unbearable."

"You're still hot."

"Fuck off."

It was all affection.

The sculptures were brutal and beautiful—twisted metal, hand-forged with detail that made your teeth hurt. Rosa had taken scrap from an aircraft boneyard in Mojave and turned it into a towering piece about grief and transference. Half the room didn't get it. The other half were philosophizing.

There were some eyes on her—someone in Docs and a chain belt, another with a fade and a carabiner full of keys.

Vee gave a soft "hey" as she passed the drink table—gentle, instinctive, barely there.

Two people looked up at the same time. Walked straight into each other.

A cup went flying. Splash. Laughter.

"Oh shit."

Someone wiped their sleeve, still smiling. "You're dangerous, you know that?"

She really didn't. But her face went warm anyway.

And then she froze.

Across the room—heels, slacks, wristwatch that probably cost more than the churro truck—Sloane Campbell walked in.

Trailing behind her was the same woman who'd sat next to Sloane during that first brutal deliberation weeks ago—quiet, composed, taking notes while grown men sweated. Vee remembered her: long legs, wavy chestnut-colored hair, warm skin that caught the gallery lights, and the kind of casual confidence that made people glance twice without knowing why.

They moved like they had somewhere better to be.

Vee took a slow sip of beer, mentally preparing herself for violence.

The gallery director appeared out of nowhere, smile stretched thin. "Rosa. Big donors just walked in. Do what you need to. I don't care if you have to sell your soul—or your ass. Just be charming."

Rosa didn't hesitate. Didn't even glance at Vee. She

handed off her glass, adjusted her earrings, and walked toward the front of the gallery like she hadn't just been offered up like a sacrificial lamb.

Vee stared after her, jaw tight.

Sloane didn't even pretend to look casual. She stood like a sculpture herself—shoulders back, eyes taking inventory like the art was an obstacle. Vee hated how good she looked under moody gallery lighting.

The assistant wasted no time. She shook hands with Rosa and the gallery director, rattled off the words "procurement," "community impact," and "sustainable narrative alignment" like they were flavors of ice cream. Vee took a breath, swallowed whatever heat was rising in her chest, and quietly peeled off toward a corner of the gallery. She wasn't about to cause a scene at Rosa's opening. Not tonight. Not over *her*.

But Rosa—sweet, oblivious, on a gallery high—dragged over the newcomers to Vee.

"Vee, look who it is," she said, grabbing her arm. "They work for Heritage too. Said they know you."

Vee didn't even look. Just sipped her beer. "Yeah. They *are* Heritage."

Sloane smiled. One of those slow, cold-blooded ones that didn't quite reach her eyes.

Then the assistant stepped forward—the woman with the chestnut waves and the don't-worry-I-run-everything energy. "We are," she said brightly. "One big happy family." She stuck out her hand. "I never introduced myself. Zora."

Vee shook it, mostly out of habit.

Zora flipped her hair as she turned. Then, almost as an afterthought, she reached out and smoothed the edge of Sloane's sleeve—quick, familiar, like muscle memory.

It was a nothing gesture. The kind you only noticed when it felt like a warning.

And just like that, half the room was watching the three of them—heat, history, and something unspoken radiating off them in waves.

Vee watched it like it was a punchline.

"You're buying art now?" she asked Sloane directly. "That's cute."

Zora answered before Sloane could. "Heritage wants something human in the lobby. So when investors or press walk through, it feels grounded. Less sterile. More 'community-rooted.' Part of the whole rebrand push since last year's...incident."

Vee raised an eyebrow. "What happened to the branded tissues?"

Zora shrugged, unbothered. "Budget got reallocated. Authenticity plays better in post-scandal optics."

Vee rolled her eyes. "Un-fucking-real."

Sloane still hadn't said shit. Just stood there, all cheekbone and contempt.

Vee stepped closer.

"Isn't this a little too real for your usual circuit?" she said. "Not many rooms left where your side doesn't set the narrative."

Sloane's mouth curved, but it wasn't a smile.

"Then consider this a rare act of humility," she said. "I'm here to observe what authenticity looks like—before we repurpose it."

Vee felt it like a slap. The way Sloane said *repurpose* like turning lived resistance into investment property wasn't shocking anymore—just business as usual.

"Owning the art doesn't absolve you."

"And sleeping with the artist doesn't make you revolutionary."

Rosa whistled under her breath. "I'll be in the back, pretending I didn't hear that."

Vee watched her go—shoulders stiff—but didn't move.

Then the gallery owner swooped in, all cashmere desperation and cloying charm. "Sloane, darling—quick question about the sponsorship tiers, if you have a sec?"

She went, of course. Didn't even glance back.

Which left Vee and Zora—alone by the champagne cart, framed in white walls and tension.

Zora just poured a flute and handed it over like a dare.

"So, are you and Sloane always this civil in public?"

Vee took the glass. Didn't sip. "Only when we're being polite."

They stood in silence, watching each other with the wary curiosity of predators who hadn't decided if this was dinner or diplomacy.

Vee nodded toward Sloane's retreating figure. "So...girlfriend, handler, or security detail?"

Zora laughed—sharp and unamused, like a cork popping under pressure. "None of the above. Try co-conspirator."

Vee tilted her head, unconvinced. "Right."

"Sloane plays long games. You throw punches," Zora said evenly. "There's no future there."

Vee blinked. "Wow."

Zora sipped her champagne. "I said it nicely."

"And you're what—her upgrade?"

Zora shrugged, cool and unreadable.

Vee studied her. The energy between them—Zora and Sloane—wasn't romantic. But it wasn't clean, either. There was a rhythm to it, something rehearsed and exacting. The kind of loyalty you didn't name because it had already cost too much. Vee couldn't place it. Couldn't dismiss it. Hated how much it got under her skin.

Before she could press further, the lights dimmed and a bell rang out. The auction was beginning.

It was casual at first—friends of the artist, chosen family, bidding in the low hundreds with soft smiles and joking nudges. A few pieces were scooped up for under a grand, the way you buy someone flowers that'll never die.

Then Rosa's centerpiece came up.

Six feet of welded chrome and burnished brass. Brutal and delicate all at once. The kind of sculpture that didn't just fill space—it claimed it.

The opening bid was five thousand.

A collector from the MCA raised their paddle.

Then someone from New York—one of those minimalist guys with round glasses and quiet shoes—upped it to eight.

Ten. Twelve. Fourteen.

It kept going.

At seventeen, the crowd buzzed. Rosa's jaw tightened.

Then, without ceremony, Sloane lifted her hand.

Zora didn't flinch. "Forty thousand," she said, like she was reading from a brunch menu.

The room stopped breathing.

The New York guy's expression stuttered. The MCA rep lowered their paddle.

Even Rosa froze, like her brain was buffering.

"Sold," said the auctioneer, voice a little too loud.

And just like that, Sloane owned the room. Again.

Photos were taken. There was clapping. Sloane didn't even flinch.

Vee couldn't say shit. Rosa deserved it. Rosa deserved all of it.

Still, the bile sat warm in her throat. Leave it to a corporation to find the one place untouched by PR—and slip a receipt under the door.

She said nothing. Just walked back toward Rosa, cool as ever, and slung an arm casually across her shoulders.

She made sure Sloane saw it.

Didn't smile or gloat. Just stood there.

Rosa leaned in. "Wanna get tacos?"

"Yeah," Vee said, not taking her eyes off Sloane. "My truck's outside."

"Lead the way."

She didn't look back.

She knew Sloane was still watching.

And that was the whole point.

9

They left together.

That was the part that lingered. Not the barbs, not the humiliation, not even the performance of it all. Just the image of Vee slipping out into the night with Rosa Márquez, easy and unbothered, like it hadn't cost Sloane anything at all.

She stood alone while the gallery's energy thinned and scattered, a hollowing of space after spectacle. Someone was clapping. Someone else was asking about tax deductions. Zora handed her the receipt with the discretion of a funeral director.

Sloane accepted it without looking. Her expression didn't shift. She never broke posture. But there was a particular kind of quiet that followed her as she exited—a hush reserved for the recently embarrassed and the very powerful.

She didn't allow herself to feel anything until the car door closed. Even then, it was just a brief tightening of the jaw. Not pain. Not yet. Just...adjustment.

The shame could be processed later.

The facts came first.

Three days earlier, the memo had arrived inside a routine strategy packet, third attachment down—titled innocuously: **Operational Streamlining Proposal.**

Sloane opened it expecting nothing of interest.

She was wrong.

Beneath its sterile language—headcount targets, cross-departmental redundancies, performance-weighted evaluations—it was very clear: They were preparing to cut senior mechanics.

And Vee Phan was among them.

There were no names, of course. That would have required courage. But the pattern was unmistakable—length of tenure, certification tier, take-home pay bracket. All of it couched in euphemism. All of it designed to pass legal scrutiny while still gutting the spine of the hangars.

Sloane had closed the document, then reopened it. Not because she hadn't understood, but because it helped to feel the shape of it again. The cruelty of it.

It would pass without challenge. The union wouldn't see it coming until the letters were sent.

At the executive briefing that afternoon, she let the others speak. She took notes. She waited.

When Lucretia Morrow finished her segment, Sloane folded her hands and said, evenly, "If this goes forward as written, you'll lose the entire west hangar before quarter's end."

Lucretia smiled in that faint, practiced way of hers. "We're prioritizing adaptability. The landscape is shifting."

"You're laying off veteran mechanics under a weak efficiency clause."

The silence was immediate.

Lucretia didn't even blink. "We're aligning labor costs with evolving operational demands."

"Stop dressing it up. You're liquidating expertise to clean a spreadsheet."

"We're building resilience."

"You're gutting the hangars."

That landed. Even Ava Thompkins finally looked up.

The woman who'd personally razed the entire board and most of the executive suite last year now sat off to the side like a guest. Technically "consulting" during the leadership transition, officially advising Lucretia. But everyone in the room knew the truth—Ava didn't need a title to run a room.

Once, she'd been Fleet Deputy Director. Morgan Delgado's mentor. The same woman who sold Morgan out last year during the whistleblower scandal, sacrificed her to clear the board, then stepped over the wreckage to install her puppet.

Now she played the long game in silk and silence.

She wasn't even at the table. Just leaning near the window, detached, almost ornamental—like queenmaker playing assistant.

Sloane didn't stop. "If this goes through, you'll hemorrhage capacity by Q4. And you won't be able to staff a holiday rotation without outsourcing."

Lucretia smiled faintly. "You seem emotionally invested."

"I'm invested in things that work. Mechanics who've kept this company functional through six restructures—they work. And if they get pushed out with no warning, that union isn't going to stay polite. We can't afford that right now."

Then Ava, voice low, said, "Lucretia?"

Lucretia tilted her head like she was weighing an ingredient. Then she gave a small, razor-edged nod.

"We'll delay implementation," she said. "Move the OKR to next fiscal year. Reassess post-Q1."

Meeting adjourned five minutes later. No further discussion. The memo was never mentioned again.

Everyone filed out, voices low. Chairs tucked in, laptops closed, scripts resumed.

But as Sloane stood, Lucretia's voice cut across the quiet.

"Sloane, stay back a moment."

Of course.

The room cleared with quiet efficiency. Chairs tucked. Laptops closed. No one lingered.

Sloane remained standing. Lucretia didn't offer her a seat.

She didn't look up from her tablet, either. Just a measured scroll, a flick of the wrist. The silence was intentional.

"We'll need a values-forward initiative next quarter," she said. "Something public. Preferably visual."

Sloane said nothing.

Lucretia's eyes flicked upward.

"If you're this concerned with labor alignment," she said, "then reflect it. Do it in front of cameras and with a press release. Even better if there is a plaque and a ribbon-cutting."

She closed the tablet with a soft snap.

"Public-facing. Artist-driven. Ideally someone with... cultural proximity to the communities in question."

Her tone made it sound like a menu order. No emotion. Just taste.

"You'll handle procurement. Have your assistant compile a shortlist."

She stepped past Sloane, unhurried. At the door, she paused just long enough to twist the knife:

"I trust you know what reads well in a lobby."

Then she was gone.

Sloane stood there a moment longer. Not stunned—just recalibrating.

She'd won the delay. And she'd been handed her punishment.

That was the trade: save the hangar, and sell the illusion of reform.

Now the elevator opened.

Sloane stepped into the lobby and stopped cold.

The installation had already been mounted—dead-center behind the reception desk, lit like a holy object. The gallery's intimacy was gone; under museum-grade LEDs, the metal caught too much light. The sculpture looked flat now. Overproduced. Embarrassed by its own sincerity.

The curves—once suggesting ascent—now read like the aftermath of a crash someone had dared to polish.

But the sculpture wasn't what made her stomach drop.

It was the plaque.

"Donated by Sloane Campbell, General Counsel, in support of Heritage's commitment to creative justice and community empowerment."

She took one slow step forward. Read it again.

The text was etched in brushed steel, flush-mounted to the wall like a verdict. No mention of the procurement process. No acknowledgment of the internal committee, the gallery, or the junior strategists who'd spent forty-six emails arguing about fonts. No Zora—though she'd done everything short of welding the damn thing herself.

Just Sloane's name. Her title. And a lie dressed as gratitude.

She recognized the move immediately.

In corporate America, you didn't need to give money to be a donor. Not if you were a woman in leadership. What the company needed wasn't her cash—it was her body language, her signature, her proximity to righteousness.

Heritage paid for the sculpture. Sloane "donated" it.

That was the game: branding through human capital. The corporation signaled virtue, outsourced accountability, and made her the face of progress—while keeping her disposable.

And when something inevitably went wrong—an inflammatory tweet, a critique calling it performative design-by-committee, a whistleblower outing Heritage for gutting pensions while funding six-figure sculptures—the blowback wouldn't touch the institution.

It would land on the name on the plaque.

It would land on her.

That polished rectangle wasn't a dedication. It was strategic liability placement. Not legacy. Insurance.

They'd quote it.

They'd say, "That was Sloane Campbell's personal donation."

All because she'd disagreed with Lucretia Morrow. Once. Calmly. On record. She hadn't even broken protocol. She'd just opposed a reckless, unethical policy.

This was the consequence.

A warning—framed in light, staged in the lobby, dressed as honor.

This is what the machine did when you challenged power.

They didn't fire you.

They enshrined you.

Then made sure everyone knew who to blame when the symbol cracked.

10

The smell of Tiger Balm and lemongrass hit Vee before she even opened her eyes. That meant Bà had beat her to the kitchen, and Kha was probably already on his third scolding of the morning. Her bedroom door was cracked, barely, and the sharp staccato of insults filtered in like clockwork. Bà was visiting from Long Beach for her cousin's birthday—a party bus to Rivers Casino loaded with sharp-tongued octogenarians with no patience for losing streaks.

"*Má ơi,*" Kha groaned from the hallway. "I told you! I'm gonna tell her!"

"Tell her now!" Bà barked, like she was prosecuting war crimes.

Vee groaned and dragged herself upright. She didn't need a translation. She knew exactly what this was about.

She walked to the bathroom and started her morning routine like she was entering sacred ritual. Face wash: pH-balanced. Toner: Korean import. Serum: niacinamide, snail mucin, and just enough retinol to burn off regret. The

sunscreen was lab-grade and absurdly expensive, SPF fifty
and light-diffusing. It smelled like chemical warfare.

She smeared on black eyeliner like she was late to a riot.
A little glitter. Red lipstick with a chipped edge. She wasn't
going for clean. She was going for Joan Jett after two cigarettes and a fistfight. The mirror flickered. She narrowed her
eyes. Then grabbed scissors from the medicine cabinet and
trimmed her bangs without hesitation.

Before the coveralls, she dressed like she always had—
same ritual since middle school. Black panties. Black bra.
White tank. A Vivienne Westwood pendant looped around
her neck. Seven rings this time. Mismatched metals—silver,
enamel, stainless steel. One coiled into a snake. Another
shaped like a broken gear.

The coveralls were black today. Fire-resistant. Slimmed
at the waist, sleeves cuffed to the elbow. Her union patch
was front and center, stitched with defiant pride. The name
badge said "PHAN."

When she stepped into the kitchen, Kha looked like he
wanted to evaporate.

The kitchen smelled like garlic and fish sauce, sugar
crackling in the pan. Bà had gone full banquet mode—rice
already steaming in the cooker, nước chấm poured into tiny
porcelain bowls, and a skillet of braised pork belly bubbling
low and fragrant. On the table: sunny-side-up eggs with
crispy edges, slices of chả lụa next to thick wedges of
cucumber, pickled mustard greens glinting in a reused glass
jar, and a warm stack of bánh hỏi still clinging to their
banana leaves. Off to the side: iced coffee with condensed
milk already sweating through the glass.

Vee took a sip. Her brain lit up like jumper cables hit it.

For a moment, just one, the chaos held its breath

"Tell her," Bà hissed again, waving a spoon like it was

ceremonial. She was four-eleven and ninety-four-years-old, but had once cussed out a six-foot GI on the Saigon tarmac and walked away with plane tickets for her children.

Kha finally muttered, "I applied to...uh, that aviation maintenance program. The one with the A&P cert."

She didn't answer right away. Just recalibrated. "You what?"

He straightened up, voice defensive. "I wanna do what you do."

"Don't you wanna go into medicine?" she said, too fast. "Something stable? You were good at biology."

It came out reflexively. Like muscle memory trained by aunties, uncles, and every nosy family friend who ever side-eyed her job title like it was a cry for help.

The silence was immediate. Even Bà clicked her tongue.

Kha just looked at her. Not angry—just wounded and a little stunned.

"Oh wow. You really said it." He shook his head. "After all the shit they gave you."

He wasn't wrong. Her whole damn life. Even now—nearly twenty years deep, specialty certs stacked, respected across the hangar like a goddamn engine whisperer—some out-of-touch family member still asked why she wasn't a doctor.

And now here she was. Repeating the curse.

Vee didn't answer.

The room went quiet. Her words sat in the air like bad insulation. Everyone suddenly remembered they had somewhere else to be.

She pulled her phone from her pocket as the kettle hissed. One unread email from Heritage Corporate. She opened it.

Subject: Site Visit — Heritage Station: Inspection & Transparency Review

In line with Heritage's renewed values commitment, legal counsel and an external third-party inspector will conduct a transparency-focused walkthrough of Hangar C. General Counsel Sloane Campbell will be on-site. Observers include associate Kenji Miwa and PR liaison. Please prepare compliance documentation and ensure visual safety standards. Thank you for your partnership.

Vee read it twice. Then again.

Bullshit.

A fake inspection. A leash in disguise. Stall tactics to keep the union docile while they played dress-up in the wreckage.

She dialed the hangar office and turned toward the door.

"Everyone on-site in thirty," she said, loud enough for the whole apartment to hear. "Emergency morning meeting. No excuses."

She didn't wait for a response. Just grabbed her boots and her gear, and walked out like she hadn't just shoved her own bullshit into someone else's future.

THE SOUND of her boots echoed through the bay like a starting gun.

Vee stalked down the central aisle of Hangar C, jaw tight, coveralls half-zipped and sleeves tied at the waist. The tank top underneath clung to her back like a second skin. Her boots—steel-toe, scuffed to hell, custom laced with matte-black eyelets and red stitching—hit the concrete with the finality of a gavel.

They straightened the second they saw her.

She didn't yell. She didn't need to.

"Ops are coming," she said, loud enough to carry over the hum of overhead lights and the whining cough of a half-gutted APU. "Not inspectors. Not auditors. Ops. Their own people. Sent to find just enough fault to shift the blame, rewrite the narrative, and walk away clean."

Everyone went quiet.

She kept walking—line by line, crew by crew—calling out names, tapping clipboards, flicking at badges that weren't clipped straight.

"You—make sure every torque check's logged. You—double check your PPE. You—fix your fucking patch, you're not a rookie."

They moved like she was gravity.

Some of these men were twice her size, half as fast, and every single one of them knew not to test her. Union stewards might get respect. Vee got obedience.

She reached the end of the line and turned.

"You think they're here to learn the truth? They're not. They're here to catch us slipping. Don't give them an inch. No excuses. No shortcuts. They want to scapegoat this hangar to get out of paying what they owe."

A beat passed.

"Don't let them pin their greed on our backs."

A murmur of agreement rippled through the line.

Then she added, quieter—knife-sharp: "Don't fuck it up."

And like that, they were dismissed.

Not with a salute. With action. Gloves snapped on. Clipboards pulled. Radios buzzed.

Vee didn't watch them go. She just turned back toward the turbine pit, wiped her hands, and picked up her wrench like a sword she'd never put down.

11

Sloane's apartment was silent, save for the low hum of Lake Michigan mocking her through the windows. A body of water that had no business pretending to be peaceful. She ignored it.

She stood in her bathroom, wrapped in a towel, head tilted as she finger-detangled under warm running water. The steam had softened her roots just enough. No shampoo this morning—just a co-wash. She'd done a protein treatment over the weekend. The balance was holding. Barely.

She sectioned, clipped, and applied her leave-in cocktail like a ritual. Aloe-based cream. Castor oil. Lightweight curl definer, but only on the ends. Her fingers moved with the precision of someone who had court by 9 a.m. and a deep distrust of stylists.

No brushes. No combs. Just her hands and the same wide-tooth pick she'd had since undergrad.

She twisted the curls she needed to behave and left the rest to dry in their own chaos. Her hair was sensitive, high-porosity, and didn't tolerate heat without complaint. So she didn't use heat. She used scarves, edge control, and prayer.

This morning, she went with a low bun—clean middle part, edges laid sharp enough to deflect lawsuits. Gold hair clasp at the nape of her neck.

The skincare was twelve steps, but fast. She applied body cream everywhere like it was a legal mandate.

Then came the clothes: a black sheath dress, knee-length. It didn't cling—it obeyed. Structured shoulders, high neckline, not a ruffle in sight. She cinched it with a matte black Hermès belt. Just one gold ring, flat and unadorned. Cartier Tank Française on her wrist, ticking with quiet judgment. Nothing flashy. Everything final.

She sprayed on her perfume—something niche, dark, laced with oud and power—and let it cling to her pulse points.

Tiberia watched her from the terrarium, unblinking. Regal.

"I know," Sloane muttered, slicking her lip balm on. "This is all beneath us."

No breakfast. Just water, coffee, and the acidic burn of knowing she'd be face to face with Vee Phan in under an hour.

Kenji had been following her. Nightly reports: location logs, time-stamped sightings, behavioral summaries dressed up as surveillance notes.

By night two, Vee lost him. Slipped down a side street in that rust-bucket truck like it had warp speed. No confrontation. No message. Just gone.

Kenji—one of the sharpest trackers she'd ever worked with—never saw where she went.

The update was terse: *Lost visual. 21:46.*

Sloane just exhaled, picked up her portfolio, texted Zora, and left.

THE HANGAR WAS chaos in a can. Hydraulics hissing, radios squawking, the heavy clank of metal on metal echoing off the steel walls. It smelled like jet fuel, sweat, and burnt rubber. Sloane stepped through it, heels clicking against the concrete.

Zora flanked her left, tablet in hand, already logging timestamps and taking notes with the efficiency of a Vatican scribe. Kenji Miwa trailed behind—nonchalant, unbothered, tracking every face in the hangar. A faceless clutch of Heritage-approved third-party inspectors buzzed at their heels like flies, useless but present.

Sloane paused near a cordoned hazard zone, eyes scanning the tangle of bodies and equipment. No clear point of contact. Of course.

She turned to the nearest mechanic—older, bearded, half-submerged in an open engine panel.

"Who's in charge here?"

He didn't even look up. Just jerked his chin toward the bowels of the hangar and said, "Phan."

And then—like it was choreographed—Vee stepped out from behind the skeleton of a stripped-down fuselage.

Grease-streaked, coveralls knotted at her waist. The tank top beneath was saturated, clinging to muscle in ways that defied structural logic. Sweat traced the slope of her neck and disappeared, inconveniently, into the kind of cleavage Sloane may have once traced with her tongue. Rings on every other finger.

Sloane's mouth went dry.

The group walked straight up to her, stopped just short of collision.

Sloane cleared her throat. "Morning. This is a third-party inspection—Section D, shareholder resolution. Internal compliance review, supervised. Findings go to Ethics."

She exhaled through her nose. Vee hadn't said a word. The way she watched her talk—mouth, then eyes, then mouth again—like she was deciphering code. Sloane resented how flustered it made her.

"If you deviate from protocol, it's considered obstruction. Understood?"

Vee wiped her hands on a rag, slow and unimpressed.

"What, you want a sticker?"

Sloane didn't flinch. Just narrowed her gaze. "Just brief us."

Vee's lips curved—too much teeth to be polite. "Yes, ma'am."

She didn't need a clipboard. Didn't even raise her voice. The script was in her bones.

"Welcome to Hangar C. All visitors are required to wear full PPE while on the floor—no exceptions. That includes high-vis vests, safety goggles, hearing protection, and steel-toe boots or approved covers. Stay within marked walkways, don't touch anything with wires, heat, or warning tape, and if you see a blinking red light, assume it can kill you."

She turned on her heel and led them down the corridor.

The locker room hit like a wall of heat—warm air, solvent funk, a trace of something floral trying and failing to cover it. A row of temporary gear bins had been laid out: mismatched vests, dented goggles, bright yellow boot covers that crinkled when moved.

"Gear up," Vee said, already tossing a vest toward Sloane without looking. "If you break a heel, I'm not carrying you."

To the group: "You have ten minutes to change. No

shortcuts. If your vest smells like death, grab a new one. If you complain about the goggles, I'll fit them myself."

She didn't wait for confirmation. She was already fixing straps, adjusting clips, barking instructions like a foreman and a field medic rolled into one.

Sloane lifted one of the vests between two fingers, turned it over like it might contaminate her. "This one's soiled.

"It's seasoned," Vee murmured, stepping in close. The air shifted with her. "Put it on."

Sloane didn't move. Not right away. She tilted her head instead, studied the vest like it was beneath her and knew it, like it ought to apologize before daring to touch her skin. But after a breath—just long enough to reassert dominance —she slid her arms in.

The fabric swallowed her. It creaked over the fine grain of her sheath dress, the contrast loud, intentional.

She reached for the zipper, but Vee's hands were already there. No warning, no ask. Just possession.

Fingers at her chest. A slow, precise pull upward. Metal teeth dragging over her sternum. The sound sharp. Contact brief but deliberate, a graze that said nothing but meant everything.

Vee didn't rush. She pulled that zipper like a secret. Like she was sealing Sloane into something that couldn't be undone easily.

Sloane held still, eyes steady, but her throat betrayed her —pulse flickering in the hollow above her clavicle. A silent tell.

Then came the goggles.

Sloane raised a sculpted brow. "Absolutely not."

"Absolutely yes." Vee's voice didn't rise. "If you go blind

from a welding arc just because you wanted to look cute? That's a liability. Not my liability."

Before Sloane could argue, the goggles descended. Cold plastic cradled her temples. Lenses clouded instantly with her breath, a bloom of heat on synthetic glass. She blinked once. Twice. The world warped.

Behind the goggles, Vee's hands moved again. This time to the back of her head, where the strap dangled loose. She adjusted it slowly, fingers brushing the nape of Sloane's neck. Then, without pause—without thinking, or maybe thinking way too much—she swept a knuckle up along Sloane's jawline. A single stroke. Casual, careless.

Like she was checking for tension. Or tracing it.

"You always manhandle visitors like this?" Sloane asked, voice lower now.

"Only the pretty ones," Vee replied, a crooked smile tugging at her mouth.

She turned, briefly, to retrieve the final indignity—hearing protectors. Oversized. Cracked. Ugly in a way that felt intentional.

"What? You trying to survive the inspection," she asked, voice slipping down a register, "or just look hot doing it?"

Sloane took them without breaking eye contact. Her fingers grazed Vee's palm—accidentally, then not. "Why not both?"

Vee didn't answer right away. She stepped in instead. Slow. Quiet. No footsteps, just the hush of friction—boot on concrete, breath on breath.

She leaned in until her lips nearly brushed Sloane's ear, breath ghosting along skin still prickled from the zipper.

"Because in this hangar," she murmured, "I run the show."

When the group was done changing into the protective

gear, Vee gestured toward the cavernous sprawl of machinery.

"To your left," Vee said, gesturing without looking, "hazard tape means stay out unless you want your obituary to say 'death by turbine intake.'"

She pivoted. "Red tags mean live equipment. Don't touch anything glowing, buzzing, or labeled *Seriously, don't touch*."

"To your right, emergency showers. Eye wash station's next to the compressor."

Then, dry: "Try not to wander. We lose apprentices that way."

Zora snorted softly behind them. Kenji said nothing—just watched with the stillness of a man mentally preparing for a legal cleanup.

Sloane adjusted the goggles. The frame pinched. The vest chafed. The air was too warm and her pulse had no business behaving like this.

She glanced at Vee again. God help her. She wasn't here to lose. She was just here to suffer through it. Professionally, of course.

AFTER THEY FINISHED GEARING UP, they had a quick overview focusing was supposed to be baseline safety—ventilation, carcinogen exposure, routine maintenance protocols. The usual.

Predictably, it split into two tracks.

Track A was the air-conditioned version: OSHA reps, Zora, and Kenji were escorted to the foreman's office to audit chemical inventories and flip through maintenance logs that hadn't been updated since the 90s. Zora held court with her clipboard. Kenji, five minutes in, was already making friends—or pretending to.

Track B was hers.

Vee had offered to guide Sloane through the hangar's "active zone"—which meant the bays, the tool cages, the break room with the permanently broken sink. And the turbine pit. That was the real destination. The place no one walked without a buddy or a badge. There were yellow safety lines painted on the floor for a reason. One misstep and you were in the drop.

Vee didn't rush the route. She moved with the kind of casual precision that said *I live here*, pausing just long enough to gesture at overhead ducts or note a spill that hadn't been cleaned up since Tuesday. Sloane followed, still in heels, and refused to flinch at every hiss of compressed air.

By the time they reached the turbine pit, the others had thinned out. A few mechanics passed behind them, heads down. Everyone else was buried in binders and admin on the other side of the hangar.

Sloane stepped up to the line. Vee stopped beside her.

"Careful," Vee said, voice low.

Sloane didn't look at her. "I'm aware."

The pit wasn't what Sloane expected.

It wasn't even called that officially, probably—but that's what it was: a sunken square of space carved into the center of the hangar, twenty feet deep and ringed with a grated walkway that creaked under her heels. Industrial, unmarked, functional in a way that felt leftover. Like it belonged to an earlier version of the company, one that still repaired engines on-site instead of shipping them out and pretending the problem never existed.

At the center of the void, a massive engine hung suspended from an overhead rig. Half-disassembled. Parts of it stripped and exposed. It looked like a mechanical carcass—cabling dangling, fan blades inert, waiting for something. The size alone was obscene. It shouldn't have been in a building with people.

Sloane stepped onto the walkway, pulse steady, hands gloved. The grate shifted underfoot with each step—subtle, but enough to register. There was a rail, barely waist-high. It looked decorative.

Vee stood at the far end, one hand on the metal bar, the other loose at her side. She didn't turn when Sloane approached. Just stared down into the pit.

"This section's supposed to be off-limits during active maintenance," Vee said, voice low, almost conversational. "But no one enforces that."

Sloane didn't answer. The air was warmer here, heavier. She could feel it on her skin, inside her sleeves. Grease, jet fuel, something scorched.

She stopped a few feet from Vee, eyes scanning the drop. "What are we inspecting here, exactly?"

Vee pointed down to a small plastic tag attached to part of the exposed engine. Red. Torn at the edges. Zip-tied to something that might've once been sealed.

"You see that?"

Sloane nodded, slowly.

"It means someone reported a fault." Vee's tone was unreadable. "Something cracked. Something dangerous. Someone flagged it, filled out the paperwork, logged it in the system. And then nothing happened."

There was a pause. Not dramatic—just real.

"It's still sitting there," Vee said.

Sloane looked at her then. The angle of her jaw. The flush at her collarbone. A dark smudge of something—grease, soot, memory—near the base of her throat.

"And what happens when people ignore those tags?" she asked.

"Depends."

Sloane raised an eyebrow. "On?"

Vee stepped closer. Just slightly. Just enough.

"On who signs off on silence," she said. "And who gets sacrificed for it."

Another step. The grate shifted beneath them.

The air suddenly felt hotter here. Thinner.

And for a moment, Sloane wasn't thinking about litigation or liability. She was thinking about the fact that the only thing separating her from a twenty-foot drop was a bolt-on guardrail and Vee's shifting sense of mercy.

Vee's gaze flicked to her mouth.

It was quick.

She didn't reach for her—of course not—but her presence tilted forward, that slight lean of inevitability, of something about to tip. Her hand was still on the railing, but her body was angled toward Sloane now. Like she could close the distance without lifting a finger. Like gravity would do the rest.

For a breath—just one—Sloane felt the heat of it. The potential. That horrifying ache at the base of her spine, that raw, reflexive anticipation she thought she'd starved out of herself.

Then Vee tilted her head.

Just a fraction.

Not enough to declare intention. But more than enough to suggest it.

Sloane's stomach knotted. Her body lit up in panic, or memory, or both. And without meaning to—without even deciding—she took a step back. A sharp one. The grate groaned beneath her heel.

She would've rather fallen into that damn pit than let their mouths meet.

Vee didn't flinch. Didn't follow.

She just watched her, like she'd expected it. Like the retreat was its own kind of confession.

Then, mercifully—*bang.*

A steel tool chest slammed shut on the floor below. The sound cracked through the hangar. Sloane startled, hand tightening on the rail, breath sharp in her throat.

Below them, a mechanic yelled something unintelligible. Someone laughed.

Vee looked away first. Back to the inspection.

Like nothing had happened at all.

Sloane didn't move. Not yet.

She needed one more breath. One more second to pretend her hands weren't shaking.

THEY BROKE for a late lunch after that. No one mentioned the pit.

The car was already idling by the curb when they stepped out. Their driver—neutral, uniformed, deliberately forgettable—opened the door without a word. Inside: cold air, tinted windows, leather seats, silence.

Zora slid into the front. Kenji sprawled across the back seat.

"They were ready for us," he said, eyes closed, head tipped back. "Too ready. Like someone prepped them with a checklist and a threat."

He cracked one eye open. "You make an entrance, Counselor. They definitely knew you were coming."

He still called her *Counselor* like they were still back in criminal court—him with a badge, her with a binder, both running on adrenaline, no sleep, and mutual contempt.

Sloane didn't rise to it. "And?"

Kenji sighed. "They played polite. Didn't give me much. But I got a couple of the older guys to meet me for beers later. That bar over by the south ramp."

Zora, still scrolling her phone, said flatly, "You're gonna get jumped."

"I'm charming," Kenji replied. "And persistent. They'll crack."

Zora finally looked up. "We didn't get through half the documentation. Maintenance logs, PPE rosters, chemical exposure timelines. We'll have to go back tomorrow."

Kenji groaned. "God. No."

"I'll go," Sloane said. Too fast.

Both of them turned toward her.

"If it's just documentation, I can move things along. We don't need to drag the whole team."

Zora raised a brow. "You don't have to."

Sloane looked out the window. The reflection stared back—immaculate and unreadable.

"I know," she said.

Zora didn't look up from her screen.

"Must've been a productive walkthrough."

A pause, just long enough to sting.

"Kenji and I got through three witness statements while you were being fitted for safety goggles."

She said it in a neutral tone. It wasn't.

Sloane didn't answer.

She didn't have to. The silence said enough.

12

By mid-afternoon the next day, Heritage's second compliance visit had already abandoned any pretense of professionalism. Sloane stood ankle-deep in cardboard boxes in Vee Phan's office, watching Zora document each battered folder and invoice.

The space was chaos—organized only in the loosest, most theoretical sense. There were outdated technical manuals, OSHA documentation annotated in red ink, and union pamphlets from at least three election cycles ago. A battered calendar from 2012 hung crooked on the wall, still frozen in June. A small Pride flag peeked out from beneath a stack of torque charts, and someone had tacked a sticker reading Solidarity Forever over a crack in the windowpane. The filing cabinet had no filing system. Instead, it appeared to function as both archive and graveyard.

Sloane's jaw tightened.

The office was giving her sensory overload. The scent of old paper and engine oil clung to everything. Nothing was where it was supposed to be. Nothing was labeled. Her eye twitched every time she spotted another handwritten note shoved into a binder at the wrong angle. She had survived final exams at Yale Law with less caffeine and more clarity.

And yet.

There was something about the space that made her feel...not unwelcome. Not exactly comfortable either, but held. It was a mess, yes—but a lived-in mess. A real one. Every inch of it bore the imprint of Vee's refusal to sanitize, to perform, to rearrange herself for anyone's comfort. It made Sloane feel something she didn't have language for. Warmth. Frustration. A sick kind of nostalgia.

Zora, to her credit, hadn't complained once. She was moving through the paperwork with terrifying efficiency, syncing each image to a shared drive where the hacker twins would chew through the data using Python scripts and a bespoke language learning model pipeline. They'd have the full document set parsed and tagged by morning.

"Got the second box," Zora muttered, snapping a final photo and kicking the lid shut. "This one's full of asbestos training certificates and something labeled 'HR NIGHT-MARES, LOL.' I don't even want to know."

She wiped the sweat from her brow with the sleeve of her blazer. Her curls were starting to frizz from the hangar's humidity.

"Want to grab the third?"

Before Sloane could answer, the office door creaked open—and Vee appeared, balancing another two boxes in her arms like it was nothing. She didn't say a word. Just smirked and dropped them on the desk with a theatrical thud.

Zora's eyes went wide. "You're evil," she said flatly.

Vee leaned in the doorway, arms crossed, grease smudged across her jaw. "Union records," she said, voice low and maddeningly pleasant. "Requested, right?"

Zora looked like she was about to either scream or cry. "I'm going home before I commit a felony."

"You've earned it," Sloane said without looking up. "Go. I'll finish this."

Zora raised an eyebrow. "You sure?"

Sloane nodded. "It's fine. I've got it."

Zora narrowed her eyes, gaze flicking between Sloane's bent head and the empty doorway Vee had just left behind. Whatever calculation she ran, the result didn't please her.

She stepped closer, voice low.

"Careful," she said.

Sloane didn't look up. "It's under control."

Zora paused—long enough to make her silence feel like commentary. Then she smoothed a stray curl back from her temple and straightened her blouse.

"If you say so." Something passed behind her eyes. "Call me if you need anything."

She left the door wide open behind her.

By 7:18 PM, Sloane had cleared the last box. Her eyes burned. Her wrists ached. She closed the final folder with a sigh sharp enough to slice a throat, then stepped out into the open hangar for air—and stopped cold.

Vee was ten yards away, bent over the guts of a half-disassembled turbine. The sun was dropping low through the high windows, casting streaks of amber across her shoulders. Her tank top was dark with sweat, clinging to the sharp lines of her back. Her sleeves were rolled up to her elbows, forearms gleaming with grease. One hand held a wrench; the other was buried wrist-deep in something that looked like it could explode on contact.

Sloane couldn't look away.

She had no idea what she was looking at, mechanically speaking. It could've been a combustion chamber or a high-stakes art installation for all she knew. It didn't matter. All she could see was Vee—focused, flushed, utterly in her element—and somehow, despite everything, that made her the hottest goddamn thing Sloane had seen since she could remember.

She took a step forward. Then another.

Vee must've sensed her stare, because she glanced up slowly, like she'd been expecting it.

"What," she said, not quite a question.

Sloane opened her mouth. No words came out.

Vee stood slowly, then peeled off the glove with her teeth. Not slow. Not sexy. Just efficient. She hooked the edge, tugged hard, and spat the thing onto the workbench. It landed with a wet slap. She didn't even blink.

She picked up a rag and wiped her hand—deliberate, almost clinical. Palm first. Then fingers. Then the stretch between her thumb and wrist.

By the time she grabbed the water bottle and crossed the floor, Sloane's mouth was dry, and her stomach was already making its own decisions.

She held the bottle out like it was a dare.

Sloane took it. Their fingers touched—bare skin to bare skin—and that flash of contact shot straight down her spine. Her breath caught.

Then, from the depths of her treacherous body: her stomach growled.

It wasn't cute. It wasn't subtle. It was the guttural snarl of a woman who hadn't eaten all day and had been surviving on tension, caffeine, and paperwork-induced rage.

Vee's smirk curled slow and mean.

"You forget to eat, Counsel?" she asked. "Or is starving part of the Heritage values initiative now?"

Sloane grit her teeth. "I'm fine."

Vee raised an eyebrow, not buying it for a second.

"Sure you are."

Sloane turned back toward the desk with quiet resignation and resumed reorganizing the final box of files. Her body ached in places she refused to name. Her silky forest green sheath dress clung damply to the back of her neck, and her shoes—black leather, narrow, Ferragamo—had long since stopped offering support. But she refused to take them off. She wasn't about to let Vee Phan see her barefoot and defeated in the middle of a hangar.

She'd nearly reached the bottom of the box when a sudden thud behind her made her flinch.

She turned—and froze.

Vee stood at the doorway with a plastic shopping bag, one of those opaque white ones with faded red lettering and a cheap-looking logo. She dropped it onto the work desk. The scent hit Sloane instantly—rich, savory, unmistakably Italian. But not the curated kind. This was the kind of food that came in foil containers, with cash-only receipts and prices that made no economic sense unless something else was on the books. It came with a side of marinara in a Styrofoam cup.

The logo on the bag read Giuliano's Authentic Cuisine, but the word "Authentic" had been scribbled out with a Sharpie and replaced—badly—with "Better." The bag sagged with the weight of its contents.

"That's a lot of grease for one person," Sloane muttered.

Vee unpacked the food with casual precision, setting out a suspiciously impressive spread: burrata in a plastic clamshell, neatly arranged antipasto, enough carbonara to drown a grown man, a full order of chicken marsala, and what looked like eggplant parmesan smothered in enough sauce to glue a wall together. And bread. So much bread. An irresponsible amount of bread. Warm. Steaming. Probably garlic-laced and criminally underpriced.

Vee handed her a paper plate and plastic utensils.

Sloane cleared her throat. "I'm good, thank you. I'll eat when I get home."

Vee didn't bother looking up. "You're eating now."

"No, I'm—"

"I don't want you passing out in my office so you can sue me. I'm not in the mood for litigation tonight." She peeled the lid off the carbonara and set it aside like a woman absolutely not taking no for an answer. "It's not like I ordered it for you. I'm pulling a double. I ordered food for myself. My ancestors would haunt me if I didn't offer some, even to the enemy."

Sloane glared at her. "That's absurd."

Vee shrugged. "Tell them that. I don't make the rules."

They stared each other down in silence, locked in yet another exquisitely controlled standoff—this one fought over plastic cutlery and a pile of suspiciously generous carbohydrates. Neither woman reacted.

And then, predictably, mortifyingly, Sloane's stomach growled again. Louder this time. No way to play it off.

Vee laughed. Not a smirk. Not a scoff. A real laugh—low and bright, almost girlish, with a musical lilt that felt wildly out of place in a hangar full of steel and solvents. It slipped through Sloane's ribs. Her entire chest went tight.

Embarrassing. Absolutely embarrassing. She needed her body to stop reacting like this was a date and not a hostile worksite.

But Vee was still going. Still uncovering more food.

Pulling open the foil. Unwrapping garlic bread. Tearing off a piece with her hands and eating it with the smug satisfaction of someone who knew she was winning.

"Mmm," Vee said, eyes closed as she chewed. "God. So good. You're really missing out."

Sloane didn't look up. "Must you do that here?"

Vee's eyes snapped open, full of mock innocence. "It's my office. I'm allowed to eat in my office." She took another bite, exaggerated her chewing just slightly. "Unless you've got a new meal break policy I haven't seen yet. In which case, I'll need that shit in writing."

Sloane muttered something obscene under her breath—low, vicious, completely unrepeatable—and forced herself to focus on the file in front of her. Her pen twitched slightly in her hand. The letters blurred.

Vee made another pleased noise.

Eventually, and without saying a word, Sloane caved. She reached for the burrata, tore off a piece of bread, and dipped it in the oil and herbs with mechanical precision. The first bite was perfect. Warm. Salty. Creamy. Disrespectfully good. Her brain went offline for three seconds.

They ate in silence. Tension simmering, but cooling just enough to keep them in their chairs.

For a few moments, they managed harmless conversation—nothing real. The weather. A brief mention of Morgan passed between them—just long enough for Vee to raise an eyebrow and for Sloane to slam the door on that conversation. They had an unspoken agreement: their friend was off-limits. She'd just clawed her way out of the whistleblower mess, barely survived Heritage the first time. Whatever this was between them now—legal warfare, emotional crossfire, flirtation by attrition—dragging her into it would be cruel. The woman was in therapy. She didn't need fresh trauma.

They talked about the shitty lighting in the hangar. About how much worse it would be when winter came. It was empty, domestic small talk. Something that might've passed for comfort if it weren't coming from people who still couldn't make eye contact for too long without raising the stakes.

At some point, Sloane let herself look at Vee's face.

There was something absurd about how striking she still was, even covered in sweat and engine grease. Her face was so frustratingly smooth. Her skin had that annoyingly effortless glow, the kind you couldn't fake with serums or sleep. Her eyes were the kind of brown that caught too much light—quick, cutting, and far too bright for someone this dangerous. She looked like someone from another decade. Like one of those punk frontwomen from the late '70s who somehow never overdosed, never sold out, and never stopped making people want things they shouldn't.

Sloane remembered the first time she saw her. It wasn't during the whistleblower case. It was before that. A girls' weekend Morgan had thrown—half work trip, half soft-launch power retreat—at some rich friend's beach house on Martha's Vineyard. Sloane was still in law school. Vee had shown up late, already half-sunburned, in shorts that didn't even pretend to cover anything and a frayed band tee, still with her partner at the time.

And Sloane had developed an immediate, humiliating crush—the kind you couldn't admit out loud, especially not to yourself.

She remembered watching her from across a firepit, bottle in hand, laughing at something Morgan had said, and thinking: *Oh no.*

Now she was thinking those same words again.

Somehow, somewhere between the last bite of pasta and the silence that followed it, they'd started sharing the molten chocolate cake—one fork, passed between them without a word. It hadn't felt like a decision. Just movement. Muscle memory.

Vee was looking back at her.

"Don't look at me like that," she said, voice low. "Unless you want me to do something about it."

Sloane's jaw twitched. "You mistake observation for interest. That's not my problem."

Vee raised an eyebrow. "Nice deflection. You that smooth with your other distractions, or just the ones that stare back?"

They were barely a foot apart now. The food was still between them, but the energy had shifted—charged, immediate, stupid with possibility.

They were barely a foot apart now. Most of the food still sat untouched between them, giving off steam and the scent of slow-cooked indulgence.

Vee leaned in first. Not far. Just a tilt of her head, a shift in weight, the kind of movement that made you question whether it was intentional or instinct. Her mouth parted slightly, lips glossed with heat, like she was about to speak— or bite.

Sloane moved in like it was a chess maneuver. She closed the distance with all the finality of a closing argument. One hand slid up the side of Vee's body, fingers splaying wide under fabric gone damp with sweat and machinery. It wasn't tentative. It was a claim. Her grip was exacting—thumb pressing into Vee's rib just enough to command.

Vee's breath caught, but she didn't back off. Her hands

found Sloane's hips, then curved lower, dragging along the fabric of her dress like she was searching for a grip she wasn't supposed to have. They pressed together—chest to chest, heat to heat. The kiss, when it came, didn't ask. It took.

Sloane kissed her like she meant to leave a mark. Like she'd waited months and chose now—under fluorescent lighting, surrounded by bankers boxes and takeout containers, door cracked open. Vee opened under her, quick and eager, but Sloane kept control, tilting her chin, angling her body, moving them easily.

She tasted like chocolate—rich and lingering, stolen from the shared fork minutes earlier. Sweet on the surface. Nothing about it innocent.

Vee tried to catch up—hands clasping the nape of Sloane's neck, teeth just barely grazing her lip—but it didn't matter. Sloane deepened the kiss, then pushed. Not with force—with intention. Vee stumbled back a step and landed against the edge of the work desk, hard enough to rattle utensils. A plastic fork slid to the floor. No one looked down.

Sloane pressed in, bracketed Vee between her body and the furniture, one knee parting her stance slightly. The kiss broke for a breath—hot, ragged, shared—and then resumed. Harder. Slower. A kind of heat that wasn't frantic but deliberate.

When Sloane finally bit Vee's bottom lip—firm, calculated, just enough pressure to walk the edge—Vee made a sound low in her throat. Not quite a moan. Not quite a gasp. Something wild and pleased and not meant for the public.

Overhead, the fluorescent lights buzzed on, indifferent. The blinds were shut, but the office door stayed cracked, that slim slice of openness stretching wider by the second.

Then the radio crackled.

They broke apart like they'd been caught mid-crime. Breathless. Hands still half-gripped, mouths parted, heat bleeding off their skin. Sloane stepped back first—controlled, but not calm. Her dress had slipped halfway off one shoulder; she pulled it back into place. Vee straightened with a quiet exhale, jaw tight, eyes blown wide. Her hands flexed once at her sides, then stilled.

The air between them felt scorched. Interrupted, not resolved.

"Phan, you copy? We got a situation on the east lift. Something's jammed."

The moment snapped.

Vee exhaled—half sigh, half curse—and reached for her radio.

"Copy. On my way."

Sloane didn't wait for her to leave.

In the space of three seconds, she gathered her portfolio, shrugged on her blazer, and walked out—fast. Almost running. Her pulse thudded in her throat. Her lips still tingled. Her mouth tasted like heat and sugar and something she shouldn't have wanted.

By the time Vee turned back, she was gone—heels clicking a little too sharp against the concrete, her exit too fast to be casual, too slow to be a full escape.

But it was still a retreat. And they both knew it.

13

Her phone buzzed as the Uber merged onto the Kennedy. Kenji's name lit the screen. She answered with a clipped, "Yes."

"Found something," he said. "One of the mechanics cited in the meso claim signed a liability waiver back in 2017. Boilerplate, buried under safety training documentation. Weakens the timeline. Could complicate the case."

His timing was surgical. She could still taste Vee's mouth, and now she had a legal landmine blinking on the docket. Sloane closed her eyes. "Forward it."

She ended the call. No reaction. Just silence, and the faint hum of air-conditioning against her cheek.

By the time she reached the bar, Lucretia Morrow was already two fingers into her drink, laughing at something the bartender had said. Her blazer hung off the back of her chair. She wore an open-back white jumpsuit—sleek, sculpted, unapologetically designed to showcase the long, carved line of her spine. Her golden brown skin gleamed under the bar's low lighting, and her posture was insultingly good, like she didn't know how to slouch.

Everything about her looked intentional. The delicate drop earrings. The fresh, glassy manicure. Even the way she sipped her drink was calm and rhythmic.

Her face was all angles: high cheekbones, sharp jaw, a mouth curved just enough to suggest menace if she smiled too wide.

The invitation had been last-minute. Sloane still wasn't sure if this was diplomacy, seduction, or a soft threat with a lime wedge.

Lucretia didn't make her guess.

"You don't want to be here," she said, smiling. "That's obvious. So what's the angle? What does Ava have on you?"

A perfectly manicured hand landed on Sloane's knee— just enough pressure to register. Just enough to be deniable.

Sloane set her glass down, untouched. "You're wasting your charm."

Lucretia tilted her head. "We could be allies."

"I don't do allies," Sloane said, voice calm. "I do containment."

Lucretia's smile went razor-sharp. "Then contain the union. That's an order."

Sloane didn't flinch. She simply folded her napkin, stood, and left.

In her inbox, the waiver was already waiting.

BY THE TIME she made it home, it was just past midnight. Her heels hit the marble floors like gunshots, her body aching in places she hadn't even used. She didn't bother with lights—just dropped her bag, peeled off her blazer, and headed straight for the terrarium in the corner.

Tiberia was already awake, coiled in slow, silent movement under the heat lamp. Predictable. Loyal. Beautiful in the way Sloane actually trusted.

She reached for her, already imagining the weight of her against her skin, the rhythm of breath slowing down—

Her phone rang.

She glanced at the screen and exhaled through her teeth.

She let it ring twice before answering. "Daddy? It's late."

"I know," he said, gently. "I just...wanted to check in."

"Everything's handled."

"I know," he said. "It's just...your aunt was at the hospital today, visiting the OB wing. One of the new ultrasound machines caught something early in a patient. They were able to intervene. Everyone's fine. The attending said it saved a life."

She closed her eyes. Tiberia coiled against the glass.

"The Campbells built that hospital," he said. "And the schools. And the scholarships. That's what our name is supposed to mean."

"I'm doing what you asked."

"And I'm proud," he said. "I just don't want you to forget what's at stake."

She ended the call before he could say anything else.

14

Vee stayed parked for a full minute after the call ended, her hand still gripping the steering wheel. The dashboard clock glared 10:47 AM. Too early for this shit, too late to pretend she hadn't already lost. Jerry's widow's voice still clung to her like smoke—quiet, wrecked, cracked down the middle with all the grief Vee had been trying not to feel herself.

"They gutted the pension, Vee. I'm down to ten grand."

"I know," she'd said. "I know."

She'd tried to keep her voice level, factual. Heritage wanted deniability. That meant finding someone to bury in paperwork and legalese—someone to take the fall cleanly, quietly, and above all, contractually. She explained that to Jerry's wife as gently as she could manage.

The silence on the other end wasn't agreement. It was too long, too hollow.

"They already called," the widow said finally. Voice thin. Too calm to be fine.

Vee straightened up in her seat. "Who?"

"Someone from Legal. A woman. Said she was part of—of the internal review. Not the union. The other side."

Sloane.

It had to be. Or someone marching under her banner.

"What'd she offer you?" Vee asked, keeping her voice even. Flat.

Another pause. Then the sound of paper—shifting, crinkling. The widow was holding something.

"Two million," she said. "If I sign. But I have to agree...I have to put in writing that Jerry...that it wasn't *their* fault."

She paused. Swallowed. And then, quieter:

"That it was *his*."

Vee felt something twist behind her ribs. Like a bolt torqued too tight, just waiting to shear.

"I just want to keep the house," the widow whispered, finally. "He worked thirty years for them. And I just want to stay in the house."

VEE KILLED THE ENGINE, got out of the truck, and slammed the door hard enough to make herself flinch. O'Hare's wind came slicing off the tarmac, spitting jet fuel and grit into the air, sharp enough to sting. The whole place reeked of cold metal. The hangar loomed ahead like a mausoleum, and she could already feel the shift in the air—too quiet, too orderly.

By the time she made it to the break room, the damage was done.

"Legal ran interviews this morning," someone told her—grimy fingers still wrapped around a styrofoam cup. "Asked about Jerry. About who signed off on his hours. What we knew. If we saw him coughing."

Her gut went sour.

She hadn't even been on shift. Swing crew had been

staggered to cover sick calls, and she'd only dropped by to check on tooling calibration before heading out. But now the clock was ticking. Legal didn't knock twice.

She cut across the hangar, boots echoing on the concrete. Kenji Miwa was leaning against a rig cart, shooting the shit with a couple of mechanics who should've known better.

"Where is she?" Vee snapped, eyes locked on his. The man had the stupid, slow-smile gravitas of a washed-up noir detective—clean lines, clean shoes, clean lies—and her guys were eating it up like idiots.

He lifted a brow. Didn't flinch. "Salvage hangar."

"Get back to work," she barked at the crew, not bothering to hide her disgust. "Stop talking to the damn help."

No one argued.

She turned, but not before leaning in just enough. Her voice was low. Flat.

"And you. Stop trailing me, or next time you won't see me leave. You'll just feel it."

Kenji gave a small nod—sharp, professional, and unmistakably clear: *Message received. Orders unchanged.*

THE SALVAGE HANGAR was two city blocks away, and too quiet. During the long walk, Vee's stomach twisted—sharp and sudden. Not fear. Something worse.

A thought came, uninvited.

She tried to shake it off, but it held.

She knew her crew. Good people. Loyal. Earnest. Not the most strategic. Not the kind who played chess—they followed orders, trusted the chain, hoped for the best. One of them had probably folded the second Sloane tilted her head and said, "Just tell me what happened."

And God, she could see it too clearly.

Sloane leaning over the table, not aggressive—disarming.

Voice low. Hands still.

The kind of calm that made you want to confess just to fill the silence.

Tag records spread across the table. Photos of salvaged parts. Inconsistencies in the logs. Safety reports someone had definitely backdated.

No accusations—just the clean, clinical logic of a noose tightening with every sentence.

And Kenji Miwa, of course, playing the opposite.

Casual. Detached. A soft voice with just enough empathy to make it feel safe.

We get it. Corners get cut.

No one's trying to ruin a career here.

Just tell us who gave the verbal.

Just tell us who knew.

She could hear it.

Could see one of the younger guys—green, eager, stupid in the way only earnest people could be—say something like: *I didn't check the manifest. My lead told me not to worry. Said the gear came from the plane. No one said it was flagged.*

And Sloane, nodding once. Expression unreadable. Tone steady.

So you skipped PPE on the job and didn't log the part.

The tech shrinking, flinching. "I wasn't the only one," he would mutter.

Vee clenched her jaw.

The intrusive thought left a bruise she didn't have time to name.

She shook it off and stepped into the hangar.

It was cold—no insulation, no heat, just the hollow

clang of ghosts and equipment past its prime. She expected to find a clipboard army. Suits. Maybe a flustered PR coordinator pretending to care.

But no.

Sloane Campbell was already inside. Alone. She had claimed the center of the salvage hangar, standing with the ease of someone who had no intention of negotiating a damn thing.

The dress was a statement—midnight navy, sleeveless, high neck, fitted like it had been engineered around her spine. The fabric clung with intent, not elasticity, molding to her body in ways that would've violated dress code if anyone had the nerve to enforce it. Every seam had a purpose. Even the hem played games, demure at the knee but daring just enough to draw the eye.

Vee stopped just short of entering.

She stood in the doorway and took her in with the kind of gaze she hated admitting to—measured, involuntary, too practiced to be casual. Sloane was everything she remembered and worse for it. The shape of her, the precision of her movements, the complete refusal to be anything less than devastating.

There was a pressure behind Vee's ribs that felt dangerously close to hunger.

She hated how much of her body remembered.

She hated that she could still feel the slope of Sloane's lower back with her hands.

And even more than that, she hated the fact that she wanted to feel it again.

"So you're running depositions now?" Vee asked, voice flat.

Sloane didn't look up. "No," she said. "I'm done, actually."

There was something so clean about the way she said it. Crisp. Bloodless.

Vee stared at her, heat rising behind her eyes. "What the fuck is wrong with you?"

The words came out lower than she meant, like they'd dropped straight from her chest.

This wasn't detachment. This was rot with a fresh coat of polish.

Sloane didn't even blink.

"They weren't under investigation," Sloane replied, finally turning to face her. "They were answering questions voluntarily."

Vee stepped in, closing the distance just enough to make it clear she wasn't bluffing.

"You don't talk to my guys without a union rep present. Not one-on-one. Not off-record. Not ever."

She let the words settle. Not shouted, not snarled—just solid. Undeniable.

"As a matter of fact, you stay the fuck out of the hangar. Period. You want something? You go through me."

Sloane also took a step toward her. They were too close now. She could smell her lotion.

"If they had nothing to hide," Sloane said, "they had nothing to fear."

"If you're done with the interviews, what the hell are you still doing here?"

"Verifying salvage protocol," she said. "Your crew pulled unauthorized components from this aircraft and reinstalled them into active service bays. I'm assessing exposure."

"You're trespassing," Vee shot back. "This section's restricted unless you're certified or supervised."

Sloane stepped in closer, eyes sharp. "Then supervise me."

Vee stared at her. No blink. No breath. Just static.

Then she exhaled once.

Without another word, she turned and walked across the hangar floor to the aircraft's forward steps. Climbed them. Unlocked the cockpit hatch with a code she shouldn't have had memorized.

And left the door open.

Sloane followed.

15

The cockpit was a fucking disaster. Nothing about it suggested sex—not one clean surface, not one horizontal plane that didn't threaten to bruise or impale. There were jutting levers, sharp-edged panels, and a center console dense with buttons that practically screamed "do not touch." The walls pressed in too close. The ceiling hung too low. The air was stale, hot with residual fuel and sweat. It was the worst place to fuck, and it didn't matter. Not to Vee.

She needed an outlet, and this was it.

Rage throbbed at her temples, curled hot and fast beneath her skin. Her jaw ached from clenching. Her fists itched. She couldn't throw a punch—never at someone she cared about, never like that—but her body didn't want peace. It wanted ruin. Wanted pain, or power, or both. So when Sloane met her at the hatch with that smug little smirk and a flick of her perfect curls, Vee saw red and reached for her.

She shoved her inside. Kicked the hatch shut behind them.

The steel groaned.

Vee knew every inch of the cockpit the way she knew her own bad habits—intimately, resentfully. She maneuvered them through the cramped space without missing a step. Sloane stumbled, caught off guard by the intensity, but welcomed it—leaned into it, eyes sharp, lips parted, already breathless with anticipation. Vee backed her toward the console like it was a goddamn altar and she was making an offering of them both.

The dress rode up almost immediately—some obscene fabric that whispered when it moved. It bunched around Sloane's waist, and Vee caught a flash of bare ass. Smooth skin. No lace. No barrier.

No panties.

Her mind short-circuited for a second, all the heat in her face dropping directly to her core.

"Well that's fucking convenient," she muttered, dragging the dress up the rest of the way.

Sloane looked over her shoulder, one brow lifted in dry amusement. "Don't flatter yourself. I just hate panty lines."

"Oh?" Vee licked her palm in a single, deliberate motion and then cupped her, pressing in hard. Flesh to flesh.

Sloane gasped—one sharp inhale—but didn't break eye contact. Didn't flinch.

Vee wanted to climb inside that moment and tear it apart.

She shoved her forward, bent her over the central console, forcing her arms to brace against a chaos of dials, toggles, blinking lights. One switch flipped with an audible click. Another button squelched under Sloane's palm. Vee didn't care what they activated.

Let the whole goddamn system fry.

Vee eased two fingers in, sliding through already slick folds, and smirked darkly.

"Already soaked," Vee murmured as her fingers curled. "Guess even our uptight little princess likes getting handled."

Sloane muttered something that might have been an insult, face turned against the metal. Her knuckles whitened around the edge of a throttle lever.

The teasing started slow. Vee worked her fingers with infuriating patience—dragging her thumb across Sloane's clit in firm, lazy circles, dipping in shallow and pulling out again, drawing heat without mercy. She watched every twitch of Sloane's thighs, every time her hips tried to rock back into the pressure. She denied her. Again and again.

Vee's mind raced and split itself down the middle. One half locked in physical instinct, controlling every breath, every thrust, every shiver. The other side unspooled in loops of self-loathing.

What the fuck are you doing. You're not sane. This isn't how people fix things. You should be walking. You should be breathing. Meditating. Talking it out.

Instead, she was deep inside a woman she both wanted to destroy and worship.

Sloane moaned—low and broken—and Vee snapped back into her body, caught in the swell of power, the addictive high of control. She curled her fingers just right, and Sloane nearly came undone right there. But Vee pulled back at the last second, earning a strangled curse.

She kept her there, on the brink, until her own hand ached from the tension. Then she dropped to her knees, gripped Sloane's hips, and buried her face between her thighs.

The taste was intoxicating—salt and heat and something uniquely her.

Vee worked with the precision of someone possessed, dragging orgasms out of Sloane with her tongue and fingers in tandem. First one. Then another. A third that left Sloane's voice hoarse and her whole body trembling against the console.

By the time the fourth hit, it was almost too much. She came so hard she nearly collapsed, forehead hitting the panel with a thud, knees buckling.

Still wasn't enough.

"Fuck me," Sloane growled, panting, face flushed and eyes wild. "Now."

Vee didn't argue.

She rose, slid her hand back in, and started to fuck her with brutal efficiency. The back of her hand slammed into her own pelvis with every thrust, the sound of skin slapping skin echoing obscenely off the walls. Her fingers curled perfectly, hitting that spot deep inside that made Sloane's thighs twitch, made her body arch, made her sob. This angle was awful. The space was unforgiving. And yet, it worked.

Sloane writhed, practically riding Vee's hand now, the entire cockpit shuddering with the force of it. Her forearms were marked from bracing against the console. Her spine was arched in a perfect, trembling curve.

When she came again, she let go with a ragged cry and gushed all over Vee's hand and the controls. The scent hit Vee—raw and electric.

She barely had time to process it before Sloane moved.

With the quick, sudden power of someone who'd been holding back, she turned and shoved Vee hard against the opposite panel. The impact knocked the breath out of her lungs.

Before she could react, Sloane was tearing the coveralls down, exposing the tank top and underwear beneath. She shoved the fabric up, both pieces bunched around Vee's arms. Her breasts spilled free into the warm, stale air.

Sloane's mouth found them immediately. Wet heat, sharp teeth, greedy tongue.

Vee's head tipped back involuntarily.

She had hated these breasts her entire life—resented the way they demanded attention, the way they made uniforms fit wrong. She used to double-layer her shirts, wear boxy jackets, anything to minimize them. She never thought someone like Sloane—the picture of restraint and polished ambition—would touch them like this. Worship them like this.

Sloane pinned her there, one leg lifting to hook over her shoulder, and dropped to her knees with a mission written into every sharp line of her body.

Her whole body jerked at the first lick. Vee let out a shaky laugh, dragging a knuckle through Sloane's sweaty temple. "God. Everyone thinks you're untouchable. If they only knew how nasty you get for me."

Sloane didn't respond. She just hummed, mouth already locked onto Vee's clit, and the vibration nearly knocked Vee's balance off. She grabbed for anything—metal tubing, control panels, the nape of Sloane's neck. Anything to stay upright.

Sloane licked and sucked like a woman possessed. Her hands never left Vee's breasts, thumbs stroking her nipples in slow, maddening circles while her tongue flicked faster. The contrast in rhythms made Vee delirious.

"Touch yourself," Vee gasped, eyes fluttering open.

Sloane obeyed without hesitation. One hand slid between her own thighs, fingers disappearing into herself while she stayed anchored between Vee's legs, drinking her down like she was parched.

Vee's pulse went wild. Her thighs shook.

She looked down—Sloane naked now, slick with sweat, dress discarded somewhere—and it nearly unraveled her. Her mouth gleamed. Her skin glowed. She looked obscene and divine all at once.

Vee's voice cracked. "Don't you dare come until I do."

Sloane moaned in response and pumped her fingers faster. The wet sounds beneath the suction of her mouth created an echo chamber of filth. It pushed Vee over the edge.

She came. Hard.

Came on Sloane's mouth, thighs clamping down, whole body convulsing. Sloane kept going, licking through it, moaning into her, until Vee came again—smaller, but raw. Then again, just from the aftershocks.

Sloane broke apart with her, fingers still buried in herself, mouth still moving until she hit her own high, her body trembling and collapsing forward onto Vee's thigh.

They stayed like that.

Crushed against metal. Skin against sweat. Bruised. Spent. Breathing shallow.

The floor was cold. The overhead light buzzed. Something dripped in the distance—coolant or sweat or time. Vee didn't know.

She couldn't think.

She only knew that her anger had faded, but the hollowness stayed.

She'd burned the rage out with pleasure, but the ashes still tasted bitter.

This wasn't healthy. But it was all she had left.

THEY SAT in silence for what felt like an hour. Maybe more. The cockpit lights were off, but enough filtered in from the hangar windows to make shadows of everything—buttons, levers, Sloane's shoulders. The engine panels blinked their dead systems. Nothing moved but breath.

Sloane was upright, spine curved slightly as she leaned against the center console. Her arms were loose at her sides, skin gleaming with leftover heat. Her head tipped back against the cracked leather headrest, eyes closed, mouth closed.

Vee didn't know how she ended up here—like this, of all things—half-sprawled across Sloane's lap, limbs slack, face turned into her thigh. Naked. Completely, humiliatingly undone. She should have moved already. Should've dressed, said something sharp, walked it off. Instead, she let it happen. Let Sloane stroke her hair in slow, repetitive motions, fingers digging in just enough to blur thought.

It wasn't fair how good it felt. The pressure. The rhythm. The obscene comfort of it. She could've groaned aloud, and that scared her more than anything.

She hated herself for giving in like this. For needing the softness after something so violently messy. For confusing damage with desire.

Vee finally spoke without looking up.

"Why?"

The question scraped out dry, raw from her throat.

"Why this?" she asked. "Why are you talking like them? Acting like them? We were on the same side last year. Or did that mean nothing to you?"

Sloane didn't answer right away. Her fingers stilled. Then resumed, slower.

"I told you already," she said eventually. "The highest bidder wins. I'm sorry if I gave you the impression I was some bleeding-heart idealist." She paused, then added, almost casually, "You do remember I still charged Morgan for legal support during the whistleblower scandal."

Vee turned her head slightly. "At a discount."

"Not that big a discount."

Silence again. The only sound was the faint creak of the plane settling in its rusted bones.

Vee exhaled hard. "You're not made for this shit. You never cared about money. You've got more than enough, don't you?"

That landed harder than expected. She felt it—not in Sloane's voice, but in the hitch that came before it. The way her hand froze briefly on Vee's scalp.

When Sloane finally spoke, it was quieter. Less rehearsed.

"Not enough for what needs to be done."

That stopped everything.

Vee sat up instantly, as if yanked from a trance. She turned to face her, heart slamming against her ribs.

"What does that mean?" Vee asked, voice low. "What's really driving this?"

She didn't say *Are you forcing yourself to do this?*

But the question was there. Clear enough in the silence that followed.

There was something almost desperate in her tone. Something hopeful. Pathetically, stupidly hopeful.

Sloane scoffed—more breath than laugh. "Don't be naïve."

Her tone turned cold again. Smooth. Practiced.

"This is the biggest containment case of my career. I wasn't going to turn it down."

But something in her face didn't match. A flicker. A crack.

And Vee saw it.

She stared at her for a long moment, half-naked in the cockpit of a corpse plane, trying to decide if she'd just imagined it.

"I don't want to keep fighting you," Vee said finally.

Sloane drew in a slow, careful breath.

"Then don't," she said. "Let it go."

The silence that followed wasn't peace. It was brittle. Off-kilter. Something hollowed out and left unfinished.

Vee didn't raise her voice. Not at first. Her words came out too slow, too deliberate, too sharp-edged to be anything but rage.

"You mean," she said, voice catching against her teeth, "make the widow sign the two million dollar settlement."

She didn't say the rest. Didn't have to.

Let the dead man take the fall.

Let Jerry die again in silence so Heritage can stay clean.

The disgust hit her so fast it made her nauseous. Her mouth went dry. Her stomach twisted. It was regret, yes, but not just about the sex. Not even about Sloane. It was deeper.

She could feel the crash coming—like a wave she'd been trying to outrun for months. It was going to hit hard. Soon.

Sloane looked at her, confused. "What are you talking about?"

That broke something open.

"Don't act stupid," Vee snapped, the words punching out of her. "Someone offered Jerry's wife money. A settlement. Quiet cash to make her stop asking questions. And now the official story is that it was Jerry's mistake. His negligence."

Sloane straightened, visibly reeling. "I had nothing to do with that."

Vee wanted—desperately, humiliatingly—to believe her. But her body had already made the decision. She was pulling on her tank top with shaking hands. Her limbs felt disjointed. Her skin didn't fit right.

She was shaking. Confused. Burnt out from every angle. A year ago she'd gone through this same hell, this same corporate gaslighting carousel, and now here she was again —half-naked in a dead airplane, crying into the same false promises.

She needed a vacation. She needed out.

But people kept needing things from her. More than she could give. More than she had.

She was tired in a way no sleep could touch.

Then Sloane moved. She stood, crossed the narrow space between them, and wrapped her arms around Vee like it would fix anything. Like proximity could unburn what had already been scorched.

Vee broke.

The tears came fast—raw, soundless, brutal. Her whole body folded against Sloane's without permission. She hated herself for it. Hated how much it still hurt to want someone she couldn't trust.

Sloane's voice was barely a whisper. "This is what happens to good people, Vee. The world doesn't reward it. It just takes. And takes. And takes."

Vee pushed her back with both hands.

"So what's the solution?" she hissed. "That I become like you? Just shut my mouth and do what needs to be done, even if it's morally bankrupt?"

Sloane flinched. Not obviously. But something passed

through her eyes—something fragile and real, and gone a second later.

She turned away and picked her dress off the floor.

When she slipped it on, it didn't wrinkle. When she reached for the zipper, she pulled it up with clean, practiced grace. She didn't ask for help. She didn't need to. Her mask was already back in place.

When she turned to face Vee again, her gaze dropped, then snapped back—harder.

"You think I like this?" she asked. "You think I chose to become the kind of person who can walk into a boardroom and hold her own against people who'd rather erase her?"

She didn't raise her voice. But she didn't hold back either.

"I wasn't born rich, I wasn't born soft, and I don't get forgiven when I fuck up. You know what I am. You know how many games I've had to play just to survive. So don't stand there and tell me what the right way looks like. You have no fucking right."

Sloane didn't wait for a response. She walked out of the cockpit, heels echoing against metal.

Vee followed her to the hatch, stopped just before the light could spill across her face.

"We're not settling," she said.

Her voice didn't shake anymore.

"No more stalling, Sloane. No more delays. I'm going to the press. I've done this dance too many times to mistake it for something noble. And I gave you a chance because it was you. But I'm done. I'm setting the whole damn thing on fire."

She paused. Just long enough to see Sloane freeze in the doorway.

"It won't be clean," Vee added. "It won't be pretty."

Sloane turned slowly, and something in her face crumpled.

"Please don't," she said. It wasn't fear for herself. That much was obvious. It was something else. Something heavier. Something that looked like devastation.

Vee saw it. And it almost stopped her.

Almost.

Sloane took a breath. "You're powerful, Vee. You're smarter than most. But you're outgunned here. You're walking into a war you can't win. I *will* bury you."

Vee's face didn't move. Her voice didn't rise.

"We're already buried," she said softly. "All of us. But we keep digging ourselves out. Again and again. That's what we do."

16

Vee hadn't moved from the floor in almost an hour.
The cats were sprawled beside her, tucked against her sides like they knew what kind of week it had been. Eugene V. Debs was curled into a loaf on her left, purring like a diesel engine. Dolores Huerta had claimed her stomach as a throne, sharp elbows digging into Vee's ribs every time she shifted. Outside, Chicago wheezed beneath a gray sky. Inside, her apartment felt strangely calm.

Her nephew had the door to his bedroom shut but she could hear him playing Fornite and yelling into a mic.

It had been four days since the cockpit. Since the fight. Since she'd walked away.

No calls. No texts. Not even a cease-and-desist.

Sloane had gone quiet in the most punishing way possible—by simply not showing up. By letting the space between them stretch like wire under tension, thin and volatile and ready to snap.

Vee didn't know what she'd expected. Maybe anger. Retaliation. Maybe another confrontation in a stairwell or bathroom or the bones of an old plane. But this? The nothing of it? It left more bruises than any argument could've managed.

She dragged herself off the floor just before the guests started arriving. By six, her home was packed. Her crew—Kill Fee bandmates, old organizing friends, and a rotating cast of very competent lesbians (most of whom were also exes)—filtered in with armfuls of poster board and folding chairs. Rosa brought ice and markers. Someone brought their new girlfriend and three fully-charged battery packs. The widow was coming in the morning. They had signs to make, chants to rehearse, and press kits to finalize.

There was work to do. Thank God for that.

Vee kept herself moving—stirring the pot of meatball noodle soup on the stove, pouring broth over bowls. She moved through the kitchen with efficiency. The smell filled the apartment: ginger, star anise, long-simmered beef, generous and aching. Everyone ate. Everyone praised her. Someone put on a punk record and screamed into a hair-brush mic. Kha even cracked a smile.

"Hey," one of the bandmates asked, gesturing at him with a Sharpie. "Are you here for college or what?"

Kha didn't even look up. "Nah. Probation."

That earned a pause.

"I just got out of jail. Adult jail," he clarified, like it was an important distinction. "They let me transfer here from California so I wouldn't get shot."

He lifted the cuff of his jeans and tapped the ankle monitor.

"Better for everyone if I'm not in Long Beach right now."

No one spoke for a second. A spoon clinked against a bowl somewhere.

Vee listened in from the kitchen, ladle in hand, heart

tight. No one asked follow-up questions. No one made it weird. That was the rule here.

She watched her people filling her home, half-listening, half-absent. This was supposed to be comfort. This was supposed to feel good. And it did—on the surface.

But underneath?

She kept remembering what Sloane had said. Not kindly. Not cruelly. Just plainly.

The world takes and takes and takes.

And Vee, like an idiot, kept giving.

What if this wasn't generosity? What if this was just her bleeding out slowly in a room full of people who loved the way she bled?

She stirred the soup harder.

THE NEXT MORNING, they hit the streets.

The protest outside the Heritage HQ building in the Loop drew a solid crowd. Local press showed. Someone brought a bullhorn. One of the signs read, WE'RE NOT MECHANICAL. WE'RE HUMAN. Jerry's widow gave a short, shaking statement in front of the cameras. Vee stood beside her.

They found out too late.

The shareholder meeting wasn't even there. It was happening miles away—Lake Forest or some other suburb. They'd been played.

Vee didn't rage. She didn't curse. She just dumped her protest sign in the nearest garbage can, watched it settle under a Starbucks cup and a wrapper from someone else's morning.

Then she slipped out. Didn't say goodbye.

Everyone assumed she went home.

Instead, she drove west. Not far. Just enough.

The salvage yard was quiet this time of day. Sky dimming. Tools where she'd left them. The half-stripped hatchback still up on blocks like it had been waiting for her. She didn't turn on the lights.

She worked in silence—hood up, sleeves pushed back, knuckles scraped open without fanfare. Time passed the way it always did in places like that: steady, unnoticed, almost kind.

By the time she stood up and wiped her hands on her jeans, the sky had gone full black.

Her phone buzzed once. No name. Just a time and a cross street.

She didn't check the message.

She already knew what it said.

At 11:07 p.m., she slid into the other car, engine warm.

She didn't race to win.

She just needed the silence between gears.

17

The board meeting went off without incident. Better than that, actually—Sloane had executed the relocation with her usual clinical precision, rerouting the venue to a discreet bed and breakfast in Lake Forest that charged as much per night as a Plaza Hotel penthouse, but came with the added benefit of plausible deniability and curated anonymity. Security was airtight. Agenda locked. The board emerged soothed and sedated, all champagne flutes and polite applause.

The press, however, had still gotten wind of the protest downtown. A few clever camera angles, a decent turnout, and the right widow holding a handmade sign had been enough to inject doubt into the market. Nothing catastrophic—just a 2.3% dip and a threadbare mention on the business ticker. But it was enough.

Sloane hadn't been caught off guard. Kenji had never stopped sending daily reports—just changed his angle. These days he scouted from two blocks out, with binoculars strong enough to pick up Vee's license plate. They'd predicted the protest from foot traffic alone: the uptick of bodies entering and exiting Vee's house, the pattern of bandmates, organizers, old union faces cycling in and out.

"She's a liability," Lucretia said crisply in the executive war room, pacing in sensible heels. "And I don't say that lightly."

"Twenty years of disruption," Ava added, stirring her tea without sipping. "You'd think someone would've handled her by now."

Sloane kept her hands folded. "If a multi-billion dollar airline hasn't managed to get rid of Vee Phan in two decades," she said evenly, "it's not because of oversight. It's because it's not possible."

Lucretia's eyes narrowed. "You two worked together last year, didn't you?"

Sloane didn't answer. She stood, gathered her files, and left the room without a word.

By the time the elevator doors closed behind her, Ava had already texted.

Careful.

Sloane didn't respond.

The shareholders left more or less satisfied. The crisis was rerouted, not resolved. The market twitched.

And in the space between performance and silence, Sloane could feel the fault line widen.

By 9:41 p.m., the illusion cracked.

Tiberia hadn't moved from her basking rock in hours. Her eyes were filmed over. Her tongue flick was sluggish. When Sloane reached in to lift her gently, she coiled in slow motion and let out a weak hiss that sounded almost wet.

The mouse. It had to be the mouse.

Sloane's composure unraveled so fast she barely registered it. One moment she was reaching for her silk robe; the next she was cradling a half-limp serpent in one arm and speed-dialing Morgan with the other.

"She won't move," Sloane said, her voice sharp and rising. "Her eyes look wrong. She didn't finish her last meal —she never does that."

Morgan answered from the porch of some idyllic lakeside cabin in Michigan, crickets in the background and Kieran's humming faint behind her.

"Have you tried—"

"Yes, I've tried! I've misted her. I checked the humidity gradient. I even recalibrated the thermostat myself." Her voice cracked. "I don't know what to do. I think—I think I poisoned her."

"Sloane," she said. "It'll be ok. Go to the emergency vet. There's one three blocks from you. I'll text you the address, okay?"

"Okay," Sloane said. Her voice was clipped, but agreeable. Automatic.

"I can be there first thing in the morning," Morgan offered. "We just got here, but—if you need—"

Sloane froze. The implication wasn't cruel, but it was clear. They'd just arrived in Traverse. A disruption.

"No. Don't," Sloane said quickly. "It's fine."

She was already shaking her head, as if Morgan could see it. Already calculating what Morgan would notice if she came—what she'd intuit beyond the sick snake, beyond the panic. Like the fact that Sloane was now based in Chicago for the next nine months. That she was "consulting" for Heritage. That none of it made sense on paper. And that Morgan, in all her razor-sharp grace, had chosen not to ask.

She never asked. She knew the cost of boardrooms.

"Matter of fact," Sloane added, reaching for a version of

herself that still sounded unbothered, "I think she's looking better already. Probably just...tired. Same as me."

She let out a quiet, brittle laugh. Then hung up.

Then powered off her phone.

She didn't want Morgan to drive down. Didn't want to be seen like this—weeping, cracked open in designer pajamas over a sick snake and the quiet, unbearable weight of her own damn hubris.

She pulled herself together the way she always did. Lip balm. Moisturized her elbows and knees. Pulled on sneakers. Threw on her comfiest cashmere sweater and slacks. Tiberia tucked into a breathable carrier she lined with a Hermes scarf. Her clutch contained a platinum AmEx and a backup charger.

She was halfway to the door when the knock came.

Three taps. No doorbell. Familiar rhythm.

Sloane opened it.

There stood Vee. She wasn't smiling.

Of course she looked like sin—like she'd just stumbled out of a dive bar fight and straight into Sloane's hallway. Black spaghetti strap tank top hanging on by a thread, the neckline stretched just tight enough to frame the line of her collarbones and the swell of her chest with ruthless efficiency. Her shorts—if one could call those shredded denim provocations shorts—looked like they'd survived a woodchipper and lost. Barely legal, aggressively casual, and clinging to her thighs.

It was obscene.

It was infuriating.

And Sloane felt heat crawl up the back of her neck before she could snuff it out.

"Your little wife called," she said, flat and annoyed. "Wanted someone to check on you. I couldn't exactly say no without blowing up this fucked up situation we've got going right now, so—" she looked down at the snake carrier—"here I am."

Her tone was clipped. Her eyes unreadable.

Sloane blinked.

It was, objectively, the most humiliating night of her adult life. And still, Sloane Campbell insisted on holding herself upright with the spine of a woman giving a keynote —not spiraling, not unraveling, simply responding to emergent conditions with calibrated urgency.

"It's just a snake," she said, out loud, to no one. The words emerged two octaves above her usual register, tight and fraying at the edges. The lie hung in the air, crystalline and ridiculous, as she rechecked Tiberia's respiration with a flashlight app and typed "reptile neurologist IL + urgent" into her second phone.

She'd already rearranged her entire calendar, cancelled the next days meetings, and was three clicks deep into an exotic animal specialty forum that warned ominously against "wet lung" and "digestive prolapse."

Vee didn't say anything at first. She didn't have to. The look on her face was enough: part exasperation, part concern.

The walk from Sloane's apartment to the truck was the stuff of nightmares.

She moved like someone rehearsing poise with every step, chin elevated in rigid denial of the fact that she was actively, silently sobbing. Not a scene. Nothing theatrical. Just mascara warring for its life beneath high-end concealer and a mouth pressed into such a severe line it might've left bruising. She clutched the snake carrier like it contained not her pet, but her last shred of control.

On the sidewalk, Vee had the audacity to look...calm.

Worse: competent. Dressed like the inside of a rave, she guided Sloane to the truck with one hand and fielded an incoming text with the other. Sloane tried to Google "python liver failure" between hiccupped breaths, but her vision blurred.

"We can walk," Sloane said briskly, clutching the carrier. "The emergency vet is less than a mile."

Vee grimaced, visibly forcing herself not to glance at the carrier. "Pretty sure they won't know what to do with that."

"It's an emergency vet," Sloane snapped, her voice pitching slightly higher. "It's in the name."

Vee gave her a look, flat and unmoved. "They mostly see dogs that swallowed socks. I doubt they've got an exotics consult on standby."

Sloane opened her mouth to argue, but nothing came out. Just the echo of her own spiraling breath.

There was a beat of silence. Then Vee exhaled, pulled out her phone, and scrolled like someone searching through a Rolodex of poor decisions and second chances.

"Unbelievable," she muttered under her breath.

She tapped something. Waited.

Then glanced up at Sloane with a grim little smile, equal parts resignation and dark amusement. "I think I have an ex for this."

The words made Sloane blink. "You have an ex who treats reptiles?"

"I have an ex for everything."

18

They arrived in Skokie, of all places, at a house that looked like the set of a nature documentary. A pride flag in the window. Native prairie plants out front. Wind chimes. There was a cat watching them from a perch, its expression deeply judgmental.

The porch light flickered as they approached.

And then the door opened.

"Vee?" said the woman—late twenties, maybe early thirties. Steady-eyed, curvaceous in a way that made space feel smaller, like gravity bent toward her. She wore scrubs and slippers, a chipped mug hanging loose from one hand. Her undercut was growing out into something controlled and sharp, longer on top, clean at the sides.

Animal anatomy tattoos climbed both arms—bone, tendon, muscle—rendered like blueprints etched in ink. "You finally bringing me something warm-blooded, or what?"

Sloane blinked. Of course Vee had a hot vet of an ex. Because why wouldn't she? Because the universe had no intention of letting her suffer with dignity.

"Hey, Audree," Vee said, offering a shy smile that Sloane found disproportionately irritating. "Thanks for taking us on such short notice."

Audree's gaze landed on Sloane—wrapped in a cashmere poncho, lip trembling, eyes glassy and rimmed with precision mascara, clutching a designer pet carrier like a grieving widow in a Bergdorf ad campaign.

"Of course," she said, eyes narrowing. " Come in."

Inside was a horror show of comfort: eclectic furniture, mismatched mugs, throw blankets that looked suspiciously soft, and an enormous lizard basking under a UVA lamp. A leopard gecko blinked at Sloane from the bookshelf.

She sat—delicately—on the edge of an armchair upholstered in something organic and morally sourced. Her knees pressed together. Her hands folded. She dabbed at her eyes with a silk handkerchief that cost more than all the appliances in the kitchen. She tried not to breathe too much.

Audree, busy prepping a heat lamp and running diagnostics, didn't look up as she asked, "So this the girlfriend?"

Sloane froze. Blinked once. Did not react.

She adjusted her posture.

The mortification came in waves. Not theatrical, not explosive. Just...relentless. Soft and slow and deeply logistical.

And yet—when Audree took Tiberia gently from her arms and murmured something soft and competent—Sloane exhaled for the first time in hours.

Audree moved with the easy, economical calm of someone who'd done this a hundred times, her gloved hands steady as she angled the exam light toward Tiberia's slack coils.

"I'm checking for respiratory infection," she said, voice low, clinical. "The bubbling around the nares, the open-mouth breathing—it's textbook, unfortunately. We'll confirm with a culture, but I can already tell she's fighting something off."

Her fingers glided over Tiberia's scales with practiced delicacy, murmuring something reassuring. The lighting in the converted den was too warm, the furniture too lived-in.

Vee stood across the room, arms crossed, hip cocked against the doorframe like she lived there.

"You look good," Audree said without looking up, casual as breath.

"Thanks," Vee replied, smiling—open, reflexive, maddeningly clueless. "So do you."

Audree made a noise. "Oh please, you don't have to be nice."

"You know damn well I'm not nice," Vee said with a dimpled smile.

They shared a look, full of history and knowing that made Sloane's blood pressure rise.

She sat frozen on a plastic chair two feet away. Her spine was straight, her sweater uncreased, and yet she was vibrating internally with a cocktail of jealousy and disbelief. Tiberia wheezed once. Sloane swallowed.

"So," she said lightly, with the venomous tone of a woman preparing for deposition, "do you do this full time, or was it one of those...remote programs?"

Audree looked up. Her smile didn't waver.

"No. I went to Davis."

Sloane blinked. "UC Davis?"

"The one and only."

"Oh right," Vee chimed in. "Isn't that the best vet school in the country?"

"Best in the world," Audree corrected with no modesty whatsoever, stroking the underside of Tiberia's jaw.

Vee pointed to the wall behind Sloane's chair.

"That's all her certs. She's got a whole section on exotic species. Ball pythons, lizards, you name it. She wrote some paper on gecko conservation and like...something about ethical enrichment? She won an award. I think it's in Nature or something."

Sloane turned slowly toward the wall in question.

There it was: an entire gallery of institutional excellence. Licenses, commendations, framed publications bearing titles like Herpetological Ethics in Captive Care Environments. A plaque for Excellence in Emergency Handling of Exotic Pets. Another from an international symposium on reptile pathology.

Of course.

Sloane, who had once bribed a reclusive Palm Beach millionaire—half-senile, wholly negligent—into surrendering a malnourished leucistic ball python he kept under a heat lamp in a marble solarium, stood in front of the wall in silence.

Tiberia, the color of lightning caught mid-flash—who looked like an aesthetic choice but was, in fact, a rescue, a confidante, and the lone witness to several felonies and one extremely specific nervous collapse—let out a soft, rattling exhale.

Audree adjusted the scope and shifted Tiberia's coiled weight gently between her hands, examining the sheen of her white scales and the subtle rise and fall of each sluggish breath. Her expression changed—just slightly. The professionalism didn't falter, but the cadence of her movements slowed. More focused. More grave.

"She's got a respiratory infection," Audree said at last, her voice calm but firm. "You caught it early, which helps. But this didn't happen overnight."

Sloane tensed. "I thought it was the mouse—"

"Probably a factor," Audree cut in gently. "But this is about environment. When humidity or ambient temperature dips too low, even for a short stretch, it compromises their immune system. Especially if they're already stressed."

She glanced up, eyes steady. "Did you move her recently?"

Sloane blinked. It was a small thing, the question. But it landed with the weight of a closing verdict.

"Yes," she said, her voice breaking on the word. "I—I relocated for work."

"New setup?"

"Brand new. I had her enclosure custom-built but—" Her mouth opened and closed again. She couldn't find the end of the sentence.

Audree gave a quiet nod. "There it is. New temperature gradients. New smells. New light cycle. She probably held on as long as she could, and then—" She gestured toward Tiberia's heaving sides. "Crash."

The word echoed, sharp and clean.

Crash.

Something buckled inside Sloane. Her jaw tightened. Her shoulders curled, just slightly inward. She looked down at the towel, at the shape of Tiberia's fragile, laboring form, and the edges of her vision began to blur. She blinked once. Then again. But the pressure behind her eyes didn't subside —it crested. And then broke.

"I shouldn't have moved her," she whispered, barely audible. "God. I shouldn't have uprooted everything. She was stable."

"Hey," Vee started, her tone low and unsure.

But Sloane wasn't hearing her. She lifted a hand to her face like she could catch the failure before it spilled out—

but it was already too late. Her body betrayed her with brutal efficiency.

She began to cry.

Not the tidy, cinematic kind. But silent, shaking sobs, chest shuddering beneath soft cashmere, eyes clenched shut like she could will herself back into control. Her lips parted, trying to shape apologies that didn't exist. The air felt too thin. Her thoughts spun in elegant, educated circles—negligent transfer, failure of duty, proximate cause—but it all translated to the same thing

She'd let Tiberia down.

Sloane Campbell hadn't cried in front of another human being since sixth grade, when her algebra teacher gave her a C and her mother told her to get over it because "We don't have the luxury of falling apart."

And yet here she was: unraveling in a stranger's living room, mascara ghosting under her eyes, as her only dependent rasped beside her under a towel printed with cartoon lizards.

Audree said nothing. She didn't comfort her—thank God—but she didn't look away either. Just kept prepping the injection like this happened all the time. Like women cried in her house over reptiles every other Thursday.

Vee moved closer but didn't touch her. She crouched, awkward and uncertain, like she wasn't sure whether Sloane needed to be held or left alone to disintegrate in peace.

Sloane shook her head once, as if answering a question no one had asked.

"I should've never brought her with me," she whispered, voice raw now. "It was too much."

Sloane excused herself with the kind of perfect calm that only came from decades of internal triage.

The air outside hit her like a slap.

She made it down the porch steps before her knees gave out, lowered herself carefully to the concrete like it was part of some evening stretch routine. Wind chimes clinked gently above her. Something floral bloomed nearby. A cat watched her from the window with heavy judgment.

Of course this was when the regret hit.

Not when she signed the contract. Not when she buried evidence. Not even when she stood across from Vee at that negotiating table and drove the knife in with perfect diction and no visible tremor.

No, it was now. In a stranger's living room. At night. With her snake's tiny body barely breathing .

Because this wasn't strategy. This wasn't optics or plausible deniability or moral relativism wrapped in a quarterly report. This was real. This was Tiberia—warm and sluggish and dying maybe, because Sloane had dragged her across state lines into a stress vortex masquerading as duty.

She'd compartmentalized everything. Her family. Her guilt. Vee.

She thought she could compartmentalize this too.

She thought she could be owned without consequence.

God, she was so irrevocably fucked in the head.

Not because she'd betrayed Vee. Not because she'd sold out an entire hangar of honest, hardworking people.

But because this—this—was what finally broke her.

Not the woman. Not the blood on her hands.

Just one sick, silent, trusting little reptile who had never asked her for anything except care.

And somehow that was the thing she failed at.

SLOANE STOOD IN THE DOORWAY, hands neatly clasped in front of her, watching as Audree settled Tiberia into the observation tank. The room was quiet but clinical—humidified, sterile, gently lit in a way that could almost pass for tender.

"She'll be monitored all night," Audree said. "I've got my tech coming in for an extra shift. Someone will always be with her."

Sloane didn't nod. She just reached into her bag, retrieved a matte-black card, and handed it over without looking.

"Charge whatever," she said.

Audree took it with a small hum of acknowledgment. Sloane's mouth moved automatically. "Thank you. For your care."

Her voice was neutral, almost digital. Too polite. Too smooth. She turned before Audree could respond.

Vee was waiting near the front door, car keys in hand, not quite leaning against the wall. Not relaxed—just occupying space in that insolent, grounded way she always had. The set of her jaw made it clear the offer to drive Sloane home wasn't kindness. It was duty. Obligation, maybe. Or pity, which was worse.

The ride was quiet. Not the good kind.

They were halfway up Lake Shore Drive when Vee finally said, "So how's burying me going?"

No heat. Just flat and sharpened by something unspoken.

Sloane hated how much she still loved Vee's voice. Elegantly feminine, wrecked at the edges—a songbird rasp. It sounded like she chain-smoked heartbreak and rinsed with river water. The voice of someone who'd been adored on stage. That voice crawled under Sloane's skin and stayed there for days.

She kept her eyes on the skyline. Jaw tight.

Right. She'd told Vee she would bury her.

"I haven't filed the paperwork," Sloan finally replied.

Vee snorted.

When they pulled up to her building, the silence stretched itself taut. Sloane moved to open the door, hesitated. Vee's hand twitched like she might reach for her—shoulder, wrist, something—but didn't. Neither of them moved fast enough.

It was the worst kind of almost.

Sloane stepped out and closed the door too softly. It didn't latch. Vee reached across, slammed it shut with a muttered, "No worries."

The doorman greeted Sloane with a bright "Good morning."

She didn't look back.

Inside, the apartment was cold and pristine. The kind of silence that didn't feel restful—just abandoned.

She set her bag down. Pulled out her phone.

Typed five words to Kenji: *Wrap up the side project.*

A quiet command to stop trailing Vee.

The carrier sat empty on the table, a ghost of weight and warmth gone too quickly. The lake outside glowed with that weird Chicago blush: pinkish-purple, a kind of beauty that didn't try to comfort you. Just showed up, unbothered.

Sloane didn't change out of her clothes. She sat in front of the glowing screen, the draft policy already open. The language was boilerplate: hostile environment remediation, departmental restructuring, strategic redundancies. All she had to do was finesse it—make it sing, feed it to the board in the right tone.

Her team had laid the groundwork. The internal memos, the compliance matrix, the contractor audit—designed to shift liability away from corporate leadership and pin it neatly on hangar supervisors and senior mechanics. People like Vee. Legacy employees. Long-timers. The ones who stayed too long, asked too many questions, made too much noise.

It was elegant. Legally sound. Executable by Monday.

All she had to do was hit send.

This was the moment she was built for.

She didn't move.

Her fingers hovered over the keys, motionless.

Not a decision. Not yet.

Just stillness with shape. The beginning of a crack. Not mercy—but memory, maybe. A flicker of choice beneath the choreography.

A coiled possibility.

That maybe—for once—Sloane Campbell was no longer playing by muscle memory.

19

The union hall still smelled like printer ink and coffee dregs—flat and bitter, the scent of tired hope. The old West Loop building had been a union stronghold since the '60s, back when steel-toe boots marched up these same stairs chanting I AM A MAN. One of the first integrated locals in the city, the International Brotherhood of Aircraft Technicians backed Civil Rights strikes before it was fashionable. Fluorescent lights flickered overhead, indifferent to the moment.

The lobby wall was a shrine—black and white portraits printed on wheatpaste, sealed behind matte laminate, a mural that stretched almost floor to ceiling. You had to stand back to take it in: the grain of the paper, the grayscale grit of mid-century protest, and front and center, deadpan and impossible to ignore, was Vee. Welding mask tipped up. One eyebrow cocked. The caption didn't bother with dates or credentials. Just: PHAN. Crew Chief, Local 313.

She hated it, of course. Hated how they'd immortalized her mid-glare, like a martyr with a torque wrench. But people needed symbols, and Vee knew optics better than most. She understood how to construct myth—and when to step aside and let it do the work.

Today was about Noah. Noah Feldman-Bloom, the overworked golden retriever of a labor rep, had finally scored a cable news segment. A real one. Not some clip on local Channel 9 with chyron typos and fuzzy audio. This was national. And because Vee knew how the game was played, she arrived two hours early.

By the time the cable news crew rolled up with camera rigs and lav mics, the room already looked like the revolution had good taste. Vee had picked the spot herself—angled for the best light, wood-paneled backdrop softened with throwback posters in bold Helvetica: SOLIDARITY IS A VERB. WORKERS DESERVE BREATHABLE AIR. She dragged in folding chairs with vintage patina, set up a water carafe, and leaned hand-painted signs along the walls that somehow looked cinematic. She'd added fresh flowers from the 7-Eleven. Just enough to suggest hope.

One of the camera guys blinked, surprised. "This looks... good," he muttered, half to himself.

The intern nodded like he'd helped. Vee didn't even dignify it with a look. Let him think whatever. She hadn't touched a camera, hadn't run a mic check, and still managed to art direct the hell out of this moment.

She wasn't in the shot, but she was in every frame.

Noah sat stiff in the chair, tie a shade too wide, brow a little too furrowed. Vee adjusted his collar once. Lightly. No muss. "Loosen up," she murmured. "You're not apologizing. You're calling them out."

He nodded. Nervous. And hot. Which—yeah. Vee had to admit it: he cleaned up well. Kind of annoying. But she wasn't gonna hate. Labor needed a little thirst trap energy to cut through the noise.

Then the widow stepped in.

Mrs. Cortez wore black slacks, a blouse with tiny blue cranes. She didn't cry on camera. She told the story clean. Her late husband Jerry, the man who trained Vee, who kept that hangar from falling apart, who'd gone soft in the lungs from years of invisible dust. She spoke like she'd practiced, but not too much.

Vee watched from the side, arms crossed, heart running like a generator. The footage would run on the six o'clock block and again at ten. The headline was already drafted: "Airline Workers Exposed: Cancer in the Sky."

By noon the next day, Heritage stock would nosedive. And it wouldn't be an accident.

They walked Mrs. Cortez to the street corner. Noah started to say something—some big-picture, macroeconomics horseshit about how this kind of pressure could force a settlement.

"We know," Vee said flatly. "Let her breathe."

He shut up. Bless him.

She pulled Mrs. Cortez into a hug, bone-deep and bracing, and ordered her an Uber home. Vee paid for it on her own card.

Noah stayed behind, looking like he wanted to apologize for existing, but muttered about having to go back to update all the social media accounts.

Vee patted him on the shoulder. "You did okay, golden boy. Go get a massage or something. You look like a divorce attorney."

He gave her a sheepish little wave and disappeared back into the building.

She lingered. Just for a second.

The street was strangely empty for a weekday. The mural stared back at her through the glass—her own face mid-glare, frozen in grayscale, like it was daring her to keep going.

She exhaled, long and quiet, and left.

20

Her body moved on instinct. Down the block. Into the train station. She tapped her Ventra card without thinking.

She was halfway to the Loop before she even realized where she was going.

When she surfaced, she was climbing the stairs at Grand. Michigan Avenue was a fucking nightmare.

Full sun. Ninety degrees. Thick air. And every damn tourist in the Western Hemisphere had apparently made a pilgrimage to the Mag Mile just to clog sidewalks with baby strollers and flip-flops. The thoroughfare heaved with slow-moving mobs. People posed in front of Sephora like it was the Eiffel Tower. A guy in a Spider-Man suit did a backflip for a Venmo tip. There was a wedding party in front of the Wrigley Building. A bachelorette group in matching shirts and cowboy hats screamed into a phone about brunch.

It was peak summer bullshit. Loud, hot, pointless.

Vee stood at the corner and just...absorbed it. The chaos. The sensory assault of traffic and body spray and street performers banging on buckets. She didn't belong here. She didn't even want to be here.

And still, her feet kept walking. Past the plaza. Past the river. Toward the air conditioning and curated fantasy of Eataly—her personal purgatory.

She didn't need groceries. She didn't even need a snack.

She stopped at every damn floor.

First: pasta. Endless rows of artisan carbs stacked. She picked up four different bags. One had squid ink. One had saffron. There were zero cooking instructions. Into the basket they went.

Then: cheese. The guy behind the counter offered a sample of a 36-month aged Parmigiano and said "notes of caramel." She nodded solemnly. Took three more samples and walked away with two wedges she didn't remember picking up.

She found herself at the olive oil tasting bar. Again. She was holding a tin that cost fifty-eight dollars. It had gold lettering and said "single estate." What the fuck was a single estate? Did she care? No. It went in.

A bottle of wine she couldn't pronounce. Some pickled something. Biscotti. A wooden spoon she didn't need. A weird sauce she convinced herself Kha might like.

Her phone buzzed at least twice. She ignored it. Just kept walking.

By the time she hit the checkout, her basket was full of high-end culinary trauma. She handed it off, half-dazed, and tapped her card.

The total: $398.12.

The cashier smiled too brightly. "Do you want a bag?"

"Sure," she said. "Make it two."

Outside, she stood on the corner holding those chic brown paper bags like a divorced Real Housewife who just discovered cold-pressed anything. Her stomach buzzed with acid. Her hands were shaking.

That's when the phone rang again. Unknown number. She was about to let it go to voicemail when it hit her: third call in under an hour. Something was wrong.

She answered.

A mechanical voice cut in, crisp and unfeeling: "You are receiving a call from an inmate at Cook County Department of Corrections, a correctional facility. To accept this call, press one."

Vee froze on the street corner, next to a busker singing in Polish, clutching $400 worth of wine and squid ink pasta, while the robot kept talking.

She pressed one.

"Kha?" she said.

His voice came in rough, low, barely audible over the static.

"Auntie. I didn't do shit. I swear."

21

The visitation room looked like a DMV that gave up. Beige everything. Plastic seats bolted to the ground. Fluorescent lights buzzing just loud enough to make you question reality. One glass wall ran the length of the room, each station separated by scratched-up partitions and ancient phones slick with someone else's sweat. Vee sat down hard and picked up the receiver without flinching.

Kha was already on the other side. Baggy jumpsuit. Eyes a little wild. And for a split second, her brain short-circuited —because it wasn't Kha she saw.

It was her brother.

Same jaw. Eyes the color of weak tea and old sunlight— same as the whole damn family. Same shitty county-issued uniform. She remembered that last day clear as hell—the ICE van, the busted-ass parking lot in the Valley, her brother's wrists zip-tied behind him while he tried to crack a joke. He got deported when Kha was still in kindergarten. He was the only one of them who'd come to the U.S. as a kid—never got his papers in order. The rest of them were born here, citizens by default. That's how it goes sometimes. One kid gets a passport. Another gets a one-way ticket out. Vee had only seen him twice since he got deported. Meant to go to Vietnam more. Never got around to it. Flights were too long. She only got so many damn vacation days.

Now Kha was here, staring back at her like he wasn't halfway to repeating a similar fucking story.

"You good?" she asked, voice flat.

He shrugged. "You know. Best day ever. Living the dream."

"Don't get cute."

"They said I violated parole. Something about the bracelet going dark for too long. I told them it was glitching, but they didn't give a shit. I was walking home from 7-Eleven —next thing I know, six cops got me face-down on the sidewalk."

"You didn't check the signal?"

"I check it."

"You check it once a day? Twice?"

"I don't know—"

"You need to be checking that ankle like your life depends on it, Kha. Every hour if you have to."

"You think I like looking at it?" he snapped. "You think I like being reminded I'm stuck in this loop?"

"You're a whole-ass twenty-year-old man," she shot back. "Act like it. You want me to vouch for you at mechanic school? You can't even stay on top of a goddamn bracelet."

He pulled back, lips tight. "I thought you didn't even want me to apply."

"I don't," she said coolly. "But I already saw your admissions scores."

"You opened my mail?"

She tilted her head. "You voided your privacy the minute

you moved into my house. Actually—correction—the minute you went to jail."

He glared. But it cracked fast. He couldn't hold onto it, not fully.

"When you get out," she said, voice lower now, softer but not soft, "we'll finish that application. We'll get you back on track."

Kha stilled. Then grinned—like a kid, like he used to before the weight of everything bent him sideways.

It broke her heart, that smile.

She forced a breath. "Chill. One step at a time. You're not out yet."

The room spun a little. She needed a snack. Her head was starting to swim. She gripped the phone harder.

The guard tapped on the glass with the butt of his pen and motioned toward the hallway.

Vee turned, and there was Moni—half-shadowed in the doorway, oversized blazer swinging behind her. Cropped hair still damp from the morning, no makeup, ankle boots that looked like they'd marched through both court and riot. A file folder under one arm, a half-drunk Dunkin iced coffee in the other. Black slacks. Bulletproof posture.

Moni was a public defender by day and the drummer for Kill Fee by necessity—controlled chaos in a wrist brace, the only person Vee knew who could keep time and start fights at the same pace.

From a distance, she could've passed for a wiry, androgynous guy leaning against the brick wall of a bar outside Boystown—sharp jaw, buzzed hair, expression like she knew something you didn't. In reality, she had a husband, two teenagers, and a Subaru with a Coexist sticker on the bumper.

She held up two fingers and mouthed something through the opening.

Then she stepped halfway into the room. "They're pulling him for legal," she said, loud enough for the line to hear. "Tell him to hang up. I'll take it from here."

Vee nodded. "They're letting you talk to your lawyer," she said into the phone. "Don't say anything dumb."

Kha rolled his eyes. "Define dumb."

She hung up on him.

Moni vanished down the corridor without waiting for a thank-you. Not that Vee was about to give one. She'd burned one of her few favors calling Moni in—made the ask, got the answer. No guilt. Just, "I'll take it." Like it was nothing.

THEY SAT on the concrete edge of a planter outside the courthouse, half-shielded by a no-parking sign and a dead bush. Between them: two soggy wax-paper-wrapped hot dogs loaded up with mustard, onions, relish, sport peppers, pickles, celery salt—the works. No ketchup, obviously. Even humiliation had rules.

Cop cars idled by the curb, lights off but still threatening. A few angry suits were pacing the front steps, phones glued to their faces. Some guy in a neon tie was yelling at a clipboard. It was the kind of scene that made Vee want to disappear into her hoodie, but she was too hungry, too tired, and too cracked open to pretend she was above it.

Moni flipped open Kha's file. She squinted at the paperwork. "Eighteen charges in the past seven years," she muttered, wiping mustard off her lip with the back of her hand. "Let's see...assault at thirteen. Vandalism. Trespassing. Possession. More possession. Jumped in at fourteen, looks like. Gun charge at fifteen—didn't stick. Evading police. Another assault. Affiliated robbery at sixteen. Two probation violations. One count of resisting arrest. And something about a ghost gun manufacturing ring? Holy shit."

She looked up, face a mix of heartburn and betrayal. "You said 'my nephew got picked up.' Not 'my nephew fled block warfare in SoCal with enough baggage to bankrupt a therapist.'"

"What was I supposed to say? 'Hey Moni, can you fix three generations of imperial fallout by noon?'"

Moni shook her head, still scanning the stack. "I didn't think the old-school Southeast Asian sets even operated anymore. Thought ICE cleaned house after the Patriot Act."

Vee took a slow bite of her hot dog. "They have. What's left is more mixed now. Looser turf. Different rules. Still deadly."

Moni let out a low whistle. "Goddamn. It's like some shit refuses to die."

"Not when it feeds your whole neighborhood," Vee said. "Not when it's the only structure some kids ever see."

She didn't look up. Just ate like she could chew her way through it.

"We've known each other twenty years," Moni went on. "I get it—we're bandmates first, friends second. The balance is the reason we've never killed each other. But Jesus, Vee. I'm scared to know what else you've never told me." She chuckled, but it was tight.

"Yeah," Vee said, still chewing. "Imagine actually being me."

They both laughed, sharp and low.

Vee wiped her mouth. Her hands were shaking slightly, but she powered through. "My mom's family came here as refugees. Grandma brought the older kids over. Her youngest, my mom, stayed behind, had a baby—that's my brother. Mom finally came to the States and brought him with her, but nothing got handled right. Some scammy immigration lawyer. Wrong names. He stayed in California. We're born here, the rest of us. Me, my sisters."

She took a breath. It tasted like peppers. "By the time I was in middle school, he'd climbed the ladder. Running crews, moving weight, the whole thing. Not just some corner kid—he had people under him. He was locked into the life. No way out. Shot someone during a drive-by in front of me when I was sixteen."

Moni stopped chewing.

"Westminster. Outside a taco stand on Brookhurst. We were parked, waiting for our order. He was in the passenger seat. Other car pulled up and opened fire. He reached across me and shot through the driver's side window. Hit the guy in the head. I watched him slump over—just folded, right out the window. Like a movie, except it wasn't."

Moni's face was blank now.

"The gun went off right by my ear," Vee added. "Didn't mean to. Just instinct. But yeah. Hearing never came back on that side."

There was a beat of silence

Moni's eyes widened. "That's why you always stand with your left side angling towards me on stage."

"Yep."

"Twenty fucking years, Vee."

"I don't like talking about it."

"Clearly."

They sat in the noise for a while—sirens in the distance, heels clacking on pavement, a pigeon pecking at someone's discarded fries.

Moni's phone buzzed. Her thumbs flew over the screen quickly. "We've got a gig in Milwaukee tomorrow night."

Vee nodded.

"You should be able to pick Kha up the morning after," Moni added. "Assuming he behaves and no one gets creative with the paperwork. The bracelet thing's manageable—it's a common glitch. I pushed it through fast, so the processing should finish in forty-eight hours. He'll walk out with a warning if nothing else goes sideways."

Vee didn't say thank you.

Instead, she hugged her.

Hard. Bone-deep. One of those rib-cage hugs that said please don't disappear.

Then—awkward, impulsive—she kissed Moni on the cheek.

Moni didn't react, just kept chewing.

Vee pulled back and stared at the sidewalk, her face hot.

That was the problem, wasn't it? People did show up for her. Sometimes. Enough to shake her up. Enough to make her think about softening, about letting someone in past the outer layer of competence and rage.

And every time, she hated how much it meant.

22

It had been four days since the emergency vet visit. Tiberia was home now, coiled in the far warmth of her terrarium like nothing had ever been wrong. The infection had broken, her breathing had stabilized, and the swelling around her lower jaw had receded to something nearly imperceptible. But she still required injections every twelve hours—antibiotics, fluid, a light sedative to keep her from biting. Sloane administered them herself, with the precision of a surgeon and the detachment of a war medic.

She hadn't returned to the office since.

The virtual boardroom was full, the air crackling with polite, high-stakes fury. Lucretia's voice, smooth as old money and twice as venomous, cut through the call with surgical contempt. Ava didn't speak—she didn't need to. Her silence was worse than condemnation. Sloane sat in front of her laptop in a silk blouse and perfectly painted face, backlit by the matte gray daylight seeping through her Gold Coast windows, and absorbed the damage.

Twenty percent. The stock had dropped twenty percent. The widow—Katrina Cortez, fierce with grief—had appeared on three major news programs in a single day. CNN. MSNBC. Even fucking CBS This Morning. Clean, quiet devastation delivered to middle America over toast and grapefruit juice.

The headline looping beneath her face:

HERITAGE KNEW. THEY LET HIM DIE.

It wasn't just a leak anymore. It was a narrative. It was sticky.

Sloane's voice—measured, exacting—tried to offer terms. Legal firebreaks. PR offsets. Strategic restructuring of frontline leadership. But the board didn't want solutions. They wanted a scalp. And hers was the easiest to take.

She closed the laptop slowly. Deliberately. Sat in stillness as the silence in the room around her became unbearable.

Zora, arms folded and standing by the window. Kenji, pacing like he had something to fix. The twins, El and Andi, half-curled on the sectional with their laptops—muted now, but both staring at her like she'd just pulled a fire alarm in a sinking ship.

"You're compromised," Zora said finally, quietly. "This isn't just bad optics, Sloane. You've never let something get this far out of hand."

"We have the ammo to bury the union and this entire suit," Kenji said, measured but pointed. "What's going on? If Lucretia finds out you've been holding back—"

"She won't," Sloane cut in, crisp as glass.

It landed with the weight of a blade, not a bluff. The room went still. Kenji stopped pacing. Zora moved from the window to sit with the twins.

What she didn't say was louder: *Yes, I have it. Yes, I could end this. No, I haven't. And you should know better than to ask why.*

"But she will," El said. "We're good, but Lucretia has ten more teams like us—on payroll and on standby. She'll find a way."

"You're slipping," Andi added, voice gentle, which made it worse. "You're slipping and we don't know why. We've been with you through a lot of shady shit, but this? This whole contract—this job—it's extra rotten. You didn't even vet the fine print yourself. That's sooo not you."

Sloane stood up slowly. Smoothly. As if each vertebra in her spine were an answer she refused to give. "I don't need a fucking intervention from my *assistants*."

The silence hit like recoil.

Zora flinched—visibly—shoulders stiffening as if she'd just been shoved. Kenji blinked, once. El's jaw actually dropped, mouth parted around a protest that never made it out. Andi looked away, cheeks flushed, fingers clenched tight around the edge of their laptop.

No one moved. No one breathed.

Sloane never raised her voice. She weaponized stillness. She negotiated with bone-dry wit and surgical detachment. She didn't swear at her team like some panicked exec throwing a tantrum.

She had never talked to them like this.

And that made it worse. Because it meant something was really wrong.

"You're still getting paid. You're still protected. You don't need to understand what I'm doing. You just need to do your job. This is still my firm. This is still my team. You don't get to question how I keep the lights on."

The room flinched at her volume, not because it was loud—but because she never raised it. Not like that.

She didn't wait for their reply. She walked out of her own living room.

She made it to the sidewalk before she heard the footsteps.

"You think we're your interns?" Zora said—voice cool, clipped, and loud enough to slice clean through the air. "You think we're here to process paperwork while you spiral over your girlfriend?"

Sloane turned, slowly. "That's not what this is."

Zora's eyes narrowed. "Isn't it?" Her voice sharpened, her posture didn't shift. "Because from where I'm standing, it looks like you've been sitting on a legal kill switch for weeks while the rest of us run cover and bleed credibility."

Sloane's tone dropped an octave. "Zora, back off."

"Why? So you can maintain the illusion that you're still in control?" Zora stepped forward—measured, deliberate. "You're not. You're stalling. And now the board wants blood, Lucretia is circling, and we're standing here exposed— unarmed—because you decided to grow a conscience."

Sloane crossed her arms. "You're angry. I understand."

"No," Zora said, shaking her head once, clean and final. "You don't. We've followed you through every fire. We've cleaned up scandals, buried leaks, gagged whistleblowers you called 'inevitable.' And this is where you draw the line? Over a pretty mechanic with some cute backstory?"

Sloane didn't flinch. But her silence turned sharper, like she'd just swallowed something bitter.

Zora inhaled once. Evened out.

"You think she's special. And maybe she is. But she's not the one they're about to crucify."

Sloane looked away—out the window, at nothing. "I'm not going to obliterate the union just to protect myself. There's another way."

Zora let out a sharp breath. One laugh, hollow and almost stunned.

"Who even are you right now?"

Her voice didn't crack, but something frayed at the edge.

"You're the one who told me that hesitation is a liability. That if I ever let personal feelings interfere with the firm's position, you'd fire me on the spot. Your words."

Sloane said nothing.

Zora stared at her like she was trying to find someone else in her expression. She took a step closer, hand brushing Sloane's arm—not tender. Just contact. Just proof she was still there.

"God, Sloane. Just—pick a side."

Sloane responded by turning and climbing into a cab— heels sharp on the sidewalk, deliberate as a closing argument.

23

Lunch with Morgan was an uncomfortable indulgence—an appointment she should have canceled, but didn't. They sat in the back patio of some aggressively minimalist bistro in River North, sipping $18 cocktails and pretending the wind didn't exist.

Morgan looked good. Too good. Cinched halter top, lacquered, sculpted—dressed like she was about to break someone's heart in a chrome-and-leather basement.

"I've been meaning to ask," Morgan said, slicing into her niçoise salad like it had personally insulted her. "Why the hell are you working for Heritage?"

Sloane didn't look up, spooning some beef tartare onto paper thin toast.

"I've never held your lack of moral investment against you," Morgan added, tone breezy, almost fond. "Principles don't pay retainer fees, and you've always known how to pick a winning side. But this?" She paused, letting her fork linger mid-air. "This isn't mercenary. This is...desperate."

Sloane didn't flinch. She dabbed the corner of her mouth with her linen napkin and exhaled.

"Well, as a firm believer in values-driven reform," she said, voice satin-smooth and soaked in venom, "I'm simply honored to be part of Heritage's ongoing commitment to accountability and the human fucking spirit."

"Fuck off, Sloane."

Sloane just sighed.

"Not now. Please."

Morgan leaned back, chewed, then swallowed slowly. "Are you trying to protect me?"

Sloane lifted her gaze. "No."

"Don't patronize me," Morgan said, low and pointed. "I'm not some fragile Delta Theta legacy from your pledge semester who cried through rush and passed out at the Founder's Ball."

She didn't have to say the name. They both thought it: *Cameron Whitney.* The girl who broke her ankle in kitten heels and threatened to sue for emotional distress. Fragile wasn't a description. It was a shared historical fact.

"I can handle the truth," Morgan continued.

"I said no." Sloane's voice cracked on the edge of something dangerously human. "We're at an impasse, Morgan. Either trust that I know what I'm doing—or don't. But I'm not explaining myself to you over lunch like some undergrad sobbing outside a kegger because her fake ID got her banned."

Morgan dabbed her mouth with her napkin. "Fine. Just let me know when you're done *Leaning In* so I can duck."

Sloane rolled her eyes, but the laugh escaped before she could catch it—low and tired, with the shape of old friendship in it. Morgan let out a matching sound, quiet and edged.

"By the way—why are you dressed like that? I mean, you look good. You look hot. But is there, like, a...sex dungeon after this? Is that what you and Kieran are into now?"

Morgan snorted. "You're projecting."

Sloane arched an eyebrow.

"I'm going to Vee's show. Milwaukee. It's just a bunch of crusty Midwestern punks trying to outrun their mortgages and bad tattoos," Morgan said, leaning in. "You should come."

Sloane opened her mouth to decline—something crisp, final, perfectly phrased. But nothing came out.

And so somehow—by accident or inertia—she ended up in a black SUV on I-94, dressed in black on black, heading toward a warehouse venue in the industrial gut of Milwaukee at 10:06 p.m. on a Friday night.

She wasn't sure why.

Maybe it was the way her apartment felt like a mausoleum of unfinished obligations. Maybe it was that Vee Phan was about to climb onstage and sing like her blood were made of gasoline. Either way, she'd stopped at Neiman Marcus on her way out of the city and left with a black Alexander McQueen dress—open-backed, razor-cut, and designed to make a certain lead singer look twice.

Sloane was quietly relieved when Morgan dropped the subject of Heritage. She hadn't realized just how tightly she'd been bracing for follow-up questions, for the slow knife of Morgan's concern. But instead, they spent the ride trading memories—Penn in the spring, bad decisions in worse heels, the reckless confidence of women who hadn't yet learned what it cost to be taken seriously.

Morgan, by design, lived completely offline now. No current events. No social media. No push notifications bleeding through her life. It had been that way since her exit from corporate, after everything imploded. Whatever was unfolding on the news about Heritage—whatever fresh outrage Vee had coordinated—Morgan hadn't seen it. She had no idea. And Sloane had no intention of informing her.

The venue itself was wedged between a shuttered foundry and a warehouse that had once manufactured washing machine parts. Inside, it smelled like rust, beer, and hair dye. The floors were concrete, uneven and scuffed, and the stage lighting was strictly functional: red, blue, green, all dim and half-broken. The crowd skewed older—thirty-somethings in patched denim and orthopedic sneakers, former punks now waging a quiet war against sciatica and early bedtimes. People swayed, headbanged, and half-moshed with the weary precision of those who needed to drive home by midnight and be upright for their children's soccer games by nine.

Sloane didn't join them. She slipped into a booth near the back, half-shrouded in shadow, where no one would recognize her or ask her to smile. Morgan had already disappeared into the crush of bodies, abandoning decorum in favor of movement—hair loose, arms raised, dancing with the ease of someone who had nothing left to prove.

And for the first time in days, Sloane found herself—if not happy, exactly—then momentarily outside of herself. The sound was too loud, the air too hot, and the beer was flat. But she was watching strangers be joyful in public, and it was disarming.

Then Vee came onstage.

The shift in the room was immediate and chemical. The crowd pressed forward. Lights adjusted. Chatter quieted. And then Vee opened with something unexpected—sweet, mid-tempo, and sarcastic in a way that only someone with real rage under the hood could pull off.

The lyrics—sharp, clever, and unflinchingly specific—landed like tiny pins stuck into Sloane's skin. Something about "not all angels have clean credit" and "love letters typed in legalese." It was annoying, and accurate, and completely devastating.

And then, halfway through the second verse, Vee spotted her.

It should have been impossible. Sloane was practically buried in shadows, tucked behind a support beam, dressed in blackout tones and sitting like a statue. But Vee's eyes flicked to her booth and didn't look away. And then—showboating, deliberate—she dipped her mic low, leaned halfway off the stage, and pointed. Directly at her.

Sloane froze.

It was absurd. It was theatrical. It was corny.

But as anyone who's ever dated a musician knows, there are certain gestures—certain public, reckless, sweat-drenched declarations—that short-circuit the entire nervous system.

And Sloane felt herself short-circuiting, right there in the dark. One hand on the table.

She didn't smile. But she didn't look away either.

Near the end of the set, someone from the crowd shouted Morgan's name. It took a beat for Sloane to register what was happening—Vee grinning wide onstage, beckoning Morgan up with a flick of her wrist, the crowd already cheering.

Sloane didn't move. She simply watched as Morgan—eye-roll, mock groan, and all—handed off her drink and stepped up onto the stage.

They launched into a punk classic—one of those early

2000s anthems that lived permanently in the bloodstream of anyone who had ever gone too hard in a mosh pit and survived. Morgan's voice, clear and deceptively polished, cut through the room.

It was chaos, nostalgia, and a kind of graceless joy. The crowd roared with every familiar lyric. People danced like they had nowhere to be in the morning.

Sloane stayed planted at the back, still cloaked in shadow, but even she smiled. It was impossible not to. The energy was absurd, contagious. For a moment, no one in the room was calculating outcomes. Not even her.

Afterward, the bands mingled with each other in a loosely organized backstage haze—cheap drinks, sweat-damp towels, someone rolling a joint with too much ceremony. Sloane lingered only because Morgan did, and Morgan lingered only because Vee hadn't disappeared yet. The conversation was incidental. The real exchange took place across the bar: Vee, leaning against a brick wall with a beer in hand; Sloane, seated in a cracked vinyl booth on the far side of the room. Neither of them moved. They didn't need to. The tension between them pulsed. Eyes locked, then broken. Returned, then held. No one else noticed. But it took everything in Sloane not to look away first.

They didn't speak.

Morgan and Sloane left just before 1:30. By the time they crossed back into city limits, the skyline was bleeding into dawn and Morgan's heels were in her lap. She looked sideways at Sloane more than once, but didn't say anything. Not at first.

Only when they pulled off Lake Shore did Morgan finally speak—softly, almost like a concession.

"You don't have to tell me," she said. "But one day, you're going to. Just...don't wait until it's already on fire."

Sloane didn't answer. She just nodded, then opened the door to her building and disappeared into the lobby without looking back.

She knew something was off the moment she stepped into her apartment.

The air was too still. The lights were on—low, but purposeful. And then she heard his voice.

"I thought I raised you to understand debt."

Her father was seated in the armchair near the window, perfectly composed, as if he'd been waiting hours and hadn't minded.

Sloane froze. She hadn't seen him in a few months. Not since Jamaica.

He stood slowly, the way a man does when he's already made up his mind. "Ava called," he said. "She's reconsidering the terms. She says you're in violation."

Sloane's mouth went dry.

He stepped forward, measured and merciless. "You told me you understood what you were signing. That you were willing to pay the price. Now she's saying you've broken faith."

And just like that, her breath caught—not from the accusation, but from what it meant.

A flash of heat surged beneath her skin, old and familiar. Her mind spiraled, not forward, but back.

To her aunt's luxury home in Jack's Hill. The sun splitting the sky in brutal gold. The air thick with salt and obligation. And the contract—dense, archaic, and entirely too beautiful. Printed in ink that somehow shimmered faintly in the light. Words she could read but somehow feel.

"It's nice to see you too, Daddy."

24

Her father looked like he belonged on a banknote. Samuel Campbell stood tall and broad-shouldered in a white Cuban shirt, light slacks, and a straw fedora, the kind of man more comfortable in a cigar bar than in his daughter's modernist Gold Coast apartment. His bearing carried the same weight as the men whose faces adorned Jamaican currency—revolutionary, revered, untouchable.

She made him breakfast anyway.

Just as she always had. As if he hadn't broken into her life with dramatic flourish, uninvited and entirely certain he had the right.

"Zora let me in," he said casually, seating himself at the oversized dining table. "I've been here all day. All night. Where were you?"

Sloane didn't look up from the stovetop. "I'm thirty-three, Daddy. I don't have a curfew."

The breakfast was simple: cornmeal porridge simmered with milk, cinnamon, sugar, vanilla, and just enough salt to sharpen it. She brewed his green tea the way he liked it, steeped exactly four minutes.

It was what they'd eaten growing up. What her mother used to make. Her mother, who had died while Sloane was still in undergrad.

They sat in silence at the gaudy dining table, one of many furnishings paid for by Heritage—opulent, excessive, and empty of history.

After a few bites, he set his spoon down.

"What are you doing, Sloane? It's eight months. A favor to the Thompkins family, yes—but one that keeps our name intact. You think they'll let us walk away clean if you don't deliver?"

"I have it handled," she said, still calm. "You didn't need to fly here."

His brow furrowed. "What does that mean?"

She shrugged.

"Keep your head down. Do what the woman tells you," he said. "You've never been rebellious. This isn't the time to start."

A lazy backhand—not for her, but for her sister. The rebellious one. Four years younger, a filmmaker in Berlin who'd cut the cord years ago and never looked back. Estranged from their father, hostile to the family legacy. Sloane still called once a month. She never said much, but she always picked up.

"You don't understand," she said, voice steady. "You're not the one being strangled by this arrangement. I am. So unless you're here to take my place, I suggest you stay out of it."

Without warning, the bowl—and the spoon still clutched in it—exploded from his hand, hurled across the room with a force that didn't match his age or bearing. It struck the wall with a brutal crack, ceramic splintering on contact, fragments skittering across the floor.

He had never raised a hand to her. But the violence hung in the air anyway—brittle, metallic, impossible to ignore.

It wasn't the bowl. It was the pattern.

The silence after impact was worse than the noise itself.

She kept her posture neutral, hands folded in her lap, spine held taut by instinct more than intention. Her body remembered things her mind had learned to file away under *context* and *discipline*. Her father never hit. That wasn't his method. But drywall had known his fists. Tabletops, glassware, kitchen cabinets. The perimeter of every room in her childhood had at some point absorbed the weight of his failure to hold still.

After her mother died, it had almost stopped. Not enough to be called progress. Enough to be called grief.

And still, now and then—especially when she deviated, when she dared—he found himself in the old rhythms. Something sharp left his hand. Something broke. Then silence.

Sloane blinked once.

The shards lay scattered beneath the window. She could see his chest rising—too shallow, too fast—but she didn't move.

There was nothing to say. Nothing to fear. Only the growing knowledge that he hadn't come here to stop her. He'd come here to see if she was still afraid.

She wasn't. Not in any way that would serve him.

"What is this about?" he snapped. "Are you—" His voice faltered. "Are you really going to turn your back on what we agreed to?"

That was when it hit him. She saw the change in his face. Not rage. Realization.

"Oh my God," he said quietly. "You don't care. Do you?"

He stood, as if the thought physically repulsed him. "You'd let us lose everything. The name. The land. The work. The schools, the clinics. Your family still in Jamaica, who rely on that name to survive—you'd let it all go. And for what? So you can be some polished American attorney in a white man's skyscraper?"

Sloane rose without a word. She walked to the utility closet, retrieved the dustpan and broom, and began to sweep the shattered pieces into a neat pile.

She didn't say anything for a long time. Let the silence hang.

"If I'm the collateral in some legacy feud no one alive remembers starting," she said, calmly discarding the pieces, "then I'll control the terms."

She dried her hands on a linen towel.

"I don't have a spare bedroom here," she continued, evenly. "Zora will book you a suite at the Langham. It's lovely. Very modern. She can arrange a few tours if you'd like. You've always appreciated architecture."

"Is that how you speak to your father now?" he thundered, his voice now thick with heat.

Sloane met his gaze without blinking. "Yes."

25

The following week was a humiliation ritual disguised as brand strategy. A carefully sequenced, algorithm-optimized performance of degradation—market-tested, focus-grouped, and blessed by Heritage's crisis consultants. Sloane knew the shape of it before the first blow landed. She recognized the choreography. It wasn't built to punish. It was built to break.

First came the billboard.

She caught it from the backseat of a black car crossing the West Loop—a sixty-foot smear of her own face above an expressway exit, lit like salvation. Her expression was frozen mid-sentence, lips parted, eyes soft, the kind of look a man would call approachable. *Sloane Campbell, General Counsel, on Heritage Values.* Below her chin, in corporate blue: **"Accountability is our altitude."** She hadn't written the line. Hadn't approved the photo. She'd been rendered into marketing collateral overnight.

Then came the press.

The morning she flew to New York, Zora called in sick. First time in...ever. Sloane took the call while smoothing gel over her edges, palm steady, face unreadable. Zora's voice was hoarse, almost guilty. "I just need the day. I'm sorry."

There was a pause. A tonal dip. Like Zora was speaking from somewhere too far away.

"Is everything alright?" Sloane asked, quiet.

"Of course." Flat. Immediate. Like she'd rehearsed it.

Then the line went dead.

Sloane stared at the phone a moment longer than she meant to.

She landed at LaGuardia to a brittle wind and an unsmiling driver, her name misspelled on the placard. The interview was scheduled for Inside Track with Toni Vaughn, a streaming political show that fancied itself radical journalism but was, in practice, thirty minutes of tactical bloodletting with a rotating cast of sacrificial lambs. This week, Sloane was the lamb.

Nobody met her at the lobby. Security didn't have her badge ready. The front desk made her wait an hour while interns walked past and dropped names. When she finally made it through, a producer offered her coffee with a smile that didn't reach her eyes and asked, "Is your boss joining us soon?"

She didn't correct her. She was tired.

The interview was a knife fight. Toni Vaughn, all sharp angles and righteous fury, opened with a clip of Jerry Cortez's widow—her voice shaking, her hands clenched—and pivoted into a monologue on corporate complicity, labor exploitation, and the long American tradition of putting brown and Black bodies in high-risk zones and calling it opportunity.

Sloane was given thirty seconds to respond.

Everything after that was a blur of clipped rebuttals and moral indictments, her own voice sounding tinny in her ears. Toni's questions weren't questions. They were charges, delivered like closing arguments. *How many funerals have you personally attended, Ms. Campbell? Is it hard to sleep, or does the salary help?*

The camera stayed close on her face. High definition. No mercy.

By the time she stepped back onto the sidewalk, the wind cut through her dress. She didn't hail a car. She just walked, heels clicking against the concrete, mouth set in that same non-expression from the billboard.

She doesn't even remember crossing the street. One minute she was in Midtown, jaw clenched, body locked in that stiff-chinned posture she's worn since childhood; the next, she was on a crosswalk blinking at a blaring horn.

Not dashing into traffic. Not flinging herself into it. Just stepping—like she forgot that cars existed. Like the boundary between public and private space, between body and machine, had dissolved. One heel clipped the curb wrong. The light was red. Someone screamed.

It wasn't suicidal. Not exactly. Just...absent. Her mind had gone gray. Not blank—quiet. The kind of quiet that terrified her because it felt good. Like stillness. Like relief. And for one flickering second, she thought: *What if I just kept walking? What if I didn't dodge? What if I let the world decide for once?*

The brakes squealed. A hand grabbed her arm. Someone cursed her out, called her a crazy bitch.

And Sloane just laughed. Not out loud, not visibly. Just a flicker at the corner of her mouth. She thanked the man who grabbed her. Apologized. Stepped back onto the curb.

26

S he was back in Chicago the next day. No limp, no bruise, no sign she'd nearly been flattened by a town car in Midtown Manhattan. Just another near-death moment filed under Tuesday.

Now she was walking to a boardroom the length of a small runway, surrounded by fourteen other members—former governors, asset managers, tech CEOs, retired generals. Collectively, they were worth somewhere north of $12 billion, not counting the off-books money parked in private equity or shell corporations.

Sloane Campbell had sat through more board meetings than some CEOs had press conferences.

She'd watched a founder of a tech unicorn stammer through a shareholder revolt while an SEC official hand-delivered subpoenas in front of cameras. She'd once whispered "shut your goddamn mouth" to a panicked CFO during a pharmaceutical fraud spiral, moments before the FBI kicked open the door and arrested half the C-suite. She'd been flown in to clean up an energy conglomerate in freefall—the kind of place where offshore funds and human rights abuses came itemized in the same spreadsheet. That boardroom burned down three weeks later, metaphorically and otherwise.

So no, she wasn't new to crisis. She was fluent.

But this—this was different.

This was execution.

The room was already full when she arrived. Deliberately. One seat left—at the end, not at the head.

She caught it in the corner of her eye: Zora, in tailored black, murmuring something to Lucretia Morrow near the coffee credenza. Heads tilted close. Posture too easy. Too familiar.

The moment Sloane stepped across the threshold, they broke apart like nothing had happened.

Lucretia turned toward the board with her practiced smile.

Zora didn't meet her eyes.

Lucretia waved at Sloane like she was the help arriving late. No one moved to make space. No one acknowledged her.

"We weren't sure you'd still be joining us," someone said with a chuckle.

Her heels echoed too loud across the carpeted floor. Her dress—cream, expensive, strategic—felt like a costume. The kind you buried women in.

Lucretia opened with her usual controlled breath and a voice like a velvet trap.

"It's been a challenging few weeks," she said. "But that's why leadership matters. Especially now."

She didn't name Sloane. She didn't have to. She said things like legal transition and public scrutiny and narrative risk—and let the silence fill in the rest.

Sloane stood when it was time. No podium. No notes. Just the legal brief—sanitized, bullet-pointed.

She began to read.

Half the room didn't look up. One board member scrolled on his phone. Another adjusted his tie. A younger woman leaned sideways and whispered to someone beside her. The whisper was loud. Intentional.

Sloane didn't pause. She didn't flinch.

But her throat dried mid-sentence. Her voice caught. A microscopic glitch—but in this room, even air was weaponized.

The questions came next. All smiles like knives.

"Is legal coordinating directly with internal comms to minimize union confusion?"

"Have you verified that there's no personal bias influencing litigation strategy?"

"Are you confident your involvement hasn't increased our liability exposure?"

They weren't asking—they were building a case. One accusation at a time.

Someone called her "young lady" twice. Another brought up "rumors"—that she was close to certain union figures. They didn't name Vee, but they didn't need to.

Sloane answered precisely. Coldly. No emotion. The way you respond when you're already bleeding but refuse to let anyone see it.

Lucretia interrupted the inquisition at just the right moment.

"Let's not pile on. Sloane's been brave in continuing to serve."

The room clapped. Politely. Measured. As if the coffin had been nailed shut and they were applauding the craftsmanship.

The meeting didn't end. It just kept going.

Financial reports. Strategy decks. Decisions she wasn't asked to weigh in on. One slide mentioned reviewing General Counsel succession planning in Q4. Like it was just another line item. Like her name wasn't on the target.

Across the room, Vivian Yue watched her. Dressed like a wedding invitation. She hadn't spoken once. But her gaze never left Sloane. And when their eyes met, Vivian tilted her head just slightly. Not sympathy. Not threat.

A test.

By the time they adjourned, Sloane felt like she'd been flayed and stuffed back into her own skin. She stood. Smiled. Gathered her papers. Said nothing.

She was still alive.

But not untouched.

They hadn't just questioned her authority.

They'd written her obituary—and handed her the pen.

THE BATHROOM WAS TOO BRIGHT. LED white, sterile and humming, the kind of light that revealed every pore and every fray in the fabric of Sloane's carefully maintained mask. She pressed her hands under the automatic faucet, water too cold, soap too floral, and tried to steady her breathing.

She didn't hear the click of heels until it was too late.

Vivian Yue stood near the mirror, swiping a lipstick bullet across her mouth with surgical precision. Pale pink dress. Glossy curls. The sort of polished, weightless femininity that made people assume innocence. Sloane had seen her type a hundred times and had learned never to underestimate any of them. But this one—Vivian—was different.

She had money that moved silently. Legacy money. Imperial money. A seat at the table—not earned, but inherited. Her father hadn't just bought his way in; he'd bought the land the table stood on.

"Ms. Campbell," Vivian said brightly, voice light as chiffon. "You were so composed up there. Really. It's not easy, facing that room."

Sloane gave the requisite smile. Her palms were still wet.

Another exec exited, leaving them alone. The door sighed shut behind her, and something in the air shifted.

Vivian didn't move, didn't blink, but the smile dropped from her face. Her whole posture straightened, as if something reptilian had uncoiled beneath the silk.

"They're going to make you eat glass before they let you leave," she said quietly. Not a threat. Not a warning. Just fact.

"They want you humbled, discredited, and photogenic while it happens." A pause. "You're too smart to let them get away with it."

Sloane didn't respond. Couldn't. Her mouth was dry and her chest felt tight—like the tension of a courtroom just before a verdict, when you already knew you'd lost.

Vivian glanced over, satisfied. Then:

"If you're not planning to go quietly...let me know. I have notes."

She capped the lipstick, smiled again—sweet, empty— and walked out.

Sloane stared at the mirror. Her reflection looked translucent. Like she wasn't entirely there.

She'd known she was being watched. She hadn't known the vultures were already picking seats.

27

The elevator opened into a private vestibule. Zora was already there, perfectly composed, holding Sloane's overnight bag.

Sloane blinked. "You're not coming?"

Zora didn't meet her eyes. "I've got work here. Final review on the indemnity clauses."

The language was crisp. Rehearsed.

Sloane hesitated. "You sure?"

Zora nodded, too fast. "Enjoy yourself. It's good optics."

It didn't add up. Zora lived for these things—billionaire retreats, whisper-network power brokering, black-tie gossip served with foie gras. She usually led the room while Sloane hovered in her wake, all teeth and silk and small talk as soft currency.

But now she stood stiff, muted, like someone had unplugged her from the current.

Sloane tried again. "Everything alright?"

Zora's smile was clean but hollow. "Just tired."

Sloane stepped forward, gently took the bag from her.

"We haven't had dinner, just the two of us, in a while. Let's fix that when I'm back."

Something flickered.

Zora looked like she'd been handed a memory she wasn't ready to hold.

"Have fun," she said. Quiet. Almost kind.

Sloane stepped onto the rooftop helipad, the sky stretched wide and gray. Millennium Park glittered beneath them. The lake beyond stretched pale and endless.

Sloane stood at the edge, heels poised on imported limestone, clutching the wind-tight folds of her trench. Her escort—if one could call Milton Hodge anything but a leash—was late.

The helicopters arrived in staggered sequence. Black blades slicing the sky with billionaire nonchalance. Executives, laughing like Roman senators, stepped into the air with practiced ease. No one looked nervous. Helicopters were not transportation here. They were punctuation marks. A habit.

She was assigned to the last one. Of course.

It was just her, Milton Hodge, and his silent, thousand-yard-stare assistant—who was possibly a hospice nurse, possibly an enabler, possibly both.

Hodge came from one of those old-money dynasties whose name was etched into half the Ivy League—billionaire pedigree, statesman by default. He was the kind of heir you send to Washington when you don't trust him with the real empire.

Over five administrations, he'd managed to sabotage transportation infrastructure on a national scale—and profit from every collapse.

He had the wattage of a war criminal and the scent of aged cologne and dried sweat.

His walker looked like it had been stolen from a museum or a plantation house—aged cherrywood, gold-plated initials, and utterly useless on stairs.

As she helped him into the aircraft, Sloane caught a faint grunt of satisfaction. One of his liver-spotted hands brushed her hip, lingering. The pilot looked away. The assistant said nothing.

She didn't flinch. She smiled. She took her seat. If she was furniture, she could not be blamed.

They flew north to Lake Geneva, Wisconsin. An unlikely zip code for power, unless you knew where to look. Behind the curtain of pine and deer stood a lakeside compound so vast it bordered on parody—multiple residences, a private dock, a stretch of woods designated for hunting, and somewhere underground, a wine vault engineered like a panic room. There was even a water park.

Obscenity disguised as retreat. Wealth so dense it bent geography.

It belonged to board member Vic Tolliver, a venture ghoul who'd once tried to buy a U.S. territory during a hurricane. He made his fortune "disrupting municipal waste." Now he threw bacchanals for other billionaires and called them retreats.

The mansion loomed like a cursed inheritance. Inside: too much velvet. Too much money. Too much history that had never been cleaned.

Lunch was obscene.

A "casual affair," someone said. They called it rustic. Yet the tableware was porcelain, the oil was imported, and the sourdough had a waitlist.

The table had three types of caviar. A whole suckling pig was carved tableside by a man in tails. A footman—not a server, a footman—poured something golden and burning into Sloane's glass without making eye contact.

Milton Hodge wheezed beside her, chewing slowly, like it pained him to remember how his jaw worked. His hand slid up her thigh mid-sentence. No warning. No pretense. Just soft, practiced intrusion—like he had paid for access decades ago and had never been told no since.

She stared forward. Ate nothing. Let his fingers rest. It was her only card at the table, and Ava and Lucretia had dealt it for her.

They hadn't said it outright. They never did.

But when the invitation came—*you'll ride with Milton*—and Ava's manicured smile tightened just slightly, Sloane did the math. He was the godfather of Heritage. His shares could swing a coup or seal a reign. And lately, he'd been "increasingly erratic."

Keep him happy, Lucretia had murmured. *You're the only one he listens to.*

Translation: Be ornamental. Be touchable. Be useful.

She could've told them to fuck off. Could've pulled rank. Could've left.

But instead, she poured Milton another glass of 2009 Château Lafite Rothschild and whispered softly about how underappreciated he was. How modern leadership had lost its spine. How his legacy was misunderstood.

He grinned at her. Called her *his little island girl.*

She laughed. Filed it away. And slipped a hand over his to stop the next grope—not as a rejection, but as a signal. A coax. A redirect.

She was plotting.

.   .   .

AFTER LUNCH, a few board members peeled off for cigars, but Vic Tolliver insisted on giving "the full tour."

No one declined.

The house was vast, but nothing about it was new. Not gaudy. Just...established. Like it had been rich longer than most countries had been stable.

Tolliver walked them through the library first. The room smelled like varnish and paper currency, dimly lit despite the wall of windows. Sloane noted a few rare books—first editions of *Atlas Shrugged* and *The Fountainhead* shelved between Kissinger's White House Years and a biography of Rupert Murdoch.

A hallway of photographs came next. Glossy, oversized prints. Tolliver shaking hands with presidents, business magnates, one or two monarchs. In the center: a black-and-white photo of him beside Henry Kissinger, both mid-laugh. The caption was handwritten in gold ink. Tolliver said nothing, just smiled when someone slowed to look.

In the dining room annex, behind glass: a set of dishes that had supposedly belonged to a deposed royal family. "Never used," Tolliver said. "Out of respect." Sloane noticed one plate had a faint red stain near the rim.

The last stop was the vaulted lounge—all stone and leather, with a fireplace large enough to cremate a horse. A chandelier hung above a custom game table where a few of the men were already settling in with bourbon and poker chips.

"We close deals in here," someone joked.

"And bury them," Tolliver added. Quiet, but not softly.

Sloane didn't laugh. She was too busy memorizing the exits out of instinct.

. . .

THAT EVENING, the real party began.

The mistresses arrived first—pearlescent women in stilettos and strategic silence. Then came the sex workers—discreet and well-contracted, dressed in identical spa uniforms and listed as therapeutic services on the guest manifest. Their presence was understood, if not acknowledged.

Family members didn't show up until the next day, which said everything about priorities.

Someone brought out an antique rifle for clay shooting. Someone else organized a bloodsport masquerading as skeet. There was a heated discussion about buying a small airline out of bankruptcy—over poker.

During the cocktail hour, the women had changed into dresses and men into suits without ties.

When Milton's hand crept back to Sloane's wrist—bone-dry and trembling, but unmistakably claiming—she looked up. Looked right at them.

Not subtle. Not silent.

She held Ava's gaze first. Then Lucretia's. Then anyone else who'd meet her eyes.

She didn't beg. She dared.

Dared them to say something. To stop it. To even blink.

No one moved.

They turned away like it was weather. Like she was weather—unfortunate, ambient, and entirely beneath acknowledgment.

So she smiled. Let Milton's grip tighten on her thigh. And imagined burning the whole estate down with one well-timed whisper.

She stood, slow and smooth, and walked to the drink cart, letting the hem of her dress brush past a cluster of executives pretending not to notice her. Her glass was still half-full, but she needed a moment. And stronger ice.

Vivian Yue intercepted her halfway.

She looked flawless—Chanel, of course—metallic, precise, the kind of cocktail dress that whispered dynasty money and knife fights over brunch. Her husband stood a few steps behind her, scrolling absently through his phone.

Vivian barely looked at Sloane as she spoke.

"Keep plying him with drinks. He'll knock out eventually."

Sloane bit the inside of her cheek. Not hard. Just enough to stay grounded. "Excuse me?"

Vivian turned, offering the smallest of smirks. "A tip from my father." Then, after a pause: "You're doing fine."

She vanished into the room, heels soft against the carpet.

Sloane stood there a second longer, then topped off her drink. Watered it down. Grabbed a fresh pour of something darker for Milton.

CLOSER TO MIDNIGHT, the real conversations drifted poolside —into cigar smoke, hot tubs, and hands where they didn't belong.

This was the part of the night where the rich stopped performing manners and started showing teeth.

Sloane had gone to Yale Law so no one would ever mistake her for part of the furniture.

And yet here she was—helping a eighty-two-year-old billionaire to bed while his hand stayed on her ass.

She kept her expression neutral. Not blank—neutral. Just enough to pass for patience. Just enough to look like deference.

His walker clicked gently across the marble.

She steadied him with one hand, held her breath with the other.

This wasn't unfamiliar. She'd seen versions of it growing up—at family parties, on Sunday phone calls. Aunties who worked the night shift at the care home. Cousins who slipped on scrubs and vanished into other people's houses. Quiet, capable women who knew how to handle a body without drawing attention to their own.

Her father had drilled it into her and her sister that they hadn't come to America for that life. He commanded them to earn their way into the rooms where it didn't happen.

But money had a way of looping back on itself. Erasing degrees. Flattening hierarchies. Reminding you that no matter how far you climbed, someone still believed you were there to serve.

And tonight—just for a moment—she let them believe it.

THE BEDROOM WAS baroque and stale, with the faint undertone of medical plastic. He gestured for her to close the door. She did.

He sat heavily on the edge of the bed and looked at her with something between amusement and expectation.

He patted the bed beside him. "C'mon. Sit. Don't make an old man beg."

She sat. Poured him another whiskey. Handed it over.

He was already fumbling through drawers with a soft wheeze. A bottle rattled somewhere inside the nightstand, then stopped.

"Goddamnit," he muttered. "Where's that damn blue bottle—"

She kept her face still. Didn't let the nausea rise.

She knew what kind of bottle he meant. The one that came with a four-hour warning and a doctor's signature.

He was serious. He thought this was happening.

He reached for the nightstand phone. She got there first.

"Maybe you left it in your travel case," she said, her hand settling gently over his, just enough pressure to stop the movement without making it feel like a correction. "Besides…"

She tilted her head. Gave him the faintest smile.

"Do you really want your assistant barging in here? That'd kill the mood."

He paused. Blinked slowly, like he was trying to remember what mood they were in. His hand went limp under hers.

"Yeah," he mumbled. "He's a real…buzzkill. My son hired him. Damn annoying."

Sloane laughed softly, just once. She let it hang in the air, and poured him another drink with her free hand

He chuckled, leaned back a little. Took the drink.

"You know, I went to Penn too," he slurred. "Barely finished. Dad had to pull strings. Got a job offer I couldn't turn down. Government needed men with real balls back then."

She nodded, legs crossed at the ankle, hands folded neatly in her lap. Her blouse still buttoned. Her smile still patient.

"Boy," he said, "if I weren't married, I'd make you wife number seven right now." He took another sip. "Always liked 'em smart. Always more fun to—" He didn't finish. He didn't need to.

She leaned in. Touched his wrist. "Milton," she said, voice low, "I think you and I should have a meeting. Just the two of us. About your shares."

He raised a brow. "Why, you looking to buy?"

"I'm looking to make sure they stay in the right hands."

He laughed. "That's a nice way of saying 'you.'"

"I'm a good investment."

He finished his drink. Eyes drifting now, face slackening.

"I'll set something up," he mumbled.

"No assistants," she said again, gently. "Just you and me."

He turned toward her, slowly, like his bones were water-logged. And before she could brace or move or even exhale, his hand gripped her jaw—too hard, too practiced—and he kissed her.

Open-mouthed. Wet.

His lips were slack and his tongue moved like something left out in the sun. She didn't kiss back, just held still, like she was being operated on. Her mouth was open but her mind was elsewhere, perched on a balcony in her own skull watching the moment pass.

He tasted like whiskey and halitosis and something chalky underneath, like pills that didn't dissolve all the way. He moaned softly, a sound that made her stomach twist. His hands cupped her face like he was offering prayer, but there was no reverence. Just possession.

She let it happen.

Not because she wanted to. Not because she was too afraid to stop it.

Because this—this—was the cost.

She'd calculated it. Ran the numbers. Found no loophole.

When he finally pulled away, her face was damp. His

spit on her cheek. She wiped it with the back of her hand like she was fixing her makeup, and then reached calmly for her glass.

"Sorry," he said, vaguely. "Got excited. You remind me of my third wife. Or maybe the fifth."

She laughed lightly, and drank. Her glass was mostly water, but she sipped anyways. Then she poured him another.

He didn't hesitate.

They sat in silence for a few minutes. She refilled both glasses. He drank faster than before. His mouth had lost the shape of conversation.

"You know Ava's scared of you?" he slurred. "She'd never admit it. Too proud. Too—what's the word. Poised. But she watches you real close. Like a dog watches another dog that might bite."

Sloane tilted her head, expression curious but not too curious.

"She ever tell you what she did in '09?" he continued, eyelids fluttering. "No? Course not. Smart girl. But there's a file. Somewhere. Everyone has one. Even her."

He chuckled like it was an inside joke. His chin dipped toward his chest.

She said nothing. Didn't push. Let the sentence hang there, leaking meaning.

He took another sip, then another.

His breathing slowed. The glass slipped in his hand and thudded to the carpet.

And just like that—he was out.

Sloane exhaled. Slowly. Quietly. Like she had just made it to the surface of a long, cold dive.

She stood, checked his pulse out of rote habit—still

there, if lazy—and looked at him one more time. Mouth open. Crumbs on his collar.

She hated him.

But she'd gotten what she needed.

She wiped her mouth with a cocktail napkin, grabbed her phone, and walked out without a sound.

28

The kitchen exit was unmarked. No security badge required. Just a push bar with a chipped handle and a rusted hinge, groaning against the quiet obscenity of Tolliver's estate.

Sloane stepped into the smoke break like she belonged there.

Two staffers—one in prep whites, the other in a Heritage security fleece—froze mid-conversation. Their cigarettes burned lazy between their fingers, curls of ash trembling at the edges.

She didn't smile. Just said, "Can I get a cigarette?"

They stared. One of them, the older one, squinted. "Are you serious?"

"I'll give you five dollars for a stick," she said, already reaching into her dress pocket, where a credit card was useless and her palms smelled like whiskey and death.

The silence that followed was almost religious.

"Why do you people always wave money around like it's a damn party trick?" the other one said, flicking ash into the gravel. "Nobody wants your guilt tips, lady."

"I wasn't trying to be insulting," Sloane said. Voice even. Measured. A little too quiet.

Her hand stayed extended. Palm-up. Almost reverent.

"You look like you're about to cry," one of them muttered, half a joke, half a warning.

She didn't answer. Didn't move.

The older woman sighed and fished a bent cigarette from a cardboard pack. "Fine. But you light it yourself."

Sloane nodded once, took the cigarette with careful fingers.

"Anyone got a light?"

A moment of shuffling. Someone handed her a half-dead gas station lighter with a cartoon frog on it.

She lit it on the second try. No cough. Just let the smoke settle behind her eyes.

The taste hit like memory. Like exam week. Like three-day depositions and bad coffee.

"Thanks," she said. Exhaled without apology.

They watched her for a long second—like they weren't sure whether to call security or offer her soup. She wasn't charming. Wasn't warm. Just expensive and hollow-looking, like someone who'd run out of reasons to keep standing.

"Actually, I take it back," one of them muttered. "You look like you're about to kill yourself."

A muscle in her cheek betrayed her. "Not tonight."

That got a laugh. Uneasy, but real.

"You want a drink?" the other one asked. "We're off at one. There's a dive bar down the road. Strong pour, no dress code."

She didn't answer right away. Just smoked in silence, like she was calculating how far rock bottom was from here. Then she nodded.

By 2:14 a.m., she was eight miles west of the estate in a

bar called The Brass Mule, which smelled like beer, sweat, and fryer oil.

Biker bar, unmistakably. Leather vests draped over chairs. Patches for clubs with names like Dead Holler and Saints of Salt. A prosthetic arm mounted on the wall next to a vintage Schlitz sign. One guy at the end of the bar had Respect Is Earned tattooed across his neck in Comic Sans.

The jukebox was cycling through a mess of '90s country, Led Zeppelin, and a single rogue Rihanna track someone must've queued up by accident. A pool game was in progress. So was a divorce, judging by the shouting near the bathroom.

She bought a round of shots for the estate kitchen staff and two off-shift Heritage security guys. Nobody used names. They just called her "Heritage Barbie." She didn't correct them.

Someone handed her tequila. Someone else dared her to dance.

She didn't say yes. Didn't even smile. She just took off her heels, climbed onto the table in silence, and started moving.

The music wasn't anything worth dancing to—something swampy and slow, blues-adjacent—but Sloane didn't care. She rolled her shoulders back, hips loose, eyes half-lidded. She performed. Not sloppy. Every motion was deliberate, practiced.

Her dress rode up just slightly. Thigh, then more. She let the hem flirt with gravity, her fingertips trailing lazy patterns across satin and skin. One strap slipped off her shoulder. She left it there. Just a little crooked. Just a little ruined.

Someone whooped.

She didn't respond. Just pivoted, back arched, one leg bent, fingers ghosting over her neckline like she was about to pull the whole thing down. She wasn't. Not really. But she let the moment breathe. Let it drag. Let them all watch her hover at the edge of something that felt both obscene and holy.

The bartender—middle-aged, unfazed—just muttered, "If she flashes a tit, I'm calling the cops."

Finally, one of the girls shouted, "Get down before you get us arrested, Barbie!"

Sloane froze like she was waking up. Then dropped to the floor in a graceful half-spin, catching herself on bare feet and tequila haze. She laughed—sharp, breathless, a little broken.

"Relax," she said. "I was just warming up."

Then she asked for another shot and drank it.

By 3:42 a.m., she was clinging to the back of a Harley-Davidson Road King behind a man who smelled like menthols and cedar chips.

How she got there wasn't complicated. Everyone was peeling off—back to the estate, back home, back to what-ever came next. She was just standing in the lot, barefoot in a cocktail dress, clearly not okay. And when someone suggested the estate, Sloane may have lost it. Enough to make it clear she wasn't going back.

One of the cooks tipped her chin toward the guy. "That's my dad. He's headed to Chicago to see my nieces. If you need a ride, he'll take you."

No one said what they were all thinking: she hadn't asked for help, but everything about her was screaming for it.

The dress. The bare feet. The way she kept tugging the hem.

They didn't know what she'd done at the estate. But they knew the look of someone running from it.

She nodded. Climbed on. Asked if he was a murderer.

The biker just said, "Acquitted."

She laughed too hard at that. Pressed her cheek to the back of his jacket, palms to his ribs.

And didn't look back.

SHE GOT HOME AT SUNRISE.

The sky was the color of skim milk, soft and sickly, already dissolving the night behind her. The door to her apartment was slightly ajar—not gaping, not kicked in, just...wrong. A polite warning. An open parenthesis.

She walked in anyway.

Any other time—any other version of herself—she would've paused. Would've checked her surroundings, considered entry points, remembered the depositions, the case studies, the women who were found in closets and bathtubs because they stepped too confidently into the aftermath. She knew better.

But she didn't care.

She stepped in with shoes in one hand, heels clinking like loose change. Her dress stuck to the back of her legs. Her mouth tasted like tequila and exhaust fumes and sleep deprivation. She was humming with it. Hollowed out and still somehow buzzing.

The place was torn open.

Drawers gutted. Cabinets ajar. Mail scattered like confetti across the floor. A single wine glass shattered in the sink. Her laptop—gone. Her legal files—rifled through. The kind of mess that meant someone had been looking for something. Or maybe just trying to remind her she didn't have anything worth locking up.

She didn't care. Not about the laptop. Not about the files.

Not even about the feeling in her stomach like a floor had dropped out.

She ran toward the corner of the living room anyway. Straight for the tank.

And there she was.

Tiberia.

Coiled like a poem. Eyes slow-blinking. Heat lamp still on. Unbothered.

Sloane exhaled. A short, involuntary noise—almost a laugh, but not quite.

She crouched down, pressed her palm against the glass. Like it was confession. Like the snake would absolve her for surviving another night in a world that had tried, and failed, to kill her softly.

"Guess you didn't scare them off," she said, voice hoarse. "You had one job."

Tiberia blinked again. Regal. Indifferent.

Sloane sat down on the floor, back against the wall. Still barefoot. Still spinning slightly. She didn't check the damage. Didn't lock the door. Didn't move.

She simply lit another cigarette bummed off the biker. Let the smoke pool in her lungs.

There was blood on her foot from where she'd sliced it on something—she hadn't noticed. She looked at it. Objective and unavoidable.

She took another drag. And smiled, slow and mean, like someone remembering the definition of retribution.

29

Her phone buzzed somewhere under the couch cushion. Then again. Longer this time.

She didn't move at first. Just lay there, one cheek pressed to the floor, sticky with sweat and tequila fumes, dress twisted.

The phone buzzed a third time. Relentless.

She reached for it with a groan and no grace. Saw the name. Didn't hesitate. Answered with a dry, flat "Yeah."

Vee's voice came in hot.

"Are you fucking serious with this new scheduling policy?"

Sloane sighed. No greeting. No preamble. Just fire straight to the face.

"They're gutting minimum shift protections. We've got people showing up for two-hour call-ins with no pay guarantee—what is this, a grocery store? You're pushing union labor out through the goddamn floorboards."

Sloane tried to sit up. Failed. Let her head rest back against the wall.

"I haven't seen the policy," she said, voice raspy. "It's not mine."

"Don't do that. Don't play dead. Your name's all over the compliance memo. Legal reviewed and signed off—don't tell me you didn't see it."

Sloane rubbed at her temple, fingers crusted with old makeup and cigarette ash.

"I've been...busy."

"Yeah, I bet. Meanwhile, the hangar's getting eaten alive by attrition tactics. You really think we won't notice that new vendor they're 'consulting' with? Those logistics audits? This is the start of a hostile phaseout and you know it."

Her mouth tasted like metal and rot. She tried to swallow and failed.

"Can you—" Sloane paused. "Can you just give me a minute? I need to check something."

She glanced around the apartment. Her eyes landed on the splintered drawer, the torn-open bag, the empty desk where her laptop used to sit.

Her jaw tightened.

"I'll follow up. I haven't seen the updated memos yet."

A beat of silence. Then Vee's voice, sharp enough to cut bone.

"You are fucking shameless."

"Vee—"

"How many times do you think you can stall like we're idiots? Like we don't see what's happening in real time?"

Sloane pressed a hand to her face.

"I'm not stalling," she said quietly.

"Bullshit."

Sloane closed her eyes. Said nothing. There was no version of the truth that didn't sound like an excuse.

She could still smell the bar on her skin. Her wrist was

bruised from God knows what. Her dress felt like it had grown teeth.

"Are you planning to continue berating me," she said evenly, "or is there something substantive you'd like to address?"

"Yeah," Vee snapped. "You look like hell on that billboard."

Sloane closed her eyes. Let the silence hang.

"Okay," she said.

Something in her tone wasn't clipped. Wasn't cold.

It was just...flat. Not even surrender—just absence.

On the other end of the line, Vee didn't speak for a second. Then:

"Wait. What's going on?"

Sloane didn't answer.

The silence stretched again. Vee exhaled, hard.

"You sound fucked up. Are you drunk?"

Sloane looked down at her bare legs, bloody footprints on the tiles. Her phone was sticky with something—maybe tequila, maybe her own sweat.

"No," Sloane said. Then paused. "Possibly."

It was that blurred middle ground—drunk fading into hungover, reality gone soft around the edges.

"Where are you?"

"Home."

"Are you hurt?"

Sloane looked at her bloody foot and didn't answer.

"What the fuck happened?"

Sloane let her head fall back against the wall again. The drywall felt cool. Her eyelids were heavy. She didn't want to explain. Not because she couldn't. Because it would mean something.

"Nothing."

Vee went quiet. Not the angry kind. The kind with too many thoughts behind it.

"I'm coming over."

"Don't."

"Sloane—"

"I don't want you here."

"Too bad. I'm already on my way."

30

Vee ran every red light. Burned through them like they were suggestions, not law. She stuck to streets without speed cameras, where the limits didn't exist and no one was watching.

She shouldn't have called. Should've left it alone.

Sloane wasn't hers. Never had been.

But the sound of her voice—that flat, emptied-out nothing? That was wrong. That wasn't the woman who once made a roomful of lawyers revise their strategy with a five-second pause.

No. This was something else. Something cracked.

And Vee didn't do cracked. Not well. Not since Kha got out. Not when her whole damn life was already hanging on dental floss and borrowed time.

She found parking three blocks out. Didn't lock the truck. Didn't even look back.

There was no doorman at the front. Odd. This wasn't the kind of building that overlooked details.

That was a red flag.

She took the stairs two at a time.

By the time she reached the apartment, she could smell it—cheap alcohol and something sharp underneath. Blood, maybe. She didn't even knock.

Inside, the air was still.

And Sloane was on the floor.

There was blood on her foot. A crusted trail from heel to ankle. Her dress was half off one shoulder, stained, wrinkled, stuck to her skin. One hand lay palm-up.

Vee went cold.

"Sloane—"

No response.

She rushed forward, dropped to her knees—no plan, no hesitation—already checking for breath, pulse, anything. Her fingers hovered just above Sloane's jaw when—

"Hey."

Sloane blinked up at her, pupils slow to focus. And then she smiled. Actually smiled.

"Vee," she said, like it was good news. "You came."

Vee sat back, hands shaking once the adrenaline had somewhere to go.

"You scared the shit out of me."

"You didn't have to—"

"No. Shut up. We're leaving."

Sloane's smile didn't falter. She looked like death in designer, and she still had the nerve to look amused.

"I'm not leaving Tiberia," she said. "She might get sick again. The move would stress her out."

Vee stared. "Are you fucking kidding me right now?"

"She's sensitive. Ball pythons need stability."

Vee exhaled hard through her nose, stood up, already pacing. Her heart still hadn't slowed.

"I'll get Audree to set up a tank at my place. She's got all the gear. Just—please. Can we go?"

Sloane squinted up at her. Then, annoyingly, grinned.

"You know that woman's still in love with you, right? And now you're gonna make her do all that?"

Vee was already crouching again, hands on Sloane's arms, lifting her with practiced care. She was gentle, but firm. The way you handle someone too proud to ask for help.

"Get up," she said. "You smell like tequila."

Sloane let herself be pulled up, limping a little, leaning just enough. "You're so bossy when you're worried."

Vee ignored that. She was already scanning the room, grabbing what she needed: a leather duffel bag, clothes, chargers, a toothbrush, something black and sleeveless from the floor. She moved like she'd lived there.

Only one thing she refused to touch.

The carrier sat by the tank. Plastic. Latches already open.

Vee pointed at it like it might bite. "I'm not doing the snake."

Sloane laughed, low and raspy.

"You're afraid of her."

"I'm not afraid. I just don't fuck with things that don't blink."

Sloane knelt with more grace than she should've had left, cooed softly toward the tank, whispering nonsense with reverence. Opened the top. Lifted Tiberia with slow, assured hands. The python curled lazily in her grip, blinking once, then again.

She lined the carrier with the dry substrate. Checked the vents. The humidity levels. Fastened the lid gently like she was tucking in a child.

"There," she said, standing. "She's safe."

Vee didn't say anything. Just took the duffel, the carrier, and the woman—wrapped in exhaustion and bad decisions—and started walking.

31

The apartment still smelled like ginger and garlic from the last time Bà visited. Vee hadn't opened a window in two days, and there was a pan soaking in the sink she'd meant to scrub last night but forgot. The front door stuck if you didn't hip-check it. One of the cats had shredded the arm of the couch again.

"Sorry for the mess," she muttered as she shoved a pair of sneakers out of the hallway and nudged a laundry basket out of the path.

Sloane didn't say anything. Just stood there barefoot.

Vee led her to the bathroom. Flipped on the light. Grabbed a towel from the top of the dryer stack and set it on the sink. Then another.

"Shower's clean. Water pressure's strong if you twist the valve left. I'll find you something dry."

Sloane still didn't say anything. Just looked around slowly. Not judging—just...cataloguing.

"But first," Vee sat on the closed toilet lid with a sigh like this wasn't the first time she'd had to clean up someone else's mess. She patted her thigh.

"Foot up."

Sloane arched an eyebrow.

"Don't be cute. You're dripping blood on the tile."

Slowly—reluctantly—Sloane lifted her foot and set it on Vee's lap. The position was absurdly intimate. Her calf looked out of place against Vee's shorts, pale and smeared with dried blood, the kind of wound that wasn't dramatic until you realized how long it had been left alone.

Vee didn't say anything. Just flipped the latch on the first-aid kit and got to work. Saline first. Gauze. Disinfectant. Sloane hissed through her teeth, but didn't pull away.

"You're lucky it didn't go deeper," Vee muttered, dabbing at the crusted edges. "Another half inch and you'd be in stitches. Literally."

"You always this bossy with your patients?" Sloane asked, voice scratchy.

"You always this careless with your body?" Vee shot back.

Silence.

Vee taped down a clean square of gauze and smoothed the edges with the flat of her palm. Her touch wasn't tender, but it wasn't indifferent either. Just efficient. Familiar. Like she'd done this before, maybe too many times, and hated that she still remembered how.

"That'll hold," she said. "Keep it dry. I'll redo it after."

Sloane slowly lowered her foot, watching her with a look Vee didn't have the bandwidth to interpret. So she stood, snapped the kit shut, and moved like nothing had happened.

"I'll get you some clothes."

She found a pair of red athletic shorts and an old Nirvana shirt—worn soft, neckline stretched. She handed them through the door. Sloane's hand took them with that same mechanical grace she'd used to carry the snake, who was now perching in the living room by the sunlight, ousting the cats from their favorite spot.

"You okay in there?"

"Ten shots of tequila and I'm still standing," Sloane said, voice faint. "Miracles abound."

"Audree's bringing the tank supplies later," Vee said. "Don't worry about her. She's chill."

No response. Just the sound of running water and a clatter of shampoo bottles.

When Sloane finally emerged, her hair was wrapped in a towel, and Vee's clothes looked borderline lewd on her— shorts tight across her hips, ass cheeks out, shirt clinging to those broad lawyer shoulders.

The cats came first. One darted behind the couch. The other, bolder, approached and sniffed her calf before making a noise that sounded halfway between a chirp and a threat.

"That's Eugene," Vee said. "He bites if you look at him too long."

Sloane lowered herself to the floor slowly, as if she expected the cat to explode. "Noted."

Vee sat beside her a moment later, pulling the first-aid kit out again with a quiet kind of resignation. She didn't ask —just patted her lap like before.

Sloane stretched out her leg. No sass this time. Just a heavy, unspoken truce.

Vee peeled back the temporary dressing with practiced hands, inspecting the skin underneath like she was reading something in it. She didn't speak, but the silence was thick. Focused. Intimate in a way that felt more dangerous than soft.

"Doesn't look infected," she murmured, reaching for fresh gauze and medical tape. "You're lucky."

"Debatable."

A sharp look passed between them—nothing obvious, just a flicker. Heat and history and exhaustion layered into one glance. It lasted a second too long.

There was a precision to it—the way Vee wrapped the gauze, the way Sloane didn't flinch. Not trust, not tenderness. Just the old choreography of women who'd hurt each other enough to know exactly where to press, and how hard.

It wasn't care. Not really. It was intimacy by proxy—need dressed up as obligation. The kind of closeness that showed up when things were already broken.

Vee wrapped the foot tighter this time. Clean lines. Secure tape. No nonsense.

Then, like a spell broken, Kha surfaced from the hallway —hoodie up, earbuds dangling, a storm of twenty-year-old restlessness barely contained. He stopped when he saw them.

Saw her.

And in that instant, they drew apart.

Not abruptly. Not dramatically. Just enough. Sloane adjusted her posture. Vee closed the kit.

No explanation, no comment.

Just gravity reasserting itself.

Vee stood first. "I'll be in the kitchen," she said, already moving, already halfway gone.

"This her?" he asked.

Vee gave him a look. "Don't start."

"I'm not starting. I'm just—that's her?"

Sloane offered a polite, exhausted nod. Kha looked unimpressed. Suspicious, even. Like he'd read the subtext in Vee's tone and filed it under prolonged suffering.

Vee didn't entertain it. Just pulled out the skillet, and started cooking. She didn't ask what Sloane liked. Didn't need to. Nutella and strawberries were universal. Turkey bacon was safe. Pancakes were comfort—cheap, fast, and soft enough to be mercy.

The kitchen filled with the scent of butter and browned sugar, the low sizzle of bacon curling at the edges. She worked in silence, focused, pouring batter into tight circles and slicing strawberries with the kind of precision you only get from years of feeding people too tired to ask.

She plated everything without ceremony. Set it in front of Sloane like a peace offering.

Sloane stared at it for a second, then picked up her fork.

She ate like someone who hadn't eaten in twenty-four hours and didn't want to be seen doing it. Like it was a task, not a pleasure. The kind of hunger you don't talk about because then you'd have to admit how long it's been gnawing at you.

She got halfway through the stack before her pace slowed. Lifted the fork again. Lowered it. Rested her elbow on the table.

Vee didn't comment. Just sat across from her and topped off the coffee. Watched her with quiet eyes. Like she was waiting to see whether Sloane would finish, or fold.

She folded. Fork down. Eyes half-closed.

"It's too good," Sloane muttered. "That's the problem."

Vee didn't ask what she meant.

Didn't need to.

"Bed's that way," Vee said, pointing with her chin. "You can crash. Take the whole thing. Get some sleep before you pass out."

Sloane made it halfway into the bedroom before pausing.

She stared at the bed. Pressed a hand to the comforter. Then climbed in and rolled over twice, burying her face in the pillow.

"It smells like you," she murmured.

"Blackout curtains should do a good job," she said. "They're for when I'm on nights."

By the time she peeked her head back into the room, Sloane was already asleep.

One arm under the pillow. Hair wrapped. Lips parted just slightly. She looked peaceful. Not soft. Just...still. Like a woman who hadn't had stillness in years.

Vee stood there a breath longer than she meant to. Then she went back to the kitchen and started cleaning without thinking.

She didn't know how long this would last.

But for now—she was here.

And Sloane was safe.

32

By the time Sloane made it to the toilet, it was too late for dignity. She collapsed to her knees and retched violently, clutching the rim. The acid taste of tequila, bile, and shame filled her mouth. Her eyes watered. Her lashes clumped. She stayed there a moment, breath heaving, cold porcelain pressed against her cheek.

It was eight p.m.

She groaned as she pushed herself up. Her head throbbed. When she shuffled out of the bathroom, the living room lights were dim, and Kha was sprawled across the couch, gaming with the blank expression of an assassin.

He didn't even look up. "Damn. You alive?"

She squinted at him, still half-blind from nausea. "Barely."

"Mm," he said, petting the cat purring on his lap. Not Eugene. The other one. "Sounded like a demon was trying to crawl out of your mouth."

She gave him a look. He smirked.

"For real though," he added, eyes still on the TV, "how old are you? Why are you still puking in toilets?"

Sloane opened her mouth. Closed it. She didn't have an answer that wouldn't sound pathetic.

Kha grinned like he'd already won. "Grown-ass lawyer, right? With degrees and stuff?"

She didn't dignify that with a response.

Her eyes drifted past him, half out of instinct, half to avoid engaging—and froze.

That terrarium hadn't been there this morning.

It was installed. Not unboxed, not halfway done—fully set up, humming quietly. Chrome trim, touchscreen controls, digital readouts. Tiberia's heat lamp flicked on with clinical precision, basking spot locked at 88. The humidity gauge pulsed green. A spa for snakes. And inside, Tiberia: coiled, gleaming, utterly unbothered in a designer half-log.

Sloane swallowed hard. Her stomach turned again.

She hadn't authorized this.

And she sure as hell hadn't asked her to do it.

Vee was nowhere to be seen. But the apartment smelled —unfairly—like heaven. Star anise, charred ginger, long-simmered beef bones. Broth. The kind that took all day. The kind you couldn't fake. She followed the scent into the kitchen.

On the counter: a bottle of Tylenol, a glass of water with condensation sliding down the side, and an empty bowl already set out for her, complete with utensils and a neatly folded napkin. Like someone had expected her to crawl out of her hangover and still hoped she'd eat.

She didn't question it. She downed the Tylenol, slumped into a chair, and ladled broth into her bowl with the reverence of the newly converted.

The broth hit like medicine. Sharp, rich, careful. Her headache started to lift by the third sip. By the fifth, she could breathe again. She didn't need much—just a little heat, a little salt, a reminder that someone had been in this kitchen thinking ahead.

Sloane let her eyes wander.

The apartment was lived-in but curated. Punk rock posters lined the walls—original prints, not knockoffs. Protest signs leaned against the entryway: STOP CORPORATE MANSLAUGHTER, FIX THE FLEET, PAY THE CREW, and the most pointed of all: HERITAGE KILLS. A framed photo of Kill Fee dominated the hallway—Vee front and center in a mesh shirt, nipples blurred behind bold font and faded ink. Sloane tried not to stare. Failed.

"Where's your aunt?" she asked, casually, like her eyes hadn't just betrayed her.

Kha paused his game, then glanced at her sidelong. "Why? So you can mess her up again?"

Sloane arched a brow. "So I can find her."

He didn't answer immediately. His foot twitched under the coffee table—and that's when she saw it: the ankle monitor, bulky and glossy black, visible beneath the cuff of his sweatpants. The skin around it was red and rubbed raw.

She tilted her head. "You know, there's a newer model. Less chafing. Discreet. If you want, I can make a call."

That got his attention. He raised an eyebrow—cynical, skeptical, interested despite himself.

"She's in the garage," he said. "It's got the unit number on it."

Sloane frowned. "Garage?"

He didn't look up. "This is a condo. She bought it five years ago."

A pause. Then, almost offhand: "Union pay's solid—when it's not getting gutted by snakes."

He went back to his game like he hadn't said anything at all.

Sloane didn't respond. She didn't need to. The implication sat there between them, sharp and quiet.

Snakes like you.

She glanced around again. The ceilings were higher than she'd realized. The floors—real hardwood. There were signs she hadn't noticed before. This wasn't a crash pad. It was a home. And Vee—chaotic, flammable, stubborn Vee— had built something here. Quietly. While Sloane had been chasing power across cities and boardrooms, Vee had been doing this.

Chicago garages weren't just parking spots—they were property. Literal real estate. You didn't rent them. You bought a deed. Signed papers. Paid taxes. Sometimes shelled out five figures for a glorified cement box barely wide enough to open your car door without dislocating a shoulder.

But of course Vee had one. Practical, mechanical, territorial Vee.

Of course she'd claim her square footage and weld her name to it.

She sipped her water and took the back stairs. Chicago standard—exposed wood, rickety as hell, always a little damp. Half fire escape, half architectural joke. The kind of thing that looked like it shouldn't hold weight, but somehow did.

At the bottom, a row of garages. One had the unit number stenciled on the door.

Vee's.

The garage door was half-open—deliberately casual, like a leg slung over the side of a chair. Inside: fluorescent lights, concrete floor, and Vee, bent at the waist over the open hood of a late-90s Toyota Tacoma. Rusted, stubborn, and apparently immortal.

She wore navy coveralls, rolled to the waist and tied loose across her hips. The tank top underneath was threadbare and damp at the spine, clinging in places that made Sloane's mouth go dry. Her breasts strained slightly against the ribbed cotton—ungodly soft-looking, aggressively unbothered, a casual architectural feat.

It was pornographic. But subtle. The kind of thing you couldn't name without sounding like a deviant.

A black bra strap peeked out—black, utilitarian, and still somehow provocative. Her hair was up in a claw clip, streaked with bleach and balayage, neck exposed, strands curling at the nape. Oil on her cheek. Grease under her nails. A smear on her collarbone that felt...intentional.

She stopped.

Sloane thought it was an act of personal cruelty—cosmic, even—that Vee had the body of the women hired to drape themselves across concept cars at trade shows, not the ones actually building the engine. Hired to smile. To sell the fantasy. But Vee didn't need the gloss or the bikini. She belonged to the machinery. Her competence wasn't borrowed or decorative—it radiated: precise, unbothered, inevitable. She could dismantle the entire system and make you feel foolish for not knowing where to begin.

Sloane inhaled—shallow, controlled—then immediately regretted it when the scent of gasoline hit her bloodstream.

Vee still hadn't looked up. "You lost?"

"I was told you were here," Sloane replied, voice clipped, posture snapping into courtroom geometry. Precision was the only thing she had left.

Vee reached deeper into the hood. Her tank rode up an inch. Sloane stared like an amateur.

"And you thought you'd just wander down? No knock? No appointment?"

"I didn't realize garage visits required scheduling."

Vee smiled, slow and sharp. "Only when it's corporate."

Sloane said nothing. She couldn't. She was staring at the torque wrench in Vee's hand and thinking about how fast it would take for her to ruin Sloane entirely.

"Goddammit," Vee muttered, stepping back from the truck and wiping her hands on a rag that had seen better decades. "Guess I'm done for the night. Missing the auxiliary throttle linkage bracket—gonna have to hit the yard tomorrow. If they haven't gutted the Tacoma shelf again."

The language hit Sloane like a slap and a seduction. *Auxiliary throttle linkage bracket.* Her brain, treacherous, filed it away with the same reverence it once reserved for cross-examinations and lover's names.

She watched Vee reach for a water bottle and drink—just water, but Sloane stared like it was something obscene. The way her throat moved, the lazy flick of her wrist, the tilt of her head back—it all felt designed to undo her. Or perhaps she was simply already undone, and this was just confirmation.

Vee caught her gaze mid-sip, wiped her mouth with the back of her hand, and smirked. "You okay over there?"

"I'm fine," Sloane said crisply, adjusting her posture.

A silence opened between them—not comfortable, but not yet cruel. Sloane shifted her weight from one heel to the other, then folded her arms. "About this morning," she began, voice smooth but laced with static.

Vee wiped her hands again. "Yeah. That."

"I think we should talk about it."

"Agreed."

Another pause.

"You go first," they both said.

Then: "No, you."

Sloane narrowed her eyes. "Very mature."

Vee shrugged. "You're the one who cross-examines people for a living."

Before Sloane could respond, a voice echoed from somewhere above them:

"Auntie! Dolores is trying to eat the snake! I'm not fucking going near that thing!"

Kha. From the balcony. Of course.

They both froze. Then, in unison, sprinted up the wooden stairs, flip-flops and boots clattering against Chicago's worst architectural tradition.

Inside the condo, chaos: Dolores—Vee's semi-feral calico with a vendetta—had cornered Tiberia, whose tank lid had somehow come ajar. The snake was coiled defensively in the middle of the floor, head raised, tongue flicking with polite menace. Dolores was in full Halloween-cat mode, tail puffed, hissing like she was possessed.

"Absolutely not," Sloane said, lunging for the snake with a precision honed by panic and years of owning creatures more emotionally consistent than people.

"I've got the cat," Vee said, already moving.

The choreography was instinctual, practiced despite having never been rehearsed: Vee swooped in with a towel and caught Dolores mid-lunge.

They both stood there afterward, breathing hard, surrounded by the wreckage of terrarium décor, fur, and mutual disbelief.

Vee sighed. "God. We really are somebody's stereotype."

By the time the living room was calmed and the animals

contained—Dolores exiled to Kha's room with a can of tuna as hush money, Tiberia safely reinstalled with two paperweights on the tank lid—they collapsed onto the couch, shoulder to shoulder, not touching but not quite separate.

The news was playing in the background.

At some point, Sloane fell asleep—head tilted, spine curved, knees pulled in like her body couldn't quite trust the space.

She woke to Vee nudging her thigh. "Go sleep in the bed."

"I'm fine here," Sloane mumbled, not opening her eyes.

"You're not," Vee said. "You're going to wake up with a cramp and blame me."

"Maybe I will."

"Then spare us both the drama."

Sloane finally cracked one eye open. "I'm not sleeping in your bed."

"It's not my bed right now. It's *the* bed. You can take one half."

"I'm not good at sharing."

Vee crossed her arms. "You're not good at being stubborn either. Your back's going to seize up in ten minutes."

They glared at each other.

Then sighed, in perfect, exhausted unison.

"Fine," Sloane said.

"Fine," Vee echoed.

They rose, in truce. The bed waited—quiet, wide, neutral territory. For now.

33

Vee woke up sweating. Not from the laggy A/C or the headache blooming behind her eyes, but because Sloane Campbell was asleep in her damn bed.

Like, for real asleep. On her side. One arm curled under her cheek like she paid someone to teach her how to pose for REM cycles.

Vee sat up slow, blinked hard. The mattress beneath them was firm, memory foam, mid-range luxury—because Vee might cut corners on some things, but never on sleep. Sloane's thigh was warm against hers, bare skin under the hem of a sleep shirt Vee didn't remember offering. Her hair was wrapped in a satin scarf, not a curl out of place. Even unconscious, she radiated control.

Sloane never stayed the night. Hell, they'd never even fucked on a proper bed. It was always stolen moments— hallways, bathrooms, once in the bridal prep suite before Morgan's wedding ceremony—half undressed, lipstick smudged, hiding behind a rack of matching robes while the rest of the bridal party pounded Prosecco two doors down.

Even when it had been Sloane for that whole ridiculous, electric year—no sleepovers, no morning afters. Just friction and fallout and a mutual understanding that feelings were a scam.

And yet.

She couldn't look too long or she might try something stupid like kiss her forehead. So she got up. Quiet, careful. She shimmied into a black bodysuit—impractical as hell, all straps and attitude—and then yanked on her favorite jeans: loose, low-slung, shredded to shit, and clinging to life.

6:17.

She could get to the salvage yard by 7. Kha's busted-ass truck needed that part before his interview up in Wisconsin. She'd promised him it would be fixed. She didn't make promises she couldn't keep, especially not to him.

Phone in hand, she fired off a text to Woytek:

"I know you're heading out of town today. Can you open the yard early? Pls. Emergency."

He replied within seconds.

"You owe me a six-pack."

"Add it to the tab."

"It's a long-ass tab."

She hit the bathroom, ran through her morning routine on autopilot. By the time she made it to the kitchen, Sloane was already there—barefoot, hair tied up, making tea like she'd been living there for months and had strong opinions about kettle temps and steep times.

She looked good in Vee's kitchen. Too good. Like she'd always belonged there. But it was wrong—wrong in context, wrong in history, wrong in every deep-buried nerve-ending kind of way that made Vee's chest ache and her jaw clench.

"Morning," Sloane said, soft. Too soft.

Vee leaned against the counter. Tried not to stare at her legs or the stretch of her spine when she reached for a mug.

"We need to talk," Sloane said.

"Yeah," Vee said. "We do. I just need to hit the salvage yard first."

Sloane sipped her tea. Eyes not leaving Vee's face. "Can I come with?"

Vee raised a brow. "Don't you have, like, fifteen labor violations to bury in your inbox?"

"It's a federal holiday," Sloane said.

Vee rolled her eyes. "Fine. But wear sneakers. And don't fuckin' touch anything unless you're ready to get tetanus."

WOYTEK LEFT the gate half open. Vee kicked it wider with her boot and jerked her chin for Sloane to follow. Gravel crunched. The place smelled like oil, rust, and busted dreams.

Sloane hesitated at the edge—one breath too long.

"What?" Vee muttered, already moving.

"Just taking it in," Sloane said. "Charming."

"Don't lick anything and you'll survive."

Sloane didn't laugh. Just pressed her lips together and followed, silent, eyes scanning the yard like it personally offended her.

They headed straight for the back racks. Vee pulled the clipboard off the hook, squinted at the inventory scrawl. Starter motor. Radiator hose. Maybe a miracle.

A familiar shape caught her eye in the shadows—low profile, primer gray, stripped of plates. Still here. Good.

They walked deeper into the lot until they reached a half-disassembled pickup, stripped down to its bones.

Behind her, Sloane asked, "What exactly are we looking for?"

Vee didn't look up. "Auxiliary throttle linkage bracket. From an '04 Tacoma."

Sloane made a noise—half curious, half skeptical. "That's a real thing?"

Vee turned just enough to glare over her shoulder. "Yes, Sloane. It's a real thing. I didn't make it up to drag your ass to Avondale at seven a.m."

"Well," Sloane muttered, "you've always been creative under pressure."

Vee didn't answer. Her fingers closed around the bracket —still bolted in, coated in dust but intact. She grabbed her socket wrench, leaned in, and cranked hard. One bolt gave with a metallic snap. Then another. She braced her forearm against the engine block and worked the last one loose.

Just as she reached to pull the bracket free, Sloane moved in behind her—too close.

Vee felt her before she saw her. The shift of weight on the gravel. The sudden heat.

Then Sloane crouched beside her, too fast, and their hands collided over the same inch of greasy metal. Sloane's skin was warm. Her breath hit Vee's jaw.

Vee tensed.

"Seriously?" she muttered. "Can you not hover?"

"I was trying to help."

"No, you were making it weird."

Sloane stayed crouched. Didn't move. "It's already weird."

Vee stood up fast, part in hand, and stalked toward the workbench. Her pulse was a riot. She needed air. She needed distance. She needed a sledgehammer.

Or a quarter-mile and a red light.

Sloane trailed behind, sneakers crunching slow. "You've never struck me as someone who avoids conflict."

"Who says I'm avoiding it?" Vee said. "Maybe I'm just pacing myself."

They hit the counter. Woytek was waiting with a chipped mug and that permanently unimpressed face he wore.

"You found it?" he grunted.

"Yeah."

"Seventy-five."

Before Vee could argue, Sloane cut in. "Thirty."

Woytek raised one eyebrow. "You the fuckin' tax assessor now?"

"No," Sloane said. "I'm the one who knows this part's been collecting dust since the Bush administration and isn't worth more than a steak dinner. Twenty-five. Cash."

Woytek looked her over. "You got a license?"

"Do you?" she said, deadpan.

He stared. Then laughed once—bitter, surprised. "Twenty-five. But don't bring her back here."

Vee slid the cash over. "Deal."

Woytek gave her a look when she handed him the cash —pointed, unreadable. The one that said he knew exactly what she kept in the back lot—and why it never collected dust

As they left, Woytek called after them. "This ain't a damn date spot, Vee. Jesus."

Vee didn't respond. Just shoved the part in her tote bag and kept walking.

THEY'D BARELY MADE it two turns from the yard when Vee spotted the pop-up tents—half set up along the edge of a cracked parking lot near Elston, wedged between a payday loan spot and a shuttered Polish deli with a *Do Wynajęcia* sign in the window.

The farmer's market was still clinging to its working-class roots—mismatched folding tables, cash boxes held together with duct tape, old Polish ladies hawking cabbage out of milk crates. But the change was coming. One row over, a guy in a man bun was selling $11 microgreens next to a booth offering "reiki-infused kombucha."

The concrete hadn't been repaved in decades, but the espresso cart had a ring light.

Vee slowed down. "I need to grab some vegetables."

Sloane blinked like she'd misheard. "Now?"

"Might as well," Vee said, already cutting across the playground. "I'm not gonna have time later, and Kha eats like a Labrador."

Sloane shrugged. "Sure."

They stepped into the lot, gravel crunching underfoot. It was still early. Vee liked it like this—quiet, functional, a little sad.

She grabbed a mesh produce bag from her truck parked across the street and made a beeline for the root vegetables. The woman at the stall nodded, recognizing her. No words, just a transactional nod of solidarity. Vee picked up three bunches of scallions, some Napa cabbage, a sack of fingerlings.

Sloane trailed after her, quiet and visibly confused. Like the idea of Vee buying bok choy at 8 a.m. broke something in her expensive lawyer brain.

"Are you always the one cooking?" Sloane asked eventually.

Vee didn't look up. "Who else is gonna feed that kid?"

Sloane picked up a bunch of dill, turned it over in her hands. "He's not a kid. He's what—nineteen? Twenty?"

Vee stilled. Didn't answer.

"Respectfully, Sloane? That's none of your fucking business, and you just crossed about ten lines."

Sloane bit her lip like she was trying to hold back, but she couldn't help it.

"I'm not judging, Vee. I'm just stating facts. If it sounds like criticism, maybe ask yourself why."

Vee stepped in close—too close for a market full of vegetables and witnesses. "You don't get to talk about him like that. You don't know the whole story."

Sloane didn't flinch. "Then tell me."

But Vee didn't. Couldn't. Because the real answer was buried under six years of sealed court records, a shoebox of burner phones, and a prison intake form with someone else's name on it.

She turned back to the onions. Gripped the plastic bin hard enough her knuckles went pale.

"Drop it," she muttered.

Sloane listened.

And that silence burned hotter than anything else.

At the next booth, a vendor pushed forward a crate of peaches. "First pick," she said. "Real sweet."

Vee reached for one. So did Sloane. Their fingers brushed.

Too soft. Too warm. Too long.

Vee let go first.

The vendor smiled at them. "You two are cute."

Vee smirked. "Dangerously."

Sloane froze. Just for a beat. Then looked away, mouth tight.

They kept walking. Vee tossed a head of garlic into her bag.

Out of the corner of her eye, she saw Sloane check her phone. The shift was small—eyebrows twitching, jaw tightening—but it was there. She didn't say anything. Just slid the phone away and adjusted the strap on her shoulder.

Vee didn't ask. She was too busy pretending this didn't feel like a morning routine. Like a Saturday they'd done a hundred times.

They walked past the jam table. Sloane paused. Picked up a jar of cherry-thyme like she was testing her own impulse control.

Vee raised a brow. "Do you even eat bread?"

"I don't need to justify myself to you," Sloane said, dry.

Vee smirked. "That's what I *love* about you." She said it like a threat.

Sloane rolled her eyes—but her ears were pink.

They left with a bag full of produce and a silence that felt too much like peace.

Vee hated how much she wanted to hold onto it.

THEY WERE HALFWAY BACK to the truck, Vee juggling a bag of greens, when she caught it—Sloane slowing down. Not stopping. Just...hesitating.

That half-step pause she always did when something got to her.

Vee followed her gaze.

A tiny bookstore, wedged between a glass-box luxury condo and a nail salon. One of those holdouts with handwritten staff picks in the window and a chalkboard that said Banned Book of the Week like it was daring someone to care.

Sloane didn't say a word. Just stared. Long enough for Vee to know exactly what it meant.

Of course it would be a bookstore. Of course she'd get soft over something that smelled like dust and paper.

Vee adjusted the bag on her shoulder. "We doing this or what?"

Sloane made a confused noise. "What?"

"The bookstore. Go on. Might as well round out this weird-ass domestic fever dream."

Sloane gave her a look—tight-lipped, amused, a little caught. "I wasn't—"

"You were."

A breath.

Then Sloane opened the door.

The bell overhead rang, delicate as glass.

She made a beeline for the new releases, posture loose but intentional—like she didn't need to look to know exactly where everything was.

Vee wandered toward the romance section, mostly to kill time. Mostly. She wasn't looking for anything. She just needed to stand somewhere that didn't smell like expensive perfume or unfinished arguments.

She ran her finger along the spines—florals, gold script, glowing couples backlit by sunsets. A whole wall of wishful thinking. Then her hand landed on a cover so ridiculous it made her pause.

Some kind of half-man, half-lizard thing cradling a woman in a flowing gown. Talons. Glowing eyes. Muscles for days. The title? *Claimed by the Marsh King.*

She huffed a laugh.

Behind her, Sloane's voice: "That one's actually well-written."

Vee turned. Slowly. "What."

Sloane blinked, unbothered. "The worldbuilding is solid. Consent is central. There's a surprising amount of emotional depth for something with that cover."

"You've read it."

"I've read the series."

Vee looked at the book, then at her. "The series."

Sloane shrugged. "There's a prequel about his twin brother. It's...tender."

Vee stared at her like she was growing scales. "You read monster romance."

"Speculative intimacy," Sloane corrected, calm as ever. "It's a growing market."

"Girl, he has claws. There is a visible pouch on the cover."

"It's called a mating sheath. It's cultural."

Vee choked. "I hope to God you're not reading these in court."

"I read them on planes. And during board meetings. Discreetly."

"Holy shit."

Vee put the book back like it burned, then picked it up again—this time turning it over, skimming the blurb with morbid curiosity.

"You're telling me this scaly bastard falls in love with a human barista and raises her orphaned niece?"

"While leading a resistance against interdimensional slavers," Sloane added, matter-of-fact.

Vee shook her head. "No. No, this is a trap. You're trying to convert me."

"I don't try," Sloane said, smooth. "People just learn."

The silence that followed was heavy, ridiculous, charged.

Vee shoved the book into Sloane's hands. "If we're doing this, you're buying it."

"Fine."

Sloane turned to the shelves, grabbed the rest of the series without hesitation, and dropped the stack on the counter.

They stepped back onto the street in silence.

Vee was holding a paperback with an alien on the cover —eight-pack, glowing orange eyes, the works.

Vee mutters, "Weirdest fuckin' day."

Sloane: "It's not over yet."

BY THE TIME they returned home, the sun was high in the sky, bright and gold across the cracked pavement. The mesh produce bag dug into Sloane's wrist, but she didn't complain. She didn't say much at all.

Kha wasn't home. Vee had muttered something about him crashing at a friend's place—casual, like it wasn't loaded, like it didn't mean they were alone.

They stepped inside and dropped the bags in the kitchen. Vee moved without hesitation, already putting things away. A head of Napa cabbage landed on the counter. Garlic, ginger, fingerling potatoes.

Sloane stood there and watched her, silent, ridiculous, unable to move.

There was a grace to it—Vee's ease in her own kitchen, the economy of her motion, the flick of her wrist as she slid scallions into the fridge. It wasn't just competence. It was ritual.

Sloane wanted to memorize it.

Instead, she stepped back, cleared her throat, and offered—uselessly—"I can help."

Vee shook her head. "I've got it. Go sit. Or do your little

tea ceremony or whatever it is you do when you're pretending to relax."

And just like that, it cracked—Sloane's composure, her restraint, her curated detachment. This was absurd. They had spent the entire day playing out some unhinged domestic fantasy: farmer's market, bookstore, now dinner.

And she loved it.

God help her.

While Vee disappeared downstairs to work on the Tacoma, Sloane moved through the kitchen like it was hers. She washed vegetables, set rice to soak, lit the front burner. She found a can of coconut milk and added it to the pan without asking. Garlic, onion, turmeric. Fish sauce. A splash of lime.

The scent filled the house. Warm, fragrant, grounded.

She didn't realize how long she'd been at it until a sudden whoop from outside made her jump. A moment later, she heard it—an engine rumbling, proud and alive, through the open kitchen window.

Sloane closed her eyes. Smiled.

Two hours. And somehow, Vee had brought it back to life.

When Vee came in—shirt damp, hands streaked with grease—dinner was already plated. Steamed rice. Curry with eggplant and soft, slow-cooked beef. Scallions sliced fine. Cilantro arranged like a flourish.

They sat at the table without speaking. No music. Just the soft hum of the fridge and the occasional creak of old floorboards settling into night.

Dolores jumped onto the table and neither of them moved to stop her.

At some point, Sloane lit a candle she found by the sink. She didn't even think about it.

The quiet wasn't awkward. It was worse.

It was peaceful.

Like time had folded in on itself and created a version of reality that wasn't supposed to exist.

Halfway through the meal, Sloane set her fork down.

"I forgot what this feels like," she said.

Vee didn't look up. Just kept chewing. Swallowed.

"This isn't real," she said. Not cruel. Not dismissive. Just...honest.

Sloane nodded. "I know."

But it didn't stop her from wanting it anyway.

34

Steam curled off the backsplash and fogged the window. Vee scrubbed a frying pan with a little too much force, her mind already three steps ahead, pulse thrumming under her skin. Sloane was rinsing glasses like she gave a damn about watermarks, hair clipped back. Vee wanted to bite her.

They moved around each other like a dance they'd done for years—rinsing, loading, wiping down the counters. The kitchen smelled like coconut milk and heat and her, the afterglow of dinner and the possibility of something else. Vee slapped the dishrag onto the sink and muttered, "I gotta shower." Didn't wait for a response.

Water was scalding. Just how she needed it. She stood under the stream, eyes closed, trying to rinse off the burn that had started in her gut and now hummed in her thighs.

When she opened her eyes, the door opened and Sloane walked in. Didn't say anything. Just leaned against the door like she had all the time in the world, like she wasn't planning to ruin Vee's life.

Vee kept washing. The washcloth dragged down her

thigh, slow. She could feel Sloane watching her. That stare like a blade, carving her open.

"Touch yourself," Sloane said.

Vee obeyed. One hand against the tile for balance. The other slipped down, slick and needy. One finger first, teasing herself, slow just to show she wasn't too eager. Lie. She was starving.

Then two. Deeper. She bit her lip. Her knees buckled a little but she kept going. Switched to her clit, rubbing in tight furious circles, then back to fucking herself. A rhythm. Sloppy and desperate. She didn't care how she looked. No posing, no bullshit.

Sloane didn't move. Just sat on the closed toilet lid, legs crossed like they were at brunch and not in the middle of a one-woman porno. Elbows on her knees, eyes glittering with venom and want.

"Look at you," she drawled. "Fucking yourself like that. And for what? Because I asked?"

Vee groaned. Her face twisted, cheeks flushed red, lips parted, gasping.

"You're so pliable," Sloane whispered. "And gorgeous when you're wet for me."

That almost undid Vee. She felt her face go soft, all her armor dissolving. No sharp edges. Just wet eyes and trembling thighs and this breathless.

She saw herself on the fogged up medicine cabinet mirror, looking like something from an old movie. Pink-cheeked and helpless. She hated it. Loved it. Couldn't stop.

Then Sloane stood. Hair down now, walking into the spray like the water wasn't even hot. She knelt. No ceremony.

Her mouth was brutal. Fingers mean. Vee couldn't speak. Couldn't think. Sloane had her wide open, whimpering, and gripping the grab bar like it was a lifeline. The sounds—wet, indecent, echoing off the tile. Her knees gave out once, but Sloane just shoved her thigh up on her shoulder and kept going.

"Fuck," Vee choked. Over and over. It was all she had left.

Sloane didn't stop till Vee was shaking and lightheaded. Bent over her. Eyes rolled back. Too sensitive. Too spent. Skin flushed and twitching.

They didn't say anything when they quickly wiped each other down with mismatched towels. Didn't need to. They stumbled to the bedroom like survivors of something holy and wrong.

Vee was already high off her. Dizzy in the head, buzzing beneath the skin. Sloane tasted like sin made ripe—like wine left too long on the tongue.

It started with the kind of struggle that wasn't meant to be won. Teeth bared in laughter, nails biting skin—not to hurt, but to mark. Limbs tangled. Breathless gasps between kisses that turned to grunts as bodies collided like waves on stone. Neither wanted to surrender, not really. But both wanted the illusion of dominance long enough to get the other to yield.

Sloane gripped her wrists, shoved her down on the bed. Vee bit her lip and arched like it pleased her. But then she twisted, pressed her thigh between Sloane's legs, and flipped them fast, fast enough to steal a startled laugh from her mouth. She pinned Sloane by the shoulders, her hair wild, her mouth already moving south.

Vee sank lower, leaving heat behind like a comet's trail— along collarbone, between breasts, over the fluttering rise of Sloane's stomach. Sloane sprawled against the mattress, one arm thrown back, the other tangled in Vee's hair like she couldn't decide if she wanted to push her away or pull her in harder.

And then Vee had her mouth on her. Open, slow, ravenous. Sloane's body went taut, breath caught like it had barbed edges.

It should've been the finish line. But of course not. Sloane wasn't one to go quietly. With a low growl that sounded almost like a challenge, she hooked a leg around Vee's waist and twisted, flipping them until Vee was beneath her.

A wicked little maneuver. A new angle. Mouth to slick— twin hunger reflected back at each other. The position wasn't delicate. It wasn't romantic. It was filthy. Symmetry warped by desperation. She dragged the flat of her tongue in the way that always made Vee shake. Vee moaned into her, but it was Sloane that came with a snap—just like that. A little undignified, which made it worse. Or better.

Sloane pulled back between Vee's legs, panting, hair stuck to her temples, looking both satiated and irritated. Her fingers dug into Vee's left thigh as she sat up, still catching her breath.

"Unfair. I had the lead."

Vee just smirked up at her like she'd already claimed her prize, licking her bottom lip.

Sloane narrowed her eyes, lips curling with something darker now. "Alright," she said. "Enough games. I want you tied up. I want to fuck you."

It wasn't a request.

And Vee—wrecked, gleaming, and gloriously pinned— didn't protest.

They didn't say "safe word." They didn't whisper some color code or contrived buzzword from a message board masquerading as a manual. Sloane said, "If you want to stop, just say stop."

"Heard."

Simple. Direct. Human. No games, no performative etiquette. Just trust.

Then Vee blinked, still half-buzzing, her body sticky with sweat and pleasure, her limbs loose. "We've never done *that* before," she said, half-curious, half-flushed with the excitement of it.

Sloane's mouth curled, slow and knowing. "No. We haven't."

Then Vee ruined it, as she often did, not out of malice but pure, stupid honesty. "Wait—first of all, I didn't even think you were, like...packing. Or the type."

Sloane's eyes cut to her with a mix of amusement and sharp rebuke. "What does 'the type' mean?" she asked, sauntering toward her. "The type to what? Want to fuck you like you deserve?"

Vee made a sound—somewhere between a scoff and a breathy gasp.

Vee swallowed. Her thighs pressed together instinctively. "I—yes? What was the question again?"

That earned her a smile.

Sloane bent to her overnight bag—the same one Vee had grabbed off her floor without thinking in what felt like ages ago, just trying to be helpful. She didn't even notice the weight of it. But now she was watching Sloane unzip it with excruciating care, like she knew what kind of reveal this would be.

And there it was. Mounted on a pair of dark, low-profile wearable shorts that looked as comfortable as they were engineered. Black on black. It wasn't some bargain-bin novelty. It was expensive, refined, and anatomically obsessive. The kind of thing designed for *ruin*.

Vee stared. "That was in your bag the whole time?"

"You brought it to me," Sloane said sweetly. "Thanks, babe."

Then she was pulling something else—just as casual, just as lethal. A blue scarf, rough cotton, faded at the corners. One of those default accessories that people tied to their pockets to flag nothing in particular except the fact that they had hands and swagger.

Sloane stepped close. Tied Vee's wrists with it. Not tight. But *definite*. Like she was saying, *This isn't about restraint. This is about attention.*

She kissed her once, slow, full. Then lowered herself.

Vee barely had the breath to beg before Sloane went down on her again. There was nothing teasing in it this time. No easing in. Just full, deliberate worship, tongue firm and greedy, nose pressed right where she needed it, rhythm metronomic and merciless.

Vee shattered fast. Her body snapped like a live wire, thighs trembling, eyes wide and glazed over. It wasn't even resistance anymore—it was surrender. Mouth open. Pulse in her throat. Wrists bound above her. Nothing to do but take it.

It was then that Sloane entered her slowly, like a secret being told in the dark. No rush, no flourish. Just that quiet, devastating stretch of fullness, inch by inch, the kind of movement that made Vee feel like her body was being pried open with intention. Her thighs were already slick with need, already trembling from everything that had come before, but this—this was something else. She sucked in a breath like it might steady her. It didn't.

The press of Sloane's hips against hers was heavy, grounding. Their bodies aligned with an intimacy so total it felt intrusive, overwhelming—skin sliding on sweat-slick skin, breasts crushed together, heartbeats competing for rhythm. Vee could feel every flex of muscle, every exhale, every slight tremor of control in Sloane's thighs as she eased deeper, deeper still, until the air in Vee's lungs was no longer her own.

They were chest to chest, breath to breath, and then there was the eye contact—brutal, unflinching. Sloane looked at her like she was trying to memorize something permanent, and Vee, for once, couldn't look away. Her mouth parted on instinct, needing oxygen or words or something she couldn't name.

The smell of them was thick in the room—sweat, latex, skin, the musky sweetness of arousal that clung to every surface like fog. The sheets beneath them were damp. Vee's hair stuck to her temples, the strands catching at the corners of her mouth. She tasted salt—her own, Sloane's, the iron tang of something primal humming at the back of her throat.

Sloane moved with restraint, like she was holding herself just on the edge of unleashing. Each thrust was calculated, smooth, maddening in its control. Vee's arms scrabbled against the sheets, her tied wrists shifting in the fabric—the rough cotton biting gently into her skin, a reminder she'd given up control but not sensation.

It was too slow. Too precise. It wasn't enough.

"Harder," she gasped, the word cracking in her throat like glass. "Faster. Please—fuck, I need—"

Sloane didn't say anything. She didn't have to. She pulled out slow, almost all the way, and then drove back in harder—sharp, perfect. Vee cried out, head falling back into the pillow, mouth open wide and soundless for a second before it ripped out of her, loud and filthy and completely vulgar.

And still, Sloane looked infuriatingly perfect. Her hair slightly mussed, her skin flushed, sure—but she wasn't panting, wasn't shaking. Her movements were fluid, her mouth curved in something too elegant to be called a smirk but too smug to be anything else. Vee hated her for it. Wanted to ruin her. Wanted to come so hard she forgot how to be mad.

And she was close. But not quite. There was a ridge of tension in her belly that refused to snap. A knot pulled too tight, waiting for the right angle, the right pressure, the right push over the edge.

Sloane shifted again. Hands slid under Vee's thighs, lifting her legs up and folding them gently but firmly over Sloane's own shoulders. The motion was seamless, practiced. Vee's breath stuttered in her chest as her hips tilted upward, pelvis angled to meet Sloane deeper, fuller, perfectly aligned.

And then—there.

The thrust landed different now, dragging across a spot inside her that made her entire body flinch. Her back arched off the bed, fingers curling into fists, toes curling tight.

"There—fuck, right there—don't stop," she panted, eyes squeezed shut, everything tightening around the sensation like a coil.

Sloane didn't stop, her hips grinding in smaller, deeper circles. And then one hand slipped between their bodies. Her fingers were slick and sure, rubbing tight, deliberate circles on Vee's clit with that same maddening precision. The other hand rose to cup Vee's breast, her thumb brushing the nipple once, then pinching, tugging just enough to overload her already-flooded senses.

Vee couldn't think. Couldn't breathe. The pleasure climbed all at once, blinding and electric, her entire body a live wire.

The orgasm came like a seizure—violent, loud, unrelenting. Her body convulsed, gushing wet, loud enough that she swore she heard a neighbor's dog bark through the thin walls. Her scream cracked the air, deep and guttural and wild. There was nothing graceful about it. No pretty moan, no gentle unraveling. Just sound. Wetness. Shaking. Spasming under Sloane like she'd been short-circuited.

Her wrists tugged uselessly against the scarf, fingers numb, thighs trembling around Sloane's shoulders. She couldn't stop shaking. Couldn't close her mouth. Couldn't do anything but take it as her body continued to twitch through the aftershocks.

It lasted forever. Too long. Not long enough.

And when it finally started to fade, when her muscles stopped firing without permission, Vee looked up—half-dazed, cheeks flushed, chest heaving—and Sloane was still above her, composed and focused.

35

The heat between them hadn't faded—it clung like humidity. Vee lay half-curled on her side, still slick, still full of Sloane. The weight of her wasn't on the bed anymore, but the imprint was there: in the messed-up sheets, the faint sweat on Vee's chest, the half-lidded way her own body hummed like it had been tuned to the right frequency for the first time in years.

The overhead fan creaked in a lazy rhythm. Somewhere down the block, a dog barked once and shut up. The city was muffled in the way it only got around three in the morning—when even the cops got quiet and the ambulances started to sound like dreams instead of emergencies.

She didn't want to say it. She didn't even want to think it. But it sat heavy in the back of her throat, clawing its way out.

"Tell me who you think broke into your place."

Sloane didn't move at first. Just a shift of breath. A twitch in the muscle of her jaw where it pressed against the pillow. Not surprise, not denial. Just that cold calculation, that lawyer silence. Vee knew it too well. Had hated it. Had kissed it anyway.

"Don't," Sloane said, voice low, buried in linen. "Not now."

"Yeah," Vee said. "Now."

She rolled onto her back, let the sheets slip. Let her body cool, even as her chest stayed hot. She didn't look at Sloane when she said it again, quieter: "Who was it?"

Sloane exhaled. Her fingers traced a line on the sheet.

"No cops?" Vee asked.

Sloane shook her head.

"Why not?"

"Bad press," she said. "Optics. Headlines like that turn into board-level questions."

Vee's mouth flattened. She sat up. Her spine ached in the good way. Her heart in the bad.

"So you're telling me someone randomly ransacked your place, stole shit" Vee said, each word sharpening, "and you just kept it cute and didn't say anything?"

"I didn't say it was random," Sloane said.

"Oh." Vee laughed once. "So what, you think the company sent someone?"

Silence.

That was all the answer she needed.

"Sloane—"

"I don't know," she snapped. Then, quieter, "But I think so."

Vee's breath caught. She stared at the far wall like she could punch a hole in it with her thoughts. Her jaw locked. Her pulse didn't.

"My crew," she said. "The hangar—are they safe?"

Sloane closed her eyes. Like that made it easier to lie.

"I found something," she said. "A trigger. If union action escalated, they'd have justification for early termination.

Department-wide. The language is surgical. Pre-cleared by Legal."

"Sloane, *you* are Legal."

"I didn't pull the trigger," Sloane said. "I buried the memo. Delayed it."

Vee went still. Not stiff, not tense—just still. Like something in her had stopped turning.

"So," Vee said, softly. "Are my people safe?"

A long silence.

"I don't know," Sloane said.

And that was it. That was the breach point. That was the sudden, brutal loss of cabin pressure. The intimacy scattered. The warmth drained out of the room.

Neither of them said anything else. There was nothing left to say that wouldn't hurt worse.

Eventually, they fell asleep. Or something close to it. The kind of sleep that wasn't rest so much as a truce.

And when Vee opened her eyes the next morning, the bed beside her was cold. Sloane was gone. So was Tiberia—habitat cleaned out, no trace left. Like she'd never been there at all.

Only the indentation in the sheets remained. And the faint scent of someone who'd once let Vee in.

36

Kha had on the streamlined track jacket Vee picked up at Costco—the one that passed for luxury if you didn't look too close. He looked weirdly grown in it, standing next to the truck with a backpack slung over one shoulder and that wild mix of nerves and swagger.

"You sure I'm not gonna get flagged or something?" he asked, adjusting the collar like it could shield him from consequences.

"They already approved it," Vee said. Her voice felt like it had been run through gravel. "Your parole officer signed off last week. Moni verified. Stop asking."

He looked her over for a second, then gave her a little grin. "You okay?"

She didn't answer.

He nudged her shoulder with his elbow. "Women. Am I right?"

Vee jabbed him hard in the bicep with her index finger. "Shut up."

He yelped and laughed, rubbing his arm. "I'm just saying! You got that end-of-the-world vibe going. Again."

She didn't smile. Just looked at the truck, then back at him.

"Don't fuck this up," she said. "My friend up there vouched for you personally. She's cool about records, but if you ghost her or show up high or try to be slick, she'll tell me. Then I'll drive up there and end you."

"Yeah, yeah. I got it." Kha pulled the door open. "I'll text when I get to the hotel."

"You better."

He climbed in. The truck—now miraculously running after two months of half-assed surgeries—coughed awake. Vee stepped back onto the curb and watched him pull away. Her reflection caught in the window of the driver's side: hunched shoulders, oversized hoodie, bags under her eyes like bruises.

THE HANGAR SMELLED THE SAME. Grease. Jet fuel. Concrete. Sweat. But the rhythm was off the second she stepped through the side entrance. It wasn't noise, not exactly—it was the absence of the right noise. No clanging. No low cursing over a socket wrench. No one blasting music.

She didn't make it five steps before Gerald—young Gerald, with the chipped tooth—cut in front of her.

"Vee," he said, voice tight. "You—uh—you shouldn't be here."

She frowned. "What?"

Then she saw them. Security. Two of them. Not the usual union guys—they were third-party. Black polos, no names on the chest. And behind them, just out of view, a man with a clipboard looking around.

Her badge wouldn't scan.

"You're kidding me," she said, jamming it again.

"Phan," said the man with the clipboard, stepping forward. "We've been instructed to escort you off the premises. Your employment with Heritage has been—"

"No," she said. Just that. Sharp. Flat.

She turned to the crew—her crew. Half of them were just standing there, frozen. Others were mid-shift, staring like they didn't know what to do. Manny. Elena. Rick. Gerald. Diego. Every face she'd fought for, sweated with. None of them could look her in the eye.

And then she noticed. Some of them—just a few—had different patches. New uniforms. Clean. Too clean. And next to them, new bodies. Outsiders. Scabs.

The floor dropped out from under her.

"Who else?" she asked no one in particular. Her voice wasn't loud. It didn't need to be. "Who else did they fire?"

No one answered.

But she could tell. You could always tell. It was the loud ones. The union delegates. The whistleblowers. The ones who dared to stand close to her.

Vee didn't react. Not then. Not in front of the clipboards. Not in front of the ghosts.

But inside, something buckled. And it didn't make a sound when it broke.

37

The union hall was on fire, in the metaphorical way. Literal fire would've been cleaner.

Three phones were ringing at once, two of them cordless, one of them landline and held together with duct tape. The fax machine kept whirring out bad news. Someone's kid was crying in the break room. Someone else was yelling about severance in the hallway.

Vee sat in a folding chair with her elbows on her knees, half-watching Noah Feldman-Bloom pace the linoleum floor like a caged wolf with a tie.

"Get me someone who isn't a legal intern with a goddamn LinkedIn bio, please," he barked into the phone. "I'm not asking for the Pope. I'm asking for your general counsel, who by the way—wait. What? Without notice? Without a replacement?"

He yanked the receiver away from his ear, looked at it like it had insulted his mother, then slammed it into the cradle. He took a breath then picked up his personal phone and dialed again.

"Zora," he said. "Pick up the damn phone."

He paused. Listened.

"Zora, I swear to God, if you don't call me back I'm going to subpoena you."

He hung up and looked over at Vee, who hadn't moved since she sat down.

"No one will talk to me," he said.

Vee didn't answer. She was holding the printed documents in her lap—hot off the Xerox, still curling at the corners. Sloane's name wasn't on any of them, not directly. But the voice—that voice—was unmistakable. Legalese with a spine of glass and venom.

She read them slowly, one page at a time.

The cover memo called it a Safety + Liability Compliance Restructure. Real clean. Real boring. The language was pre-emptively defensive—"in light of rising regulatory ambiguity," "to ensure continuity of care," "aligned with FAA recommendations."

But the real story was tucked in the footnotes, the clauses, the amended schedules. The evil was structural.

First move: Subcontractors. On paper, Heritage said it was just to help clear a backlog—bring in some outside crews for a bit. But the fine print said if over half the maintenance work went to these third-party firms, the union no longer counted. No majority workforce, no union. That was it. They cited a clause that was written in the nineties and recently found in a dusty vendor doc no one was supposed to touch.

Second move: Job title switch-up. Mechanics got reclassified as made-up roles—"compliance specialists," "integrity analysts." Sounded fancy. Meant nothing. Except now the union didn't protect them. And if they didn't agree to the new title? Fired. For "non-compliance."

Third move: Hangar clause. Some ancient lease bullshit

from the '80s. Said Heritage could shut down union operations if the site became a PR problem. Thanks to the cancer leak and the protest, Vee had accidentally handed them the perfect excuse.

And the final knife: good faith severance. Generous packages, NDAs tucked in the back. One-time payouts for silence. The ones who refused? "Performance-based separation." The ones who took it? Gone. Complicit. Forgotten.

It was legal. Every word of it.

It was poison in a crystal decanter.

Vee sat back in her chair, the papers slipping from her lap to the floor.

She wanted to throw up. Or break something. Or call Sloane and demand to know why she'd done this and how she could live with herself.

Except she already knew.

This wasn't just Sloane's work. This *was* Sloane. All her elegance, all her cruelty. A woman who knew the law so well she could turn it into a weapon no one could see coming. A woman who could walk into a room and dismantle an entire labor movement with three footnotes and a severance letter.

It was brilliant.

It made Vee sick.

And it worked.

Noah kicked the corner of a filing cabinet, then sat down beside her with a grunt.

"Well," he said. "What now?"

Vee didn't answer.

She just stood there, hands braced on the cheap folding table in the union hall, while the walls around her buzzed with noise she couldn't hear anymore. Phones still ringing. Someone yelling in the hallway. None of it mattered.

It was gone.

The whole thing. Every year, every shift, every fight, wiped clean.

She remembered driving into Chicago more than twenty years ago in a rusted-out Corolla with expired plates and a duffel bag she didn't unpack for two months. She hadn't known where she was going. Just knew she couldn't go back. Not to Long Beach. Not to that life. She told herself it was a clean break. A restart.

Her aunties in the north side took her in. Fed her. Watched her. Didn't ask questions. One of them got her a job scrubbing parts in a tiny maintenance shop. She had barely turned eighteen. But her hands were steady. Her head was quiet when she worked.

Her aunties had only one condition for letting her stay: finish high school. She started senior year not knowing a soul. Morgan was a loudmouthed freshman with too much eyeliner and no chill. They didn't like each other at first. That changed.

Over time, everything did.

She apprenticed. Got her hours. Got her people. Built something.

When Morgan got called to testify before Congress last year, Vee had sat beside her, steady as hell, while men in suits tried to twist her words. She'd stared down company lawyers in arbitration hearings. She'd walked picket lines in ice storms. She'd held grieving coworkers after they buried Jerry. She had bled for this work.

And now?

Nothing.

No job. No hangar. No crew.

They cut her out clean. Not even a message. Just policy changes, reclassification memos, the dull language of erasure. Like she'd never been there at all.

She looked down at her hands. Still grease-stained. Still strong. Still hers.

But she felt hollow.

Not broken—just scraped out. Like the core of her had been scooped clean and left behind somewhere on the shop floor.

It didn't hurt. Not yet.

There was just the quiet.

And she didn't know what came next.

VEE STEPPED out into the heavy heat, the air thick enough to chew. She lit up her vape without thinking, thumb tapping muscle memory. Morgan had asked her to quit. Begged, actually. They'd pinky-sworn over a bowl of popcorn. And here she was. Hiding in a puff of synthetic mango because there was nothing left worth keeping a promise for.

The union hall sat on a corner in the West Loop, made of pale limestone and red rage. Grand as hell. Ridiculous even. With those dramatic-ass steps—thirty of them, maybe more.

She took them slow. Not because she was tired, but because the world had gone numb. Her hands shook. Her legs didn't feel like hers. Her heart was a radio stuck between frequencies.

She reached the bottom just as the black town car screeched up to the curb.

Vee didn't flinch. Didn't even blink.

The back door flung open like a movie. Like some twisted rom-com timed to ruin her actual life. And then there she was—Sloane. Hair undone, heels uneven on the pavement, panic painted across her face. She wasn't walking so much as storming, like she'd run the whole way from Gold Coast to West Loop fueled on guilt and five espresso shots.

"I heard," Sloane said, breathless. "Vee—are you okay?"

Vee stared at her. Blank. Wondered how she even found her.

"Are you—" Sloane started again.

Vee took a long, slow drag. Blew the smoke out between her teeth. "Are you fucking serious."

Sloane froze.

"You destroy my life with a goddamn Word document and now you want to check in?"

"I didn't know," Sloane said, voice tight, eyes wide. "Zora —my assistant—circumvented protocol. I had a strategy. I did. I was going to stall implementation, reframe the terms —God, I was preparing to turn the entire thing against them—"

She reached out like she was going to grab Vee's hand. Vee jerked back so hard she almost dropped her vape.

"I will fix this," Sloane said. Her voice cracked on the word fix. "Just give me time. Please. Please. I didn't know they would pull the clause—I didn't know they'd throw me out too—"

That stopped Vee cold.

"You got fired?" she asked.

Sloane gave a brittle laugh. "People like me don't get fired. They announce a 'strategic transition' and 'step back to explore other opportunities.' It's the same thing. Just with better lighting."

Vee stared at her. Then rolled her eyes so hard it hurt.

"Great," Vee said. "Tragic."

Sloane's breath hitched. And then—like she couldn't hold it in anymore—tears.

Not a single, tasteful tear either. Full, choking, messy sobs. Her mascara was already smudged, her dress wrinkled. Vee had never seen her like this. Not even close.

And it made her sick.

Because her heart—the stupid thing—wanted to reach out. Wanted to gather Sloane in her arms and fix her hair and tell her everything was going to be okay even when it wasn't. It wanted to remember the night they danced barefoot in the hotel room after Morgan's wedding reception, matching bridesmaid dresses puddled on the floor, lipstick smeared on collarbones. It wanted to go back to two days ago, Sloane sleeping soundly in the passenger seat of the truck, her damn snake on her lap, as they trusted her to get them to their destination.

But Vee couldn't. Not anymore.

She stepped back, spine locked, voice flat. "You're not sorry. You're just scared."

"That's not true—"

"It doesn't matter," Vee said, cutting her off. Her voice trembled, but she stood steady. "This is what you do, Sloane. You're too good. I spent twenty years building something you erased in twenty minutes. And the worst part? You didn't even have to pull the trigger. You just trained someone else how to aim. You wrote the killshot in twelve-point font and buried it in a footnote."

Sloane looked wrecked.

"You don't fix things," Vee said. "You finish them."

Silence. The kind that split atoms.

Then—quiet, clear, absolute: "Don't ever speak to me again."

She turned to walk to her truck parked across the street. Didn't look back.

Sloane didn't follow.

38

M organ didn't ask questions when she opened the door—just pulled Sloane inside.

The house was one of those old West Side Victorians with opinions—tall, narrow, and proud of it. The handcrafted staircase alone looked like it had taken some artisan thirty years off their life. Crown molding carved so intricately it bordered on petty. Rosettes. Dentil work. Patterns no one bothered with anymore.

But the grandeur was unfinished. Boxes still everywhere. Paint swatches taped to the walls in test patches—deep greens, cool grays, moody blues. The signs of two lives merging, cautiously but unmistakably. It was disgustingly domestic. It mocked her with its hope.

Morgan was barefoot, wearing nothing but a forest green oversized Michigan State Spartans T-shirt, full of dog hair and probably sleep. No makeup. No armor. Daisy and Scout —Kieran's rescue mutts who'd somehow become Morgan's —sniffed Sloane's ankles and sneezed like they didn't think much of what they found.

The house smelled like fresh paint and black tea.

She didn't make it two steps past the threshold before her face crumpled. The tears came fast, hot and humiliating. Her body gave out in pieces—first her shoulders, then her knees. She would've hit the hardwood if Morgan hadn't caught her, arms tight around her ribcage, anchoring her with one hand and smoothing her hair with the other.

"Vee told me everything," Morgan murmured into her scalp.

Sloane's voice cracked. "You don't hate me?"

Morgan pulled back just enough to look her in the eye. "Right now? I actually do."

Sloane flinched. Fair.

"I'm really holding back from slapping the shit out of you," Morgan went on, tone flat. "But that's not what this moment is for. This is the part where you tell me what the hell is going on. And if you're honest—truly honest—I won't tell you to get out of my house and never come back."

Sloane's mouth opened. Closed. She couldn't get the words out.

Morgan's expression didn't soften. "You can."

"I don't know."

Morgan crossed her arms. "Please. You made a U.S. congressman cry last year. In four-inch heels. On C-SPAN."

That got a broken, pathetic little sound out of Sloane. Almost a laugh. Almost.

So she told her.

Everything.

39

The next thing she knew, she was in Jamaica.

Not the Jamaica of her childhood—hushed verandas, cane furniture, rum in dark glasses while adults whispered politics—but a cloyingly cheerful resort on the north coast where everything smelled like mango-scented chlorine. There were matching shirts. Buffet stations. A steel drum cover of Coldplay echoing faintly across the lawn.

She sat perfectly poised in a linen sundress, legs crossed at the ankle, espresso in one hand, and an encrypted tablet in the other. She looked like someone's estranged wife on a solo vacation to 'find herself.' Which, in a way, wasn't wrong.

Across from her, Kenji reclined on a lounger in a pair of flamingo-printed swim trunks and mirrored sunglasses, sipping something violently orange through a paper umbrella.

To his left, El and Andi were curled up on pool chairs with their laptops out, cables snaking into portable batteries, Bluetooth keyboards clacking. El wore a shredded neon rash guard over bike shorts, her pink braids piled into two buns like antennae. Glitter sunscreen streaked her cheekbones like war paint. Andi had a lime green crochet halter over black swim trunks, mirrored sunglasses perched on her buzzed head. She was eating a popsicle.

Sloane's group was the only one not smiling.

The steel drum cover had changed twice a day. The breakfast buffet rotated on a four-day cycle. By now, Sloane knew both by heart.

The weather stayed perfect—sunrise like a slap, sunset like a dare.

She no longer flinched when a child screamed. She no longer noticed the couples taking anniversary selfies beside her with ring lights and forced grins.

By day five, they'd mapped the entire estate network. Pried open the backend of two shell corporations. And unearthed a clause the Thompkins family had buried so deep in the contract it required both legal fluency and a working knowledge of the occult mechanics of power.

Around them, life unfolded with insulting ease. Children screamed over water slides. A bridal party squealed near the photo backdrop. Someone's aunt was already drunk on mimosas and recounting her divorce.

Sloane tapped her screen. A set of documents loaded. Her pulse stayed steady.

She wasn't here for nostalgia. She wasn't here for absolution.

She was here to make a problem disappear.

THE CABANA'S FAN HUMMED. Somewhere outside, a child shrieked with laughter while a steel drum cover of "Shape of You" mangled the concept of joy.

Inside, the four of them stood in silence around a teak table that still smelled faintly of varnish and rum.

The letter sat at the center.

It wasn't in an envelope. It didn't need one. The paper was unnaturally smooth—like parchment, but colder, like it had been pressed under something heavier than time. The ink shimmered when it caught the light.

Sloane didn't touch it. She just stared.

The contract had no logo. No watermark.

El leaned forward first. Read a line. Then pulled back like she'd been slapped.

"This isn't a contract," she muttered. "This is a curse."

Andi said nothing, but reached for her laptop.

Kenji sipped his coffee, then turned his head and squinted through the gossamer curtains at the pool deck.

There was a white guy outside in a Rasta wig. One of those mesh beanie things with fake dreads sewn in. Sloane followed his gaze. Rolled her eyes.

He didn't blink. "You want me to make him disappear?"

Sloane didn't look up. "We're busy."

"Copy that," he said, and went back to scanning the letter with the intensity of someone reading a bomb schematic.

Outside, someone cheered. A conga line started. A blender roared to life.

Inside, the air felt wrong.

And the contract stared back at her.

She had read it perhaps a thousand times, and still it raised the hairs on her arms.

El was the one who finally said it, her voice low and a little dazed.

"So just to be clear—your best friend's old boss is part of

the family that's been trying to destroy yours since independence?"

Sloane didn't look up from the contract. "She *is* the family."

Kenji gave a dry, humorless laugh. "Aviation's a small world, huh?"

Sloane's eyes flicked toward him. "A small, rigged one."

Outside, the conga line kept moving. Inside, no one moved at all.

Memorandum of Agreement and Restoration

Between the House of Thompkins and the Campbell Estate
Kingston, Jamaica

Witnessed in the Year of Our Lord and the Turning of Fortune

Let it be known:
In recognition of debts outstanding, accrued by the Campbell family in matters of taxation, liens, and fiduciary default—debts which now total $18,403,200,000.00 JMD, compounded annually over five generations—and in solemn acknowledgment of lands held by the Campbells in trust, including but not limited to:

- *17.2 hectares in St. Ann Parish*
- *6.5 hectares in Westmoreland*
- *The clinic site in Clarendon*
- *The Ridge Road property presently held in partial title*

...the House of Thompkins, with mercy and foresight, offers forgiveness in full, upon the fulfillment of the following terms:

I. Term of Service

Ms. Sloane Eralia Campbell, eldest living heir of the Campbell line, shall enter into a binding period of service under the sole direction and authority of Ms. Ava Clemence Thompkins, acting matriarch of the Thompkins estate and majority shareholder of all related corporate entities, for a period of three hundred sixty-five (365) days, commencing upon date of signature.

During this term, Ms. Campbell shall act in the role of General Counsel to Heritage Airlines International, with full legal over-sight, strategic compliance duties, and discretion as determined by the employer. Travel, hours, and personal autonomy are at the employer's discretion.

II. Terms of Silence and Loyalty
No details of this agreement shall be disclosed to any outside party, kin or otherwise.
Violation of said clause shall incur immediate reinstatement of all debts, legal action across relevant jurisdictions, and forfeiture of ancestral land holdings without recourse.

III. Authority and Enforcement
This agreement is binding under:
- The Civil and Commercial Laws of the Commonwealth of Jamaica
- The customs of inheritance and right upheld by both houses
- And the unseen court of God and the Ancestors, whose names are not written here but are known to all parties involved
- Let no man interfere. Let no daughter run. Let no legal scholar unravel what was woven before their birth.

Signed in Faith and Finality

Ava C. Thompkins

For the House of Thompkins

Sloane E. Campbell
For the Campbell Estate

Witnessed and sealed, this document to remain active in spirit and in law until the term is completed, the debts are paid in sweat, and the name Campbell is once again cleared.

The road narrowed until it was barely a suggestion —no more than a strip of gravel, pressed into the earth by decades of tires and rain. The hired car protested with every turn. Suspension groaned. Brakes hissed. But it kept going, nudged forward by Kenji's hand on the wheel and Sloane's silence in the back seat.

They were deep in Cockpit Country now, though no sign announced it. Only the land itself—unyielding, unpaved, unbothered by their presence. The terrain had shed its colonial politeness. Asphalt gave way to packed clay and limestone outcrops. The trees leaned in, branches low and interwoven, filtering the light into something dappled and deliberate. Sunlight arrived here in fragments.

And with every mile, the noise of the world fell away. No billboards. No hum of generators. No ambient machinery. Just the sound of the wind threading through ferns, and the occasional snap of a twig underfoot—a natural quiet, but not an empty one.

It felt like the land was listening.

Sloane sat straighter. She didn't fidget. Her hands

remained folded in her lap, nails immaculate, blouse still too crisp for the air around her. But she felt it. In the marrow.

The place was lush, yes—but not decadent. This was not the curated greenness of resort gardens or colonial estates. This was a landscape grown with memory. The orchids here did not bloom for beauty; they clung to tree bark like confessions. The ferns unfolded in the heat —each one a gesture repeated for centuries, unacknowledged but never abandoned.

The dirt was red, stubborn, slick where it shouldn't be. The air was thick with heat and something else—an awareness, low and steady, neither welcoming nor hostile. Just present.

The villages came and went without preamble. Houses painted in sun-faded colors, roofs patched with whatever metal was closest. People moved at a pace entirely their own. No one smiled reflexively. They nodded instead—once, if at all—and returned to their tasks.

A boy walked barefoot down the roadside with a basket of cassava balanced on his head and a phone in his hand. He didn't look up. An old man selling breadfruit from a folding chair didn't speak, didn't motion. Just watched.

They passed the first marker without realizing it—a signpost half-swallowed by vines, the painted wood warped and illegible, its message long since surrendered to rot and moss. No replacement had been installed. No GPS pin registered. The map didn't acknowledge it. As if it had never mattered.

Further in, the drone swept low over what remained of a perimeter wall—crumbling stone, a rusted chain that trailed into soil, and a clearing that might once have been a garden or a battleground. The terrain offered no clarification. A machete protruded from a tree stump nearby, blade still clean, like it had been planted there with intention rather than forgotten.

Nothing was labeled.

Everything spoke.

Sloane remained silent.

She stepped carefully over an exposed root, the soles of her sandals muffled against the loam. Every sound she made felt wrong—too crisp, too recent. The air hung heavy, but it wasn't heat alone. There was gravity here. She could feel it at her sternum.

She wandered toward the edge of the property, not out of aimlessness but out of a need for stillness. The others were somewhere behind her—Kenji in his endless calibration, the twins being absolutely useless—but here, past the brush line, the land felt...untouched.

The slope curved sharply downward, a ridge giving way to lowland cleared long ago but now overtaken by ferns and banana trees. Beyond that, the mountain rose —not majestic, but stern, as if it were tired of being looked at. Sloane didn't need a plaque to know what had once been grown up there. Cane. Always cane. She could feel it in the stillness. Not absence, but residue. The past hadn't left—it had simply ceased to explain itself.

A woman sat near the base of the hill, beneath an ackee tree, peeling fruit with the kind of knife that didn't shine anymore. Her hat was wide-brimmed and shapeless. She looked like she'd been sitting there for a hundred years. And might keep sitting, long after Sloane was gone.

Sloane approached cautiously, but the woman didn't flinch.

"Well. Look who's surveying her kingdom," she

murmured, the knife still moving through fruit with deliberate ease. "Come to count your trees?"

Sloane didn't bristle. She just stepped closer, the hem of her maxi skirt brushing the grass, her posture untouched.

She knew that voice. Older now, sanded down by time—but unmistakable. This wasn't a stranger.

Summers spent in Port Antonio, before the clinics, before the contracts—she remembered a small house painted blue, a stern hand on her shoulder. The woman who brushed out her hair with coconut oil and told her to stop acting like a foreigner. The woman her mother once called family, but never treated like one.

Her old nanny never left. She'd just stopped waiting.

"The land is in my hands now," she said quietly. "I just don't know what it means to stop carrying it."

That made the woman pause.

Only then did she glance up. And just like that, the rhythm of the moment shifted.

"You came late," the woman said, not unkindly. Her voice was even, musical in a way. She didn't look up. "But you're here now."

And then, as if deciding Sloane could keep up, she switched. Not in sound—the words stayed English—but the rhythm changed. The grammar bent. The melody behind her speech shifted into something older, something shaped by mountains and survival. She was speaking in *patois* now, or near enough.

Sloane said nothing. She sat—knees together, spine held in habitual, exhausting posture.

"You know this place?" the woman asked, slicing cleanly through another fruit. "This land you step on, this is not just bush. This here was a rebel yard. A place for the ones who ran, who wouldn't kneel, who wouldn't stay."

She gestured lazily toward the slope.

"People used to run from that hill. There was a plantation up there—sugar, plenty of it. Sweet for England, bitter for everyone here. They came down at night, bleeding, broken-backed, but still moving. Hiding in the caves. Fighting when no one could see."

Sloane's throat tightened. She didn't respond.

"Your people," the woman continued, not asking, just stating, "were the ones who helped lead them. The Campbell name carries plenty of stories."

She sliced another fruit. The knife made no sound against the skin.

"But stories get messy. Time passes. Blood dries up. Revolutions cost money. So your people took a loan—from the same ones whose fathers once claimed everything here, down to the bones. That's how it always starts. A signature. A favor. A name on a line."

Sloane blinked, once. Hard.

"The Thompkinses," the woman said, voice steady, "learned early how to live between things. Between upstairs and out back."

The knife moved, slow and certain.

"They were born close enough to the house to learn its rules. And close enough to the kitchen to know who really kept it warm—because they came from both."

She sniffed and offered a piece of fruit to Sloane. Sloane took it wordlessly and ate.

"They got just enough to stay quiet. Just enough to inherit."

She spat that last word like it offended her mouth.

"Everybody broke," she added. "Just differently."

Sloane didn't argue. She knew.

Her chest felt too tight. Not with panic—something

denser. Older. The contract. The debt. The land that neither forgave nor forgot. Her mother's voice echoing in the back of her mind, telling her to take care of the family, always, always. There was no line between loyalty and sacrifice when you were the daughter chosen to hold it all together. First-born meant last to rest.

The woman studied her—not with interest, but with recognition.

"Chain's a chain. Could be rope, could be gold. Still tight all the same."

Sloane's voice caught behind her teeth.

The woman didn't seem to expect a reply. She turned back to her fruit.

"So what now?" she asked. "You here to keep the cycle runnin'?"

A pause. Wind tugged gently at the hem of Sloane's skirt.

"Or you here to break it?"

Sloane didn't answer.

But the land, dense and humming around them, already knew.

THE BUNGALOW, with its tasteful stucco and manufactured charm, sat just above the tide line—close enough to hear the surf, far enough to pretend they were still in control. It was meant to be a reprieve. A beachside detente. The moon cast its path across the water in soft, deliberate silver, and the breeze smelled of salt and hibiscus and something faintly metallic. The kind of night designed for peace.

Sloane felt anything but at peace.

El and Andi had just returned from a massage—oiled,

smug, and suspiciously quiet. Their shoulders looked looser. Their tempers had cooled. Neither said as much, but Sloane knew what it was: they were giving her a second chance. She had disrespected them back in Chicago. And now, here she was, footing the bill for a five-star Jamaican beachfront villa while letting them hurl encrypted PDFs at her face.

They were gathered on the bungalow's veranda now, perched on lounge chairs and uneven wicker stools, the air humming with insects and tension. Paper was everywhere— maps, deeds, shell corporation filings printed in duplex to save space. A Bluetooth speaker played something ambient and forgettable. Kenji muttered to himself over a set of planning schematics, adjusting the brightness on his screen with the measured irritation of a man who already knew the answer and resented the need to prove it.

The sound of the waves was a metronome.

Sloane didn't move. Her eyes drifted over a printout beside her elbow—standard formatting, Helvetica header, stamped with Heritage's digital seal. It was familiar. She'd signed it weeks ago without blinking. Something Zora had routed to her iPad while she was in proceedings. She remembered the phrasing now only because it was so innocuous.

Redevelopment Access Agreement

She'd thumbed it through on a flight. Clicked to sign. Never questioned it. Zora had flagged it as routine.

Now, under the glare of the moon and a highlighter-yellow beach lamp, it was anything but.

And now, Port Antonio—the ridge, the clinic, the land held in trust since before the emancipation papers were even dry—was marked for "redevelopment."

Her father's voice came back to her without permission —cutting across time, across oceans.

"You know what you've done?" he'd asked, the last time she'd answered his call. "That land is the only reason the clinics are still open. Ava made sure the banks didn't take it when your grandfather died. You think this was free? You think she kept that land safe out of kindness?" He had laughed then—dry and humorless. "You've given it away, Sloane. After everything. You've destroyed us."

She had tried to speak, but he'd already hung up.

Kenji held out a tablet now. On it: aerial footage, tight resolution, drone-shot. Stakes in the earth. Marked boundaries. Survey tape already laid.

"They've broken ground," he said. "Quietly. But it's begun."

Sloane didn't flinch.

She leaned back in the chair, letting her head tilt toward the moon, letting the shame settle, acidic and slow. Her voice, when it came, was even.

"I can't save the land," she murmured. "But I can stop them from owning it."

No one responded. They didn't need to.

The truth had already laid itself out across the table: The Campbells had always owed the Thompkinses—money first, then favors, then blood. Two old families with too much history that spanned across international borders and not enough forgiveness. The Thompkinses came to collect in the form of a single, brutal contract. Sloane's signature was the key. Her legal brilliance was the weapon. She had agreed, and then she'd hesitated. Fallen in love. Broken rank.

Now the land was in jeopardy. And with it, the schools

and clinics and everything her family had ever claimed to stand for.

THE NEXT MORNING, en route to a government office in Kingston—Land Trust and Indigenous Heritage Preservation—Sloane's phone buzzed.

Everyone in the car wore suits. Kenji and Sloane sat in the front. The twins occupied the back.

Andi picked up the phone from the cupholder, the screen glowing as she tilted it toward the light. A smirk crept across her face.

"Oh, look," she said. "It's your boyfriend."

Before the words had even landed, El jabbed her sharply in the ribs. Andi winced.

"Not cool," El muttered, still facing forward. Her jaw was tight. "Don't joke like that."

No one asked why Sloane still took calls from a man halfway to the grave—a man who had once treated her body like an open entitlement. Who touched without permission. Who never flinched, never apologized. The room already understood the cost of being close. And the currency she was willing to spend.

Kenji had seen it firsthand.

He was the one who drove her to the Hodge estate in the Hamptons the day before they boarded the plane to Jamaica. He watched her walk in with soup and civility.

"Off the record," she'd told him.

Then she let the old man ramble, uninterrupted, about the glory days—when deals happened with handshakes and winks, when HR was a back-office formality, not a power broker.

She allowed his hand to linger between her thighs. Answered it with a gracious nod. She played the role they always expected: deferential, unthreatening, grateful. The perfect mentee. The decorative kind.

Kenji handled the rest. He played chauffeur. El and Andi tapped in remotely. They pulled probate files, sealed trust documents, and decades of medical records riddled with euphemisms—all siphoned through the estate's unsecured Wi-Fi. They found gaps in the bylaws no one had touched since the Clinton years. Sloane began annotating them that same night.

And Vivienne Yue—always luminous, second-generation billionaire, and disturbingly polite—was no longer circling. She was in position.

All it would take was one signature from Milton Hodge. Once that ink dried, the shares would transfer. Along with them, the voting power he had held on Ava's behalf for decades. That was the move—not just equity, but authority.

What Ava once commanded through loyalty and unchecked male entitlement, Sloane was dismantling piece by piece. All of it, stripped with a smile and a pen.

Sloane answered the call. Her voice came out smooth, even, practiced.

"Milton," she said, tone soft and honeyed, as though the hour were tender, not ruthlessly corporate. "You're up early."

A rough chuckle came through the line, thick with scotch and sleep.

"Was just thinkin' about you, sweetheart."

She smiled into the speaker, cool and controlled.

"I hope you weren't dreaming about bylaws again. You always get tangled."

By some miracle, Milton hadn't been informed of

Sloane's current status with Heritage. He was a vote, not a liability, and Heritage didn't waste strategy on the nearly-dead.

He laughed, more wheeze than humor.

"You're trouble. You know that?"

"I've heard," she replied, crossing her legs and leaning into the car's leather seat.

Kenji didn't glance over. He kept his eyes on the road. He knew the scene. He'd seen the script.

Milton rambled.

He launched into a monologue about loyalty, about how the board had grown spineless and "too woke." He griped that no one shook hands anymore, that he used to close billion-dollar deals on eye contact and gut instinct. Back when, in his words, men were men—and that meant something.

Sloane let him talk. She offered just enough—soft murmurs, the occasional hum of agreement, polite laughter timed to fuel the fire without stoking it too high. She gave him room to decay in real time, letting the rot air out on its own.

He talked like no one had really listened to him in years. Which was, depressingly, just reality. His kids hadn't invited him to Thanksgiving in a decade. His grandkids only tolerated him—eyes darting to clocks, clearly bribed to stay.

Milton didn't just smell like money and bitterness. He reeked of decline. Not merely aging—decomposition in slow motion.

By the time he finished, they had reached Kingston. The government building rose ahead of them, sun-washed and bureaucratic, unmoved by the hour and a half of generational rot she had just endured.

Kenji stayed silent, both hands steady on the wheel. He didn't even cut the engine.

El and Andi had dipped the minute they parked—claimed they were heading to a smoothie shop to check Wi-Fi. But really, they had no appetite for the spectacle.

It had been ninety minutes of verbal embalming.

When Milton finally sputtered to a halt, the silence felt like a fracture.

That was when she moved in.

Her voice dropped—warm, slow, almost tender.

"Milton," she said, as if his name were something delicate, "I know things have changed. The board. The industry. Everything. That must be disorienting."

He grunted. "No loyalty left."

"Oh, I wouldn't say that," she replied, her tone still sweet. "Some of us still remember what it means to protect one another. To act discreetly. To preserve legacy."

That word always landed. Milton still believed he had one.

She dialed her voice down further, the way you would if you wanted to sound caring but not condescending.

"You've done more for this company than most people will ever understand. But the vultures are circling, Milton. You know it. So do I."

He didn't interrupt. She had him now.

"I just think," she said gently, "you deserve to choose where your power goes. While you still can."

A pause. Then:

"You think Jack Yue's kid is serious about that offer?"

"I know she is," Sloane said. "And I'll be with you every step of the way. No red tape. No drama. Just a clean transfer. You get to leave on your own terms. No one rewrites your ending for you."

He let out a breath, slow and shallow.

"You always did talk pretty."

"That's why they pay me." Her smile didn't reach her eyes. "Now. Shall I have my office send over the revised draft?"

He hesitated—just long enough to convince himself he still had a say. Then he offered it up, offhand, like the words weren't laced with rot:

"Not like the board's gonna stop Jack anyway. His people are buying up half the damn country. One more Chinese billionaire snapping up old American blood—what's the difference?"

She didn't flinch. Sloane had learned how to absorb men like him—quietly, efficiently, without leaving a trace.

And finally, he landed where she had been steering him all along.

"Yeah," he said. "Let's do it."

The line went dead.

Sloane turned to the window. Her reflection hovered faintly in the glass—blurred by sun, motion, and the weight of what had just shifted. Behind her, the city was starting to stir. Ahead of her, a name was about to vanish from the voting roster.

Kenji glanced over, calm as ever.

"Soup worked?"

Something flickered across her face—then vanished.

"Every time."

41

The team had wrapped it all with surgical precision.

Probate filings submitted. Voting shares transferred. Statements drafted in three tones—neutral, apologetic, and preemptively litigious—depending on how Heritage chose to spin it. The entire operation had been executed with such crisp, methodical grace it almost felt antiseptic.

Kenji was already on his second espresso martini, lounging on a rented jet ski. El and Andi were shrieking in a loop around the bay, their personal brand of victory lap involving water sports, Bluetooth speakers, and enough SPF to arm a coral reef.

Sloane remained on shore.

The preservation order sat in her bag, quietly stamped and filed under the Land Trust and Indigenous Heritage Act. Technically, the Campbell land had been reclassified as a protected ecological and historical zone. Legally, no development could break ground on it now—not without triggering a media and international diplomatic firestorm. The paperwork had been signed in the Kingston office.

Once it hit the press, someone would be livid. Probably several someones from the House of Thompkins. Good.

She stayed where the sand met the water, hands braced behind her, sunglasses hiding most of the damage. Her heels were off, her dress was wrinkled, and her eyes felt like they'd been sandblasted. Devastated wasn't the right word —it was too delicate. She felt hollowed out. Gutted with polish.

Her phone buzzed.

A Google Alert. *Vi Anh Phan.*

Sloane's stomach dropped. She opened the link with the quiet dread of someone peeking into a wound.

There she was—Vee, on-screen, mid-interview with local news. No uniform. No hangar in the background. Just Vee in a denim sleeveless dress, wearing her reading glasses, and speaking with quiet fury about Jerry Cortez, about toxic exposure, about the workers still in the fight. Even after being fired, she hadn't stopped. She'd gone louder. She was dragging the lawsuit into the spotlight with bare hands and a steady voice, one appearance at a time.

Sloane's throat went tight.

The tears came without warning—hot, soundless, ridiculous. Salt on top of salt. She laughed once, bitter and quiet, as the irony landed—an exquisitely dressed woman alone on a beach in Jamaica, weeping over the one person she could never outmaneuver.

She tipped her head back, let the wind dry her cheeks, and watched her brilliant little team circle the water like sharks that could afford vacation.

42

Vee didn't have a job, technically. No badge. No clock to punch. Still, she hadn't had a free afternoon in weeks.

There was always something—another interview, another courthouse walk-through, another call with the lawyers or the Cortez family or some reporter asking if she'd comment "on background." She said yes too often. She didn't regret it.

Her finances held, for now. No debt. No loans. No degree, either, but she'd made her peace with that years ago. She lived lean. Always thrifted and wore hand-me-downs. The work didn't pay, but it fed something steadier than money.

Kha was back, orbiting close. He'd gotten into mechanic school, aced the interview, even smiled about it. Vee had told him she was proud—and she meant it—but something twisted in her gut every time he talked about torque specs and toolboxes. She hoped he'd have a better time of it. She hoped he'd get out clean.

He'd started tagging along to press events, helping with

setup, holding her bag, sitting in on strategy sessions like it was a class he didn't know he'd already enrolled in. They weren't talking about it, not directly, but something between them had softened. Rebuilt itself out of small errands and quiet loyalty.

Her name was starting to travel. People were reaching out—mechanics, organizers, widows, lawyers. Some wanted advice. Some just wanted someone to pick up the phone. She tried to do both.

She hadn't planned to be the face of anything. But here she was. And she wasn't backing down.

VEE HADN'T SHOWERED. Hadn't eaten anything green in three days. Her phone was on five percent. She was about to go over case files on the couch, again, when Morgan called.

"Get in, loser," Morgan said. "We're going shopping."

Vee blinked. "I'm not wearing pants."

"That's fine. We're not actually shopping. You're coming to my house. We're watching trash TV and eating carbs."

"I—"

"Don't argue. I already ordered food. Kieran's flying. I have wine. And popcorn. And MILF Fight Club Season 26 on queue."

And just like that, Vee was off the clock—sort of. She pulled on some old basketball shorts, and headed out the door.

By seven in the evening, Vee was curled up on Morgan's couch, knees tucked to her chest, a shared bowl of popcorn resting precariously between them. The TV was on—some garish, hyper-edited reality show neither of them were following. It buzzed in the background, loud enough to muffle the silence but not sharp enough to demand their attention.

The house looked different. Not bad, just in transition. The walls were streaked with dark paint samples, half-rolled patches of charcoal and oxblood and something green that bled almost black in the low light. Morgan had clearly committed to redoing the entire place and then lost steam halfway through.

"You're back in your goth phase," Vee said, nodding at the chaos on the walls.

Morgan didn't take her eyes off the screen. "It never left."

Kieran was gone—on a flight somewhere, working. Or maybe just giving them space. Hard to say. But he was good at not hovering. The house felt easier without him in it. Like it was back to just the two of them in the beforetimes. They'd ordered takeout without discussing it. The way you do when you've been friends long enough to know what kind of grease someone needs.

At one point, Morgan said, "How funny. We're both unemployed now." She laughed, but it came out thin.

That was when Vee noticed the tank in the corner, half-covered with a silk cloth that shimmered under the lamp. Inside, coiled like a comma made of bone, was Tiberia. Sloane's leucistic python. Pale as smoke and just as unsettling. She looked like a bolt of lightning that had decided to nap in a pile of wood shavings.

"She's yours now?" Vee asked, nodding toward the tank.

"Oh, God, no." Morgan made a face. "I'm just babysitting. Kieran's on snake duty when he gets back. I'm not thawing rats in my kitchen. Disgusting."

Then she turned to the tank and hollered at Tiberia, "Call your mother to pick you up when she's done being mysterious and tragic."

Tiberia blinked once.

Vee didn't respond. She just watched the slow movement of the snake's sides as it breathed. Barely there, like it might not be alive at all.

Morgan's voice softened. "She's trying. That doesn't mean anything yet—I'm not saying it should. I'm just saying...I won't tell you how to feel."

Vee stayed quiet. Kept her eyes on the tank like it might answer for Sloane.

Morgan tried again, gentler this time. "If you ever want me to stop talking to her—I will. You're still my number one ride-or-die. I love her, sure. Sloane's my sorority trauma bond or whatever, but you and me? That's something else."

Vee finally looked over. Her face unreadable. Not warm, but not cold either.

"You wouldn't," she said. "And you love her."

Morgan didn't argue. Didn't deny it. No one said anything else.

The episode ended. Credits rolled. The silence between them settled into the couch cushions.

The dogs stirred first, ears perking up, tails thumping. Then they trotted to the door in unison, alert and eager.

"He's home," Morgan said, without checking the clock.

Five minutes later, the front door creaked open.

"Well," Kieran O'Hara said, sighing as he kicked his boots onto the mat. "That was an ordeal."

Morgan didn't move. "You get the feeder mice?"

He stepped into the kitchen slow and heavy, like a man returning from battle with nothing but a paper bag to show for it. His pilot jacket hung half off one shoulder, his tie undone, face road-weary and blank in that particular way people got after too many flights and too few hours of sleep.

"I flew two legs into Atlanta," he said, like he was reciting it for a court. "Landed at nine. Could've gotten a hotel. Nearly did. But then I remembered I had to go mouse-hunting. For the snake."

He set the bag on the counter like it was carrying precious cargo.

"Spent forty-five minutes driving backroads trying to find frozen feeder mice. On a Sunday. In Illinois."

Vee raised her eyebrows. "And you actually found some?"

"Bait shop off Route 55," Kieran said. "Guy behind the counter didn't even blink. Told me they keep 'em near the worms."

Morgan made a face like she'd just bitten into something rotten, then let out a sharp, involuntary gag.

He cracked a dry smile. "I tipped him five bucks and said it was for my wife's other woman's snake."

He paused, then added, "Guy just nodded and said I wasn't the 'first fella today to say that.' Still not sure if he was joking."

Morgan chuckled. "See? Romance isn't dead."

"May this kind of love never find me," Vee muttered, reaching for another handful of popcorn.

"No," Kieran said, opening a can of ginger ale. "This wasn't love. This was commitment. Love would've let me sleep."

He leaned against the counter and took a long sip before adding, "Also, I'm not feeding it. I don't care how long she's been gone. I draw the line at handling thawed rodents."

Vee groaned. "You're both babies. I'll do it."

Morgan and Kieran both turned to her, eyes wide with mock surprise, and said nothing. But the look they exchanged said plenty.

Vee rolled her eyes and lobbed a popcorn kernel at Morgan's forehead.

"Shut up," she muttered. "Nobody asked you."

Then she stood, crossed the room, and yanked the silk cloth off the tank. Tiberia flicked her tongue once—slow, disinterested.

"All right, creepy girl," Vee sighed. "Let's get this over with."

She disappeared into the kitchen and came back a few minutes later with a plastic container and a pair of tongs. Morgan immediately covered her eyes like a kid at a horror movie. Kieran had already fled upstairs—the groan of old pipes and the hiss of the shower his chosen alibi for cowardice.

"Don't narrate it," Morgan groaned. "I'm serious. I will throw up."

Vee popped the lid and retrieved a thawed feeder mouse —limp, pale, its tiny claws curled.

"Your loss," she said. "This is quality enrichment content."

She dangled the mouse into the tank. Tiberia struck fast, silent. It was over in seconds. Vee snapped the lid shut.

Vee tossed the tongs in the sink with a little too much force. "And that officially maxes out my ex-girlfriend bull-shit quota for the night. I tong-fed a corpse to her emotional support reptile. I'm going home."

She grabbed her jacket off the back of the chair and slung it over her arm.

"Meeting Jerry's widow tomorrow. Press is at seven."

Morgan blinked, caught off guard by the turn. "Jesus. That's brutal."

Then, quieter: "He was a good man."

She sank back into the couch, voice softening as the

memory caught up with her. Across the room, Vee shoved on her combat boots, yanking the laces tight.

"You remember that one Thanksgiving when I was home from Penn?" Morgan said, eyes fixed somewhere past the TV. "We ended up drinking with Jerry's crew at that awful sports bar near the airport. The one with the mechanical bull and the flammable wings?"

Vee snorted. "Jerry headbutted a guy for grabbing your ass."

"Sweetest man," Morgan said, grinning. "Looked like my tío, until he unleashed violence."

"I would've done it myself," Vee said. "But I was projectile vomiting behind a Hertz shuttle."

"And you still went to work the next morning. With glitter in your eyebrows."

Vee grinned at that. Then quieted.

"...Jerry made us all come in. Said we had to impress some outside compliance guy. Thought he was full of shit."

Morgan frowned. "Wasn't that the guy who looked like a substitute teacher and asked too many questions about the coffee machine?"

Vee froze. The grin slid off her face. Her eyes went sharp, wide—the way they did when her brain latched onto something it didn't like.

"Yeah," she whispered. "Except...I don't think he asked enough."

THE CAB SMELLED, and the dome light above her flickered. Vee leaned her forehead against the window, watching the streetlights smear into long amber blades. Her breath left fog behind, dull and steady.

She couldn't stop thinking about him. That guy.

The auditor.

What was his name?

Something bland. White guy, forgettable face. Wore a tie with little blue airplanes on it and smiled like he wanted you to know he wasn't a threat. She remembered him handing out business cards. Said he was doing a "compliance sweep" on behalf of HQ. That would've been—what? Early tens. Somewhere in the thick of it. Back when the air in the hangar felt denser, heavier. When guys started coughing dry in the breakroom and nobody said a word.

The audit itself was a blur. But Jerry had been on edge—not paranoid, just watchful. He'd wanted everything clean. Organized. "Let's show them we're better than they think," he kept saying. That was Jerry. Still believed that if you followed the rules, the rules would take care of you. Still gave people the benefit of the doubt.

She'd followed his lead. Everyone had. Jerry was the kind of guy who stuck around after his shift to help someone replace a blown valve. The guy who remembered your kid's name and whether they liked Legos or dinosaurs. You trusted him. You just did.

But the auditor hadn't asked about the insulation in Hangar B. Or the way the solvents sprayed, or why the ventilation kept shorting out in winter. He'd asked about the coffee machine. The break schedules. The proper signage for emergency exits.

The wrong questions.

All the wrong goddamn questions.

Her stomach turned—not from the cab's lurching or the smell, but from something old and sour rising in her throat. He'd smiled and nodded and filed his report and then what? Disappeared? Got promoted? Got paid?

She pressed her tongue to the roof of her mouth, trying to keep the bile down.

By the time the cab turned onto her block, her hands were fists in her lap.

She threw cash at the driver without looking, slammed the door behind her, and didn't wait for change. The night air hit her like a slap—cold, wet, thick with the stink of trash day and damp leaves. She didn't care. Her boots hit pavement.

Inside, the apartment was dark except for the under-cabinet light and the high-pitched mewl of one of the cats, pissed about her lateness. Kha was snoring behind his bedroom door. She kicked off her boots, peeled off her jacket, and went straight to her bedroom—the one that used to be a sanctuary, and now looked like a crime scene archive.

Boxes lined the wall. Some labeled neatly. Others scrawled in grease pencil, duct-taped shut. She hadn't touched most of them since the day she got canned. She'd packed fast—two days before they "eliminated the position." Loaded everything into her truck like she was fleeing a crime scene.

Because maybe she was.

She yanked the top box open. A mess of loose papers. Manila folders. Spiral notebooks with dog-eared corners. Post-its with half-legible handwriting. A photo of Jerry at a union cookout, grinning wide, barbecue sauce on his cheek. She set it aside without looking too hard.

The grief pressed against her ribs like a bruise. She ignored it. She had to.

She dug deeper. Old maintenance logs. Her own scribbled notes from safety meetings. A laminated contact list. And then—bingo. A folder marked AUDIT – Q4 FY2012, scrawled in Jerry's blocky handwriting.

She dropped to the floor and flipped it open, cross-legged like a kid in detention.

There it was.

Martin G. Halberstam.

Third-party contractor. Based out of D.C. Subcontracted by a subcontractor. On paper, everything looked legitimate. Corporate white noise.

She stared at the report.

Halberstam had signed off on everything. No notes on air testing. No mention of solvent exposure. Just friendly language about "general compliance with federal standards" and "recommendation for continued self-monitoring."

Her hands curled around the edges of the folder. Her jaw locked.

She didn't touch the grief. Not yet. That could wait.

Right now, she had a name.

43

His email wasn't hard to find. When Vee reached out, he responded right away and offered to meet. He lived in Cedar Rapids now. She made the four-hour drive without hesitation.

The house was big—too big for one man—and quiet in that hollow, echoing way that meant no one had really lived in it for a while. The kind of quiet where sound didn't settle. Vee stepped inside and immediately smelled stale air, over-ripe fruit, and something vaguely chemical.

He met her at the door already looking like a man who hadn't slept through the night in months. His tie was off, his shirt half-untucked, socks mismatched. He didn't offer her a drink, just muttered something about the A/C not working right and waved vaguely toward the living room.

It wasn't even ugly. It was worse. It was dated.

Tuscan beige walls with crown molding that tried too hard. Oil-rubbed bronze light fixtures. Faux-marble coun-tertops that had once screamed wealth in 2004 and now just whispered: *you peaked during the Bush administration.* A wrought-iron wine rack that hadn't been restocked since his family left. The furniture was all tan leather and dark wood, oversized and deeply uncomfortable—like a Pier One showroom abandoned mid-divorce.

The place looked expensive and exhausted.

She followed him through the house and caught glimpses of old lives in the mess. Framed degrees in Latin. Family portraits turned facedown on a side table. A single child's drawing stuck to the fridge—faded with time, corners curling.

The man himself had aged like milk left out. Still technically in a tailored shirt, but sagging around the edges. His skin gray, hair thinning, the kind of misery that had gone past dramatic into static.

He sank into the leather couch and stared at the floor.

"I thought you'd be someone else," he said.

Vee stayed standing. "Who? A ghost?"

He flinched.

She scanned the room again. There was money here— enough to redecorate, to move on. But the house felt paused. Stuck in the exact year he'd stopped being a person.

"I keep thinking someone's going to come back," he muttered. "That there'll be a knock at the door and it'll all just...reset."

He looked up, almost smiling. "But no one's coming. I guess except for you."

Vee didn't offer comfort. That wasn't why she came.

She looked around one last time—at the dust, the driedout houseplants, the heavily used liquor cart—then met his eyes.

He didn't look at her when he started talking. Just stared down at his hands, like if he kept them still enough, maybe they wouldn't be stained.

"I worked for Heritage," he said, voice low and almost apologetic. "Internal compliance. Fifteen years."

Vee didn't respond. Didn't nod. She didn't plan on making any of this easier.

"I found the pattern," he continued. "The exposure. Long-term illness. It was clustered—mostly hangar workers. Guys like Cortez. I wrote it up. Flagged it. Attached medical logs, shift records, component lists. Everything they needed."

He paused. Something flickered in his throat—not a swallow, something smaller. A wince made of memory.

"Then a rep from the executive team showed up. Gave me a new directive. Sanitize. Reframe. Destroy the originals."

Vee bit the inside of her cheek. She knew exactly who he meant. That old guard—now half-dead, half-senile, or sealed away behind gates in Florida, breathing filtered air and hiding from lawsuits. The ones who signed the memos, cut the corners, smiled in the annual report, and vanished before the blood hit the floor.

He exhaled, long and hollow. "I did it. I complied. I kept a copy."

He finally looked up. Red-rimmed. Hollowed out.

"I told myself it was just for my own protection," he said. "I never did anything with it."

His hand moved—slow, deliberate. He slid a folder across the table. No ceremony. Just gravity.

She didn't reach for it right away. Just looked at him— this man who once wore power like armor, now slouched and sunken in a house that smelled like lemon cleaner.

Then she took the folder.

It was paper. No flash drive, no password-protected cloud. He didn't trust digital. Inside were timestamped scans, charts, metadata trails. The original audit report, unedited. Everything they'd need to back the union's demands with a tactical nuke.

She flipped through the first few pages just to be sure. She didn't thank him.

She stood.

No closure. No absolution.

At the door, she paused. Just for a breath. Not because he deserved it. Just to make sure he remembered.

Then she said, quiet and brutal:

"You don't get credit for cracking now. You were always broken."

He just nodded slowly and poured himself a drink.

She turned to leave, halfway through the doorway, when his voice caught again—small, almost embarrassed.

"There's one more thing," he said. "The safety video."

Vee paused. Didn't turn around.

"They made us reshoot it after the audit. Said the original version was too 'panic-inducing.'" He let out a dry laugh. "The first cut actually explained the exposure risks. Real charts. Real cases. One of the narrators was a hangar mechanic. Died two years later."

He stared down at his hands.

"They shelved it. Said it didn't align with Heritage's 'culture of resilience.'" His hand tightened around the glass. "They replaced it with animation. A cartoon wrench named Wally."

Vee didn't move. Didn't blink.

He tried to smile, but it cracked halfway. "Wally teaches you to wash your hands and hydrate."

She stopped in the doorway again. Just for a second.

"Where is it?" she asked, still not facing him. "The video."

He shifted behind her. "Legal archive. That's where they put the stuff that's too sensitive for ops. Red-label, physical only. No digital backup. Locked filing. Might still be sitting in a vault under HQ. Or in one of the auxiliary buildings in Aurora. Who knows."

"That's not helpful."

He shrugged. "Wasn't cleared for that level. I just watched them pack the boxes."

Legal archive.

The words sat heavy in her gut.

She exhaled through her nose. Steady.

I wonder if Sloane—

No.

Don't you dare open that door.

She walked out without another word.

44

Sloane Campbell had not known decadence, not truly, until the Gulfstream skimmed over Biscayne Bay and descended toward an island that didn't appear on commercial aviation maps. From above, Fisher Island looked less like a neighborhood and more like a tax shelter in bloom—red-tile roofs tucked between imported palms, golf greens manicured with the neurosis of royal gardens.

The ferry terminal, visible only if you knew where to look, buzzed with quiet luxury. No signs. No lines. Just armed calm in navy polos and mirrored sunglasses.

The estate was set back from the marina, flanked by white stucco villas owned by minor oligarchs and hedge fund escapees. Vivienne's compound—because it was absolutely a compound—sprawled like a dare: part Brutalist monolith, part Balinese hallucination. There were koi larger than toddlers in the reflecting pools, eucalyptus-scented misters tucked into the bougainvillea, and someone had arranged Sloane's initials in white orchid petals by the front door.

Inside, the air was cool with the chill of engineered wealth. A Matisse sketch leaned against travertine like someone had forgotten it there. The Murano glass chandeliers had been rewired by artisans Vivienne flew in from Venice. The "indoor slippers" offered at the door were Prada, naturally, and monogrammed in her exact font.

She had assumed it would be a party. One of those sprawling carnivalesque fundraisers where people in caftans whispered about SPACs between microdoses. But no. There were five women in the room.

Six, counting her.

Vivienne Yue stood in a sunken conversation pit upholstered in suede the color of spilled champagne. Her linen dress looked hand-woven by virgins in the Pyrenees.

"You're here," she said, like Sloane had been summoned.

The other women turned with slow, devastating grace. Sloane knew the choreography. One was a Hong Kong cinema legend with a jewelry line discreetly valued at $300 million. Another owned half the shipping lanes in the Strait of Malacca. The third designed gowns worn only once, exclusively by people whose deaths made headlines.

The fourth woman didn't bother with a greeting. She and Vivienne had been suitemates at Dartmouth, back when her father still held office. The Secret Service was somewhere on the island. Still is, if you know where to look.

Sloane sat. Crossed her ankles. Let the silk hem of her dress fall with studied elegance.

Vivienne lifted a glass of something that cost more than most cars.

"I'd like to propose a toast," she said, her tone lacquered in the kind of fluency you can't fake.

"To Sloane Campbell," she said. "Who got me my first

dominant share. Who read the fine print. Who caught the buried clause. Who delivered the Heritage board to *me*."

Five pairs of eyes turned toward her, all measuring value.

Sloane smiled. Not with charm—with precision.

The air tasted of guava, salt, and bloodless war.

She raised her glass.

"To firsts," she said. "And the fools who think they're final."

Vivienne leaned in, her tone veering into that dangerous lilt—half debutante, half guillotine.

"Oh," she added, bright as spilled champagne, "you also helped me beat Daddy's stake."

She held her glass aloft.

"He only had ten percent. I've got twenty-two now." Then the smile: all teeth, no warmth. "It's not a majority— but it's enough to make the board check my mood before they piss."

A ripple of laughter. The kind that meant they knew. That kind of stake didn't buy control—it bought deference.

Sloane didn't react.

Vivienne sipped again. "He was mad. And proud. But mostly mad."

Sloane had come armed with briefs. Not legal ones—those had already been committed to memory—but strategic ones. A soft pitch folded into a conversation. She had assumed Vivienne invited her here to talk shop in the language of trust: asset maps, proxy swings, soft power plays over citrus and spa water.

But Vivienne refused to speak business. She refused to speak, period, unless it involved shoes.

"No spreadsheets," she'd said that morning, already in head-to-toe white linen, sunglasses large enough to signal a lawsuit. "You're overdressed. We're going shopping."

Sloane opened her mouth to object, but Vivienne had already swept out of the villa. Two minutes later, they were in a private car, seats scented faintly of vetiver and wealth. The driver did not ask for a destination.

They started in Bal Harbour. Of course. Where else did billionaires pretend retail was spiritual? Chanel first, for ceremony. Then Saint Laurent, because Vivienne thought Sloane's existing wardrobe was "too prosecutorial."

"You dress like a threat," she said, gently draping a dove-gray coat over Sloane's shoulders. "Which is hot, but like...exhausting for brunch."

At Hermes, Vivienne demanded champagne and got it. Sloane didn't ask from where. The staff knew not to speak unless spoken to, and the jewelry came out like weapons—delicate, stupidly heavy, curated for people who never paid retail.

"Vivienne," Sloane said, fingers brushing the edge of a price tag she refused to look at. "You don't need to outfit me like I came in off the street."

Vivienne's smile didn't shift. "Of course not," she said. "But let's not pretend we're all working with the same baseline."

She said it gently—like a kindness. Like facts. She then tossed three Cartier boxes into the growing pile of soft tissue and bespoke sin. Her AmEx hadn't been swiped once. Everything was just...noted. Charged to the ether.

"I don't have very many friends," she said, languidly,

twirling the stem of her glass like it was someone's neck. "The ones I do have are mostly leveraged or hostile."

Sloane arched an eyebrow. "And you're trying to buy me?"

Vivienne grinned. "No. I'm trying to adopt you.

"Have you tried a local animal shelter?"

Vivienne rolled her eyes.

"I want a friend. A real one. You're like me—quietly fucked-up, brain running twenty degrees above normal, and smart enough to act like it's nothing. People never see us coming."

"I'm not—"

"You are," Vivienne interrupted, setting the glass down. "You just won't admit it. And that's fine. I'm patient with emotionally repressed women who destroy men for a living."

Sloane opened her mouth again, but Vivienne cut her off once more—only this time, her tone shifted.

"I know you're planning something," she said, light as air. "Something about the board. And I'm telling you now: if you think I'm going to be collateral damage, I'll take you down with me."

Sloane didn't move. Didn't even breathe, for a second. That grin was still there. So was the threat.

"I'm not going to burn you," Sloane said, quiet but steady. "The mesothelioma cover-up happened before you came onto the board. I can prove that. You're clean."

Vivienne tilted her head. "How do you know I didn't know? How do you know Daddy didn't?"

"I don't," Sloane replied. "And you're not going to tell me. So I'm going to do what I came here to do, and you're either going to help me, look away...or get very uncomfortable."

Vivienne let out a soft breath—almost a laugh.

"This isn't really about the board, though, is it?"

She swirled the champagne, eyes sharp. "It's about Ava Thompkins. And her board pets. You're not aiming for the company—you're aiming for the woman behind it."

She smiled, almost admiring. "I get it. She's mythic. Dangerous. The kind of woman you don't look at directly."

She giggled.

"You're lucky I'm too...comfortable to be one of hers, Sloane."

Vivienne stared at her for a long moment. Then smiled —wider this time. Almost fond.

"Well," she said, reaching for a ring she had no intention of wearing, "I do love a purge."

Sloane exhaled, just barely. "So you'll help?"

"I'll help," Vivienne said. "But I'm not saving you. I'm saving myself. And if you ever even think of throwing me under the bus—"

"You'll take me with you. I know."

Vivienne smiled, all silk and scalpel. "Please. I don't sink —I displace."

Something dropped in Sloane's stomach. It always did when Vivienne uncoiled just enough to bare teeth.

"Now," Vivienne said, "can we stop pretending this is a strategy meeting and grab lunch? I'm starving."

"Of course. We're adjourned."

"Fantastic. To girls like us." Vivienne lifted her glass with unbothered grace

Sloane tilted her head, almost fond. "I suppose the real tragedy would be believing we're above any of it."

They clinked.

There were no friends in this room. Just two women circling the same fire, trying not to be the one who burned first.

45

Chicago, again.

Sloane Campbell now had three roommates staying with her in her Gold Coast apartment overlooking Lake Michigan The glass-wrapped tower was still paid off, but the energy had changed. Budget cuts. Pay reductions. Full-on fixer austerity. Kenji had taken the guest suite. The twins split the office, each claiming half like it was Berlin. Even though Sloane, in her silk robes and eye masks, had lied to her father about not having space just a couple of weeks ago. The man had already returned back to New York.

She was sleeping fine. On Pratesi sheets, with room to spare.

What she didn't have was peace.

The apartment had transformed into a low-budget war room. Laptops on the kitchen island. Whiteboards in the hallway. Late-night ramen next to top-secret binders. No one said it out loud, but they were all in it. Again. The same way they had been in three years ago. And seven years ago. And in that disgusting East Coast church basement with the rats and the burner phones.

Kenji Miwa, former top New York City detective, now full-time disappointed uncle, had given up half his retainer and most of his patience. He sighed every time Sloane did her midnight pole routine to Philip Glass in the living room —shirtless, focused, perfect.

"You know, Counselor," he said, flat, "some of us are trying to eat."

"You have a perfectly nice space to retreat to," she replied, not missing a beat.

The twins didn't mind. Andi sat cross-legged on the floor, sipping green tea. El hovered behind the couch, suspiciously quiet, both of them harboring respectful, delusional crushes on their boss like it was a team-building exercise.

The team plotted over dinner. Wine, burgers, and asset maps. Andi opened her laptop with a soft chime. El pulled up encrypted chat logs. Kenji dragged a chair over and dropped a manila folder on the table.

"New strategy," Sloane said. "We bait the board."

She slid her phone across the table. Onscreen: a redacted investor memo. Real, damning, dangerous—but just enough to cause a stir, not a coup.

"Private equity wants the hangars," she said. "Short-term returns. Sell the land. Half the board are getting kickbacks."

Kenji skimmed it. "That's real?"

"It's real. But not filed. Still whisper-level. If it leaks, it panics. And I can be the one to clean it up."

El grinned. "So you're pushing a new scandal to fix the current scandal."

"I'm reintroducing demand," Sloane said. "Make them scared without me."

She'd already sent the memo—along with a few other things—to the only person she trusted to move it with precision and malice.

Three nights ago, she'd emailed Noah Feldman-Bloom under a burner alias:

Subject Line: The Enemy of my Enemy

Attached: a cluster of internal audit docs she and Zora had buried months ago. Sloane hadn't read all two-thousand pages—just skimmed for buzzwords like "asbestos," "ventilation," "noncompliant." Zora had flagged them before her betrayal. Which meant anything inside could be a trap—or worse, a dead end.

But Noah had read every single line. Probably within a day of receiving them.

There was a line buried deep in a summary note from several years back:

Refer to training tape 119F. Per HR, video not retained.

That sentence alone had probably ruined his week.

Tonight, Noah showed up in jeans and a T-shirt, eyes sharp.

"This better be worth it," he said, stepping into the kitchen. "I read that audit packet three times. And I swear to God, if you're holding back—"

"In due time," Sloane said, already setting the table. "Try the appetizer. Bacon-wrapped dates."

Andi offered him a bowl. El poured wine. Kenji gave him a nod like, *you're brave for showing up.*

Dinner was chaotic, but the agenda wasn't.

They laid out the plan. Leak the investor memo anonymously. Let Noah circulate it to union-tied outlets. Let the press catch wind. Let Heritage panic. Let Lucretia reach out. And when she did—

Sloane already had the text ready.

You don't need to rely on Ava's to keep your seat. You don't need to rely on Ava at all.
Let me back in—and I'll give you something better than control.
I'll give you a agency.
—S

It wasn't a threat. It was a coronation.

Noah leaned back in his chair, expression unreadable.

"This is cute," he said finally. "But you and I both know the investor memo's a fart in a wind tunnel. It'll scare the board, maybe. But it won't win the public."

Sloane arched an eyebrow. "What will count as a win for you then?"

He leaned forward.

"That tape. Training tape 119F. I know what it means. It shows faulty filtration during onboarding. Probably shows Jerry. Maybe others. And if it's missing? That's obstruction."

Sloane stayed quiet. Kenji looked at her, then at the twins.

"You knew this was coming," Noah said. "You baited me with the documents *your team* buried. Now I'm here. So where is it?"

"We're don't have that one," she said.

He stood up, grabbed his coat.

"You want my help? Find it. You don't find that tape, you're not serious. You're just another fixer with a savior fantasy."

The door shut behind him.

"He's hot when he's angry," Andi said.

El looked up. "He didn't even stay for dessert."

Sloane poured herself more wine. "He wasn't here for the food."

Kenji spoke next, voice low. "You think the tape's still out there?"

Sloane stared into her glass.

"I think if it is," she said, "it's the match."

46

Vee didn't knock.

She never did, not for people like this. She slid in on muscle memory, let the soft-close door seal shut behind her, and kept walking.

Noah had called last-minute. Bubbe sick again—delirious, coughing, calling him names in Yiddish he wouldn't translate. "I'd go," he'd said. "But I trust you more than anyone."

"Not comforting," Vee had muttered.

Now here she was, standing in Sloane Campbell's surgically perfect apartment, and every pair of eyes in the room said what the fuck.

She saw the hacker twins first.

She didn't know what she expected when Noah said "the hacker twins" like they were underground folklore—but it sure as hell wasn't this.

One had pink braids twisted into a crown and wore an oversized vintage tee that had clearly seen some shit. The other had a razor-sharp green bob that framed their jaw like a blade, and a blazer with chains hanging off it.

Vee didn't need names—Noah had given her the cheat sheet. El was pink braids. Andi was green bob. Noted. Didn't matter. What mattered was how they moved: like one lethal organism split in two. No wasted motion. No repeating themselves. Just sync.

A breath later, Kenji Mura drifted behind them—too casual to be casual—tucking something back into a holster under his windbreaker like he'd just changed his mind about pulling it. They'd been waiting. Too long. Noah was two hours late, and no one had heard from him. She knew how that kind of silence read in a room like this. Badly.

Nobody spoke.

Vee didn't even scan for Sloane. She knew where that woman was without looking—could feel the tension coming off her in waves.

But it wasn't just her. It was all of them. El, Andi, Kenji— the little brain trust behind the glossy fall of everything she loved. These were the ones who'd buried the union in NDAs and counter-narratives. Who'd helped Sloane spin worker blood into compliance metrics.

They didn't hang her personally.

They just built the scaffold.

And here they were, lounging like it wasn't all still on fire.

A room full of the people who ruined her life—and now she had to collaborate nicely?

No.

Fuck that.

Let them flinch.

She walked into the middle of the room and parked herself against the wall.

"Noah's out," she said. "I'm here."

El opened her mouth, then closed it again.

"Emergency?" Kenji asked carefully.

Vee nodded once. "His grandma's sick. Like, hospital sick. I was closer."

The silence that followed stretched like bad insulation.

"Someone tell me what's going on," she added. "Now."

Andi cleared their throat. "Right. So. We found a recurring entry in the Director of Security's sandboxed calendar —encrypted and obfuscated. It ties to a storage unit in DuPage. Changes name every quarter, but the location's stable. We think it's a stash site. Could be the training video."

"El scrubbed the metadata," Kenji said. "It's not linked to any active employee address. But the payment trail routes back to a holding company tied to Heritage."

"It's deliberate," El added. "This is placed. Hidden, but findable. Which means either it's real—"

"Or bait," Kenji cut in. "Might be one of our friends, Ava or Lucretia, laying traps. Misdirection. Classic disinfo shit."

"It could also be Zora drawing us out," Sloane said from behind her glass of something amber and expensive. "I taught her to layer false trails."

Vee didn't flinch. Didn't look at her. Didn't even breathe in her direction.

She focused on the twins.

"You run the camera sweep on the facility yet?"

"We're getting into the backend now," El replied. "External surveillance is old-school. Analog feeds. Should be easy to interrupt. We're working on storage unit blueprints and zoning permits."

Vee nodded once, already planning.

She could feel Sloane staring, waiting, like a pressure valve no one had the guts to twist.

"I'll drive," Vee said.

Two words, clean and loaded.

Sloane exhaled like she was bracing. "No."

That got Vee's attention—not Sloane herself, but the nerve.

She turned slightly. Not enough to meet her eyes. Just enough to speak.

"You don't even know what part of Illinois this is. You think a GPS will be enough?"

"We don't need—"

"I'm the only one who's actually from here." Her voice cut like wire. "I know which streets have cop cams. I know which county patrols ignore what after midnight."

Sloane said nothing. But her posture went rigid.

Vee stepped forward, still not facing her. "Also, you can get your little team in the door. But Noah and I get first look. No chain-of-custody bullshit. No private archive. We get the tape. We hold it. Before any of you touch it."

El and Andi shifted in their seats. Kenji ran a hand down his face, quietly.

Sloane didn't argue.

Which meant she agreed.

Vee turned back to the wall, her job done.

The decision had been made—quiet, sober, no room for flair. Hit the DuPage storage unit at 2:00 a.m. the following night. No backup, no noise. No heroes.

Vee stood at the edge of the kitchen island and cracked her neck once.

"Give me everything you've got," she said, leaning her hip against the counter. "Blueprints, parcel numbers, camera placements, any zoning irregularities or unregistered traffic sensors. We're building a route."

The others hesitated. Kenji shuffled over and dumped a bunch of street maps on the counter. The twins looked like they were waiting for a reason to leave the room. They both just got back on their laptops and started sending things to the printer.

Vee began sketching.

Not some "mind palace" bullshit. Just raw logistics. Pen to paper. Inked lines and escape branches fanning like arteries across a map of western Chicagoland. A web of muscle memory.

She spoke in short, clipped bursts.

"This lot connects to two back alleys—one's blocked off with city trash, but there's a four-foot gap if you're not useless. Traffic cam on the northeast corner—can't cut it. But if we time the light right, it won't catch anything that matters. This intersection right here? Don't turn. Loop the industrial park, cut through the bread factory lot. I'll confirm in the morning, but pretty sure their third shift clocks out at 2:15. Nobody questions a car sitting there."

Andi blinked. "How do you know all this?"

Vee didn't look up. "This isn't storytime."

That shut them up—but only just. They had that look: sharp, half-smirking. Like the suspicion was already blooming, and it'd take maybe two keystrokes to trace the truth.

They mapped in silence after that. No talking. Just strategy.

Kenji offered questions she didn't answer. Andi tried to guess her process, then gave up halfway. El looked like they were caught between fascination and mild fear.

Vee didn't perform. She calculated. She charted. She cut the city open and laid out its guts, street by street, warehouse by warehouse, until every arterial exit had a plan and three backups.

By the end, no one said thank you. They just backed away like they were afraid she might draw blood if touched.

She liked it better that way.

El and Andi wandered off to annotate the printouts. Kenji mumbled something about crashing.

Vee walked to the balcony. Lit her vape. Pulled in something synthetic and sharp. Let the streetlights simmer below her—flat, low, wide open like an old scar.

She was scared at how fast it came back.

Not just the instincts—but the hunger.

She didn't drive getaway anymore. That part of her life was over. These days, it was cash races and closed streets, midnight loops through industrial parks with no spectators, just engines and ego. Still illegal. Still fast. But no crew, no cargo, no consequences beyond her own.

Just speed, raw and loud. Just control—for once, hers.

The tech was newer now—better cameras, sharper patrols, plate scanners that blinked before you hit the gas. But her brain still mapped the city like it had teeth. Speed traps, blind corners, warehouse lots with just enough shadow to vanish into.

She learned all that when she was seventeen—running jobs for her brother. No questions, no second chances. One wrong turn back then didn't mean a warning. It meant years behind bars.

Now?

Now it was different. Kind of.

Maybe a ticket. Maybe a night in lockup.

But she still clocked patrols without blinking. Still read traffic patterns like a second language. Still knew how to slide from one county to the next without touching a single lens.

The risk was smaller.

The thrill wasn't.

And that was before this job.

Before tomorrow.

The life didn't need her full-time to come knocking.

THE BALCONY DOOR slid open behind her.

Sloane stepped out carrying a glass of water. "You okay?"

Vee didn't turn. Didn't take the glass.

"You didn't eat."

"I'm fine."

"I just—" Sloane paused. "Did you...get a new ear piercing? It looks..."

Vee exhaled smoke into the sky. "Let's not do this."

Sloane hesitated. "Do what?"

"This. Small talk. Nostalgia. Whatever this is." Vee's voice dropped into something low and serrated. "I'm here for the tape. For Noah. For Jerry. That's all. Let's not pretend this is anything else."

Silence.

When Vee finally glanced sideways, Sloane looked like she'd just been slapped. Stiff shoulders. That tired mask cracking right at the mouth. A blink too slow to hide how hard it hit.

And fuck, that wasn't what Vee wanted.

She turned back to the skyline. She hadn't meant to gut her—just cut clean. Boundaries. She needed them. She had them. Sloane no longer had the right to climb over the fence around her heart.

Even if sometimes, in the quiet, Vee still remembered what it felt like—being seen by her. Held in that piercing, exacting way Sloane had of watching people like she was solving them.

No.

No, no, no.

She stayed outside a minute longer after Sloane left. Watched the lights blur along Lake Shore Drive, all movement and no meaning. Let the vape burn her lungs raw, just to remind herself what pain was supposed to feel like.

Inside, El handed her the marked printouts. "Here. It's all annotated."

Vee nodded, didn't thank them. Tucked the folder under her arm.

She glanced back once on her way to the door.

Sloane stood at the edge of the living room, alone, unreadable. Her posture was perfect, her face composed. But her eyes—god, her eyes—looked cracked down the middle.

Like she'd expected something from Vee.

Like she was still waiting.

Vee left without a word.

She barely slept that night.

Not because of nerves. Not because of fear.

Because that fucking look stayed etched behind her eyelids like a scar.

47

Vee spent the late afternoon under the hood of her car in the back of a shed no one ever used in the salvage yard. The floor was oil-streaked concrete, lit by a single work light. Her hands were raw, the skin around her knuckles split and darkened with embedded grease. She didn't wear gloves. The car—a lowered sedan with gutted rear seats, reinforced panels, and a rebuilt engine—was built for torque, built for silence, built to move fast when it mattered and disappear when it didn't. She knew every inch of it. Every mod was intentional.

Across the garage, Woytek was hunched over a folding table stacked with preprinted temporary tags. He was muttering to himself while feeding fresh sheets through a desktop printer patched together with duct tape and exposed wiring. The tags looked good. Clean fonts. Legit serial sequences. Every single one could survive a quick scan.

She worked fast but checked everything twice—tire pressure, brake response, coolant levels. Nothing fancy. Just efficient, brutal readiness. Her hair was pulled back in a

French braid tight enough to give her a headache. She didn't notice. Didn't care. When the wrench slipped and caught her thumb, she didn't flinch. She didn't even look up.

She didn't stop until the sky went black and Woytek's poker crew started showing up—guys in oil-stained jeans and warehouse hoodies, hauling Żywiec six-packs and off-brand kielbasa-flavored chips from the corner store. Someone fired up disco polo on a busted Bluetooth speaker.

The call came in. "Ready." She changed in under a minute and drove.

By 1:30 AM, the streets were stripped bare—only the hum of city infrastructure, distant sirens, and the crackle of occasional static through comms. The industrial park was silent. Sterile rows of corrugated metal buildings under sodium lights, all indistinguishable from one another except for the one that mattered. "Genesis Records." No signage. No branding. Simply a keypad by the door that looked new enough to belong somewhere else.

Vee cut the lights and dropped Kenji off without a word. He slipped out of the car with a backpack slung over one shoulder and walked like he belonged there. She eased the vehicle back onto the road and circled the block, slow, methodical, not drawing attention. Andi's voice checked in over comms. They were parked a few hundred feet away in the recon van with El, who was already running interference on the cameras.

Inside the facility, Kenji's breathing came through the earpiece—steady, shallow, quiet. The space was climate-controlled, sterile, and silent enough to hear the soles of his shoes press against the floor.

"Motion sensor already tagged you," El's voice crackled over the comms.

"Doesn't matter," Kenji replied. He kept moving.

Silence followed, then a soft mechanical hiss. She guessed he had popped the lock.

Static thinned. A low, grainy thump came through—probably a door swinging open—and then Kenji spoke.

"Steel walls. Shelves. Nothing labeled."

She pictured it as he moved, step by step. Boxes. Dust. Whatever climate control that place had, it wasn't for comfort. He exhaled once, too close to his mic.

"There's a container. Fireproof. Got a film reel next to it. Label says 'OSHA Training 2003 – Master Cut.'"

Vee's pulse kicked. She didn't say anything yet.

"That's it," Sloane said through comms, voice clean and cold.

Vee's head jerked slightly.

What. The. Fuck.

She hadn't known Sloane would be around. Wasn't supposed to be. Last she checked, the plan had her holed up in that Gold Coast apartment with a VPN and a glass of overpriced wine. This wasn't for her.

But Sloane did what she wanted. She always had.

Just showed up in places she was never invited to—and expected the world to rearrange itself around her.

Vee gritted her teeth. Didn't say a word. Because she wasn't an idiot. She would never waste energy on ego when someone else was inside with live rounds in the mix.

Instead, she said, "Grab all of it. Then get out."

They could hear Kenji move quickly. Something clattered against what sounded like metal. A short pause. Then Kenji's voice: "Got the canister. And the drive."

His footsteps shifted—quicker now. A sudden surge of static hit the channel—short, sharp, like power snapping on. Vee leaned in.

Kenji muttered, low and tight, "Lights just came on. Fuck—"

The sound that followed wasn't clear. The audio feed distorted—clattering, something falling, a scrape, then a gunshot.

"Kenji? Say something."

No answer.

"Kenji—"

"Got it. I'm out." His voice was tight. Sharp with pain. Something was wrong.

Vee swung around the block in time to see the side entrance crack open. Kenji burst through it, one hand clutching his backpack, the other pressed tight to his arm. Blood was streaming through his fingers, soaking the cuff of his sleeve.

Vee hit the brakes, popped the door. He dove in, hard, shoulder-first, knocking into the console. His foot slipped on the mat—blood. She caught the tang of iron in the air. He hissed through his teeth but said nothing.

Door slammed shut. No seatbelt. Just motion.

Behind them, a black SUV surged out from the far side of the lot. No plates. No headlights. High beams flashed once before cutting off completely. The men inside didn't yell, didn't demand surrender. They opened fire once, the shot hitting pavement shy of the bumper.

Kenji grunted. "They got my arm."

Vee said nothing. She shifted gears and gunned the engine. Her car responded immediately—silent and brutal acceleration as they took the first right, then another. The SUV kept pace.

No music. No chatter. Only the sound of tires gripping asphalt and the low thrum of a calibrated engine doing exactly what it had been built to do.

She took them off the main road, jumped a curb, and veered onto a narrow service lane that ran parallel to the expressway. The SUV followed, engine snarling behind them.

Then—sirens.

From the other end of the lane.

"Shit," Kenji said, barely able to hold himself upright in the backseat.

Vee didn't say anything. She checked the mirrors, downshifted, and recalculated. Her hands stayed steady. Her focus didn't waver.

The squad car came out of nowhere—no siren, only the flash of lights behind a delivery truck and the howl of tires a half-second too late. Vee didn't slow down. She tapped the brake enough to feint, then yanked the wheel into a hard right, cutting down an access road behind a shuttered daycare and punching it past the faded yellow caution tape.

Behind her, the SUV didn't hesitate. Whoever they were, they weren't spooked by cops. Which meant they were either better armed, better paid, or had someone higher up in their pocket. Probably all three.

She kept her hands steady on the wheel, eyes sweeping intersections faster than the onboard GPS could process. Cops behind the SUV, SUV behind her. She threaded the car through the back end of a strip mall that had been gutted. Glass crunched under the tires as she cleared the loading dock and took the corner wide to avoid a dead fridge that had been dumped behind a payday loan storefront.

Kenji groaned from the back seat.

She risked a glance. His hand had gone slack over the wound, blood pooling under his elbow.

Not fatal. Yet.

"Still breathing?"

"Yeah."

She couldn't tell if it was bad, not from this angle. She scanned the mirror—there was blood on his shirt, smeared across his ribs. Not pumping, not pooling. Enough to escalate things but not enough to stop.

Comms crackled again. Sloane's voice came through the earpiece, too sharp, too loud. "Is Kenji alright?"

"He's fine," Vee said. She kept her voice flat. No heat. No panic.

Sloane didn't shut up. "Vee--"

Vee yanked the earpiece halfway out before Sloane's voice could wind her way into her mind and take hold. The SUV was still behind her, barely holding traction. The cops weren't even aiming for it anymore. They were locked onto her vehicle.

She threaded through the construction zone fast enough to jolt the undercarriage—metal groaning over uneven concrete—then veered behind a barricade marked NO THRU ACCESS – CITY WORKS. The SUV followed, tires grinding dust and debris, still gaining.

Half-hidden beneath a collapsed scaffold and a rusted-out Bobcat was a chain-link gate, half torn from its frame. She clipped it with the bumper, punched through, and dropped them down a steep service ramp that wasn't on any map.

No lights. No signs. Just black tunnel and the echo of their own tires.

The SUV crept forward, high beams skimming over a turn that wasn't a turn—just a drop, sudden and unmarked, maybe fifty feet down. They stepped on the break hard right before they could tip over the edge.

Too steep. Too unknown.

That bought her four seconds. It was more than enough.

She killed the headlights, let the engine roll on idle, and steered by memory. This place had been a Cold War fallout tunnel, or a trolley repair line, or a city lie—depending on who you asked. What mattered was: the kids who ran the midnight quarter-mile swore you could ditch a cop in here and not leave a trace.

Or so claimed the barely-legal adrenaline junkies who treated hearsay like gospel. Vee knew better. She did. But tonight, she'd taken their word—and now she was hoping to hell it held up.

Two rights. A left. Then up a ramp lined with busted halogens and moss-cracked walls.

She let out a shuddering exhale.

She emerged on the second sublevel of a shuttered parking garage. It had been sealed from the main entrance for over a decade.

She cut the engine.

Kenji coughed behind her, wet and close to cracking.

"I need pressure on that," she told him. She popped the glove compartment, tossed a sealed trauma kit into his lap without looking back. "Now."

Outside, she could still hear the sirens. They were heading south now. Wrong direction. Perfect.

She stayed behind the wheel, jaw locked, hands steady. The adrenaline hadn't dipped yet, but her focus hadn't cracked either. Not even close.

The garage stank of mold and piss, lit by flickering overheads that hadn't seen maintenance since before the pandemic. Vee pulled the car into the far corner, behind a line of broken concrete barriers and a busted ticket machine. The second vehicle—a gray Camry with temporary tags and a quarter tank—was parked two levels up, tucked behind a column.

She cut the engine.

Then the comms went sideways.

A sharp pop of static. Then shouting—El or Andi, it was hard to tell. High-pitched, clipped off fast. Movement. Something metallic crashing.

A yell.

It was so garbled it could have been anyone. It could have been Sloane's.

Then silence.

Vee's body locked. Every part of her went still.

She forced her fingers to move. One at a time. Back to the now.

Kenji stirred beside her.

She didn't speak. Not yet.

She opened the door, stepped out, and told him, "Out."

Kenji groaned but moved, one hand still pressed to the side of his ribs. Blood had soaked through his shirt and was starting to dry at the edges. Not deep enough to kill him, but messy. He stumbled once getting out of the car, muttered something low and ragged, then caught himself on the door frame.

Vee yanked the pack from the backseat and shoved it against his chest. "You're taking the Camry. Second level up. Go north till you hit 47th. Switch to surface streets. Then disappear."

Kenji blinked, his face unreadable in the dark. "You're giving this to me?" He patted the bag once, lazy. "You're serious?"

She didn't react.

His hand finally closed over the strap. "Huh."

She started the car. "Try not to die in the stairwell."

That got a grunt. Maybe agreement. Maybe not.

He didn't respond. She heard his boots on concrete as he limped off into the dark, dragging the pack and muttering something too low to catch. The moment he was out of sight, she exhaled. Then she pulled her backup phone from her boot.

One text from an unknown number.

We lost Sloane.

Vee stopped breathing.

Her body didn't go limp—it locked. Like something inside her snapped taut and refused to let go. The phone stayed in her hand, screen burning against her skin, but the rest of her went cold. She sat there, rigid in the driver's seat, listening to the sound of nothing. A full minute passed like that. Maybe longer.

Then the world started dripping back in.

She swallowed. Once. Then forced her fingers to move.

She tried Sloane's burner.

Prayed it was still with her.

48

They were still parked on a forgotten side street, deep in the industrial guts of DuPage County.

No one reached for the ignition. Not yet. Not until word came through that Vee and Kenji had made the switch.

The van sat next to a rusted sign that hung on one bent screw and read: Permit Parking Only. 11PM–5AM. Violators Will Be Ticketed.

No one actually enforced that ordinance. Everyone knew that. Everyone with a life knew that. But of course—tonight, of all nights—a municipal parking officer emerged from the dark like divine punishment in a neon vest. City-issued Prius. Flashlight. Attitude. A man who thought a badge-shaped patch made him the final arbiter of civic order.

Sloane clocked him the moment he stepped into the beam of the van's headlights—late thirties, the gait of someone who failed his psych eval for real policing but couldn't quite let the dream die.

"You can't park here," he said, shining his light directly at the windshield. "This is permit-only past eleven."

El rolled the window down halfway, gave him a slow blink and a flat "Didn't know."

Andi muttered, "We'll move," without looking up from the burner laptop.

That should've been the end of it. But El rolled her eyes. And that—that—was the mistake.

His posture transformed completely—suddenly calculating and predatory, but with an unsettling theatrical quality that felt entirely performative.

He stepped closer. His expression shifted as he shined the flashlight in El and Andi's faces. Not just suspicion—something smaller, uglier. A flicker of amusement, maybe. Or contempt.

Five years ago, this man wouldn't have looked twice. Nothing to see. Just two quiet shadows in oversized hoodies. That was before the hormones. Before the twins stopped trying to make themselves smaller.

He walked around. Flashlight scanned the cab. Then the back. Then the rear tag.

A paper license plate. Slightly waterlogged. Not issued by anyone reputable.

He tapped it with his finger. Squinted.

"This looks bogus," he muttered, using his scanner to read it. "This tag ain't right."

Sloane felt her pulse spike. She shifted in the back seat, legs folded under her, dressed head to toe in black—Asics worn down to soft soles, Lululemon top cinched tight against adrenaline, her hair yanked back so hard it tugged at her temples. Everything about her was legal-adjacent. And failing.

"You're not law enforcement," she said coolly, her voice low and clipped.

But the man was already reaching for his phone.

"Don't need to be a cop to call one."

Andi didn't wait.

She moved like it was reflex, like the part of her brain that processed morality had gone offline the minute his flashlight hit the tag. She opened the door, stepped out, and in a single fluid motion, put him in a rear chokehold so quiet it bordered on surgical. His phone hit the ground. His flashlight spun wildly, beam slicing across the cracked pavement. Then he slumped.

He was breathing. Unconscious. Mouth slack.

"He's fine," Andi said. "We're not."

Panic detonated inside Sloane's chest.

"They'll track his GPS," El said, already unhooking the power bank from the server stack. "We have ninety seconds."

Sloane didn't move.

Couldn't. Her brain was still parsing statutes while her body refused to respond to reality. The meter guy was slumped on the sidewalk, semi-conscious and softly groaning, the phone beside him blinking.

And then El's voice—sharp, high-pitched, unlike anything Sloane had ever heard from her.

"Move!"

The back doors swung open.

"You need to run," El hissed. "Now."

Andi grabbed Sloane's upper arm hard—too hard—and dragged her halfway to the side door before shoving her forward with both hands.

"Go. GO. You don't wait, you don't look back. GO!"

Sloane stumbled, heart slamming, ankles folding over cracked concrete. They had never—ever— spoken to her like that.

She twisted halfway, breath catching—the man on the

pavement groaned again—soft, pained, slowly returning to consciousness. His flashlight had rolled out of reach. One sneaker was off. His phone lay face-down beside him, its screen cracked.

Sloane stood in the van's open side door, half-shadowed by the dome light. Her brain was backfiring in all directions —estimating their exposure, the felony count, the likelihood of federal escalation. The law had never felt this physical before.

El didn't stop moving. She was at the back of the van, hunched over the baby server rig they'd mounted just yesterday. It was already half-stripped. Drives slid into a strawberry-print tote bag. RAM sticks clattered against cables. A coiled ethernet cord was yanked and stuffed with one hand while she rummaged for a USB dongle with the other.

"Grab the mirror set," El muttered. "Don't need anything else. Let it melt."

Andi was crouched by the side crate purposefully mislabeled FIRST AID. She had a lighter clenched between her teeth and a glass bottle already half-filled with gasoline. The rag was denim. She twisted it tight with muscle memory.

"Not the whole thing," El called out. "Just enough to panic the cameras."

"I know," Andi snapped, jamming the rag into the bottle neck. "It's not my first fucking rodeo."

El zipped the tote shut and jumped down from the bumper. She didn't even glance back.

Andi stepped into the street. She lit the rag in one slow strike and lifted the bottle like a bartender giving last call.

The man on the ground moaned. Andi didn't look at him.

"You're wasting time," she barked at Sloane. "RUN."

Sloane ran.

Her Asics slapped the pavement. Her arms ached. Her lungs filled with night air. She vaulted a curb, clipped a chain-link fence, caught herself on a hedge. She kept going. Didn't look back.

Somewhere behind her, the van would ignite. That man would wake up. Sirens would follow.

But right now—just for this minute—Sloane Campbell, former clerk for a federal appellate judge, was fleeing a Molotov cocktail.

She didn't even know where she was.

Only that Andi's grip still burned. Sharp, deep, fingers like a brand. She knew there'd be bruises by morning— because it already hurt like hell. The twins hadn't hesitated —not for a second—as if it were life or death.

And it probably was.

Still, she ran.

She didn't have a plan. Her limbs carried her through backyards and cul-de-sacs, over fences, through plastic play-houses and uncollected recycling bins. She vaulted a low wall, crossed two empty driveways, and finally collapsed behind someone's suburban trampoline—breathless, quivering, body pressed flat against the dew-wet lawn.

She could hear her own heart, loud as sirens. Her Asics were soaked through. Her hands smelled like melted rubber and metal casing. The van would be on fire by now. They'd agreed on that contingency. El would light it. Andi would ghost. And Sloane would hide.

Somewhere behind her, a dog barked.

She exhaled through her nose, sharp and slow, trying to remember her name and not her GPA.

Former Editor-in-Chief of the Yale Law Journal, she

thought grimly. Now accessory to arson, assault, and God knows what else.

She curled into herself under the trampoline and waited for the sound of sirens—or silence. Whichever came first.

49

She sat with her knees to her chest, forehead pressed to her thigh like in high school—after cross-country practice, no food, willing herself not to pass out. Same posture. Same breathless, vibrating stillness. Her whole body was a tuning fork for fear.

Grass stuck to her leggings. Sweat pooled at the base of her neck. The trampoline above her sagged, and somewhere nearby a sprinkler clicked on like nothing had happened. Like she hadn't just become accessory to a crime scene.

Her burner buzzed in her bra.

She answered it without thinking.

"Where are you?" Vee's voice, low, crackling with static and urgency and something unnameable. Something that made her stomach turn inside out.

"I don't—I don't know," Sloane whispered. Her throat was thick. "Are you okay?"

"Yeah. Yeah, I'm good. Still in the area. El and Andi told me what happened. I'm coming to get you."

"Wait—no, Vee. That's—are you serious? Did you even change out the car yet?"

A pause. A long one. Then Vee's voice again, calm like water before a storm.

"No. But they're not gonna catch me. Just tell me where you are."

Sloane swallowed. Her pulse roared in her ears.

"I don't know—I cut through two yards with busted fences and a row of garages sinking into the alley. Might be near a gas station."

"Okay," Vee said. Her voice gentled. "Look around. Slowly. What do you see?"

Sloane lifted her head. Her neck ached. Her hands shook.

"A trampoline. A shed. A fountain. One of those putrid cherub ones pissing into a cracked basin."

"Good. Okay, good. Now go out. Quietly. Look for a number—on the garage if there is one, facing the alley."

She crawled out from under the frame, scraped her knee on a rock, staggered to her feet. The air felt different out here—too open. She scanned the alley.

"Three-four-seven-two," she whispered. "Spray-painted under the eaves."

"Okay, one sec" Vee said. A minute passed "I know where that is. Don't move."

And then came the sound.

It began low—just a murmur at first, like a throat being cleared two blocks away. Then it built: a low-end growl, subterranean and carnivorous, an engine with bad manners and worse intentions. It echoed off the alley walls like something alive.

And then it turned the corner: a plain white sedan. Fake taxi medallion sticker peeling at the edge. Blue door numbers smudged with road dust. Vee behind the wheel, one arm flung over the seat, eyes scanning for her like a missile locking on heat.

She stopped hard, tires whispering against gravel.

The door opened.

"Get in."

THE SECOND they pulled out onto the main road, Sloane knew.

Gas station lights burned overhead like interrogation lamps. A strip mall blurred past, empty but watching. And behind them—too casual to be casual—came the state trooper. A white Ford Interceptor with a spotlight mount and government plates. Tinted windows. Lights off.

Vee spotted it in the mirror without a word. Her jaw twitched. Hands loose on the wheel. Calm as ritual.

Then the trooper lit them up—red and blue slicing through the night.

Sloane's breath hitched. Her whole body tensed.

"Vee—"

Vee didn't answer. Didn't react. Just drove.

Her right hand dropped to the stick. The car dropped a gear with a deep, throaty growl—then launched forward.

One second they were on the main drag. The next, Vee snapped the wheel and took a hard right between two construction barricades marked DO NOT ENTER, tires skidding just enough to thrill—but not enough to lose control.

Sloane's shoulder jolted against the door. The seatbelt bit across her chest, holding her fast, forcing the breath from her lungs. Vee drove like she touched—decisive, exacting. Not tender. Not warm. As if reassurance had never been the point. Control was.

Something jolted loose—a magnetic cab number plate peeling off and spinning into the gravel as they cut down a service road behind a shuttered outlet store.

An eighteen-wheeler crossed the lane just as they veered off. Perfect timing or divine chaos. Either way, the trooper had to brake—or plow through.

"Holy shit—"

Still, no answer. Just precision.

She took another turn without slowing, tires humming as they kissed the edge of a curb. They plunged into a dark side street. The trooper was nearby. Lights cutting wide.

She killed the headlights mid-turn—custom mod, rigged last winter. Brake lights went dark too.

Then she hit the handbrake—just for a second. The rear end slid, kissed a dumpster, then re-stabilized. She threaded the car through the narrow alley behind a bail bonds office and a muffler shop, then cut across a parking lot.

Gone.

No sirens. No lights.

Just breathing. And the sound of the engine purring low and hot between them.

Sloane was silent.

Then she looked at Vee. Not just looked—devoured.

Those angular cheekbones. That focused scowl. One loose strand of hair stuck to her cheek from the wind.

"Oh my god," Sloane said finally, voice hoarse.

"I told you," Vee murmured, eyes still on the road. "They won't catch me."

She didn't smirk. She didn't gloat.

She just drove. Wrist loose over the wheel.

And Sloane, knees pressed together, still tasting adrenaline, suddenly realized she wasn't breathing because her entire nervous system had rerouted into pure, unfiltered want.

50

The decals were gone. The dome light, the fare chart, the fake QR code—they'd ripped it all off in the alley behind the check-cashing place. Vee had kicked the plastic taxi grill off the Mazda herself, jaw clenched, hands trembling from the aftershock.

Sloane had climbed onto the hood, breath ragged, and worked the magnetic roof topper loose—one of those cheap fiberglass domes, sun-bleached and sticky from residue. It wasn't wired in, just bolted and banded down with elastic straps Vee had rigged that morning. She hissed through her teeth as she pried them off, palms burning from friction.

They moved fast, no words, just motion.

The suction mounts let go with loud, flesh-like pops. The Velcro flaps peeled with resistance, every sound loud in the quiet alley. Vee rolled up the fare sheet and shoved it into a crumpled Arby's bag. Sloane snapped the fake medallion sticker in half.

The car was just a car again.

The disguise—cheap, dirty, perfectly forgettable—now

lived in a dumpster behind a Popeyes, buried under wet napkins, bone-dry biscuits, and a cracked baby swing.

And now, here they were.

Pulled into a drive-in, sitting low in the seats of a plain blue Mazda 6 Turbo. Anonymous enough—for now. The car's dull body was still warm from its sins, too hot to take straight back to the meeting point.

The screen stood where the old meatpacking plant used to rot—concrete gutted, fencing still half up. A local organization had cleaned it up last summer, turned the ruin into a pop-up movie lot. Free shows, donated projectors, folding chairs for whoever didn't have a car. Families came out. Teens on bikes. Someone was selling elotes and fruit cups from a frutería cart, the air thick with lime, butter, hot cheese, and gossip. Kids chased each other between car bumpers.

On screen: *The Notebook*, playing like it hadn't ruined generations of soft-headed romantics. Ryan Gosling was screaming in the rain, and Sloane was too overstimulated to laugh. Her chest was still reverberating with the erratic percussion of post-heist dread. She could feel her own heartbeat behind her teeth.

Her palms were slick. Her thighs still pressed together.

She popped the console open just to do something with her hands.

Found a switchblade.

Of course.

The moment fractured when red and blue lights bloomed across the windshield, swallowing the projector's flicker in a wash of civil authority.

A squad car. The rookie trooper. His dome light blazing like divine judgment.

Sloane exhaled once, sharp and brittle.

A car door slammed. Footsteps crunched gravel, slow and deliberate.

"He's close. Thumbs on his belt." Vee murmured, her voice carved from smoke.

And then she moved—quick, practiced, shameless.

She climbed onto Sloane's lap like it was muscle memory and captured her mouth with the kind of kiss that short-circuited language. Sloane froze for half a heartbeat, then dissolved. She tugged down Vee's top below her bra, the cup exposed, curved and flushed and utterly obscene in the strobe of red and blue.

They were flushed, panting. Lit by the siren's garish strobe. Mouths open, greedy. They looked like they'd been doing this for hours.

The trooper reached the window, tapped the glass with the back of his knuckle.

They didn't stop.

Another fifteen seconds passed, shameless and silent but for the slick sound of kissing.

The trooper tapped again, more forceful.

"Ma'am?" he said, awkwardly. "Can you two step out of the vehicle?"

Vee didn't move. Sloane shifted slightly—just enough to brush a knuckle along the inside of Vee's arm in a gesture that looked casual.

"Is there a reason for the stop, Officer?" she asked, her voice low, measured, calm as a scalpel.

"Your vehicle matches a description from earlier this evening. We're looking for a woman, or a man matching the build."

Sloane bit the inside of her cheek to keep from laughing.

"That describes about more than half the population,"

she said, petting Vee's hair like they were post-coital in an indie film.

The trooper's eyes narrowed. He stepped back slightly. His flashlight arced down across the side of the Mazda—and paused.

A fragment of blue. The ghost of a decal. Torn at the edge, missed in the flurry. Adhesive still clinging like guilt.

Sloane saw it the moment he did. So did Vee. Neither flinched.

The trooper bent closer, studying the residue.

And then: the honking started.

"Hey, man!" someone shouted from three rows back. "They're watchin' the movie!"

"They're not bothering nobody!" another voice added, older.

"Go harass a Jeep or somethin'!"

"This ain't Naperville, bitch!"

The trooper straightened like he'd been slapped. The crowd was turning. Headlights flickered with indignation. Someone tossed a half-full ICEE at the edge of the squad car. It bounced.

The flashlight dropped. The trooper muttered something unintelligible into his shoulder radio, glanced once more at the Mazda, and turned back to his car like a man escaping a bar fight with his ego intact but his soul in pieces.

Silence returned.

The projector flickered on. Gosling was still screaming. And Sloane—still breathless, still half-pinned under a woman who tasted like fire and cinnamon gum—looked out the windshield like she'd survived something divine.

.   .   .

THE POLICE SCANNER crackled from the glove compartment, low and jittery.

"Unit 426 reporting back—false alarm at 47th and Damen. No vehicle match. No suspects."

Another voice chimed in, bored and annoyed: "Copy. Moving on."

They both let out a sigh of relief.

There was silence again. Just the hum of the projector and someone's baby crying two rows back.

Vee didn't move.

"We wait," she muttered. "If they're still circling, they'll double back here last. It's the only soft target nearby."

Sloane didn't argue. Better to let the city forget them for an hour before they moved.

They'd been watching in silence for thirty straight minutes, tucked low in the seats, when Sloane finally shifted —just slightly, just enough to look deeply, irrevocably pissed.

Vee caught it in her periphery. "What?"

Sloane didn't answer right away. She just stared at the screen.

"I've seen this movie...many times. I thought this—" she gestured toward the screen, where Gosling was mid-breakdown in the rain, "—was romance. I thought this was what love was supposed to look like."

Vee blinked, caught off guard by the sharpness in her tone.

"And now?" she asked.

Sloane scoffed. "Now I see a manic, codependent wet man yelling at a woman with clear signs of an undiagnosed mood disorder."

"Whew," Vee muttered. "Okay."

"It's gaslighting, Vee. It's damp, heterosexual gaslighting

with woodwork and a sepia filter. She had a fiancé who respected her boundaries and paid his taxes. And she gave it all up for some unhinged boatboy with abandonment issues and a two-by-four."

Vee let out a low whistle. "You've been sitting on that for thirty minutes?"

"I've been sitting on that since I was in middle school," Sloane snapped. "But now I have the vocabulary."

A few more minutes passed. Vee reached down to adjust the climate controls—more to give her hands something to do than anything else.

Then Sloane added, "Also, where the hell did you learn to drive like that?"

Vee didn't answer right away. She adjusted the air vents like she hadn't just taken a sedan through a tactical evasion at eighty miles per hour.

"Long Beach," she said finally. "Rough part. A lot of refugees. You either stayed useful or you got fucked."

She paused.

"My brother taught me. Back in California. I used to run jobs for him. Teenager shit."

Sloane froze mid-breath. "Oh."

"After he went to jail, I moved here, got a legit job. Started working under Jerry. But I didn't stop—not right away. Still ran side shit. Dumb stuff. Cash pickups. Couriers. Nothing high-risk."

Sloane was watching her closely now.

"Jerry found out when I was twenty-one," Vee went on. "Told me if I didn't quit, I was done. So I quit."

"For how long?"

"Ten years," she said. "Didn't touch it. Not once."

"And now?"

Vee let out a breath. "After a bad break-up, it started

creeping back in. Street races. Kids with too much Red Bull and too little fear. It was dumb. I know that. But it was something. Felt like control."

"Until tonight."

"Yeah." A pause. "Tonight wasn't for fun."

They went quiet again.

On screen, Gosling was still flinging himself into the river of delusion.

Then Vee's phone lit up. Andi. Calling. Then again. And again.

Vee answered. "What—"

Andi was sobbing. Sharp, wet, gasping. Not even words at first.

"Breathe," Vee snapped. "What happened?"

Sloane was already tensing beside her.

"It's Kenji," Andi got out, cracking down the middle. "He's not—El says he's still breathing, but he's not moving. There's blood. A lot."

Vee went still, then threw the Mazda into reverse so hard Sloane's body jolted.

"We're twenty minutes out," Vee said, voice cold now. "Keep him alive."

She hung up. Sloane didn't ask. Didn't need to.

Behind them, the screen was fading to black—final shot, final breath, lovers dying old in bed.

The Mazda pulled out just as the credits rolled.

They didn't look back.

51

The night before had collapsed under the weight of too many mistakes.

After the drive-in, Vee drove them back to the temporary loft in Old Town, the one they'd secured as a staging base. She lectured Sloane the entire way back, voice clipped, knuckles white on the wheel. Something about abandoning protocol, nearly blowing the operation.

No mention, of course, of straddling Sloane in the front seat, of their mouths colliding in what could technically be described as a last-minute tactical distraction.

Sloane hadn't bothered to respond. She sat in silence, limbs crossed like a closing argument.

Not even when they opened the door to find Kenji unconscious on the floor, one arm flung out like a broken clock hand. A discarded pawn.

At first, they thought it was just his arm. Clean through the bicep. Messy, but survivable. But there was blood in his mouth. Turned out a second bullet had grazed his lung. Slipped in under his ribcage, almost missed on the first sweep. El found it. Andi packed it. Vee tore through the

West Side in the spare Corolla, headed for a clinic that didn't ask, didn't judge, and took cash folded into a paper bag.

Kenji didn't die. Barely.

Sloane watched the sunrise from a plastic chair while they gave him oxygen. Slid a needle between his ribs and winced when the air hissed back. No anesthesia. Just gauze, a bucket, and fast hands.

Her own hands wouldn't stop shaking. Blood caked under her fingernails. Vee hadn't looked at her once.

Time didn't so much pass as fracture.

There hadn't been time to process. Just blood, then this.

Now she was here.

Some underground dining concept—part bunker, part postmodernist hallucination—where the menus came projected on glass and the ceiling dripped with filament bulbs.

She had been sitting in the same molded walnut chair for fifty-eight minutes. No cushion. Her back ached.

Zora was late. On purpose. And Sloane, exhausted and humiliated, was still here. Waiting.

The room did not announce itself. No name, no signage. No maître d', no menu. Just a whisper at the elevator, a retinal scan behind a partition near the Art Institute's conservation lab, and a descent into curated silence. Supposedly, the Institute's basement housed lecture rooms, storage vaults, maybe a kiln. In reality, below the academic detritus and grant-funded dust, there was Table 0—a dining chamber so rarified it refused the label "restaurant." It was not open to the public. It did not exist. The only way to dine there was to be invited by someone whose net worth could topple a government.

She had been served ten courses already, each more

conceptual than the last—gastronomy as spectacle, cuisine as psychodrama. The first plate arrived suspended on an invisible thread, slowly descending from the ceiling: a sphere of smoked tamarind reduction encased in a gelatin shell of "black pepper air," resting briefly on her palm before imploding into vinegar and heat. A dish of compressed heirloom radish followed, served atop a mirror polished so highly she could see the fatigue in her own pupils. The utensils changed with each course. One was magnetic. One vibrated softly, "to stimulate the tongue."

There was music, of course—live, but unseen. A composer's dissonant quartet pulsed through the space like an arrhythmia. Somewhere behind the walls, a scent artist piped in alternating whiffs of saffron, old paper, snowmelt, and something that hinted—uncomfortably—at blood.

She tapped one manicured finger against the side of her water glass. Her other hand remained in her lap, balled into a fist.

Course eleven arrived in silence. A single quail egg, hollowed out and filled with liquid foie gras, balanced precariously atop a ring of shiso leaf.

Then—Zora.

She appeared with no fanfare, sliding into the chair opposite Sloane like she belonged to the architecture. Black blouse, no jewelry, her hair sleek and severe. Her presence had the smug finality of a closing argument.

"You are, without question, an extraordinary piece of work," Sloane said, her voice low and restrained.

Zora didn't blink. "You taught me."

She unfolded her napkin.

"You taught me to win. You taught me not to flinch. You said emotion was weakness. And then you—" Zora's eyes narrowed. "You got sentimental over a damn mechanic. You blew the whole timetable because you wanted to play savior instead of strategist."

Sloane stared at her.

"I didn't fall," she said quietly. "I chose. And I don't regret it."

Zora's smile faltered. Just slightly.

She looked at Sloane like she was seeing something she didn't want to recognize.

"You weren't supposed to change," she whispered. "You were the one thing that didn't."

For a second, Sloane wasn't at the table.

She was twenty-six. First year out of law school. A suit that didn't quite fit. Hair pulled back so tightly it ached. She'd taken the case on a dare, really—a senior partner tossing it her way like a cigarette someone else didn't want to finish. Domestic violence, sealed hospital records, no visible support from the family. Rich girl. Disgraced boyfriend. A tangle of wealth and silence.

Zora had two black eyes. A fractured rib. Bite marks she hadn't tried to hide. And a non-disclosure agreement drafted by her father's firm.

The DA offered a plea deal before Sloane even filed motions. Probation. Anger management. Restitution in quarterly checks.

Sloane burned through three restraining orders, hired a private investigator out of pocket, and dragged the case back into court every time it was quietly buried. She subpoenaed phone records, medical histories, old security footage that was never meant to see daylight. She wrote briefs until her knuckles locked.

When the sentence finally came—two years inside, with conditions so strict the man couldn't hold a passport— Sloane hadn't even stayed to hear it read. She'd walked out before the verdict.

Zora came to her office not long after. She stood in the doorway for a long time, silent.

"No one ever made him say sorry," she whispered. "They always said it wouldn't stick. But you—" her voice caught— "you made him go away."

She didn't cry then. Just stared at Sloane.

That look in her eyes—Sloane had told herself back then it was gratitude. Maybe awe. But it had never been that. Not really. It was hunger. The kind that clings. That turns reverence into possession.

Over the years, Zora had followed her like gospel. Shadowed her arguments. Modeled her cadence. Absorbed her power and wore it like armor.

But lately—something had shifted.

The cracks started months ago: Zora getting short when Sloane hesitated. Picking fights after briefings. Making snide remarks whenever Vee's name came up.

Then that day at the apartment—Sloane told her not to file, not yet. To wait. Zora's face had gone tight with something she hadn't named then.

Now she recognized it.

Betrayal.

Zora hadn't wanted a mentor. She wanted something fixed. Unbreakable. Something that wouldn't flinch when the world did. Sloane had been that once—her axis. Her compass. Her proof that survival could be engineered.

Sloane blinked. The memory dissolved, and the scent of saffron returned like a slap.

Zora was no longer composed.

Her lips were parted like she was about to speak, but no sound came out. Her eyes shimmered in the flickering light

—blinking too fast, like she could force the tears back with calculation alone.

"You were supposed to be above all this," she said, voice cracking once, then hardening. "You were supposed to know better."

Sloane understood, finally.

Zora hadn't healed. She'd survived.

For her, love hadn't been a feeling. It had been an illness she nearly died from.

And now Sloane—her cure, her compass—was back inside the contagion.

A server appeared between them without warning, gliding into the emotional wreckage like a drone. He presented a single langoustine tail, suspended midair by a wire rig and spritzed with something that smelled faintly of ozone. "Course twelve," he murmured, before squeezing a vaporized citrus mist over the plate and vanishing.

Neither of them moved.

The silence that followed felt unholy.

Then—like a switch flipped—Zora straightened her spine. Her mouth drew a perfect line. She pulled the envelope from her bag, fingers too precise.

She slid it across the table.

"If you give us the tape," Zora said, voice syrup-smooth again, "Ava will forgive the debts. We put you back as General Counsel. The Campbell lands go back to your family. We make the story go away."

"And if I say no?"

Zora leaned in. "Then you take the fall. Publicly. We name you as the cover-up. We fire you for cause. You could be disbarred before the year ends. And no one will hire Kenji, or El and Andi. We'll salt the earth behind you."

Sloane didn't move.

Kenji had been one of NYPD's finest until he put a bullet in a predator who walked on a technicality. The case never stuck, but the stain did. He'd lost everything but his instincts.

El and Andi came from something louder. Their dead names were buried under classified redactions and different pronouns. Before the firm, they'd crashed a defense network for sport. The kind of breach that doesn't get tried—just erased.

They were hers. Built not bought. And without her, they'd be back running ghost jobs for men who paid in fear and threats.

Sloane lifted her wine glass, stared into it like it might hold an answer. Then: "I don't have the tape."

Zora studied her. Long enough to make it uncomfortable. Long enough to wonder if Sloane was lying or had simply outplayed her again.

Zora's smile twisted. "You're pathetic."

"Probably," Sloane murmured. "But I trained you well."

"By the way, I know it was you. There was no need to trash the apartment. You gave Tiberia a good scare."

Zora didn't flinch. "You care more about that snake than you ever cared about the rest of us."

Sloane looked at her, finally. Not with anger. Just pity.

That was the problem. That was always the trade. Zora would follow orders, mimic tone, memorize every move. In return, Sloane just had to stay—unchanged, undivided, hers.

"You never officially resigned, by the way. So consider this your termination."

Zora laughed. A real one. Throaty, cruel.

She'd meant to say something smart. Something sharp. But what came out was, "Fuck you, bitch."

Sloane picked up to grab her bag and turned.

Zora's face stilled. "Your career's over. The firm's finished. You've torched every bridge and romanticized a dead cause. What are you going to do?"

There was hunger in her eyes—not empathy. Not grief. Just the sharp-edged curiosity of someone dissecting a lesson in failure. Like Sloane still owed her a final case study.

Zora didn't want guidance. She wanted to witness collapse up close. To chart the trajectory. To replicate the power, and dodge the cost.

Sloane met her gaze across the table. The room had gone silent. Even the music paused.

"You'll see," she said.

And then she walked out.

52

The next morning, the union dropped the OSHA training video.

Grainy footage from the early aughts: a training room with cracked tile and a whiteboard still marked from last week's meeting. A supervisor giving a shrugging walkthrough of asbestos protocol, barely skimming the script. A mechanic coughing—wet, deep, gutting—off-camera. Executives in suits laughing in the background, one making a joke about "lungs as a line item."

It was all there. Proof the board knew. Proof they lied.

By noon, it was everywhere. TikTok clips, YouTube breakdowns, grandmother-fueled Facebook rage reposts. CNN looping the footage with grim commentary. A comedian turned political commentator doing a three-part series. A health worker in Detroit started a GoFundMe for impacted families and raised six figures in a day.

And the day after that? The Heritage comms floor earned their hazard pay.

Every chyron. Every push alert. Every feed.

Disgraced General Counsel Implicated in Corporate Cover-Up

The Sloane Campbell Scandal: Embezzlement, Malpractice, Murder-by-Mesothelioma

They didn't just fire her.

They lit the match and watched her burn.

Her name was ash before noon.

There was footage. Forged invoices. A leaked executive memo tying her name—her signature—to the fake charitable fund that supposedly purchased the Rosa Márquez sculpture now sitting like a cursed icon in Heritage's lobby. The press called it a monument to corruption.

They blamed her for the cancer.

Never mind she was in grade school when it started. Facts don't matter when people are pissed.

They said she signed off on the cover-up—and that was enough.

The documents were ready: backdated, cross-referenced, strategically "found." Planted with care. Buried like landmines.

Zora's work. But under Sloane's authority. Which made it Sloane's crime.

By noon, both the Illinois ARDC and the New York State Bar had opened formal proceedings. Her limited in-house admission under Rule 716 was now "under urgent review," and the New York Office of Attorney Discipline had flagged her license for possible suspension.

D.C. hadn't weighed in. Yet. But it would. They all would.

No verdict—just the quiet machinery of professional death, beginning to turn.

By one p.m., a formal ethics complaint had been filed.

By two, Lucretia Morrow stood on a press platform and

said, flatly, "Ms. Campbell's conduct does not reflect the values of this company."

Zora stood beside her, in cream silk, looking mournful.

They'd cut Sloane loose. Made her the face of every sin they'd spent twenty years cultivating.

The summons came an hour later.

Polite, of course.

Tempered with regret and wrapped in the crisp language of bureaucratic necessity. A simple request for cooperation—just a brief statement, Ms. Campbell, nothing formal at this stage. The tone was apologetic, deferential even. But the venue was the Chicago field office of the FBI, and the subtext was clear: Heritage was on fire, again, and someone had to hand over the matches.

The agent who met her—white shirt, plain tie, deliberate vowels—looked vaguely horrified to be doing his job. "We understand this is all very sensitive," he said, as if delicacy could disinfect the optics. "But in light of the whistle-blower leak and the financials connected to the art acquisition fund..." He trailed off. The implication hovered.

She did not deign to respond.

Her counsel arrived five minutes later—*the* counsel, in fact. Not merely high-powered, but constitutional-law-textbook-appendix, nationally ranked, terrifyingly unbothered. A woman who charged by the hour in five figures and made federal prosecutors forget their own names. Sloane had made precisely one phone call that morning, and the woman had flown in from D.C. without blinking.

The statement was handled with surgical efficiency. No, Ms. Campbell had not authorized the creation of any fraudulent accounts. No, she had not misrepresented the nature of Heritage's charitable funds. No, she had not participated in or condoned embezzlement of any kind. The language was clear. The delivery, glacial. The entire meeting lasted twenty-six minutes.

She emerged into light and chaos.

Kenji was waiting. In a plain windbreaker and dark sunglasses. He didn't speak. Just stepped in beside her and began quietly displacing bodies.

The press was already there, a sea of glass eyes and grasping hands.

"Ms. Campbell, were you aware of the fake invoice scheme—?"

"Is it true your signature was on the memo—?"

"Are you being charged, or cooperating voluntarily?"

"Ms. Campbell, were you acting alone?"

She didn't flinch.

Didn't pause.

Didn't respond.

Kenji moved like a blade, cutting space where there was none, ushering her down the concrete steps without so much as a glance at the noise. The cameras followed, of course. The flashbulbs, the live feeds, the speculations already coalescing into headlines.

The town car arrived late. Unsurprisingly. No one was early for her anymore.

She got in, still composed, still upright, and the door shut behind her with the finality of a tomb.

Then—silence.

Then the shaking started.

Not theatrical. Not loud. Just a fine tremor, fingers to forearms, like her nervous system had decided to start peeling away at the edges.

Her pulse was erratic. Her breath, too shallow. A pressure behind her ribs began to crescendo—dull at first, then burning. She tried to steady it. Count backward. Nothing helped. The images kept replaying: the flash, the press, the stain of accusation. Her name, detached from her body, dragged through chyrons she couldn't scrub clean.

She reached into her bag with practiced precision and retrieved the bottle. Xanax. Prescribed. Low dose. Emergency only.

Her hand hovered.

She hated this.

Hated the idea of chemical stillness.

Yale Law had been littered with classmates who'd taken this same step, once. One of them—brilliant, terrifyingly so —started with something mild. Just something to sleep. Then something to wake up. Then something stronger for the in-between. Now he was somewhere in Long Island, still calling her once in a while from borrowed phones and borrowed time. A golden résumé still tucked in his glove compartment—five years at one of the BigLaw firms. The kind with $215k starting salaries and 4 a.m. emails. He made it to senior associate before heroin did what the hours couldn't.

Sloane wasn't him. She had sworn she wouldn't be.

But she had to land in San Francisco composed.

Not cracked. Not sweat-slicked and unstrung.

She had to present herself to Vivienne like a weapon, not a warning sign.

She swallowed the pill with the complimentary water bottle from the side door.

Not quickly. Not without shame. But deliberately—like a woman staging her own intervention.

Like if she didn't make it ceremonial, didn't imbue it with gravity, she might one day forget the first time—and become someone who medicated her own unraveling without blinking.

The rest of the ride passed in silence. Kenji didn't speak. The driver didn't look back. Outside, the city blurred.

Inside, she held herself together by the edge of a thread.

53

Vivienne Yue's favorite property wasn't on the books. A "wellness estate" in the Marin hills— stone, glass, and negative space. The kind of place that required NDAs just to approach the gate. The board called it *The Orchard*. The staff called it the compound.

Sloane arrived with her back straight and her lipstick sharp, but she felt it—the void behind her name. The absence of inboxes. The silence of deactivated logins. The hollow hum of a career amputated in real time.

She stood in the guest washroom for fifteen minutes before the meeting, palms flat against the marble counter, trying to convince her reflection she was still a weapon. That she wasn't unraveling by inches. That she hadn't, for one sick second on the flight over, thought about disappearing entirely.

Then she adjusted her earrings, reapplied her lipstick, and walked into the adjoining conference room.

It had one-way glass, turning her into a ghost in heels. Not unseen, exactly—just unacknowledged. That was the arrangement. Vivienne's orders. No visible alliances. No witnesses to their partnership. Not yet.

The boardroom on the other side was awash in soft leather, old scotch, and weak men pretending to have spines. Half the board had been summoned by sunset. The rest trickled in, blinking at the Zoom wall like it might bite. A grid of pale faces projected ten feet high, all nodding, all waiting for their instructions.

The interface looked like a chessboard. And every single one of them was Vivienne's piece.

She stood at the head of the table in a white silk dress. She didn't raise her voice. She didn't need to.

"I hold majority interest now. Some of you sold. Some of you were...encouraged. The rest of you failed to read your emails, which is on brand."

There was a shuffling, a throat cleared, someone unmuted and re-muted by accident.

Then came Hodge's son.

"This is fucking absurd," he spat. "You spoiled cunt. You think you can steamroll us because you now have my father's shares? We know what this is. You got that whore of a general counsel to manipulate him. She got in his ear, fed him bullshit, took his proxy like a fucking gold-digging parasite."

Sloane blinked, once. Let the word slide down her back.

Vivienne didn't flinch. She just raised one eyebrow, then nodded at tech support. The Zoom call abruptly lost one tile. The Hodge heir was gone.

"Anyone else want to test the firewall?" Vivienne asked, not looking up from her folder.

Silence. Then murmurs. Then fear.

She let it hang a moment longer before flipping to the next page.

"There's a corruption investigation brewing. Has to do with hangar redevelopment approvals. Environmental negligence. Falsified maintenance logs. Some of you signed off without reading. Some of you didn't bother showing up. It's amazing what stacks up when no one's paying attention."

A few directors shifted in their seats. One older woman looked like she was about to throw up into her Hermès scarf.

Vivienne smiled, cool and clean. "Your signatures were on the redevelopment files. All I did was connect the time-stamps. The rest? That's between you and the press."

That did it. Panic—controlled, silent, exquisitely corpo-ratized panic—rippled across the room like static. No one wanted to be the next name trending under a whistleblower hashtag. And none of them had the bandwidth or the moral clarity to untangle whether Vivienne was bluffing.

"Effective immediately," she continued, "the board will approve settlement in the mesothelioma litigation. Full OSHA-aligned reform package, with an independent third-party inspector selected by union leadership. We'll eat the costs. Call it ethics. Or call it survival."

A pause.

Then: "All in favor?"

Hands raised. Digital tiles flickered affirmative. One abstention. Vivienne didn't even glance at it.

Sloane leaned back against the cold wall, arms crossed, heart steady.

Vivienne had made her move. And she'd done it with a smile, a scalpel, and the bones of a bluff sharpened into truth.

Check. Not mate. Not yet.

But close.

. . .

TWO HOURS LATER, they agreed to settle by a slim majority. Barely.

Legal counsel murmured behind clenched teeth, their voices pitched low. The room reeked of resignation and disinfected money.

One by one, the votes fell. Not with thunder, but with silk—soundless, expensive, inevitable.

Then—Lucretia Morrow.

The screen focused on the Chicago boardroom. A sterile mausoleum of glass and chrome. Lucretia sat at the head, posture perfect, wine-red lipstick flawless. Around her, Ava's pawns had already fallen into place—two former heads of state in their oxygenated hush, a former CEO blinking like he'd forgotten where he was, that new finance girl still too green to realize she'd been bought. Ava stood in the back, unspeaking. As if she'd orchestrated the entire thing from a chaise lounge in hell.

And just to her left—Zora.

Poised, polished, and pretending to belong to no one. Her tablet was folded under one arm, her blouse pristine, her gaze locked on the boardroom table. Not defiant, not obedient—just present. Neutral. Forgettable, if you weren't looking.

But Sloane was looking.

And she saw it.

Zora wasn't watching the room. She was measuring it. Weighing the fall of one empire against the rise of another.

The final vote.

Then—Lucretia nodded.

A few gasps. Zora's mouth dropped. Her eyes flitted between Ava and Lucretia.

Sloane already knew the answer. Not because Lucretia

was loyal, but because she'd been offered something sweeter than obedience.

Last night, it had gone differently.

"No," she'd said, smooth as a stone dropped in a still pond. "I won't sign."

The private suite was soundproofed and shadowed, sealed tight as a tomb. Lucretia stood by the minibar, one manicured finger circling the rim of a crystal glass. Scotch untouched. She wasn't posturing—she was calculating the odds.

Sloane didn't move. Neither did Vivienne.

They didn't need to.

Vivienne Yue spoke first, voice barely above a whisper, honed to a scalpel's edge. "We remove Ava. And every single pawn she installed."

The silence after was wrought with tension. Lucretia didn't answer right away. She didn't need to. Her gaze slid from Vivienne to Sloane—measuring, calculating—and for a split second, they saw it. The future she'd already mapped behind her eyes. One where Ava's heel was off her neck. One where she answered to no one.

And it was ravenous.

Lucretia set down the empty glass with a soft click. "It's always musical chairs with tyrants, isn't it?"

She said it like a joke, but no one laughed.

Vivienne didn't blink. Just smiled, slow and feline. "Then sit in my lap next time."

A moment passed—quiet, not tense, just...suspended. The kind of silence that suggested a temporary equilibrium. Like the tectonic plates of ambition had settled, for now.

Sloane said nothing. She didn't need to. If no one got greedy, the balance might hold.

But no one in the room was built for stillness.

Now, in that Chicago boardroom, Lucretia cast her vote with the steadiness of someone who'd already rewritten the rules in her favor.

And this time, she wasn't voting for Ava.

She was voting for herself.

Ava Thompkins didn't even flinch. She just smiled—tight, unblinking.

Lucretia, freed from under Ava's heel for the first time in her entire executive life, didn't hesitate. "Do it."

The board turned. Quiet and efficient. Ava was stripped of power in four minutes.

Zora stood at the edge of the boardroom, half-shadowed by the frosted glass wall. Not center stage—just close enough to witness the tide shift.

She watched Lucretia lean into power like she'd always had it. Watched Ava fall without a single scream. Watched Vivienne smile like she'd already picked the next body to bury.

Zora's expression didn't change.

But her hand—just briefly—tightened on the edge of the table.

Ava rose from her seat as though it were a throne, not a boardroom chair.

"You'll regret this, Lucretia," she said. Calm. Prophetic. "You're not free. You're just next."

It wasn't loud. It wasn't cruel. It just...landed.

Something shifted. Imperceptible, but real. A beat too long between breaths. The faintest ripple across the boardroom glass. Every person within earshot felt it—like static under the skin. Even Lucretia looked ill, her gaze suddenly fixed on some invisible middle distance, like she'd caught the echo of her own future.

No one spoke. No one dared.

Ava didn't wait for permission. She smoothed her sheath dress, adjusted a bracelet, and walked out like she'd just passed a sentence the room would spend the next decade serving.

Lucretia looked at the contract in front of her. The settlement papers. The full reparation figures. The cancer fund. The widow's trust. Jerry Cortez's name typed cleanly in black ink.

She signed.

By morning, Lucretia Morrow was installed as permanent CEO. The wolves were fed. The fire, briefly, quelled.

No one dared call it peace.

54

Vee had done more press this month than in her entire life. Still hated every second of it.

The cameras, the posture, the artificial calm of media-trained voices—it all set her teeth on edge. But this? A union-led press conference on their turf? This was different. The headquarters wasn't much, just cinderblock bones and outdated carpet, but it had a hell of a view of the skyline if you stood near the east windows. You could see all of the Loop laid out under mid-morning sun, steel and glass gleaming like a promise they hadn't been paid for yet.

Vee kept to the back for now. Her jacket was the navy one—union-issue, patched at the shoulder, and broken in at the cuffs where her gloves used to rub. She'd earned it. Not just in years but in funerals, broken gear, and backroom deals she didn't live-tweet. Underneath, just a black camisole and black jeans—clean lines, simple. She'd done her eyeliner the same way she had since she was sixteen— sharp wing, no smoke. Clean slash up the side. A look born from stolen Wet n Wild at a Long Beach Walgreens, perfected in the backseat between gigs and garages.

Noah came up behind her, all nerves and clipboard energy. "You see the Heritage people yet?"

They were supposed to be presenting some new unity bullshit—airline and labor finally locking arms after years of bloodshed. Vee didn't trust it. But she didn't trust a lot of things lately.

She scanned the main room—cameras, mics, every outlet from WGN to MSNBC shoved into cheap folding chairs, all aimed at a sad little podium. The flags were lined up behind it: state, federal, union. No sign of the suits.

She ducked out of the room, moving through the narrow halls. Second floor. Break room. Then, a low sound. Voices. She slowed her steps and let the door crack just enough to see.

There it was.

Back room. Dim light. One overhead bulb flickering with the kind of hum you could feel in your fillings. Lucretia Morrow stood behind Sloane, too close, too casual. Her hand wasn't quite on Sloane's waist, but the intent was radiating off her. Sloane stood ramrod still, jaw clenched, staring ahead at nothing—at everything.

Then Lucretia leaned in, lips brushing the space just behind Sloane's ear. Not a kiss, not exactly. Just a quiet weapon of intimacy.

"You keep pretending it's only your brain that's valuable," Lucretia murmured, low and knowing. "But the real leverage? The soft kind? You know it's real. I used it. You should, too. It's not shameful. It's...strategic. You want to hear what I had to do when I was your age? What kind of favors get you past locked doors? This isn't about seduction. It's about survival. If you think brilliance is enough, baby girl, you're already bleeding out."

Sloane didn't flinch. But Vee saw the vein in her temple jump.

Vee pushed the door open the rest of the way with the side of her boot. Loud enough to break the spell. "Hope I'm not interrupting the mentoring session."

Lucretia straightened without alarm, glanced back. "Ms. Phan." That infuriating smirk already back in place. "Always on time to spoil the mood."

Vee crossed her arms. "Funny, I thought we were here for reconciliation, not...whatever that was."

Lucretia only chuckled, that velvet-laced derision of someone who'd outlived bigger scandals. "Enjoy the cameras, ladies." She tapped Sloane's shoulder on the way out—territorial or just plain patronizing. Either way, it made Vee's skin crawl.

Once she was gone, the silence pressed in like a closing tomb.

Sloane turned to face her. Perfectly composed, like nothing had happened. Like Vee hadn't just seen her neck get treated like a submission hold.

"That was unnecessary," Sloane said, voice cool.

Vee raised an eyebrow. "Was it?" She let the air stretch between them, thick and biting. "Seemed like you had it handled."

Sloane didn't answer. Just stood there, hands loose at her sides, not looking away.

It would've gone on longer if Noah hadn't stepped in, dragging the moment back to earth. He peeked into the room and blinked like he regretted it instantly. "Everyone's assembled," he muttered. "We're starting. Let's—uh—do this thing."

He gave them both a look—the kind that screamed, *Why*

do I work with this many women who could stab me and get away with it?

Vee didn't laugh. But she did shoulder past Sloane, brushing against her, then falling into step as they moved toward the stage.

Side by side. Publicly united. Privately unraveled.

Sloane stepped up to the podium. No notes. No script. Just breath, poise, and the sharp scent of survival.

"I made decisions with the information I had. I signed off on what was presented as clean. It wasn't. And now it's public record."

A pause. No emotion. Just precision.

"This isn't about absolution. It's about truth. And truth, like rot, doesn't stay buried."

She looked at Vee, just once—a brief, intimate glance that revealed everything. She was completely wrecked but somehow still standing.

"I'm not here to beg. I'm here to name. Jerry Cortez. Every mechanic exposed. Every family that buried someone while Heritage executives cashed bonuses. You don't have to forgive me. But you will remember them."

The silence that followed Sloane's last word was brief— like a sharp inhale before the crush of a wave.

Then the room broke.

Reporters shouted questions, none of them listening to the answers. The human interest buzzards were circling, already high off the scent of her guilt. The union's press liaison tried to corral them, but it was useless. This wasn't about unity. It was about spectacle. They'd come to see the high priestess of Heritage Airlines bleed on the steps.

Vee watched the feeding frenzy from her side of the stage, arms folded, jaw set. Nobody cared anymore that Jerry had died slow and brutal. That the press only showed up after the scandal got glossy. Now they were all here, pretending to care, scribbling soundbites like they'd known all along.

Sloane had barely stepped off the dais when she was swallowed. The alderman from the 12th ward had her by the elbow, whispering something performative and oily. Then came the Heritage reps, pretending they were confused about the timeline. A PAC strategist tried to pass her a card. Someone else shoved a mic in her face. She looked like she might vomit or vaporize—maybe both—but she held it together.

Vee was pulled the opposite way. Union brass dragged her toward the local TV crews and Spanish-language media, backslapping her like she'd just finished a marathon and not watched her old situationship admit to weaponized silence on national television. Her phone buzzed nonstop in her jacket pocket—texts, alerts, probably more media requests. Noah tried to shield her, but it was chaos. Everyone wanted a quote, a reaction, a goddamn hero.

She and Sloane locked eyes once more in the chaos. No emotion. Just the sharp, exhausted clarity of people who'd once known each other in the dark.

And then—without ceremony—they turned.

Sloane disappeared into a wall of handlers. Vee walked out the back—fists in her jacket pockets, boots scuffing the concrete.

No goodbye.

No clean ending.

Just two women pulled apart by the machine they tried to dismantle.

55

She waited until the room had emptied—until the murmurs had receded, the cameras powered down, the lights dimmed to something approximating anonymity. Only then did she allow herself stillness.

Her heels made no sound against the carpeted floor, her breath caught somewhere just behind her ribs. She was not crying, but her entire body felt as though it had been hollowed out, scraped clean with surgical precision, and left open to the air.

She had named names. She had told the truth. And it had changed nothing.

No reaction from Vee. Like Sloane hadn't laid herself bare in front of national press with a trembling voice and an apology stitched into subtext.

Even now, the echo of Vee's voice hung in the air—cool, unreadable, final. That last glance between them had said everything and nothing. It had ended her.

So she walked outside.

The rain was cinematic. Naturally. The sky, cruel in its timing. Her dress soaked through instantly. Her heels slipped slightly on the stone steps. The wind was punishing. Her vision blurred, not from tears, but from the sheer density of what she could not contain.

She thought, absurdly, of *The Notebook*.

The last time they'd been together—really together, not just glancing off each other in meetings and headlines—they'd been hiding in plain sight. After stealing that tape. Chicago behind them, adrenaline still in their teeth. They parked in that drive-in, Vee's hand still trembling from whatever came after survival. Sloane had scoffed, called it drivel. Vee smirked and turned up the static-ridden audio. And then they sat in silence. Watching the rain fall on-screen. Letting the moment stretch too long.

And now here she was. Soaked, humiliated, watching Vee vanish.

She had always hated that movie. She had eviscerated its sentimentality, its predictability, its fraudulent premise of romantic inevitability. It was manipulative.

And yet—she had watched it forty-two times the summer she was fourteen. Hidden in her bedroom in Queens with the lights off, the volume low, the shame constant. She had memorized every beat of that final rain-soaked chase long before she had ever been kissed.

And now she was living it. Again. Against her will.

She found Vee.

Still there. In her truck. Lights off. Engine running.

Sloane ran. Through the rain, through the ache, through the bone-deep humiliation of it all. She didn't care who saw. She had given the world everything already—what was one more public display of ruin?

She reached the driver's side just as Vee looked up.

"Is there—" Her voice cracked, then steadied. "Do we

still exist in theory? Or am I the only one who hasn't let go yet?"

A pause. Too long. Too silent.

"I don't know," Vee said. Quiet. Not cruel. Just true.

And then the truck pulled away.

No screech of tires. Just taillights swallowed by rain and the sound of Sloane's own breathing, sharp and uneven in the dark.

She didn't move. Didn't scream.

She stood there, soaked to the bone, curls flattened, her leave-in defeated—an entire routine undone by one woman and ten uninterrupted minutes of rain. She whispered, almost laughing, "God. *Fuck* that movie."

And then she stayed. Because there was nothing else to do.

56

One year later.

I t was already over.

The air in the penthouse boardroom was climate-controlled and clinically quiet, the sort of curated sterility that cost twenty-five thousand a month in maintenance and made its occupants feel both powerful and vaguely nauseous. Outside, it was already dark. The Bay flickered—red, gold, occasional static. Nothing organic. Vivienne's preferred battleground.

The Shanghai team was dialed in, calling from a room soaked in too much light—glass, chrome, morning sun, and smugness. Bright suits. Bone-white teeth. All of them peacocking from the hundredth floor like the distance would insulate them from consequences. It didn't.

Sloane didn't sit. She never did in moments like these. She stood near the head of the table, tablet in hand, manicured thumb tapping once to advance the next clause on-screen. Her tone was glacial and exact, every syllable a needle threaded through silk.

"...and since your board never formally disclosed the F-round buyout cap in your last shareholder report—buried in Appendix D, if memory serves—this merger is either a hostile takeover or a quiet euthanizing. Your choice."

She did not raise her voice. She did not look around.

"Either way, Vivienne gets your IP."

She simply let the silence sprawl after that—weaponized, intentional. The kind that couldn't be interrupted because no one wanted to be the first to breathe wrong.

The CEO—a man with too many degrees and not enough instincts—shifted in his seat like something primal in him had started to sweat. His tie was a half-inch too tight. He reached for his water glass and didn't drink. The Shanghai execs went quiet on the feed, their delay lagging just long enough to register their horror in slow motion.

At the far end of the table, Vivienne reclined ever so slightly. Her expression wasn't gloating; it was something worse. Amused. She tapped a fingernail against her espresso cup, then looked up, all cheekbones and chill.

"We'll be in touch," she said, voice sugar-glazed and full of bone.

"Enjoy the liquidity event."

Sloane gave no reaction. Her work was done.

Across from her, Kenji sat with the casual indifference of a man who'd already been paid. His roller bag leaned against his leg. He was scrolling through the final PDFs. His job was to witness. Her job was to win.

Outside, the fog had started to rise off the bay like it, too, was coming to collect.

∼

THE PLANE WAS QUIET. The hum of altitude kept steady in the background. A glass of water sat untouched near her elbow. She'd changed in the bathroom an hour earlier—out of the heels, into black sneakers and a structured zip-up that cost more than a mortgage payment. Courtesy of Vivienne, of course. The lipstick stayed. She didn't remove it. She hadn't decided if the night was over.

Vivienne had stretched the evening past its natural ending. Dinner in a restaurant with no signage. Dessert at a rooftop bar that required retinal scan entry. After that, drinks somewhere unlisted, invitation-only, and crawling with VCs trying not to look impressed. Sloane stayed for all of it. She smiled when she needed to. Laughed once. She didn't remember why. She knew better than to decline anything outright. Vivienne hadn't crossed a line yet, but the possibility stayed in the room, folded into every offer. Sloane hadn't decided if she cared.

Kenji had stayed in the car the whole time. He didn't like to mix settings. She didn't blame him. When they boarded the plane, he was already on his second ginger ale.

"I bet they're still cursing the day you got reinstated," he said. "And that California bar didn't know what hit it."

He raised his glass. The ice clinked once. The rest of the cabin was dark except for the overhead light above his seat.

Sloane leaned back and closed her eyes. She could still feel the heels in her arches, even though she wasn't wearing them anymore.

Her license in Illinois and New York had been temporarily suspended after Heritage let her take the fall. Not disbarred—just put on pause while the state bar did its hand-wringing. Nothing illegal had stuck. No charges filed. Just questions about ethics and silence and whether a woman like her could ever be fully clean.

It didn't stop her.

Vivienne Yue had work lined up before the hearings even ended—enough deals, acquisitions, and strategic warfare to fill a second career. Sloane applied for the California bar mid-investigation. Passed on the first try. Didn't wait for permission to start working.

Vivienne had five black card lawyers on retainer full-time. Sloane wasn't even primary. She was secondary when the first one was busy. She never asked who was number one.

"Law school trained me to win," she said. "They didn't specify who for."

Kenji didn't reply. He didn't need to. The statement wasn't meant for discussion.

She pulled the blanket over her lap but didn't recline. She didn't expect to sleep. If she was lucky, she'd get forty-five minutes—enough to fake rest, not enough to dream.

Chicago was three hours away.

The next meeting was in six.

She'd change again in the airport bathroom. She'd be fine.

There was no version of this job where she wasn't tired.

THE PLANE TOUCHED down in a crosswind. There was no sunrise—just a gray band of sky trying and failing to become morning. Her curls were flattened at the crown and frizzing at the ends, but she didn't care enough to fix them. Presentation mattered. Perfection didn't.

Kenji scrolled through real estate listings he had no intention of following up on. He got out near the South Loop, nodded once, and pulled the door closed behind him.

The Uber peeled off toward the South Side, tires humming against frost-rutted asphalt. She sat in the back, sunglasses on despite the absence of sunlight. Her trench still carried a trace of San Francisco—sterile, sharp—but Chicago was already bleeding through: exhaust, salt, something burnt. She didn't mind. Luxury always wore off fast.

She skipped home. Just a cavernous industrial loft, condiments in the fridge, and mail sorted by weight and irrelevance. She wasn't in the mood to curate the silence.

The steelworkers union hall sat in the shadow of an overpass, tucked between an empty currency exchange and a church that doubled as a soup kitchen four nights a week. She'd been here before, but always after dark, always through the back. This time she used the front door. It stuck halfway open and let out a low mechanical groan.

Inside, the room smelled like overbrewed coffee, dust, and years of frustration. A box fan whined in one corner despite the cold. The folding chairs were already half-full—men in layered flannel and union jackets, women with clipboards and expressions that said they'd read every document twice before breakfast. Sloane stepped inside without announcement.

El and Andi were in the back corner, halfway through turning the hall into a low-budget war room. Wires snaked across the floor like trip hazards, one monitor already glowing with a static test screen. Andi sat cross-legged on the floor, typing at a pace that suggested neither sleep nor restraint. A gas station energy drink balanced against their knee. El stood on a plastic chair, adjusting the projector while texting with the hand that wasn't holding a wrench.

They'd built a simulator. From scratch. OSHA data, AI models, Blender assets, and three weeks of sleep-deprived spite had resulted in a fully operational tool that could visually re-create workplace safety violations in 3D—complete with incident triggers, citation overlays, and editable layouts for organizers to use in presentations, negotiations, or lawsuits.

"Red Dead Reclassification is live," Andi said, still typing. "I fixed the blood physics."

"We added forklifts," El said. "Real ones."

"Too real," Andi muttered. "Noah almost threw up."

"Hey! That's not true. I just got a bit of motion sickness."

Noah Feldman-Bloom met them at the entrance to the main meeting room, still wearing his coat, a styrofoam cup of sludge in his hand. He looked at her like a man grateful to see backup but too stubborn to admit it.

"Jesus. I thought you were still in Silicon Hell."

"I was," she said, brushing past him. "Now I'm here."

The corporate lawyer was already seated at the table. He looked fresh—too fresh. New suit, expensive haircut, no visible fatigue. He smiled when he saw her, like they were on the same side. She didn't return it.

She walked straight to the end of the table and set her bag down. When she looked at the room—at the union reps, the organizers, the printed packets already curling at the corners—she didn't think about legacy, or redemption, or even justice. This wasn't about that. Not anymore. It was just work.

THE OFFER to the steelworkers was fifteen pages long and printed on company letterhead designed to suggest civility. Sloane read it once, standing. She didn't annotate it. Didn't circle anything. She turned each page carefully, without urgency, allowing silence to accumulate. The room had settled into a reluctant hush—someone coughed, someone else shifted in their chair, and the young man across the table kept adjusting his sleeve cuffs.

The company's lawyer had gone through his prepared remarks already. They were vague but pointed, full of phrases like shared resolution and forward-looking compromise. The kind of rhetoric meant to imply progress while reinforcing power. He was speaking to the room, but watching her the entire time.

She did not acknowledge him.

When she finished the last page, she folded the packet, set it on the table, and remained standing.

"There's a mistake," she said.

"That clause you added—Section Five, Sub A. It's binding, yes. But it's unenforceable under Section Seven of the National Labor Relations Act. Which means that not only is the no-strike provision invalid, you've also opened the door for a coordinated walkout and a class action suit."

A pause. Still no eye contact.

"If I were your general counsel, I'd fire you."

She didn't raise her voice. She didn't need to. The man blanched—not dramatically, but enough that it registered. His posture broke a little, the beginnings of a response forming and dying in his throat.

The union rep—gray around the temples, face like gravel—stayed quiet. He just looked at her with the grim satisfaction of someone who'd lived long enough to see history repeat and knew the value of watching it crack open.

From somewhere near the back of the room, a voice murmured: "Jesus."

No applause. Just the quiet movement of chairs, the sound of someone exhaling through their nose.

Sloane sat, finally. She didn't lean back. She didn't loosen her coat.

By late morning, the room had emptied.

The chairs were half-stacked. A clipboard leaned precariously on the edge of the radiator. Noah was packing cables into a duffel, muttering to himself about missing lunch. El and Andi hovered near a folding table, transferring files to USB drives for the organizers—whistleblower templates, union-safe cloud logins, two different versions of the simulator, one stripped down for Android.

Sloane sat at the end of the table with a paper cup of coffee that had gone cold an hour ago. She drank it anyway.

Noah dropped into the chair next to her, jacket half-zipped, hair unbrushed.

"You ever figure out what side you're on?"

She didn't answer immediately. She didn't fidget. She looked straight ahead at the blank wall across from them. There was a cracked outlet plate and a strip of masking tape over a light switch that said DO NOT TOUCH in faded Sharpie.

"You'd feel it if I wasn't on yours."

Noah snorted.

"Damn. Ok, that's fair."

She didn't argue.

Outside, the wind had picked up. It cut through the gaps in her coat and clawed at her collar. She walked without gloves. The corner lot across from the steelworkers building had been leveled last week—construction fences were up now, blue vinyl signs advertising luxury condos starting in the low sevens. The brickwork on the surrounding buildings was original. You could still see the outlines of old signage beneath the grime.

She still wasn't sure why she hadn't left this city. She had other options. San Francisco, New York, D.C. Places with better weather, cleaner glass, quieter corruption. But this city—with its bureaucratic rot, its relentless beauty, its rusted systems and impossible kindness—fit her better than any of them. It was hostile and loyal. It was transactional and full of ghosts. It didn't pretend to be fair. She understood that.

And of course, her people had stayed. El and Andi, Kenji —drifting toward her orbit and never really leaving. They weren't family. Not exactly. But they were hers. And she was the one who kept the lights on.

She didn't slow down.

She was still here. Somehow, that made sense.

57

Vee stepped off the jet bridge into the stale breath of O'Hare. New terminal, different airline, same air. She didn't go back to Heritage even after they won the suit. She'd switched over months ago—senior mechanic at their biggest rival. Better contract, better shifts, fewer lies.

She'd flown standby on the company rate, just like every off-duty airline employee does. Got bumped twice. Finally made it out on a red-eye from LAX. She could've bought a full-fare ticket, but Bà taught her better than that. Waste nothing. Take the hit if you can carry it.

She had just buried her.

Three days ago in Long Beach. Closed casket. Monk chants and paper offerings. Quick, quiet, no drama. That was how Bà wanted it. No spectacle. No fuss.

Turns out, she'd had congestive heart failure for months. Never told a soul. Not her children. Not Vee. Not even the cousins she called every Tuesday night to talk shit about politics and egg prices. She just kept going. Flew to Chicago two weeks before the end, like she always did—sat on Vee's couch with a heating pad and a bag of shrimp chips, heckled Korean dramas, hugged Kha like he was still eight. Then she borrowed someone's van and went to Hammond with the aunties to play penny slots and order lemon drops with extra sugar on the rim.

Vee didn't know it then, but Bà had come to say goodbye on her own terms. No pity. No doctors hovering. Just her girls, bad lighting, and a casino buffet crab leg that nearly cracked a crown.

Vee had been in the middle of rewiring a panel when she got the call. Her hands kept working. She didn't cry until that night, and when she did, it was like a valve releasing. Since then, everything felt thinner. The noise of the world, the line between here and whatever came after. Jerry was in that space too, probably laughing his ass off. They were both close. Close enough she could feel it in her teeth. It made her quiet. Not calm, but softer. Less fire, more smoke.

Kha had flown back the day before. Apprentice now. Doing real work. Wiring harnesses. Preventative maintenance. Getting grease under his nails. She didn't say it out loud, but she was proud as hell.

She shouldered her bag and moved through the terminal. Her gate dropped her on the far end of Terminal 5. Her back hurt. She hadn't eaten. She wanted her bed. She expected Morgan or Kieran and the ugly Tesla that squealed when it turned. She wanted to groan, toss her bag in the trunk, and talk shit about the TSA for twenty minutes.

Instead, she saw the car.

Matte black Lexus RX350 mid-size SUV, recent year. Not flashy, but the kind of crossover that screamed *I read the manual and took notes.* Seats that probably heated in twelve zones. Doors that closed like vaults. No smudges on the handles. Cabin so quiet it probably had cathedral acoustics.

Vee stared at it for a second, jaw tight. Practical luxury. The kind of thing you buy when you're pretending you're still modest.

And then she saw Sloane—leaning against the passenger side door. Coat cinched. Coffee in hand. Curls perfect. Of course.

Vee stopped walking.

"No. No, no, no. Where's Morgan?"

Sloane's expression didn't change.

"She was asked to fill in for a last-minute vacancy on a guest panel at Kellogg. Something about sustainable logistics."

She let out a controlled exhale.

"She sends her apologies."

Vee rolled her eyes and slid into the passenger seat. "Great."

Sloane closed the door behind her.

Vee forgot to buckle her seatbelt. Sloane waited a few seconds, then spoke without looking.

"Seatbelt please. I know you've danced with death and drag races. That doesn't make me less liable if your skull meets the dash."

Vee snorted and clicked it in. The engine was already humming low.

They pulled out of the curb in silence. The roads were half-empty, full of frost patches and construction cones. Sloane turned on the radio. NPR. Some panel show about civic engagement.

Vee turned it off with one jab of her finger. Sloane didn't say anything.

"Let me guess," Vee said. "You drew the short straw?"

"It was either me or Kieran," Sloane said, eyes on the

road. "I wanted to spare the man. He's been working back-to-back rotations and sounded like a zombie."

Vee didn't answer. Just shifted in her seat and leaned against the door. Her head hurt. Her neck was stiff.

They both opened their mouths at the same time, then stopped.

"Oh my God," Vee muttered. "This is weird. You've never driven me before. I didn't even think you knew how to drive. You look like you were born to be a passenger princess."

Sloane chuckled low. "I needed a car. I live here now. My new boss offered me a driver. But I'd rather keep costs down."

Vee raised an eyebrow, didn't look over. "I heard you're clocking in for a billionaire now and helping Noah and the other union organizers on your lunch breaks."

"My schedule's efficient," Sloane said.

"That part of the plan, or just where you landed?"

Her mouth twitched, but she didn't smile. "Maybe a little bit of both."

Vee's face remained impassive.

"Noah mentioned you've aligned yourself with the competition," Sloane said carefully. "One of their senior mechanics now, I take it?"

"Yup."

"Is it what you wanted?"

"It's fine."

Nothing after that. The car moved through Schiller Park, past warehouses and truck stops and motels. The heater hummed. The road cracked beneath them.

At the next light, Sloane reached into the passenger side footwell and set a small plastic bag between them.

"Snacks."

Vee glanced down. Granola bars. An electrolyte drink. A packet of almonds. Fancy packaging.

She grabbed the drink and cracked the seal. Didn't say thank you.

The light turned green. Sloane drove.

Vee rested her head against the glass. She didn't feel angry. She didn't feel good. But for the first time in a long time, she didn't feel like breaking something just to prove it was hers.

They remained silent for the next ten minutes. It was the closest they'd been in a year.

Vee looked over at Sloane from the passenger seat. She still looked the same—perfect posture, clean lines, not a hair out of place—but something was different. Less glossy. Less performative. More worn-in, like she'd stopped trying to be above it all. It wasn't weakness. It was the opposite. She looked like she gave fewer fucks, and somehow that made her hotter.

Desire shot right through Vee—low, unexpected, chemical. Her face flushed. She looked away fast, annoyed with herself.

What the fuck. She'd just come back from a funeral. Wasn't that a thing? People getting all messed up and horny when they're grieving? Something about biology and the dumb body trying to create life next to death. It was gross. It was real. She didn't want to think about it.

Sloane glanced over. Her voice was clinical.

"Too warm?"

She reached for the climate control, already lowering it by a few degrees before Vee could answer.

"It's fine," Vee snapped. Sharper than she meant it.

Sloane didn't react.

They drove the rest of the way in silence.

When they pulled up to her place, Vee didn't move. She unbuckled her seatbelt but stayed seated, hand resting on the door handle.

"So...what now?" she said, still looking ahead. "You gonna text Morgan and tell her you did your civic duty?"

Sloane didn't hesitate. "No. I'm going to see if you invite me in."

The car settled around them. The engine ticking. The air dry.

Vee opened the door.

"Fine. But bring the rest of the snacks."

And that was it.

58

Vee's place looked the same, mostly. Same scratch on the entryway wall. Same crooked light fixture in the kitchen that buzzed when the microwave ran too long. But something about the air had shifted—calmer now. Settled.

Vee kicked off her boots. Sloane hesitated in the doorway. Coat still on, her hand hovering over the hook by instinct, like she was trying to decide whether she belonged in this space again. She took it off eventually and folded it over the back of a chair, precise as ever.

One of the cats—Eugene—brushed against her leg. Sloane didn't flinch. Just looked down, blinked, and let it happen.

On the table, the ankle monitor sat like a paperweight—black plastic, scuffed at the edges, unplugged and dead.

She didn't touch it, but her posture shifted—shoulders eased slightly, something subtle let go.

"It's off," she said with a smile. "Good."

It wasn't dramatic. Only fact, stated with certainty and the smallest trace of satisfaction. Like she'd been tracking the outcome from a distance and was relieved to see it resolved.

Vee's chest went tight for a second. She looked away.

"Thanks," she said. "For getting your ACLU friend to push him into that parole trial program."

Sloane didn't blink. "It was the right fit. I just made sure they saw that."

Vee gave a short nod. "Well. It worked."

No one said anything else for a while. The monitor stayed on the table, inert and ugly, but it didn't feel heavy anymore.

She opened the fridge, pulled out two cans of soda. They hissed as she cracked them open. She held one out to Sloane.

Their fingers brushed—barely—and the contact sparked something sharp and immediate. A jolt. No warning, no buildup.

Vee looked away before it could show on her face.

"Kha's still here," she added, clearing her throat. "At work right now. Saving for his own place once the apprenticeship starts paying steady. He's doing good."

Sloane nodded once, approving. Took a sip from the can.

"That's sensible. The rental market's untenable right now. Staying put while he builds savings is the only rational choice."

Vee let out a short laugh—at the words, at the tone, at the way Sloane always made everything sound like a policy memo.

Sloane tilted her head to one side like she missed a joke.

"Feel free to take a seat," Vee said. "I really need to get the smell of funeral incense out of my hair."

Sloane nodded. When she walked to the living room. She froze.

"Oh."

"What's up?" Vee asked.

Sloane was staring toward the window. The tank was still there. The one she'd kept Tiberia in when she stayed with her over a year ago.

It was different now. No heat lamp. No branches. The glass had been cleaned, lined with moss, bark, and bits of stone. A whole little world. Someone had turned it into a fairy garden. There were gnomes tucked between clusters of begonia. A tiny gravel path cut through the middle like a trail.

Sloane stepped closer. Her expression didn't shift much, but her breath caught. A small thing.

Vee said nothing. Simply watched her. The light from the window caught the curve of Sloane's jaw, the stiff line of her mouth.

She turned and walked down the hallway to the bathroom, closing the door behind her with more force than necessary.

She stepped into the shower and cranked the water hotter than she could stand. Steam rose fast, filling the space. She stood there too long, letting it scald her skin before she moved. Then the routine kicked in—scrubbing, exfoliating, shampoo, conditioner. Twice. Everything with more pressure than required.

She didn't need to be this clean. She needed something to do with her hands. Her body wouldn't stop remembering the last time Sloane was in this bathroom with her—how she'd made Vee touch herself first, slow and precise, drawn out to the edge of cruelty. How she'd pressed her against the tile and dropped to her knees like it was nothing. Like it was routine. Like she'd always known exactly how to make her fall apart.

Vee squeezed her eyes shut. Pressed her forehead against the wet tile.

"You fucking pervert," she muttered to herself. "She's out there. Get a grip."

The water kept running. Her skin stung. The shame didn't help.

A quiet part of her—buried deep and wild—waited for the sound of the door opening. For Sloane's voice, low and unreadable, telling her to leave the water on.

It didn't come.

The door stayed shut.

VEE CAME out of the bathroom barefoot, hair still damp. She'd thrown on the biggest shirt she owned—an old band tee that hung past her thighs and smelled faintly of lavender detergent.

The TV was on low, tuned to the local news. Background noise. Headlines about weather and traffic filled the silence she hadn't figured out how to break.

Sloane hadn't moved from the couch. She sat upright, knees together, hands folded like she was prepping to deliver closing arguments. Eugene and Dolores flanked her from opposite corners of the room, watching her like security detail. She met their stares with the same blank expression she reserved for hostile witnesses.

Seeing her like that—so composed, so...Sloane—threw her off balance. The air between them felt thinner now. Closer to breaking.

"Why are you sitting like you're in court?" Vee asked.

Sloane turned her head slowly. Not smiling. "Because I'm waiting for a verdict."

That landed with a thud in Vee's chest. She didn't have a response. Didn't try for one.

Instead, she walked over and sat beside her. Not close enough to touch—enough for the edge of their shoulders to brush. Bare skin meeting fabric. A single point of contact, quiet and live.

They didn't speak for a long time. Just two bodies, barely touching, holding the silence together.

Vee should have walked away. She knew that. It would've been the smart thing, the sane thing, the self-respecting thing. But she wasn't feeling smart, sane, or particularly proud of herself at the moment. She was feeling starved. And maybe it wasn't about reconciliation. Maybe it wasn't about trust or healing or any of those noble things. Maybe it was about admitting—without shame, without overthinking —that she wanted Sloane. Needed Sloane. Right here, right now. The craving was physical, cellular. Something gnawing through her gut.

One look and they lunged for each other.

Vee was in Sloane's lap before she realized how fast she'd moved. Her thighs bracketed Sloane's hips, knees pressing into the couch cushions. Their mouths collided hard, all teeth and friction, breath dragged between them. It was fast and messy, the kind of kiss that had no shape—only need. She pulled at Sloane's clothes with clumsy urgency, tugging the black sleeveless turtleneck over her head and tossing it aside, revealing skin that always looked too smooth to be real. The cream trousers came next, expensive fabric sliding down long legs. But then—of course—Sloane wasn't wearing anything underneath, save for a ridiculous lemon-yellow thong with daisies on it.

Vee smirked. "Seriously?" she murmured, breathless, already pulling it off with a sharp tug.

"Shut up," Sloane said, breath hitching, lifting her hips in sync with Vee's pull.

The joke died the moment skin met skin.

Sloane's hand was already under the hem of Vee's over-sized t-shirt—nothing on underneath—and long fingers were curling against her breast. Playing, pressing, tugging. Vee's head dropped back involuntarily. The way Sloane touched her—remembered her—it was like no time had passed. Like they hadn't been strangers for the past year. Just this endless heat unfurling across her spine, settling between her legs. She was already wet. Already throbbing. It was humiliating how little it took.

And then Sloane's fingers found her again—lower this time—and Vee buckled forward with a gasp, body curling into the touch like it was oxygen. She clenched around nothing and everything. Climax slammed into her fast, too fast, but she didn't care. She shook all over, mouth parted, eyes rolling shut. It wasn't elegant. It wasn't performative. It was honest.

Before the tremors even fully passed, she pressed Sloane flat against the seat cushions and climbed on top again, straddling her with purpose. Their mouths found each other, slower now, drunk on heat. Vee's shirt stayed on—something about it felt right. Like a dirty little secret.

Sloane's thigh pressed up, firm and warm, right where Vee needed her. The pressure was immediate—undeniable—Sloane's warm, slick folds against hers. Vee sank into it with a low exhale, her whole body tightening around the contact. She rocked her hips forward slowly, testing it. The friction was perfect: steady, just coarse enough to catch her clit in a way that made her legs tremble.

Every slow drag sent a ripple up her spine. A taut little burst of electricity, sharp and pulsing. Her inner thighs were already slick, sliding against Sloane's skin, and the wet sound of it—filthy, honest—only made her grind harder. Her breath hitched with every pass, every roll of her hips meeting Sloane's. Her nerves were overstimulated and hungry at the same time, overwhelmed and asking for more. There was no rhythm, not really—only a frantic, aching pace that kept building. Heat coiled low in her belly and bloomed outward with every grind.

Her clit throbbed with every rub—just enough pressure, just enough friction to ride that razor-thin edge between pleasure and collapse. It wasn't graceful. Her thighs shook. Her hands clutched at Sloane's shoulders like she might fall apart without something to hold onto. And the eye contact? That was a whole other thing. They didn't break it. Didn't dare. Like if one of them looked away, the spell would snap. Pupils wide, lips parted, flushed cheekbones—Vee could feel herself mirrored in Sloane.

Hands everywhere. Mouths grazing skin. Nipples rolled between fingers. Breaths caught and released.

Every time their pelvises met, it was louder. Wetter. A little less controlled. The pleasure grew sharper, more precise, like being pulled taut across a string. And still—Vee didn't stop. Couldn't. She chased it, chased her, until her whole body clenched up again, back arched, mouth open, her climax coming hard and fast and shaking her down to the bone.

She didn't say a word. Just let it take her.

Vee grabbed Sloane's wrists and pinned them over her head, leaned down and kissed her. And as their hips rocked together—slick, raw, pulsing—they came again, tangled up in each other, chests heaving.

After that, there were no words. Only the sound of skin and breath and everything that hadn't been said.

THEY DIDN'T TALK about it.

There was no post-mortem. No "what does this mean," no "are we doing this again." Just movement. Just staying close.

Vee wandered into the kitchen and started picking through the snacks Sloane had dumped on the table—granola bars, dried fruit, some off-brand electrolyte drink. She ate without thinking.

Sloane got dressed in the other room, methodical and quiet. Vee watched her move like nothing had happened. Her eyes lingered longer than they should have—on the flawless sweep of Sloane's skin, the clean curve of her hips, the sharp, unfair swell of her ass. She'd waxed of course.

Vee tugged down her oversized shirt, suddenly aware of her own body—unshaved, unprepped, too busy to bother. It wasn't shame, exactly. Simply the quiet discomfort of contrast.

Sloane helped feed the cats, refilled their water bowls, and noted they were low on kibble. She paused at the automatic feeder, checked the settings, and gave the lid a skeptical tap, like she didn't quite trust it. Vee muttered that she'd pick up more later. It was already programmed through the weekend.

Sloane didn't argue. Nodded once, like she'd done the math.

They passed each other in the kitchen a few times. No touching. Never far apart.

At one point, Sloane looked down at the half-eaten

granola bar in Vee's hand and said, "This doesn't qualify as a proper meal."

Vee shrugged. "It's food."

Sloane didn't argue. She simply grabbed her keys and took her to the diner down the block. Vee got a patty melt. Sloane ordered a veggie egg white omelette and didn't comment on the chipped mug.

They ran errands like it had been on the calendar.

Stopped by Walgreens to pick up a cheap pack of thank-you cards—plain, blank inside. No cursive. No flowers. Vee scribbled short notes to relatives and neighbors who'd shown up, dropped off food, or Venmo'd for incense. Her handwriting was garbage and she cursed every time she messed up a name, but she did it anyway. Bà would've expected that.

Sloane didn't comment. Just stood beside her in line and silently paid for the stamps.

They dropped an envelope off at the union hall, then swung by Woytek's to grab a part Vee had forgotten over the weekend. Sloane stayed in the truck for that one—apparently the man was serious about her being banned from the yard.

Sloane moved through each task with quiet precision, like she was trying not to overstep but couldn't help showing up anyway.

At one point, Vee looked up and had to confront the quiet absurdity of it—they were standing side by side in the pet aisle of the grocery store, both reaching for the same brand of cat food she'd been buying since forever. Her hand brushed Sloane's. Neither of them flinched. She pushed the shopping cart forward and kept moving.

It was easier that way. No explanations. No risks. Only

the kind of rhythm that shouldn't have existed after what they did—but did.

By evening, they drove back to Sloane's new apartment to feed Tiberia.

It was a loft in Fulton Market—too pretty to be practical, the kind of place people posted about but rarely lived in. The neighborhood was all brick sidewalks, overpriced bakeries, bikes chained to wrought iron fences. The building used to be a textile warehouse. Now it had a name in all caps and a locked package room.

Inside, the space felt open in a way Sloane's old corporate apartment never had. No drywall partitions. Only air. Light came in through the old warehouse windows—those thick glass blocks from the eighties that blurred everything on the other side. No view, just brightness, soft and directionless. The bed was visible from the spiral staircase that led to the open second floor, the sheets crisply tucked, untouched.

Sloane opened the door. Tossed her keys into a ceramic bowl by the entry without comment.

The snake was fine. Coiled under her heating pad, unbothered. Vee crouched near the tank while Sloane checked the thermostat and humidity levels.

They didn't talk about where they were staying that night.

They meant to.

But then Sloane was standing too close in the kitchen, rinsing the snake's water bowl, and Vee leaned back against the counter long enough for their arms to brush. Just enough to feel it again.

No one made the first move. It simply...happened.

The second time wasn't frantic. It wasn't tender either. It hovered somewhere in that strange middle—measured, sharp-edged, like they both believed if they just *pressed hard enough*, it might burn itself out.

Vee dropped to her knees on the cold concrete while Sloane leaned back against the kitchen counter, breath already hitching. Vee didn't hesitate—just buried her face between Sloane's thighs, mouth hot, relentless. Sloane tasted like sweat and something sweeter, almost metallic, like the edge of a bitten lip. She tangled her fingers in Vee's hair, tugged hard enough to make Vee moan into her. That moan vibrated straight through her, and Sloane made sure Vee looked up while she worked—their eyes locked, pupils blown, mouth slick.

Sloane shattered with her head tilted back, a jagged gasp ripped from her throat as her thighs clamped around Vee's face. She trembled through it, fingers still fisted in hair like she was afraid to let go.

Then they were in Sloane's ridiculous bed—oversized, over-everything, suspended above the rest of the loft like a throne room. Vee sprawled across silk sheets while Sloane strapped in, all cool precision and nothing soft. When she pushed in, it wasn't gentle. It was a claiming.

Vee clawed at the sheets, body dragged up the bed with every thrust until she had to brace herself against the carved teak headboard. The wood creaked under her palms. Sloane held her hips and drove into her, brutal and unrelenting. Their sounds—ragged breaths, wet slaps, choked-off curses—bounced off the high ceilings, ricocheting through the open space like confession.

Afterward, they lay tangled and naked in Sloane's bed, too exhausted to move.

The room was dim, lit only by the spill of streetlight through the blurred glass blocks.

She didn't ask to go home.

Sloane didn't ask her to stay.

It was ridiculous, if she really thought about it. Two grown women fucking like the world was ending and then tiptoeing around it like it hadn't happened.

This was what passed for intimacy between two people pathologically opposed to surrender—no apologies, no distance, only presence.

By Sunday, it was obvious neither of them was going anywhere.

They didn't talk about it. No decision was made. They just kept staying close. Doing things together. Moving as a unit.

Vee woke up to Sloane upside down on the pole, legs split like a geometry lesson, moving slow and precise to whatever moody, cello-laced bullshit she played at sunrise.

She watched from the bed, jaw tight, limbs aching, unsure if she'd just lost the war or won it.

Hard to tell from this angle.

Then she rolled over and went back to sleep.

When it was time for Vee and Morgan's usual reality TV night, they went together. No conversation. Got in the truck and went.

Morgan and Kieran's West Side Victorian was finally starting to look lived in—somewhere between Gothic and homey, full of new furniture that was both gorgeous and suspiciously multifunctional. Vee made a comment about it that made Sloane chuckle and elbow her lightly.

The popcorn was already on the coffee table, still warm.

When they walked in—together, unannounced—

Morgan looked up from the TV, didn't blink, didn't pause. Only smirked and stood up.

"I'll make another batch of popcorn."

Then she disappeared into the kitchen like nothing about it was surprising at all.

THEY STOPPED at the gas station on the way back.

Vee went in to pay. Sloane wandered off—purposeful but aimless—in search of snacks with a shelf life longer than a workweek. Vee let her. She was the one who insisted they keep the truck stocked "in case of emergencies."

They looked like a couple. An old one. The kind who knew how to move around each other without speaking.

Vee grabbed coolant from the rack outside, popped the trunk, and started checking levels. It was habit. Her hands needed something to do.

When she came back in, Sloane was standing at the register, holding a sad little armful of dried fruit, trail mix, and electrolyte drinks, looking around like she'd misplaced her anchor.

The clerk clocked Vee immediately and said, "Oh, your wife was looking for you. She's right there."

Vee froze.

Sloane did too.

Neither of them corrected it.

Just held eye contact for a beat too long.

Sloane looked down, pulled out her card, and tapped without a word.

Vee picked up the bag. Didn't say anything.

They walked out together, side by side, not touching. But they didn't drift.

Back in the truck, the silence wasn't tense anymore—simply full.

Sloane shifted in her seat. Still looking out the window when she said, "You didn't say anything."

Vee didn't look over. Kept driving.

"Was I supposed to?"

She didn't raise her voice. She didn't have to. It was tired honesty, flat and frayed around the edges.

Sloane exhaled slowly, like she'd been holding her breath for a year.

"I don't know. But if we're going to keep pretending we're not circling the drain again, it would help if we stopped lying by omission."

Vee pulled the truck over. Not hard. Not dramatic. Just decisive. She put it in park. Stared straight ahead.

"You want me to name it? Fine," she said. "I never stopped wanting you. Even when I hated your fucking guts. Even when I was sure I wouldn't survive another week of seeing you on the other side of the table. I still wanted you next to me. That what you needed to hear?"

There was no venom left in it. Only truth.

Sloane turned to her. Her voice was smaller now.

"Yes."

A long pause.

Vee let out a slow breath.

"I did."

Sloane nodded once.

"So did I."

That was it. No one apologized. No one begged. Nothing collapsed.

They sat there. Two stubborn women in a truck full of snacks, blinking too hard and not saying another word.

Vee finally reached for the ignition.

"You still want that sundae from Margie's?"

Sloane didn't miss a beat.

"Obviously."

And that was it. It was the closest they were ever going to get to closure.

No declarations. No ceremony. Only this—body heat, shared errands, and a quiet agreement to stay in each other's orbit a little longer.

Maybe even for good.

EPILOGUE

Six months had passed since she picked Vee up at O'Hare. They hadn't spent more than twenty-four hours apart since. Even when Vivienne Yue summoned her to San Francisco for work, Vee made sure someone covered her shift and came along on the jet—claiming, flatly, that she "didn't trust that rich bitch." Sloane let her be territorial. She even enjoyed it. A little.

And now, here they were in Jamaica—two women who had survived the detonation and the debris, driving into the belly of heat and light in a battered four-wheel drive with a cracked dash and no side doors. The wind clawed through their hair, powdered dust rising behind them like incense from a long-dead altar.

No NDAs. No contracts. Just wind and limestone.

Vee drove with a casual ferocity, one foot slung over the open frame where the Jeep's door should've been, her other hand gripping a plastic bottle of Ting. Her mouth, stained faintly from the syrup, quirked like she was chewing on a secret or a lyric. No makeup. No armor. She looked like herself—Vee Phan, unrepentant, unbrushed, alive.

They crested a rise, the road giving way to cliffside, and the horizon fractured into cerulean and foam. Below, the sea roared with unmediated joy, and the wind was no longer gentle—it was sovereign. They pulled off the road, tires grinding into coral-sand gravel. Sloane didn't say anything as Vee killed the engine.

Somewhere nearby, there was a plaque. Engraved in her own lawyerly hand, though she now found the prose overwrought. It noted that the land—this particular stretch of limestone bluff and fertile lowland—was held in an irrevocable trust, shielded from corporate redevelopment. Not for the Campbells. Not for the Thompkinses. But for the farmers. The teachers. The herbalists and nurses and children running barefoot between sugar cane. A community commons. A defiance etched into stone.

"This is what I did it for," she said. "The thing I couldn't name. The thing I thought would make the damage... worth it."

She paused. Her throat caught. She swallowed it down.

"I betrayed you to protect this. Or at least, that's the lie I told myself. But the truth is—" She glanced down at her own hands, curled now into fists inside the linen. "I was protecting a version of myself I couldn't stand to lose."

The silence that followed was full, not empty. Breath. Sea. The soft scrape of Vee's sandal against stone. Sloane kept going.

"But I found a way not to lose everything. The land's in trust now. For the community. Not just for my family. For everyone."

She didn't look back. Couldn't.

"I don't get credit," she said. "Just peace."

Vee said nothing for so long that Sloane started to think maybe that was the answer. Silence. A kind of mercy.

Then, finally: "We went all the way out here just for you to show me this?"

Sloane let the question hang. She didn't move. Didn't blink.

"No," she said. "I brought you here because...I didn't want to see it alone."

Her father had not spoken to her since. His silence was not rage—it was worse. It was administrative. And yet, in the crucible of that exile, her younger sister had emerged from the wreckage and texted her, unprompted, from Berlin: *I want you to visit. Both of you. Bring her.*

Sloane had stared at the message for an hour before answering.

Now, she leaned against the front of the car, arms folded, sunglasses tilted just enough to register Vee's smirk.

"You remember," Vee said, tearing into a piece of fruit with her teeth, "almost two years ago—you said you wanted to talk. Said you'd find me once you got to Chicago. Then you landed and acted like you never said a word. Like a damn coward."

She glanced at the view, then back at Sloane. "Were you standing here before that lie?"

There was no accusation in it. Not anymore. Just curiosity. Dissection. Autopsy-level calm.

"Yes."

Sloane exhaled slowly, jaw tightening, not in defense but in admission. "This was where I decided to euthanize the fantasy."

Vee snorted, but Sloane wasn't done.

The wind shoved the car hard enough to rattle the frame. Neither of them flinched.

She leaned forward slightly, elbows on her knees, sunglasses slipping down the bridge of her nose. Her fingers moved absently to adjust them, then dropped. Her hands wouldn't sit still.

"My uncle was dying," she said finally. "I thought I was just going to bury him. Sign a few land revisions. Be back in Chicago in a week."

A pause. She reached into the cupholder for a bottle of water, found nothing.

"Ava Thompkins was already there. Contracts printed. Notarized and dated. They didn't even pretend it was a negotiation."

Vee didn't look at her. She was peeling a piece of fruit slowly with her thumbnail. The juice ran down her wrist, but she didn't lick it off.

"They offered me a deal that would protect everything. My family's land. The clinics. The schools. Everything my ancestors built for two-hundred years." Sloane rubbed her thumb along her palm like it itched. "All I had to do was sign."

A breeze lifted her dress. She didn't fix it. Just stared straight ahead at the water and let the next words rot in her mouth a little before saying them.

"So I did."

Silence. The fruit tore in Vee's hands. She finally glanced over, eyes narrowed—but not angry. Just clinical. Scalpel-ready.

"You really thought that would be cleaner?"

Sloane gave a breath of something close to a laugh, but it broke halfway through. Her voice cracked, not dramatically —just enough that one syllable dropped off.

"I thought...it'd be easier. To disappear."

She didn't look at Vee. Couldn't. She pinched the bridge of her nose, then let her hand fall back to her lap.

"I killed it early. Us. Whatever it was. Killed it before it curdled."

The ocean answered with a wave that slammed against rock hard enough to spray mist. It kissed the edge of her sandal. She didn't move.

"I told myself I did it for the land. For the legacy. That I traded my heart for duty."

Vee leaned back, sunglasses low, watching her now. Not hostile. Just present.

"You could've told me."

Sloane turned to her.

"I wanted to. I almost did."

Vee's expression didn't change.

She exhaled hard, as if something inside her collapsed just from naming it.

"But the moment I landed, the deal was already in motion. I wasn't even a person to them. I was a signature. A legal instrument."

She blinked down at her lap, at her hands balled into the linen of her dress. The fabric was damp with sweat.

"I was scared," she said again, quieter this time.

Vee didn't say anything. Just pulled a beach towel from the backseat and tossed it over the hood. Climbed up. Lay back. Took her time.

Eventually, she closed her eyes.

"Unbelievable," Vee said lazily, and put on her sunglasses. "Next time you try to be kind, ask first."

Sloane sat beside her on the hood, not touching, but close enough that their shoulders warmed the same patch of air. Her dress was backless, and when Vee dragged her fingers down the line of her spine, it raised goosebumps— despite the heat.

"I'm over it already," Vee said. "Doesn't mean it stopped hurting."

It was then that Sloane moved. A shift forward, inevitable as gravity. She curled her hand around the back of Vee's neck, fingers threading into sweat-damp hair, and kissed her like she finally had nothing left to prove. No audience. No script. Just truth and breath and heat.

She hadn't dared touch Vee until now—not really. Not until they were alone in the full sense of the word. Out past the last paved road, past reception towers and curious gazes and the curated theatre of womanhood.

Here, the only witness was wind.

Even now, her hand moved slowly—not from hesitation, but from memory. The muscle memory of danger. Of knowing, deep in the spine, what it meant to be seen loving the wrong person in the wrong place. To reach out and be punished for it.

But Vee didn't flinch. She didn't retreat or brace. She leaned in with the quiet defiance of someone who had outlived shame. Pressed her body into Sloane's like the world had never punished a woman for wanting. Like the story had already been rewritten.

Later—how long later, Sloane wouldn't have been able to say—she lay back first, one arm tucked behind her head, the other reaching without looking, until her fingers found Vee's and threaded through. Vee joined her a breath later, shoulder brushing shoulder.

Without a word, Sloane adjusted—shifting just enough to rest on Vee's left. Not her dominant side. Just the side that could hear.

She didn't say anything. Just settled there like she always had.

Vee noticed, of course. She always did. But she didn't

mention it—not with words. She just turned her head, let the weight of Sloane's voice curl against the part of her that could still catch it.

She'd stopped expecting that kind of consideration from anyone.

She never had to ask it of Sloane.

The sun had started to fall, and the ocean burned gold beneath it. Their clothes and bikinis were somewhere on the dash, forgotten. Salt still clung to their bodies, the kind that only comes when there's nothing between you and the air. Vee was beside her, half-propped on one elbow, lazily dragging her fingers along the dip in Sloane's stomach—not as seduction, but as fact. As ritual.

"Okay. So what's our cover story if we get pulled over again?"

"We're friends from law school."

"Sloane, I barely graduated high school."

"We met on a leadership retreat?"

"You think I scream leadership?"

"Fine. We met at church."

"Girl. What church?"

They cracked up, Vee muffling her laugh against Sloane's neck, breath warm, body shaking.

And just like that, the air shifted. Something raw and reckless surged up in her chest—not hunger, not longing, just the unbearable knowledge that she still had permission to touch her. She rolled Vee beneath her without thinking.

She'd wrecked this woman's life. Not once. Not metaphorically. And still—Vee let her close.

They didn't forgive each other. They just stayed. And somewhere beneath the sun, the sweat, the salt—that counted for something. Maybe not redemption. But mercy. The kind you don't ask for. The kind you bleed into.

There was no plan. No next move. Just breath. Just skin. The wind moved over the cliffs.

They hadn't fixed what they broke. They never would. But they lay beside the wreckage anyway. And called it enough.

AFTERWORD

If you made it this far, thank you—and if you see yourself in these pages, I hope it felt like care, not extraction. That said: I wrote characters with lives and lineages outside my own. I did my research, I asked questions, I stayed up late over tiny choices—but if something in here missed the mark for you, I accept that. This isn't an apology. It's an acknowledgment. I don't take your trust lightly.

ABOUT THE AUTHOR

Kim Serrano writes messy women, moral gray zones, and the kind of queer stories that refuse to behave. She's a former organizer, a forever Midwesterner, and believes in justice, pettiness, and plant care in equal measure. *Pressure Breach* is her third novel. More at kimserrano.com.

ALSO BY KIM SERRANO

Burn Rate

Hold Control